DEBBY HANDMAN

The Gambler's Wife

Season of the Wilderness

This book was professionally typeset on Reedsy.
Find out more at reedsy.com

This book is lovingly dedicated
to my sister Becky,
whose bravery and strength
during difficult times
truly inspires me.

"To everything there is a season, and a time for every purpose under heaven."

ECCLESIASTES 3:1

Contents

III   Part Three

Acknowledgments

With every book, there are so many people to thank. A big thank you, Mom. You are always my go to person for writing advice. Thank you for all the time and effort you put into reading my manuscript and giving suggestions. You never make me feel like you're too busy to help me. Dad, thank you for always being my biggest fan and your continuous support. Alesha, thank you for the feedback, and eternal patience. Your encouragement has helped to keep me writing even when I half want to quit forever. Thank you for always listening to my ideas, even the half baked ones. Melissa, I appreciate your honesty and giving me the hard feedback. It is the writer's greatest friend. A big thank you to all of my praying sisters at CFC and for the small group of praying women where it all started. I still pray for every single one of you today. Loving thanks to my dear cousin, Eli for your support and teaching me so many important things about the world of marketing. Finally to my sons, Seth and Isaac, thank you for being the greatest lights in my life.

I

Part One

Playing the Game

Chapter 1

You Gotta know when to hold 'em
Know when to fold 'em
Know when to walk away
Know when to run.
—*Kenny Rogers*

Fold 'em

"Um, is this Lauren Westbrook?" His voice was deep and rich like glazed honey.

Lauren rubbed her eyes with one hand while grasping her cell phone tighter to her ear with the other. "Yes. Speaking."

"I'm Officer Hernandez calling from the Lincoln City Sheriff's Office. Is your husband Marcus Westbrook? Minister of the First Assembly of Disciples Church in South Salem?"

"Yes. Can I help you?"

"Are you able to talk now?"

"Yes, I think so," she stammered as she forced herself upright in bed.

"There's been an accident. A man with your husband's ID passed away last night. He was in an accident driving Hwy 101. There was bad weather, a freak spring storm with intense hail. We believe he missed a corner and drove off the road. I'm so sorry to tell you this over the phone."

"No, that's not possible. He's right here." Lauren turned toward Marcus's side of the bed. Her eyes lingered on the depression in the sheets where he had been moments ago. The cotton was cold to her touch. He was gone.

"There's no good way to tell a person, so I find it's best just to be up front. We're going to need you to come down to the police station in Lincoln City to identify him. Unfortunately, we're not able to confirm from the state of his body that this is in fact Marcus. We are going to need a family member to confirm his identity."

"Oh." Her voice was frothy like sea foam, almost inaudible. "I'll be there as soon as I can... Thank you."

She didn't cry.

* * *

The Lincoln County Sheriff's Office was the definition of drab. From the outside, there was almost a stately quality to the domed structure, a relic of government buildings from the 1960s. Inside, it was in sore need of renovation. Police officers were divided from the general public by a glass partition planted into a solid mahogany beam that ran the length of the room. The walls were painted a pale blue that was dull, chipped, and faded in spots. A receptionist directed her to the waiting area near the bathrooms, defined by a few makeshift dividers.

The officers moved about purposely as Lauren stared through them wondering when she would wake from this nightmare.

"Mrs. Westbrook?"

She recognized the voice and looked up. "Officer Hernandez?"

"Yes, ma'am. Did you come alone?"

"My daughter's at school. It's her last day, so I needed to take care of this before she gets home."

"I see. This is an upsetting thing. I don't recommend driving. You should call someone."

She waved her hand dismissively. "I didn't have time. I don't even know if this is true."

Mechanically, she followed him down a flight of stairs into a dimly lit room. The cold metal table and the white sheet held her eyes hostage, freezing her blood.

"Mrs. Westbrook, you don't need to see all of him if you don't want to. It might be better just to look at the right side of the chest where there's the least trauma."

Lauren shook her head. "No. I need to know. I need to see everything."

He nodded and together with the man in the blue lab coat, they pulled the sheet from the dead man. She recognized nothing of Marcus. The figure on the table was not remotely human.

"Take your time," the coroner said.

Officer Hernandez guided her to the other side. "It's the side with the least damage."

The patch of skin from underneath the armpit to the hip was smooth and without disfigurement. Lauren stopped breathing.

"Is it him?"

She nodded but couldn't speak.

"How do you know?"

"His tattoo. The one with the cross and the rose. He got it the summer he decided to be a minister," she choked.

"I'm so sorry." Officer Hernandez offered her a hand, but she didn't take it.

* * *

Two Weeks Later

Lauren bit her bottom lip as she stared across the cherry wood desk at Reverend Martin.

"Mrs. Westbrook, you realize that you have no money."

"I thought he was in remission," Lauren said slowly. "Marcus received counseling for gambling about five years ago. We were on a payment plan. That's why I took the teaching job at the high school."

"I'm afraid he never left the page of his destructive behavior. These documents show that Pastor Westbrook took nearly forty thousand dollars from the congregation's treasury."

Lauren's face flamed hot. "I didn't know. How much?"

"Nearly forty thousand dollars."

She added the sum to the ninety thousand she was already helping him pay.

"His insurance policy of one hundred thousand dollars should allow you to pay back what he took."

Lauren nodded. After repayment, about sixty thousand would remain. Thirty thousand short of clearing the larger debt.

"When tragedies like this happen, widows are usually secure. This is not how I like to see things unfold."

"When do we need to leave the parsonage?"

"We have a new family arriving in five days."

"So I have three days?"

"I'm sorry."

"I know you are. We'll manage."

* * *

The parsonage was half hidden in the shadow of a massive oak tree.

The house stared back at her from the driveway and she could feel it grieving in the heat of early summer.

"Mom, are we going to have to move?"

"Yes. I'm sorry."

"It's okay. I want to remember him, but maybe not here all the time."

A silver Toyota Corolla pulled into the parking lot. Lance Tenley climbed out, sweating.

"Do you know everything?" Lauren asked. "About the additional forty thousand?"

"I do. Marcus told me a week before the accident."

"So what brings you here?"

"I thought you should know something."

Lauren waited.

"Lauren, you were a pastor here too. On the books, you never stepped down. You're still the co pastor of this church."

She blinked. "What?"

"You kept doing the work. Youth group, choir, newsletters, even filling in for Marcus. You just stopped getting paid. The church owes you about twenty six thousand dollars in back salary."

Lauren stared. "Reverend Martin didn't say anything."

"He's trying to move past all this. But you're still an active minister. That matters."

"What am I supposed to do with that?"

"You're a widow with a daughter. If you're a minister in good standing, the General Ministry has to place you in a church with a salary and housing allowance. Standard pay is fifty thousand plus housing."

Lauren felt a chill despite the heat. "Do you think they would do that?"

Lance smiled. "I wouldn't be telling you if I didn't."

Chapter 2

Money Won
Is Twice as Sweet
As Money Earned

Walk Away

The twilight made him luminous, like an angel. The sheets were cool, but Lauren was warm in his arms. She turned her head to look into his eyes.

"I thought you left me."

"Never. I would never leave you." He traced her nose with his fingertips and tilted her chin. His mouth was firm, then gentle. The kiss lasted only an instant before her eyes shot open.

Her lips seared with pain. "Marcus?" she whispered. But he was gone.

Lauren awoke to a pillow stained with red. She tasted the copper of blood in her dry mouth. She brushed her teeth and showered hastily, trying to scrub the dream away before opening the door to Lance, his wife Ellen, and Melanie—the only female elder in the congregation.

Melanie tackled her in a bear hug, smelling of sweet, flowery perfume. "Oh, my dear girl. I'm going to miss you."

"Thank you, Melanie. For everything," Lauren managed, muffled against Melanie's shoulder. "You guys really went to bat for me."

"It was nothing," Melanie said, her blue eyes wide behind thick mascara. "You promise to visit the second I need you, you hear? I'm going to miss our Saturday coffees."

Sydney poked her head from her bedroom. "Are you guys the movers? Mom said Reverend Martin was sending deacons."

"That was before your mother took them for twenty-six thousand dollars and demanded a job," Lance said with a sly smile.

"Mom did that?"

"She did," Lance said. "And yep, we're the movers."

Ellen looked small but authoritative next to her husband, her hair still damp from the shower. She put her hands on her hips. "It was the right thing to do. Now the 'holy' deacons are licking their wounds and won't help you pack. I've had it with this church."

"Ellen, don't," Lauren warned. "This place needs you. Because of you three, I have a job and a place to go. I don't care if my name is mud with the Reverend. You were there for me."

"They were disappointed in Marcus," Lauren added, her shoulders tensing. "I was married to him, so I'm painted with the same brush."

Melanie laughed in disbelief. "Darlin', no. We don't do jail time for other people's crimes. There should be compassion here, not a ledger."

"The church got a dose of real life," Ellen said. "Their minister wasn't perfect. Shocker. If they'd shown an ounce of care, maybe he wouldn't be dead."

Lauren winced.

"Oh, Lauren. I didn't mean—"

"It's okay, Ellen." Lauren waved it away. "I don't blame the church. I really don't."

Melanie pulled Lauren aside toward the hydrangea bush at the corner of the parsonage. "Are you sure you're okay? As a social worker, I've worked with hundreds of people in grief. I'm concerned."

"I'm fine," Lauren insisted, the question sparking a familiar irritation. "I have Sydney to focus on."

"And you're putting yourself on the back burner. I haven't seen you shed

9

a single tear, Lauren. That's denial. It isn't healthy."

"I'm dealing with it in my own way," Lauren said, her voice sharpening. "My first concern is making sure we aren't on the street. Now is not the time to break down."

Melanie bit her lip. "You're just so stoic. It's okay to cry."

Lauren couldn't tell her the truth. She wasn't being stoic; she was numb. At night, when she searched her soul, she felt nothing. Or worse—a tiny, flickering part of her felt relieved.

* * *

The KIA Sorento was packed to the roof. Lauren cranked the air conditioning and gripped the steering wheel. Marcus had always been the one in the driver's seat. Now, watching the Starbucks and the parks of her old life roll back in the rearview mirror, leaving Salem felt... good.

"So, what's this town like?" Sydney asked, her eyes wide with expectation.

Lauren knew next to nothing about Vernonia, Oregon. She breathed deeply, forcing her body to relax. "The church has had some issues," she confessed. "Five pastors in four years. But it's beautiful. There's land with the parsonage—maybe enough for a pet."

"Seriously?" Sydney squealed.

"Seriously."

As they hit the highway, Lauren recalled Reverend Martin's face during the meeting two days ago. He had been flanked by the three elders most critical of Marcus. Lauren had focused on the cross behind his head, bolstered by Melanie's saccharine perfume and Lance's steady presence beside her.

"I never really stepped down," she had told them, her voice surpisingly steady. "I have the Master of Divinity. I've served faithfully. I can do the job, and the General Ministry needs me as much as I need them."

"And you believe the church owes you twenty-six thousand dollars?" the veteran elder, Bob Whitaker, had asked.

"Melanie and Marsha went through the books," Lauren replied. "Based on the *salary schedule, it's exactly $26,527."*

Reverend Martin had grunted, delivering the news like a verdict. *"Vernonia is on the verge of being shut down. It's a congregation of twenty. This is their last shot, and you're the last minister we're sending."* He had smiled then—a sly, private joke of a smile. *"And Mrs. Westbrook? They specifically requested a male pastor. Just thought you should know."*

Lauren had ignored the red flag. She was too grateful for the seed money to pay down the debt. For the first time in years, the weight on her shoulders felt lighter.

"Mom? How did Dad really die?"

The car felt suddenly cold. "Sydney, you know he lost control of the pickup on the coastal highway."

"Why was he there? You didn't even know he'd left. I heard you guys fighting that night."

Lauren's knuckles turned white on the wheel. "We were angry. He was struggling with a problem he couldn't overcome."

"Gambling," Sydney said flatly.

"Yes. He needed to feel powerful, I suppose. I don't think he was happy."

"Why weren't we enough?"

"Oh, sweetie. If I had that answer, we'd be living different lives. An addiction is a monster you can't control."

"I hate gambling. It's stupid."

"It is stupid," Lauren agreed. "I guess I feel the worst about not being able to help him. I've spent my life training to help people, and I couldn't save the person most important to me."

"I don't think you made a mistake, Mom. That's just life," Sydney said, patting her arm. "Do you think he was thinking about us? In the truck?"

Lauren's voice caught. "I think he was thinking about us the entire time."

"Then why would he do it?"

Lauren watched the road, trying to find the words. "The police say it was an accident. But maybe he thought the monster had gotten too big. Maybe he thought he was keeping us safe by facing it alone on that road."

Sydney broke then, the sobs coming in jagged waves. "He's never coming back."

Lauren pulled the car to the shoulder and held her daughter, patting her back as the girl wept. "You've got me," she whispered. "And I've got you."

As she held her daughter, Lauren felt a sharp, physical pain in her chest with every breath—but the tears still wouldn't come.

Chapter 3

Nobody is always a winner,
and anybody who says he is,
is either a liar or
doesn't play poker.

New Game

Nobody is always a winner, and anybody who says he is, is either a liar or doesn't play poker.

Lauren watched the landscape transform as they drove northwest. The flat, open spaces of the Willamette Valley baked in the heat of the summer sun, but suddenly, without warning, the terrain turned green and lush. They entered a world of misty mountain forest. Lauren rolled down her window and breathed the cool, wet air.

They drove for sixty miles through winding forest roads before they approached the crest of a hill. From this vantage point, Lauren spotted Vernonia for the first time. The small town was a snapshot of the past, classic Americana with its statuesque brick buildings. At the center of town was a church with a large white steeple nestled in rolling green hills. Foggy patches dressed the valley like lace on a windowpane. From the west, the sun pierced through the clouds, creating a halo of golden light.

Lauren said a quiet prayer. "Lord, I pray that this will be a good place for Sydney and me. Help this to be a place of healing."

She followed a small gravel road to the top of a hill where she viewed the church for the first time. The building was classic in style, not too different in appearance from the Presbyterian church below. But where the church in town was neatly maintained, the First Assembly of Disciples Church of Vernonia had fallen into obvious disrepair.

"Oh boy," Lauren said under her breath. "What am I getting myself into?"

Beautiful purple and white stained glass windows reflected light from the setting sun, but several were boarded up. One could tell the wooden siding had once been a pristine white, but over time a gray tinge had covered the entire structure, giving the appearance of permanent cobwebs. The drab exterior was further accentuated by pronounced cracks in the stressed wood.

The church was past its prime, stewing in neglect. Lauren's father, a contractor by trade, would have said the church had "good bones." He had built a few churches himself in his day before a heart attack took him too young. He would have noticed the strong beams and beautiful arches that reflected the love and care of the original engineers. No doubt they were working people who had built their church to reflect the love they had for their God. They believed their place of worship would stand strong through the passage of time. Lauren wondered how those original builders would react to seeing their church, so lovingly constructed, now looking so dilapidated and forlorn.

She passed the church and drove about a hundred yards further north on the gravel road, up to higher ground and a small, modest white house. On second thought, Lauren thought "cottage" was a better word. Overgrown hydrangea bushes and rhododendrons that looked more like trees grew wild in the front yard. The parsonage was in better repair than the church and boasted a large covered front porch. The wood siding looked freshly painted, and someone had planted purple and pink irises around the entire structure.

"Things are looking up," Lauren whispered.

From the outside, the parsonage felt cozy and welcoming. A woman sat smoking on the front veranda in a white porch swing. She was slim, and her outrageously red hair was styled in a fancy up-do that looked out of place in the natural setting. Lauren parked the car in a patch of yellowing grass and nudged her sleepy daughter.

"Alright, Syd. Get out and stretch your legs. We're here."

Sydney removed her earphones, wrinkled her nose, and then looked out the car window. "We're here? Oh, wow. Is this our house?"

"I believe so. I need to talk to this lady. Do you want to stay in the car?"

Her daughter's tired eyes now looked fully alert. "No way. I want to explore. Can I?"

"You've got to stay within my vision. This church and parsonage look like they're on a pretty steep hill. I don't want you rolling down and breaking your legs on our first day here."

Sydney rolled her eyes. "Mom, seriously. You act like I'm five. I know how to walk."

"Just be careful. That's all I'm saying. And wait—you need to meet this nice lady from the church first before you go running off." Lauren's heart tightened in her chest as she opened the car door. She took a deep breath and waved to the woman. "Hello? Gloria Ketchum?"

"Well, hallo. Yes, that's me." Gloria stubbed her cigarette into what appeared to be a metallic silver lighter in her hand. She put the lighter back into her pocket and threw the discarded cigarette into the yard. She removed a small box of Tic Tacs from her canary-yellow purse and quickly popped one in her mouth. Gliding down the steps, she greeted Lauren in front of the house. "I'm not supposed to be smoking," she confessed. "Please, don't tell my husband, Henry. He'd have an absolute fit, and I wouldn't hear the last of it fer a month."

Lauren smiled and suddenly felt at ease. "Your secret is safe with me. It also helps that I don't know Henry, so I certainly wouldn't tell him."

Gloria laughed, revealing yellowed teeth beneath her red lipstick. "You might not ever know him. He ain't much of a church-goer."

Lauren thought Melanie wore a lot of makeup, but Melanie looked practically *au naturel* compared to Gloria. There was so much mascara clumped on her synthetic eyelashes that one could hardly see her eyes.

From afar, Lauren thought Gloria was in her mid-forties. Her movements were quick and agile like a young woman's, but up close, Lauren could see the etched crow's feet around her eyes and the lines around the corners of her mouth. Upon greater scrutiny, she guessed Gloria to be in her sixties. Likewise, Gloria looked Lauren up and down, assessing her.

"Well, I am as close as you're going to get to a church secretary, or whatever you want to call it. In truth, I'm just the last gal standing."

"What do you mean?" Lauren asked, confused.

"I don't mean to discourage you none, but we've just had people leaving this church in droves. When they heard we had a woman pastor coming... well, I don't think that stopped the exodus any."

"I'm sorry to hear that. I hope the people here will give me a chance." Lauren sighed. She had just arrived and already felt defeated. She took a breath and forced a smile. "This is my daughter, Sydney."

Sydney remembered her manners and stretched out her hand. "Hello."

"Why, hello, young lady. You're just as pretty as a picture, aren't you? It's nice to meet you. Welcome to Vernonia and welcome to your new home. You want to see it?" Gloria gestured toward the cottage.

Sydney's eyes opened wide. "I very much do!" she almost shouted, forgetting her manners.

Gloria chuckled, pulled a key from her pocket, and unlocked the door. The lock was stubborn, and she had to push with her shoulder to budge it open. Lauren was greeted by the slightly musty smell of an old home as she followed Gloria and Sydney into the living room.

"My son, Luke, did some work in here to get the place ready. He took out the old carpet and put in new flooring and did some refurbishing. It smelled a bit like the old pastor, and I didn't think that would help you in feeling welcome."

Sydney wrinkled her nose. "What does 'old pastor' smell like?"

Gloria's eyes sparkled even as she deadpanned. "It's hard to track down exactly, but I assure you, it's not a good odor."

"Oh," Sydney shrugged. "Wow, this is kinda nice."

Gloria laughed. "Well, what did you expect?"

16

Lauren's eyes widened. "Honestly, I don't know, but I'm with Sydney. I wasn't expecting this."

Gloria smiled. "It is kinda special, isn't it?"

Lauren felt a strange warmth and peace as she surveyed the space. The beautiful woodwork struck her. The hardwood floors were smooth, freshly sanded and finished. The color was a rich caramel that made Lauren think of molasses, apples, and spices. The warmth contrasted with the white walls that looked freshly painted, just like the outdoor siding.

The kitchen was small, but her eyes lingered on the brand-new cupboards in the same caramel maple wood. There were cupboards to spare. Lauren had never been in a home with enough cupboard space, and as she looked at the kitchen, she felt almost pampered by the idea of calling such a kitchen her own. The cathedral-shaped cabinets looked expensive and meticulously crafted. She placed her hands on the countertops and allowed her fingers to glide over the lustrous surface. "These are beautiful. What is this made of?"

Gloria laughed. "That's good old concrete."

"Really? How did they get the counters to look so smooth?" Under her fingertips, the concrete was as cool, shiny, and slick as marble.

"Luke is a bit of a perfectionist," Gloria sighed. "If he can't do the job to his satisfaction, he doesn't feel like it's worth the effort. He's always been that way. It's been worse since his divorce." Gloria gave Lauren a knowing look. "It's just one floor. Only about 900 square feet. The master bedroom is over there, and the spare bedroom, which I'm guessing will be Miss Sydney's, is on the other side of the house."

"I didn't realize it would be furnished," Lauren said.

"Most of the things were my mother's," Gloria sighed heavily. "She liked beautiful things."

"Gloria, is it okay for us to use them? That's very generous. These items are lovely." A green velvet Victorian sofa was positioned against the wall. Lauren ran her fingers over its cherry-wood frame. Her eyes were drawn to a colorful Tiffany lamp that sat on the end table. She reached over and clicked it on, and the colored glass lampshade sparkled with purples and greens.

17

"Ma loved irises. That was a special gift from her second husband, Vern."

"It's beautiful. The colored glass is striking. Are you sure it's okay?"

"Well, if they weren't here in the parsonage, they'd be in storage and I'd be paying out the nose for that. So, if you don't mind being the caretaker of her things, I'd be appreciative."

"Gloria, I certainly do not mind. This is unbelievable. Sydney and I will have to be very careful with these lovely items, but... why don't you want these things in your own house?"

Gloria's eyes clouded for a second, and the corners of her mouth twitched ever so slightly. "Let's just say my mother and I had a complex relationship. Sometimes it just don't feel right to have someone else's things in your house. In my mind, those things will always be Mother's, not mine."

Lauren nodded with understanding as she thought of her own mother. "Well, I get that, Gloria. Now that you mention it, I'm not sure I'd want too many of my own mother's things in my house, either."

Gloria raised her eyebrows as if reconsidering Lauren. She exhaled suddenly. "Well, don't worry yerself too much about any of it. You have to live and be comfortable. Mother's up in heaven now and she won't be needing any of these things anymore. I like to remember her in my mind, not with things. So, it works out fer the both of us."

Lauren nodded her head, impressed. "That's quite philosophical."

Gloria laughed. "When you reach sixty-five, hopefully you got some wisdom to show for it."

"Thank you, Gloria. You have no idea how much this means to both of us."

Gloria's mouth formed a solid line as she frowned. "Don't be thanking me yet. I wouldn't wish this church on my worst enemy."

Lauren set to unpacking. She smiled as she listened to the sound of Sydney humming in the next room. The windows were open, and a cool breeze filtered through the house. Suddenly, there was a knock on the door.

"I'll be right there," Lauren called.

She opened the front door but saw no one. *Maybe it was the wind,* she thought. But there had been a distinct sound—the sound of knuckles on wood. She was sure of it. As she glanced around the front porch, she heard only the breeze through the trees, but when she gazed down at her feet, a beaten cardboard box sat on the porch in front of the door. Inside the flimsy box was a mishmash of what looked like old, forgotten junk.

Lauren picked up the box and brought it to the kitchen table. She wrinkled her nose as she gazed at its contents. She felt a chill move up and down her spine—an ominous, dark presence she could not explain. She grabbed a can of Lysol and sprayed it over the contents of the container, standing back for a moment. The box was filled with old pictures, most from the seventies, she presumed, based on the frequency of jean jackets, bell-bottoms, and mustaches worn by the subjects. She grabbed a washcloth, dampened it under the faucet, and proceeded to wipe the dust from the frames. She recognized the First Assembly of Disciples Church of Vernonia in what must have been its heyday.

The church stood white and pristine in the background of the largest framed photo. More than two hundred people were gathered for the picture. They looked like happy people for the most part—families and children in the front and older, more stately figures in the back. Most of the women wore floral dresses and the men suits and ties. *Perhaps this was an Easter Sunday?* Lauren thought. The other pictures in the box highlighted different individuals and families. Lauren assumed they must have all been members of the church during that time. A relative of an old church member or a local history buff must have dropped them off. These items surely had historical and sentimental value to the church, and she was now entrusted with their safekeeping. Lauren was the new pastor, after all. Surely her address wasn't a secret from the community. But as a single woman and mother, Lauren didn't feel comfortable with uninvited guests dropping in unannounced.

She shuddered before poking carefully at what looked like a bundle of dirty, disheveled washcloths in the corner of the box. Not wanting to touch the wad of fabric with her bare hands, she grabbed a fork from a kitchen drawer. Cautiously, she jabbed at the bundle.

When she detected sudden movement, she screamed. The rags moved up and down as if they held a living heart, and then a spider the size of a baseball skirted its way from beneath the wad of fabric and moved across the largest picture frame. It settled there, poised to jump. Lauren couldn't help herself; she screamed again.

"What is it, Mom?" Sydney called as she ran into the living room.

"Stay back, Syd. There's an enormous spider in that box."

Sydney laughed. "How big is it?"

"It's as big as you," Lauren whispered in terror.

Sydney rifled through one of the moving totes and handed Lauren a fly swatter. "Kill it," she said.

Lauren stared at the enormous black spider. Her skin crawled as she registered all eight of its black, beady eyes staring at her. The hairy bristles quivered on its back. "I can't kill it, Syd. I just can't," she whispered.

Sydney took the fly swatter back. She held her chosen weapon daintily and considered her angle. She moved to the left of Lauren and then suddenly brought the fly swatter down with force. Lauren heard the smack and winced. As Sydney slowly lifted the fly swatter, Lauren felt her stomach lurch as she identified a large blot of spider blood and guts. The remains of the insect were now smeared across the Easter Sunday photo.

"Got it!" Sydney yelled.

"God bless you," Lauren whispered as she grabbed a paper towel to wipe away the spider corpse.

"What a creepy doll," Sydney said as she lifted the wad of dirty fabric out of the box and turned it around to reveal a white porcelain face, the shredded remains of a nineteenth-century house dress, and scuffed patent-leather shoes.

"Syd, don't touch that! Oh, never mind." Lauren's eyes widened as she took in the doll. She absorbed the pale porcelain and the jagged crack that ran down its face from the forehead to the jawline. "Sydney, that doll is totally creepy, and I definitely do not want it in the house."

Sydney smiled. "What, this?" She shoved the flopping figure of the doll toward Lauren.

"Don't! Just don't!" Lauren shrieked.

Sydney laughed. "Don't worry, Mom. It's the creepiest doll I've ever seen, and I don't want it in the house either." She threw it back in the box.

"You know, I think Gloria told me that the church has an attic that they use for storage. I'm going to take it down there." Lauren took the box off the kitchen table and carried it back to the porch, leaving the cardboard box and its creepy contents outside. *Out of sight, out of mind,* she thought.

Chapter 4

When something unlucky

costs you a win.

Bad Beat

W hat are you waiting for?" Sydney asked.

Lauren squinted up at the church from outside and recorded to memory where the steeple was located. She set the box full of pictures topped with the forlorn doll on the hood of the car. "I'm just trying to figure out where the attic is before I go inside."

"Did you ask Gloria where the attic is over the phone?"

"Yes, of course, but her instructions were kind of confusing," Lauren admitted.

Sydney wrinkled her nose. "You're not a very good listener."

"That's not true!"

Sydney gave her mom a harrowing look before laughing. "You know, Mom. This church is almost as creepy as that doll."

Lauren bit her bottom lip and sighed as her eyes settled on the boarded windows. "You're not wrong. That's what happens when you don't take care of a building. Grandpa would have blown a gasket if he saw this place. He hated it when people didn't take care of historic buildings."

Sydney's eyes were wide with disbelief. "So, we're really going to church here?"

"It will be okay, Syd. You know I'm lucky to have this job and just think, we don't have to live with Grandma."

Her face brightened. "That is good news. I guess it's not the creepiest. I mean... grandma is creepier."

Lauren's lips tightened. "That's not kind, Syd. Grandma tries." Anxious to change the subject, she handed the key to Sydney. "You open the front door. I'll carry the scary box."

"Deal," Sydney bolted the stairs to the front entrance. She struggled with the key for several moments. Lauren breathed in through her nose reminding herself to be patient and to allow her daughter the opportunity to wrestle with the key. Finally, the door opened with a loud creak.

"Nice job, Syd! That lock looks like it was made in 1792."

They made their way into an enclosed foyer area. Lauren was overcome by a stifling musty odor and held her hand over her nose. Several of the windows were covered with wooden boards and the room was dark. "Sydney, do you see a light switch anywhere?" Her daughter scampered around the room, her hands tracing the walls.

"Got it!" She cried. A dull yellowish glow emitted from the rectangular fluorescent bulb on the ceiling. The light it cast illuminated, but didn't necessarily brighten the room.

"Hmm," Lauren grunted as she surveyed the space. "I think we're going to need to open some windows. It's hot and musty in here." An abundance of floral carpeted furniture filled the cramped space. The chocolate wood paneling draped in dust cobwebs made her wonder for just a second if she had time traveled to a forgotten movie set from the 80s. Old books in bookshelves caked with dust lined most of the western wall. To the right, someone had made a sad attempt at creating a coffee bar. Lauren ran her fingers along the surface of a Mr. Coffee machine. The pot was stained a rusty brown and emitted a foul, rotten odor. "Ooh. Wow!" Lauren took a step back and raised her eyebrows at Sydney. "Girl, we got some work to do."

Sydney's eyes opened wide. "I'm not the pastor. Don't you mean, you've got some work to do?"

Lauren opened her eyes wide in mock surprise. "I'm hiring you to share the job. Plus, I didn't know being a pastor meant also being the custodian."

"Nice try, Mom," Sydney laughed. "I don't want your job. Plus, I know you're broke and couldn't pay me."

"Touche," Lauren chuckled.

Lauren picked up a container of powdered vanilla flavored coffee mate that was sitting next to the machine and read the label. "This expired in 2012. Goodness! Maybe I should add it to the spider box and put it in the attic as an artifact?"

Sydney yanked the creamer from her hand and shook it. "Mom, it's got something lumpy and hard in it."

Lauren grabbed the container back from Sydney and also shook it. She grimaced when she realized the powder had turned into a congealed mass of goo. "See if there's a garbage can, you can throw it into." She tossed it back to Sydney.

"Your bossy, Mom," Sydney whined, but she complied.

Lauren spent about an hour exploring the church. Sydney was long gone. To her credit, she had grabbed a duster and helped Lauren all of thirty minutes, but the call of the outdoors had lured her. After promising to phone Lauren in the event of an emergency, she had agreed to let her explore the hillside around the church and parsonage. Lauren gave herself a tour and discovered her study which was in the back of the main office. The 200 square foot room looked a bit like a glorified closet with no windows and the same dark wooden paneling. Lauren made a hasty list of what she would need to clean up or remove to make the space habitable. Despite the overall disrepair, the sanctuary was charming. High arched ceilings and beautiful purple and white stained glass windows created a tone of grandeur. *It's not without potential,* Lauren reminded herself. Beyond the sanctuary there were several classrooms, but most were not being used for anything but storage. In a 6000 square foot church, only 20% of the available space was actually being used by the congregation for active ministry.

The office, the foyer, and the sanctuary were the only rooms that showed any sign of life, the rest of the rooms sat silent gathering dust. Lauren's heart felt heavy as she discovered a baptismal behind the sanctuary. The tub was filled with linens and old costumes. Likely, it had not been used to actually baptize a living soul in years. The piles fabrics smelled of dust and mothballs. The book of Ezekiel came to Lauren's mind, the Valley of Dry Bones. "I will make breath enter you, and you will come to life…" She whispered the words under her breath trying to capture Ezekiel's vision. God reminded the prophet that only the Lord himself could restore life to the people of Israel who were in exile, their faith and spirit dead. Would God choose to work a miracle in Vernonia? *I sure hope so*, she thought. Could He bring this pile of dead bones back to life? Lauren had not met anyone in this body of believers besides Gloria, but she already knew that this church for all practical purposes was dead. Nothing in the building showed evidence of a life in the spirit, but only the vague ghosts of a faith now dead.

Behind the baptismal, Lauren finally discovered the hatch to the attic. She ran back to the office and grabbed a ladder. She struggled as she carried it awkwardly through the chamber of rooms and finally placed it by the opening. She returned for the spider box. Lauren vowed to use the ladder carefully. She wasn't taking any chances. Sydney needed at least one healthy, living parent. If she fell, no one would hear her in the abyss of back rooms and forgotten junk. If she broke her neck, she might be hidden in this church for days before her dead body was discovered.

Lauren set the ladder firmly in place and carefully climbed and pulled the hatch revealing the dark hole of the attic. Lauren coughed as dust coated her lungs and held her arm over her nose. She climbed down again and grabbed a utility flashlight that she had found in the office and made her way cautiously back up the ladder. On the fourth rung, a cold chill moved through her body from the top of her head to her toes. Suddenly she felt off balance and shivered. She closed her eyes and focused on her breathing. *Lauren, you've seen way too many scary movies. Get it together. You're a grown up and you've got a job to do.* She focused on the texture of the metal frame of the ladder and reminded herself that her hands were firmly gripping the bars. *I'm okay*, she repeated. *God, give me courage*, she whispered. Her mind settled and she no longer felt the dizzy sensation. She opened her eyes and climbed further up. After a deep breath, she poked her head into the darkness. She cast the beam of her flashlight across the room.

What she saw surprised her. Every room in the church that was not currently in use was a bit of a mess. Most of the rooms had stacks of furniture, books, and papers cluttered about with an occasional stained drop cloth over the piles. Likewise, the attic was filled with junk, but there was some order to the madness. Through the uneven light, Lauren could see a corner filled with Victorian furniture, not so different from the couch and lamp in the parsonage. A bookshelf looked about ready to burst with books that were stacked to the ceiling on top of the bookshelf. An oriental carpet appeared almost strategically placed at the foot of the bookshelf and even through the shaded light, Lauren could tell the carpet was a rare antique. *That could probably command a hefty price on eBay,* she thought. The room was not as dusty as she expected considering the state of the rest of the rooms. After making her way back down the ladder, she grabbed the spider box balancing its weight against her hip. Cautiously, she pulled herself up the ladder.

The box wasn't heavy, but awkward and she maneuvered one rung of the ladder at a time. When she reached the top, she placed the box on the floor and then pulled herself up. She stood up with her flashlight and surveyed the space again. A small pile in the corner of the room filled with pictures caught her eye and she lugged the box in the same direction. The pictures were neatly organized in a plastic tote and surprisingly free of dust. *One of the church members must have been up here not too long ago organizing,* Lauren thought. *It seems odd to start your organizing in the attic, but whatever floats your boat.* The beam of her flashlight lingered on the top of the picture pile. A five by seven rested on the surface, an older man holding a little girl. The picture was in color, but had the same faded, yellowing of the other pictures in the spider box. The child was quite beautiful with long, dark curly hair and striking deep set blue eyes. Lauren shivered as her eyes rested on the porcelain doll the girl was holding. *Is it the same one?* Lauren recognized the emotionless expression, the petticoat, and patent leather shoes. The doll was out of place even in the photos. It was not a doll from the last half of the 20th century. There was something both ancient and foreboding about it. Lauren picked up the photo and read the handwritten inscription at the bottom: Pastor Byron Worth. Lauren placed the photo back on the pile. She felt the sudden need to step back.

The rafters creaked under the pressure of her feet and suddenly she felt a presence in the room. Terror seized her. She whipped around. Something, someone was moving. She saw a glimpse of dark fur, fabric? She screamed. She couldn't help it.

Lauren felt the dizziness return. She was off balance as she continued to step back in the desperate effort of regaining her equilibrium coupled with the frantic desire to escape from whatever creature was in the room with her. Her feet slipped between the wooden beams of the attic floor. The surface gave way and she was falling, falling through the ceiling. Lauren heard a terror induced shriek, before realizing she was the one screaming.

Lauren thought she was dead for a moment. As she opened her eyes, she realized she was still in the attic at least from the waist up. Everything below her waist was dangling from the ceiling. She was caught between the legs by a rafter and she felt fire and pain in her groin, but the rafter had saved her from falling at least 12 feet to the ground below. The beam was still holding her up, but the damage was obvious in the cracked misshapen wood that was now bending under her weight. Remembering the movement in the attic, the panic returned. Moving her flashlight wildly, her eyes scanned every corner of the room. She saw nothing.

The room was quiet, dead as a tomb. Her legs felt moist, from blood or urine she wasn't sure. Lauren was not able to see her legs through the attic floor, only the broken, splintered wood and plaster where she had fallen. Lauren tried to reach for her phone, but she needed her arms to hold her up. It didn't matter anyway. She had left her smartphone in the room below before climbing the ladder. *You idiot! Don't panic,* she repeated in her head as her thoughts spiraled. She gave herself just a moment to think before croaking out, "Help!" She took a deep breath again. "Help! Help!"

* * *

She wasn't sure how much time had passed. For the first few minutes she had screamed herself senseless, but when no help came, she had to rest. Her voice was raspy and frail. Periodically, she called out, "Help, Help! I'm in here!" Surely Sydney would be along soon to check on her. She was growing tired and weak. She was not sure she had enough energy to keep herself upright.

"Where are you?"

She heard his voice cutting through the fog of panic. Lauren's mind had been so focused on inhaling and exhaling, that she struggled to find her voice.

"Here. I'm in... I'm in the attic," she managed to say.

Lauren heard the sound of steady footsteps approaching as they resonated through the attic space. From her vantage point, she could only see the dust settling on the rafters through the dim light of one murky attic window as her legs dangled beneath her. The weight of her lower body strained her chest and arms, but she was determined to pull herself up instead of falling all the way through the rafters. *One must maintain what little dignity they have even in the worst of situations.* Lauren heard the door creak as the stranger entered the room below her. She heard a surprised intake of air and perhaps just the hint of a chuckle. "You alright?"

The voice was deep and calm. His presence revived the dead air and Lauren found she was able to breathe. She couldn't restrain the sarcastic edge in her voice, "Yeah, everything's just fine and dandy. I'm just hanging out. Maybe you should come back in an hour or so."

He was silent for a moment. Lauren could only imagine what he was seeing. She was wearing shorts and her bare legs up to her thigh were exposed. *I pray to God this man is not some pervert, but a gentleman.* Her face was hot with humiliation. She struggled for every shred of dignity.

His voice filtered upward. "I'm going to pull you up. I'm coming up there. Hang tight." She heard the slight grunt of laughter and then, "no pun intended."

"Ha, ha," Lauren deadpanned.

She heard his footsteps as he climbed the ladder and then through the glare of the window she saw his face. He rested on the ladder, his strong upper body poking through the entrance so they could face each other eye to eye. There was no question he was handsome, but not in a conventional way. His features were strong, but not quite symmetrical. He had broad shoulders, sandy hair, and deep brown eyes that hinted at keen intelligence. "Well, hello. I take it you're the new pastor."

Lauren couldn't help herself. She rolled her eyes. "Please, would you just get me out of here?"

"Yes, ma'am," he said with a hint of humor. He climbed all the way up the ladder till he towered over her and then slowly tested his feet on the rafters. Approaching cautiously, he planted himself in front of her on a strong beam and squatted down to her level. His brown eyes narrowed on her face. "Okay, I'm going to lift you under your arms and pull you up. I'm going to do it slow and easy. We don't want to get you more scratched up than you already are."

Before she could respond, he was in her space. His arms were wrapped beneath her arms, around her back. His face was so close to hers she shuddered from the intimacy. Then, they were moving upward together, her heart beating erratically in her chest. She winced as her legs met the resistance of sharp plaster. He read her face and stopped. He shifted her slightly to the left and then the right before continuing to pull her upward. He set her firmly on the platform, but did not release her from his grasp. "You, okay?" he asked.

Lauren's legs were numb. She felt woozy from hanging from the ceiling and then there was the scent of him. He smelled like forest, shaving cream, and a hint of coffee. The new and familiar surrounded and overwhelmed her. The dim light in the attic did not provide enough illumination to fully examine the damage to her legs, but as she ran her hands down the bare skin of her thighs she felt sticky and damp. "I'm not sure," she admitted. The truth was she felt lightheaded and the idea of staying secure in his strong arms was not exactly unappealing.

He released her slowly. "Are you okay to stand?"

"I think so."

"Wait," he said with authority. He took off his button down plaid shirt. Lauren's eyes opened wide. *What is he doing?* Beneath his shirt he wore a plain black dress T shirt. His biceps were working and she could see how strong he was. She knew this first hand. He had lifted her with such ease and control. From his back jean pocket he removed a small knife. With the blade, he ripped into the fabric of the shirt.

" Your shirt. Don't do that," Lauren protested.

He held out the large swatch of plaid cloth. "You have a nasty gash on your upper leg. It looked like it had mostly stopped bleeding when I saw your legs dangling from the ceiling, but put some pressure on the wound just in case."

"Thanks," Lauren said apologetically and took the remnant of his plaid shirt and held it against her leg.

The hint of a smile flickered across his face. "You're not putting pressure on the wound." He placed his hand almost roughly over hers and moved her hand about four inches to the left and higher. "Don't you even know where you're hurt?" He asked.

Lauren shook her head. "To be honest. I can't feel my legs."

The smile spread slowly across his face. "I guess that explains it."

She was dizzy again and her legs trembled unsteadily beneath her.

"Woh. I got you." He held her again briefly as she found her center again. "We gotta get you out of here."

She nodded her head. "Yes, please."

He angled himself behind her and made his way down the ladder about half way. "I'll spot you as you come down. Take it slow."

She followed him down more than aware that her rear end was practically staring him in the face. *This guy's probably a church deacon or even better an elder and this is how we meet?* Lauren was too overwhelmed to fully process the awkward nature of their first meeting, but focused instead on taking one step at a time down the ladder. She sighed with relief the moment her feet hit the floor. The sight of the gaping hole in the ceiling and chunky plaster on the floor stunned her back to reality. "Oh no! You have got to be kidding me! First day on the job and I've already caused thousands of dollars of damage to the building. What am I going to do?" She buried her head in her hands and tried to keep the tears from falling.

He laughed easily. "Breathe. It's okay. That's probably about a $500 fix. Don't worry about it. I'll fix it right up. The place is a dump anyway. This building hasn't had any proper maintenance done on it in the last two decades at least."

"Thanks for helping me. I don't know what I would have done...Oh no. Sydney. My daughter's outside playing. I've left her out way too long."

"Little girl with a ponytail about 8 or 9 years old?" The man asked.

"She's 10. Yes, that's my daughter."

"Well a little girl fitting that description was out on the swing set before I came in. She looked like she was doing a whole lot better than you."

She sighed with relief. "Oh, thank the Lord. Thank you."

"Not sure if the Lord had anything to do with it," he said. "In any case, let's get you to the church office. I'm pretty sure there's a first aid kit under the sink."

Lauren trailed behind him and limped her way back to the church office.

"Sit here," he ordered as he indicated a metal chair next to the desk. He made his way to a utility sink and rifled in through a cupboard before returning with a metal first aid kit that looked like an artifact from the WWII era.

"I guess the first aid kit came from the same store, where they got the coffee maker," Lauren said.

The man laughed. "My mom keeps meaning to update the office at least, but she never seems to get around to it." He opened the metal box and removed a bottle of antiseptic while also grabbing a clean cloth and a metal basin from a drawer.

As she observed his movements, her eyes opened wide with understanding. "You're Gloria's son."

He nodded his head as if to introduce himself. "My name's Luke Reid.

Nice to meet you, pastor."

Lauren returned the smile. "Not Ketchum like your mom?"

"No ma'am."

"I see. Well, it's nice to meet you too. I'm Lauren. Lauren Westbrook. You did the renovations on the parsonage?"

He knelt down in front of her. "I did, Pastor Westbrook."

"Please...just Lauren will do. Syd and I. We love it. I can't tell you. When we walked into that room it was like...Well, like we were home. Oh and the cabinets and the counters in the kitchen! They're just beautiful. I think they're maybe the most beautiful cabinets I've ever seen."

Luke smiled despite himself. "So, you like my work?"

Lauren laughed. "Yes, I would say that. It was pretty amazing and...well, honestly just what Sydney and I needed, so thank you for that."

Luke poured antiseptic on the clean cloth and gently reached under her knee to extend her leg.

"Oh, you don't have to do that." Lauren reached her hand for the antiseptic. "I can do it myself."

"No. Sit back." The firmness in his voice surprised her. "You're going to be doing enough by yourself at this place. You might as well take help when you can get it."

Lauren did not know how to reply to his odd statement. She watched as he used the cloth to clean her bloodied leg. His hands were rough and lined, but yet somehow gentle. Her heart beat unsteadily as he touched her. He removed the remnant of his shirt from her leg and cleaned the wound gently prompting fresh blood. He held the pressure for a long moment and then lifted the cloth. He tilted his head to blow on the wound.

"What are you doing?" she gasped. Her voice sounded light and inconsequential in the still air.

He smiled. "Oh, sorry. That's just a trick my mom taught me. I got scraped up pretty good when I was a kid. Probably about every day. I learned all her tricks for dressing a wound. Makes it dry faster, I believe."

Lauren could not resist, "but...not exactly sanitary."

Luke raised his eyebrows and smirked. "You know where most people

32

die?"

She shook her head.

"In hospitals. They pride themselves on being sanitary."

"There's some logical fallacies there, but…."He glared at her.

"Okay. Point taken." Lauren nodded.

His warm brown eyes moved from the wound on her leg and studied her face. "This one may need a stitch or two."

Lauren's eyebrows inched closer together as she wrinkled her nose. "I hope not. I'm not sure I have health insurance."

Luke raised an eyebrow. "If you don't mind me asking, why did you take this job exactly?"

Lauren considered several diplomatic responses before blurting out, "Desperation is really the only word for it. My husband died just, well a few weeks ago. He was a gambler. He left me and Syd with nothing, well… nothing except a pile of debt and this job. I guess this church is what my husband left me. It's a chance for a new life. One where I get to parent my own daughter and don't have to live with my mother."

Luke's mouth tightened. He studied her silently as he reached into the tin first aid box and pulled out gauze and tape.

Lauren felt the heat of regret. "I'm so sorry. That was way too much information. I don't know what I was thinking of dumping all that on you."

His frown deepened, as he stared at her with an intensity that unnerved her. "Don't ever apologize for speaking the truth." The silence between them returned as he wrapped her leg in gauze. He finally spoke. "You see…I just wouldn't wish this place on my worst enemy."

Lauren frowned. "That's exactly what your mom said."

Chapter 5

An instance of unfair treatment

Raw Deal

Lauren rose early Sunday morning, her nerves rattled. She debated between dressing casual or dressy, knowing that older congregations still expected a certain Sunday formality. She finally selected a black knee-length skirt, black tights, and a blue blouse, paired with her favorite Mary Janes. Most evenings she was still tormented by the loss of Marcus, but this morning, the terror of preaching managed to shove thoughts of her husband into the recesses of her mind. She was grateful for the break.

As she stepped out the door, Lauren felt something hard under her shoe. She drew her foot back as her eyes caught a flash of metal. Sydney bent down and retrieved a ring.

"Where did this come from?" Three prongs held a large round ruby resting in a tiny circle of diamonds.

"It's so pretty," Sydney cooed. "Can I have it?"

Lauren took the ring gently. "We'll take it to church and ask Gloria. Maybe she dropped it." Lauren wore a chain around her neck with a small golden cross. She unlatched the clasp and added the ruby ring to the chain. "I'll keep it here for now so we don't lose it."

They walked together from the parsonage to the church. Lauren ran a protective hand across Sydney's back, admiring the tight braids her daughter had managed for herself. Since moving to Vernonia, Sydney seemed different—as if she had grown into a teenager in the span of a week. It made Lauren proud, but also frightened. Sydney wasn't a baby anymore, yet looks could be deceiving; the girl's face was often puffy in the morning from the tears she hid. The road ahead was not going to be easy.

Lauren almost did a double-take when she met Gloria at the door. The older woman's red hair was piled high in an intricate twisting of layers, lacquered into the shape of a football. Gloria clearly had an up-close-and-personal relationship with her hairspray bottle. Her Sunday makeup made her weekday look seem restrained; she wore a pineapple-colored dress suit with white trim, matching yellow pumps, and bright green eyeshadow with a slightly askew cat-eye liner.

"You look like a big pineapple," Sydney said.

"Sydney! That's rude," Lauren scolded, her cheeks heating with embarrassment.

Gloria laughed. "Why, I like pineapples. They're one of my favorites. I'll take that as a compliment, Miss Sydney."

Sydney smiled back. "I like pineapples too. I think you look pretty."

Lauren breathed a sigh of relief as she helped Gloria with the sticky door. Once inside, the pervasive darkness of the foyer struck her. "Gloria, it's summer. Why don't we leave the doors open? Bring in some fresh air."

Gloria raised an eyebrow. "You could do that. Some people aren't gonna like it."

"I think they need to stay open," Lauren insisted, "not just for appearances, but for public health. It's stuffy in here."

Gloria shrugged. "You're the boss." She threw open the swinging doors, casting a beam of light into the foyer.

Sydney found the light switch, and Lauren surveyed the space. The drab paneling remained, but the books had been thinned and organized. The space had been dusted, and the windows cleaned. The horrible old coffee pot was gone, replaced by a shiny red machine—the one bright object in the room. Next to it sat a silver tray Lauren had brought from the parsonage, stocked with fresh creamers and stir sticks. Luke had volunteered an afternoon to fix the attic floor and had hauled off two truckloads of junk.

Lauren's eyes narrowed with emotion as they settled on two large bouquets of flowers.

"Hydrangeas from my garden," Gloria said. "A celebration for our new minister."

Lauren flushed. "They're beautiful. How do you get them so vibrant?"

"Aah, a little trick with the soil. You gotta increase the acidity. I find natural, organic matter works the best, not the store-bought crap." Gloria placed a hand on Lauren's shoulder, demanding her full attention. "You know, I always find it interesting how some of the ugliest, godforsaken garbage can create the most beautiful colors."

Lauren caught her meaning and nodded. "I'm going to do my best, Gloria, but I'm not sure it's all in my hands."

"It never is," Gloria sighed. "If I'm being honest, there are days I'd like to call it quits. We might just be the people sent to close up shop."

"I'm not ready to open that can of worms yet," Lauren said.

Gloria tilted her head toward the parking lot. "You haven't met *them* yet."

Lauren ignored the remark. "Gloria, by the way, do you recognize this?" She lifted the ruby ring from beneath her blouse.

"Beautiful," Gloria mused. "Where'd you find that?"

"Stepped on it leaving the parsonage this morning."

"No, don't recognize it. But someone is sure likely to want that back."

At that moment, an older woman bustled into the foyer. "I'm here. I'm here."

The energy in the room shifted; Gloria visibly tensed. "Lauren, this is June. June, Lauren—our new minister."

Lauren extended her hand, but June ignored it. Clad in a burgundy velvet tracksuit, June looked Lauren up and down. "You? You're the minister? You look like you just came out of grammar school."

A shocked laugh escaped Lauren. "No, I'm actually forty-two. I graduated from Fuller Theological Seminary over a decade ago."

"So you're the one with the dead husband, desperate for a job?" June maintained her power pose, hand on hip.

Lauren's jaw slackened. She had no idea how to respond to this force of nature. June's raven-black hair was styled in a bouncy "Rachel" cut from the nineties—odd on a woman in her seventies, but meticulously groomed. Where Gloria was colorful and spontaneous, June was a soldier preparing for battle.

"It's nice to meet you," Lauren said, omitting the handshake this time.

"Where did you get that?" June snapped abruptly.

"Where did I get what?"

"That ring around your neck."

Lauren touched the chain. "Do you recognize it?"

"Who gave it to you?"

"I found it outside my porch this morning. Do you know it?"

"No," June snapped, squinting at it. "I thought it looked familiar, but now that I look closer, I don't recognize it."

"Well, if you could ask around, I'd appreciate it."

"Getting back to where we left off," June interrupted, "I'm the worship leader. My husband is Porter Lee. He was an elder for decades before the dementia got him." She spoke of the disease as casually as the weather.

"I'm sorry, June. You have a lot on your plate."

June waved her hand dismissively. "Life is life." Her eyes darted to the sanctuary. "Who's that?"

"My daughter, Sydney."

June frowned as Sydney jumped off the platform steps. "She's a little old for that. I hope she knows better than to jump around during practice."

"I haven't figured out a children's program yet," Lauren said. "There's a lot of trusting God at this point."

"Well, I see you've already made changes. Nobody drinks coffee here. You didn't need to use church funds for a new maker."

"It cost thirty dollars," Lauren said softly. "I meant no offense."

"And these doors? We keep them closed. Elderly people get chilled. We wouldn't want anyone pressing charges for getting sick."

Lauren recovered quickly. "June, it's a dry day and the church is musty. We might have black mold—at least, that's what Luke told me. Fresh air is key. We wouldn't want a lawsuit over mold, would we?"

June's dark eyes felt like lasers.

Gloria coughed, her eyes twinkling. "Where is Porter, June?"

Alarm flashed across June's face. "He's in the car! I better get him." She bustled out.

Lauren turned to Gloria. "Is she handling him by herself?"

"She's a control freak," Gloria whispered. "She's fired every nurse they've had. Porter is a sweet man, unlike that old bat wife of his. Don't worry about her; that's just June being June." Gloria sighed. "I'm gonna get the bulletins. You sure you want to greet everyone at the door?"

"I should start getting to know them," Lauren said, though her nerves were frayed. She thought of Marcus; he would have charmed June in two minutes. Lauren didn't have that "it" factor. She felt the fingers of hopelessness creeping in.

June returned, guiding a frail, hunched man. Porter looked at Lauren with bloodshot eyes and gave her a wide, toothy grin. She waved, watching June direct him to a front pew like a drill sergeant.

A few minutes later, an older African American man in a blue wool jacket entered. He had a refined, educated air and a charming smile. "Pastor Westbrook, I take it?"

"Yes. You are?"

"Paul Lu Roe. I'm the sound guy—or, when June's leading, I'm 'doing my time.' I'm on the Ministry Team, so we'll be getting to know each other."

"Lovely," Lauren smiled, warmed by his energy.

"You're a brave woman moving out here. Fortune rewards the brave."

"Does it reward the stupid?" Lauren gasped. "I'm sorry, that was rude."

Paul laughed with delight. "They go hand in hand! If we were all smart, no one would be brave. I'm an optimist, so let's stick with brave."

Rehearsal began. Sydney returned, scowling. "That woman told me I was a nuisance."

"Stay clear of her, Hun," Lauren whispered. "I need you to sit still today.

We don't want to live with Grandma, right?" Sydney nodded, the rebellion beneath her surface momentarily stilled.

The congregation trickled in—about twenty-five people in total. They dispersed in uneven groups, many scowling or looking on with vacant eyes. Lauren felt a looming darkness.

She took her place in the front pew. Linda, the pianist, plunked out the first chords of *O Sacred Heart Now Wounded*. The tempo was inconsistent, the chords wrong.

"Mom, what is this song?" Sydney whispered. "It's the worst thing I've ever heard."

"Ssh!" Lauren cautioned. She felt a sudden, inappropriate urge to laugh. A few weeks ago, she and Marcus had been the "perfect" family in a thriving church. Now, June was singing in a piercing mezzo-soprano that sounded like a rabid owl. Lauren bit her lip, her eyes wet with a confusing mix of laughter and grief.

"You okay, Mom?" Sydney asked.

"Just thinking about Dad," Lauren whispered.

Lauren prayed as the music continued. *God, help me. I don't know why Marcus died. I don't know why my life withered. How can I preach when I have nothing to say?*

June moved to the pulpit with a plastic smile. "Church family, I am absolutely thrilled to welcome our new lady pastor, Ms. Westbrook. I'm sure you'll make her feel welcome. Pastor, come introduce yourself."

Lauren's legs held as she walked to the front. She saw the stone-cold faces but remembered her own advice to Marcus: *Don't take it personal.* She looked at Porter, who was still bobbing his head to music that had ended, and Sydney, who gave her a thumbs up.

June handed her the microphone.

"Hello everyone."

Silence. The mic was dead. She tapped it. "Hello?"

Suddenly, her voice boomed like a tornado siren, making the front row jump. Paul gave her a thumbs up from the booth.

"Good morning," Lauren tried again.

"Well, good morning!" Porter shouted from his seat. Sydney giggled.

"It's a blessing to be here," Lauren began, but June seized the microphone back.

"And we are just so happy," June said, her voice dripping with noxious honey. "Normally we'd have a potluck, but with budget cuts and paying your salary, we don't have money for extras. But we do have cards." She handed Lauren a basket with three sad envelopes.

"Thank you," Lauren said, squaring her shoulders. June glared at her beneath the frozen smile as Lauren headed toward the pulpit.

Chapter 6

*To offer a proposition bet in which
players accepting the offer
would win less
than they wagered.*

Taking Odds

As she walked up the three steps toward the platform, Lauren could not rid herself of the thought that absurdity had become her new normal. The weight of the world was on her shoulders, a familiar burden she had carried many times before. *I will rise to the occasion like I always do,* she thought. *Sydney needs me to be strong.* She turned to face the congregation and took a moment to breathe. From this short distance, her scarce parishioners looked frail and benign. *I don't need to be afraid,* she reminded herself. But then, movement from the furthest pew in the left corner drew her eye.

Through her peripheral vision, she registered a presence that felt feral, almost animal-like, tucked into the shadows of the back row. A woman of indeterminate age sat there, wearing a battered navy rain jacket despite the bright summer sun outside. Her long brown hair was tied in a haphazard bun—an abandoned bird's nest of frizzy strands that concealed most of her face. Lauren assumed she might be homeless, but her presence here was odd; the First Assembly of Disciples wasn't exactly convenient to downtown.

You had to climb the foothills and follow a winding gravel road to find this place. A piece of Lauren's heart stirred with sympathy. She felt a palpable pain emanating from the woman's deep-set, hooded blue eyes—the only feature visible between the bulky coat and disheveled hair.

Lauren forced her gaze away and addressed the room. "Good morning."

A mass of blank, oatmeal-colored faces stared back. Paul Lu Roe raised his thick eyebrows with interest from the sound booth.

"I can't tell you how nice it is to be here. I'm really thankful... well, grateful to you all for having me." She hesitated, smoothing the three pages of sermon notes on the angled pulpit. Vaguely, she remembered how natural Marcus had always been. Lauren did not own his effortless confidence. Instead, her stomach churned. *I feel just like I did in the first two months of my pregnancy with Sydney. What if I just threw up right here on the congregation? That would certainly make for a memorable sermon.* The dark humor brought a hint of a smile to her lips. It was a quality Marcus had always appreciated about her—the ability to realize that if you could survive the worst-case scenario, the current reality wasn't so bad.

At that moment, her eyes fell on Luke Reid. He was attempting a subtle entrance, but discretion was impossible in a sanctuary with only one large door. The entire congregation shifted to look at him, some with visible disapproval. His eyes darted around the space before locking onto hers. He shook his head in a silent, shamed apology for the disruption. Lauren smiled and nodded toward Gloria. Luke bowed gratefully and slid into the pew beside his mother.

His presence broke the tension. Lauren was surprised to see him; he'd previously indicated he didn't attend church, even saying he "wouldn't wish this place on his worst enemy." Yet here he was. His presence, however brief their acquaintance, eased her nerves. *Focus, Lauren. You're here to preach.*

"Um, so I think some of you know my story already," Lauren began. "My daughter Sydney and I have come to you from Salem. Many of you know we experienced some tragedy recently. My husband, Marcus, died a little over a month ago. It was a car accident... sudden and a surprise to everyone. We co-pastored a church in South Salem for many years. I have to be honest and tell you, the grief is still pretty raw."

The back of her throat felt tight. Her voice broke. Spilling her guts hadn't been the plan, but she felt an overwhelming urge to explain herself. She had to adjust their expectations: she was no Marcus.

"I know you have been looking for a pastor for a long time. I wish I could say you were getting the perfect pastor in me, but you're honestly getting someone who's pretty broken."

The sound of rustling filled the room. Several people shifted uncomfortably. Gloria's brow furrowed, but Luke continued to watch her with rapt, unreadable attention.

"You know, we all have different spiritual gifts," Lauren continued, finding her footing. "Marcus was a gifted speaker. If someone said the word 'minister' to you, he is exactly what you would picture. He made church feel like the most exciting place you could be. But… he wasn't perfect. None of us are."

Her gaze drifted back to the woman in the navy raincoat. "When you're in pain, grieving… like I am, and like I suspect some of you are, the scripture can give us comfort. I think of Joseph in the Old Testament. He endured an unbelievable amount of suffering—sold into slavery by his own brothers, the very people supposed to love him. Then, after rising to a position of stewardship under Potiphar, he was falsely accused and thrown into prison."

Lauren looked at Sydney. "But in every hopeless place, he found the light. He continued to walk with God even in the dark. Joseph was a great manager, a gifted administrator, and eventually, he became second to Pharaoh. He stored food when there was plenty so that when famine hit, there was enough for everyone."

She paused, looking down at her notes, then back up. She went off-script.

"You know, I'm not like Joseph. He was a good steward. Marcus and I… we struggled to make ends meet. A lot. We lived paycheck to paycheck. He had a gambling problem, and it was hard for both of us to be honest about what was wrong."

The room was pin-drop silent. Porter Lee continued to beam and nod, while June's face hardened into a mask of disapproval. Lauren's knees felt weak.

"Now, without my husband, I've got to be better for myself and for my daughter. I think it's easy to be discouraged. But when I look at the people God used in the Bible... they were not perfect. They were broken. Like me. Like you."

She locked eyes with June. For a split second, she didn't see judgment there, but something that looked like fear. June broke the contact and stared at her feet.

Lauren opened her Bible with shaking hands. "2 Corinthians 12:9 says: *My grace is sufficient for you, for power is perfected in weakness.* The Apostle Paul is reminding us that when we are weak, we are opening the door for God to be strong. You might be thinking, how could God revive this church? I might be thinking, how can a grieving widow like me pastor a congregation of strangers? I don't know the answer. But I have to walk through the one door that opened. Vernonia was my door. So I'm walking through it. I'm asking you to trust God and walk with me."

The sanctuary was as silent as a tomb. Lauren signaled for June to come up and close the service.

Later that afternoon, Lauren groaned as she put her feet up on the parsonage coffee table.

"What's wrong, Mom?" Sydney asked.

"Your mom's a disaster," Lauren whined, burying her face in a sofa pillow.

"You weren't a disaster! I thought your sermon was kind of awesome. The singing, though? That was a train wreck. Someone call 911." Sydney opened her eyes in mock horror. "That lady sounded like Georgie's pet poodle—the one that sang for beef jerky." Sydney began to howl with a strident, wounded-dog yip.

Lauren covered her ears. "Go ahead and laugh, but if this church fires me, we're going to Grandma's, and you won't be hooting then."

Sydney wrinkled her nose. "Seriously, Mom, why do you think you stank?"

"Remember our old church, Syd? After Dad would preach, we'd get four invitations to lunch. Did you notice what happened today?"

Sydney shook her head. "People went to their cars?"

"They sneaked out of there like criminals leaving a crime scene," Lauren muttered.

Sydney flopped down next to her. "Who wants to go to a boring lunch with wrinkly people anyway? Except for Luke. He's alright. He asked me what I thought of June's singing, and when I mentioned the poodle, he practically died laughing. He said she sounded more like a goat."

Lauren choked out a startled laugh. "Well, she does over-pronounce her vowels. He's not wrong; it sounds more like bleating."

That night, the memories wouldn't stay buried. In her dreams, Marcus was stroking her arm. She was half-asleep, feeling his strong arms pulling her close. She felt the roughness of his unshaven chin against the nape of her neck.

"Stop," she murmured, but she turned to face his broad, amber-eyed smile.

"What were you dreaming about?" he teased. "You shouldn't need to dream when I'm right here to fulfill all your fantasies."

She had tossed a pillow at him then, laughing. But then the dream shifted. The memory of the truth flooded her.

"Marcus? What? How?"

"Lauren, I don't have excuses. I've had stress… with the elders. I started going to Spirit Mountain a few days a week. I thought I'd just blow off steam and… well, one thing led to another."

The darkness had descended then. "What kind of gambling?"

"I started with slots, but blackjack became my game. I start playing and I… I just can't stop. There's a rush, Lauren. You feel like the whole world is there for the taking. I don't feel trapped when I'm playing."

"I make you feel trapped?"

"Not you. The church. The expectations." He had looked so small then. "I took out a loan. A company called Fratello Loans. They give to anyone, but the interest… Lauren, in two weeks, that $30,000 will become $60,000. It's a loan shark. Technically legal, but super shady."

She remembered collapsing into a kitchen chair. She had offered to get a job, to use her good credit to bail him out.

"Marcus, if we tell the elders, they might have resources. They know ministers are people, too."

"Damn it, Lauren! You're so naive!" He had slammed the table. "We aren't people to them. My image is all I have. If I'm not the perfect spiritual mentor, I have nothing."

Lauren had believed him. She had bet on Marcus. She had taken the odds, thinking she could save him. Every aspect of grief was strange—the shaking, the nausea, the disconnect.

Marcus had been an addict. But Lauren was a gambler, too. She had bet her life on him, and just as her mother had warned, she was still paying the price for the bad beat.

Chapter 7

A person or thing whose
influence is unpredictable or
whose qualities are uncertain.

Wild Card

Lauren sat at the kitchen table, eyebrows furrowed. A liturgical calendar was sprawled before her, its dog-eared corners a silent parting gift from Marcus. Should she preach the suggested texts? On one hand, the calendar was a relief—it insured balance between the Old and New Testament and kept ministers from playing favorites. On the other hand, allowing a chart to choose her message made her feel closed off to the Spirit. Did the Creator really want every minister in the Christian world preaching the exact same words?

Marcus had rarely followed the calendar, preaching on whatever struck his fancy. Lauren, never having been a lead pastor, wasn't sure what kind of speaker she would be. Based on the radio silence and the lack of lunch invitations after her first sermon, she assumed she wasn't a very good one.

Suddenly, Marcus's presence filled the room. His voice echoed in her mind, transporting her to a past conversation. "Pretty soon you'll be able to order a robot minister through Amazon."

"Oh, Marcus," Lauren had protested. "That's ridiculous."

"No, it isn't," he countered. "They'll be programmed with the right scriptures and correct doctrines for any denomination. They'll preach a perfect sermon that offends no one and affirms everyone. They'll sing and dance, maybe even a little tap number. It'll be terrific."

"We'll be unemployed," Lauren said with mock despair.

"No." Marcus shook his head and laughed. "We'll win the lottery and move to Fiji or Hawaii. We'll do church our way."

"And what would that look like?"

"Well, we'd keep God, but we'd get rid of the church part," Marcus chuckled.

"And how exactly do you take the church out of the people?"

Marcus's expression became solemn. "You make them honest." He sighed. "That will take the church out of almost anyone."

The conversation was classic Marcus—light and humorous, but with a quiet brooding beneath. He had become so hopeless toward the end. As he struggled for his faith, Lauren fought to maintain her own. Ministers always had their dirty little secrets, but when a pastor doubts the existence of God, they become a hypocrite by trade. Marcus was a thinker; he was a fraud even in his own eyes.

Lauren tossed the calendar aside and opened her Bible to the text she couldn't stop thinking about: *Now faith is confidence in what we hope for and assurance about what we do not see.* Hebrews 11:1 was a verse she knew well, but today it sparked a conversation with the Almighty himself.

I'm out on this limb, God. I have all my eggs in this basket. Please, for Sydney's sake, come through for us. Help my time here not to be a complete disaster. Sydney depended on her, but everything about her life felt tenuous. She was hanging by a thread.

Lord, help me to hold it together. Beneath the facade of calm, Lauren sensed a hurricane of emotions. *I'm in a job where I have to minister to others and I feel so alone. Marcus left me; maybe you have, too?*

A knock at the door broke the silence.

"I'll get it!" Sydney yelled. "Grandma?"

"Oh no you don't. I'm no one's grandma. You call me Nana. Geez Louise, no one told me my granddaughter's hair had turned the color of a carrot. It used to be such a rich auburn."

"No, it's not." Sydney's voice betrayed her shock.

Lauren's heart fluttered wildly. "Mom?" She bolted from the kitchen to the living room. "Ma, what are you doing here?"

Vivian gave Lauren a winning smile, standing on the porch with a hand on her hip. "Well, are you gonna invite me in?"

Lauren hesitated. "Of course. Come on in, Mom. I didn't even know you knew where I lived."

Lauren gave her mother a once-over. Vivian looked good, though dressed inappropriately for a woman her age. A leopard-print blouse with a low neckline drew deliberate attention to her decolletage. She looked half her age. Her white skinny jeans and gold sandals showed off perfectly pedicured coral toenails. Slimmer than Lauren by twenty pounds, with bleached blonde hair cut in an angular, streamlined bob, she could pass for thirty from a distance. Every aspect of her appearance reminded Lauren of how different they were. Lauren shuddered at the cream-colored luggage behind her. "So, I'm taking it you're not just here for the afternoon?"

Vivian gave her trademark laugh. Lauren's neck muscles tensed like the springs on a trap. Her mother accentuated each syllable in slow motion, almost like a cartoon character. There was nothing genuine in it.

"Oh honey, aren't you happy to see me? You just lost your husband. Is it so terrible to want a visit? Isn't that what families do—help each other in times of grief?" She snapped her fingers at Sydney, who eyed her with suspicion. "Sweetie, make yourself useful and grab my bags."

Sydney gave Lauren a mournful look and scampered out to the porch.

Vivian scrutinized the living room. "Kind of small, ain't it?" She walked through the room, running manicured nails over the green sofa, inspecting the Tiffany lamp, and opening kitchen cupboards. "For a little country place, this ain't half bad. Where'd you get the sofa and lamp? They look expensive."

"They're loaners," Lauren said quickly. "They belong to a woman at the church. She's just real generous."

"I see. Where am I sleeping?"

"Ma, I didn't even know you were coming."

Vivian frowned and tapped her foot. "Well, I would have, but you didn't give me your phone number. I had to pump that woman Melanie at your old church for information. I was hurt by that, you know. All I want to do is support you. My little girl has been through hell. I've been through hell, too." She surveyed the shelves and glanced at a wedding picture. "So, you're still trying to preserve his memory, I see." She spat the words.

Lauren was triggered. "Well, he was my husband and Sydney's father. It's only been a month." She bit her lip to keep from saying more.

"Oh yeah, of course it is," Vivian said dismissively, settling on the Victorian couch. "Well, I'm parched. You wouldn't believe how hot it is in the valley—close to 97 today. You think, dear, you could get me some iced tea? You got Sweet and Low?"

"I have Stevia in the Raw."

"I guess that will work," Vivian said icily.

Lauren retreated to the kitchen. Sydney rolled her eyes as she passed by, dragging the heavy bags.

"Well, that's sure nice of you, Laur Bear," her mother called out. "You gonna let me stay in your room? You didn't have to do that."

The saccharine tone grated on Lauren's nerves. *She's been here two minutes and I'm already annoyed.* "I'll stay with Syd while you're visiting for a couple days. A couple days, right Mom?"

Vivian's youthful energy evaporated. She hunched over the sofa, her back shaking.

"Mom, are you okay?"

"Oh Laur Bear, I just can't lie to you."

Lauren brought the iced teas into the living room. "What's going on, Mom?"

"It's… it's just… just Bill." Vivian began to sob.

"Ma, who is Bill?"

"My boyfriend. I told you about him at the funeral."

Lauren shook her head. "The funeral is a blur. Tell me what happened."

"He took me for everything I had," she sobbed.

"What?" Lauren felt overwhelmed. "Last time we talked, you were still with Jim. Who's Bill?"

Vivian stopped crying, her brows creasing in agitation. "I haven't seen hide of Jim for over a year. I've been with Bill for six months. That just goes to show how much you care about my life. Hmm, some daughter I have."

"Seriously, Ma, it was an honest question."

Vivian sighed and dropped her voice to a stage whisper. "I stopped seeing Jim because he was a lady's man. He was seeing half of Portland, it turns out." She gulped her tea greedily. "Anyway, a girlfriend told me a good place to meet a man was at a cattle auction. So, I dressed in my Saturday night best rodeo bunny getup and went to Molalla. That's where I met Bill. I thought he was a rancher, but he was just a smooth-talking schemer. He paid for everything at first, but it turns out he was worse than old horny Jim."

"What did he do?"

"He said he wanted us to get married, but he needed $30,000 to buy stud bulls for his business. Our seed money. We were gonna be home free once he was renting them out and selling their fluids across the country." Vivian swallowed a large chunk of ice.

Lauren swallowed the lump in her throat. "Did you give him money?"

"Well, you know I did," she barked.

"How much?"

"Fifteen thousand. The money I saved from the Roth IRA my brother Rich invested for me."

"Oh, Ma. I'm sorry."

"Bill said it was perfect—I'd put in my half, he'd put in his, and we'd be equals. I'm an old fool." She buried her face in her hands.

Lauren was filled with empathy. Vivian looked like a frail bird, a line of mascara streaming down her cheek. "You're not a fool, Mom. You just want to believe the best in people. We all want to believe that."

"You're not going to tell me my dream man is still out there? That if I pray enough God will lead me to him? That's what you've always told me before."

Lauren shook her head. "Mama, I think the problem is there is no dream man. Every guy out there is going to be flawed—Jim, Bill, and even Marcus."

Vivian raised her eyebrows. "So you don't think Marcus was the perfect husband? You've said that since the time you ran off with him in college."

"No, Mom. I married a gambler. What right do I have to judge you? But I did love him, and I miss him. Syd and I have been struggling."

Vivian sniffled. Lauren found the tissue box. "So, you're here for..."

"I need to get back on my feet, hon. A couple months tops."

"What about your apartment in Portland?"

"I lost it, Laur Bear. Bill and I were living the high life. I thought he'd take care of me. I wasn't careful with my money and I'm on a fixed income."

Lauren's heart sank. She had moved to the middle of nowhere to avoid living with her mother. Some ironies were just too much.

* * *

Vivian had been with them for two days, and Lauren already felt the whirlwind of her mother's moods. The days began with a burst of frantic activity; today, it was an immediate need to redecorate the bathroom in French blue. Vivian nagged until Lauren loaded everyone into the KIA and drove downtown for new curtains. By afternoon, Vivian would watch daytime talk shows before retreating into Lauren's bedroom for a nap. Between the bursts of energy and the naps, she barked a chain of commands. "Sydney, I need water," or "Laur Bear, run to the pharmacy for my Claritin." Sydney was smart enough to hide outdoors, but Lauren, trying to work on her sermon, found no escape.

After showing Vivian how to work the TV remote for the twenty-seventh time, Lauren reached her limit. She pulled Sydney onto the porch. "It's time for a day trip."

Sydney tilted her head. "Are we telling Nana where we're going?"

"Absolutely not."

Sydney's grin spread across her face. "Good."

While Vivian was engrossed in a *Judge Judy* rerun, Lauren stuffed protein bars, apples, a first aid kit, and water into her backpack. "Back in a few!" she called out, fleeing the house before her mother could reply. "Let's go!"

Since moving to Vernonia, they'd had little time to explore. Gloria had mentioned the trails, pointing out the path that led from the church to the main trail. "It's a famous hike," Gloria had said. "Goes all the way from Banks to Vernonia. When Henry and I first married, we walked the whole darn thing."

It was a beautiful July day, and they hit the dirt path with a spring in their step. Lauren inhaled the fresh air, grateful for the rustle of wind instead of the cloying pitch of her mother's voice. The trail led down a steep hillside shaded by majestic virgin firs. Sunlight filtered through the needles, shifting shadows with every breeze. Deer ferns and moss spread out like a lush green carpet.

"It's like being in a fairy tale," Sydney said.

"It sure is. I can't believe this is right outside our front door."

"Dad would have loved it," Sydney said, twirling in a circle.

"Yes, he would have, but be careful not to trip over a root."

Sydney ran ahead, her laughter echoing through the trees. For a moment, Lauren felt a flash of blinding joy, imagining Marcus there with them. But the feeling vanished as quickly as it came. *Marcus, forgive me,* she whispered into the breeze. The heaviness had been with her since the moment she knew he was dead—or rather, since the moment she discovered the truth about his gambling and the other things she didn't want to imagine. In her anger, she had once thought she would feel better if he were dead. It was a disturbing, freeing, and ultimately horrible thought. Now that he was gone, the guilt was a complex, suffocating darkness. Would Marcus ever forgive her? Could God?

She swallowed hard and forced the thoughts down. The trail led into a clearing, and she gasped. Below them sat the brightest blue lake she had ever seen.

"Mom, can I go swimming?" Sydney yelled.

"Hang on," Lauren cried as Sydney approached the rocky ledge. "You don't have a swimsuit. Come back here."

Lauren surveyed the loose rock. They were supposed to be on the main path. "We must have gotten turned around."

"Luke!" Sydney cried, bolting toward the trees.

He was sitting in the shade on a rocky overhang, legs relaxed, a white T-shirt revealing his golden-bronze skin. He held a fishing rod, a large blue cooler by his side. He smiled when he saw Sydney. "My partner in crime."

Lauren felt suddenly shy as she walked toward them.

"Want to see what's in the cooler?" Luke asked Sydney. Inside were four gleaming, spotted fish on a mountain of ice.

"What kind are they?" Sydney asked.

"Three rainbow trouts and this big guy—a largemouth bass." He pulled the darker fish out and forced its jaw open and closed. "Hello, Sydney. I am a largemouth bass. Have a nice day."

"Gross!" Sydney laughed. "Can I hold it?"

Luke glanced at Lauren. "Is it okay?"

"Yeah, sure."

"Hold your arms out." Luke demonstrated the proper form and placed the fish in Sydney's arms.

"It's slimy," she said, unmoving.

"And one of the most delicious game fish in the world," Luke said with a wink.

"I want to eat it," Sydney decided. "Have you ever gutted a fish?"

"No way."

"You want to try?"

Sydney nodded eagerly. "Oh, yes."

Luke laughed. "When I was a kid, I wouldn't eat any fish. Then my uncle took me out to live off the land for a week. I didn't eat for two days until we caught one of these guys. We sliced it, gutted it, and cooked it over the fire. It was the best thing I'd ever eaten."

"Starvation is a good motivator," Lauren laughed.

"You guys out for the day?"

"We thought we were headed toward the Banks trail. We're lost."

"I know what you did. You turned right at the Candelabra tree when you should have turned left. It's a Sitka Spruce, about two hundred years old. Big trunk, curved branches—some call it the octopus tree."

"It looks like it's got tentacles," Sydney agreed.

Lauren nodded. "Oh, I saw that. Weird-looking, but beautiful."

"Famous with us locals. Left takes you to the paved Banks trail; right brings you here to Vernonia Lake."

"Rookie mistake," Luke teased. He gestured toward Sydney. "Does she have time to try the rod?"

"We have all the time in the world. My mom's at the house."

Luke raised his eyebrows. "I got ya. Hey Sydney, sit here. Want to see if you can catch something?" He patted the ledge.

"Yes! I've never been fishing before." Sydney sat and pulled her knees to her chest.

"Hang on, Syd. Let's get a seat for your mom." Luke stood up, and they were face to face. Lauren felt flushed, her eyes tracing his features. In the sunlight, his eyes weren't just brown; they held flecks of green and gold. He looked rugged and manly, yet his gaze was sensitive.

He knelt, unrolled a flannel blanket from his pack, and laid it on the ground. "That should be a little more comfortable. Have a seat."

"Oh, thanks." Lauren realized then how much she'd wanted to rest her feet.

Luke sat between the two girls and opened his bait box, showing Sydney the feathered lures. "I like this one!" Sydney pointed.

"Good choice." Luke placed a neon orange pellet in Sydney's hand. "This is what I used to hook that bass. Let me help you put it on, and next time you can do it yourself."

Lauren watched him teach her daughter. Seeing Luke with Sydney didn't make her melancholy; it made her hopeful. Sydney settled into a fisherman's patience, gazing out at the water. "When will they start biting?"

Luke chuckled. "Didn't you listen to your mother's sermon? That's where you have to have faith."

Sydney shook her head. "But what if I don't catch anything?"

"Sometimes you don't," Luke said, his tone turning serious.

"Well, that's stupid."

Luke looked at Lauren with wide eyes, and she burst out laughing. "She'll keep you honest," she admitted.

They sat in a comfortable silence. Lauren was usually shy with strangers, but Luke's presence felt easy. Perhaps it was because he'd already seen her dangling from a ceiling in short shorts. Her face heated at the memory. Luke fished inside the cooler and pressed something cold into her hand: an IPA.

"Do you drink beer?"

Lauren caught the sly smile on his lips. "You're offering beer to a minister? You know you could go to hell for that."

Luke sprayed beer as he tried to stifle a laugh. Lauren handed him a dish towel from her pack.

"Thanks," he said. "I was not expecting that response."

"I don't drink a whole lot," she confessed, twisting the cap and taking a swig. "We ministers consort with people who don't approve. But I discovered my husband did more than his fair share. I have a theory now that people who practice complete abstinence are more prone to losing self-control. You feel like you've missed out on every pleasure, and eventually, you go crazy."

Luke nodded. "A theory based on experience?"

"Absolutely."

Luke leaned back on his triceps. "That was some sermon you preached the Sunday I visited."

Lauren tensed. "It was my first attempt as a real pastor. I should probably apologize to the congregation this Sunday."

"Why? It was good," Luke said softly. "I never heard a sermon like that. It was so honest. To tell you the truth, it kind of hurt to hear it."

Lauren's interest was piqued. "What do you mean?"

"I don't really go to church," Luke said. "I decided as a teenager it wasn't real. Every Sunday, I saw a preacher trying to make the world seem tidy and neat. Black and white. If you followed the rules, your life would be perfect. But there were the things they said, and then there were the things they were actually doing. They weren't the same." He put his empty bottle back in the cooler. "None of it was real."

"Maybe just too real," Lauren countered.

"Maybe… but what you said on Sunday wasn't like that. You moved all the way here to this godforsaken place. It's like you really believe or something."

Lauren chuckled. "Most days I do. There are days I don't."

"There you go again." Luke laughed. "Don't you know you aren't supposed to say things like that? June would crucify you."

"Now, that would be ironic."

Suddenly, Sydney screamed. "Luke! There's something pulling! What do I do?"

"Hurry! Stand up!" He was behind her in a second, guiding her elbow. "Start reeling!"

"It's yanking harder!"

"Don't let go. Slow and easy. Keep it going."

Lauren was on her feet, staring at the rippling water where the line thrashed. "Come on, Syd! You got something good!"

Sydney reeled hard and steady. Out of the water emerged the fattest largemouth bass Lauren had ever seen, fighting for its life.

Chapter 8

A term referring to
the strongest poker player in a poker game.
Used to describe someone who demonstrates composure
even in the most stressful situations.

Alligator Blood

Saturdays were difficult for ministers. Sunday service was drawing close and Lauren was desperate to put the finishing touches on her sermon. Finally, she had resorted to locking herself in the bathroom, so she could have a few moments of peace. Vivian had agreed to watch Sydney while she was at the staff meeting today, but Sydney was clearly not happy about the decision.

"Mom, can't I go with you? I won't cause any problems. I promise."

Lauren bit her lip with impatience. "I know it's not a perfect situation, but it's only for a few hours. I don't want you running around the church. You know about my mishap with that building. It's not a safe place for unsupervised children."

Sydney stomped her foot and ran off to her room.

"Ma, thanks. I appreciate it," Lauren called as she grabbed her keys at the front door.

"Oh, she'll be fine. It won't kill her to watch TV for a couple hours with her Nana. I was thinking we could even go into town for ice cream at the

Dairy Queen."

"Sydney will like that. She'll never say no to a Butterfinger Blizzard."

Lauren left the house with a sinking feeling in her chest. Her own childhood had left her with so many scars. Leaving her daughter with her mother did not feel good. She vowed she would only leave Sydney as a last resort. *She isn't the same woman she was,* Lauren insisted in her head. She wanted to believe her mother had grown up, at least a little.

Gloria's car, a white Ford Escape, was the first vehicle she saw as she drove into the parking lot. There was a large black Cadillac Escalade parked next to it. She assumed the fancy SUV was June's. There was also a gray Toyota Camry. *That's Paul's,* Lauren thought with a smile. The Camry was understated and classy, much like Paul himself. *Great, I'm the last to arrive. I just can't seem to make a good impression here to save my life.*

She made her way into the foyer and heard Gloria call, "We're in here, Pastor Westbrook." The motley crew sat in the church office around a large oval table. There were four of them: Gloria, June, Paul, and Porter who was still bobbing his head and swaying back and forth as if dancing to an invisible rhythm.

"Paul and I've just been enjoying a cup of Joe from the new coffee maker," Gloria said warmly as Lauren entered. She was dressed in a bright green pant suit and white Converse sneakers. Her red hair was piled in a high ballerina bun. Lauren stifled a smile. Gloria had her own unique style that was for sure.

"I prefer tea," June said hastily as she stirred whatever was in her mug with a silver spoon. She glanced up at Lauren briefly and frowned. June was her polished self. She wore fitted jeans and a short sleeved lacy black top that Lauren had to admit was sleek and stylish. It wasn't often you considered raiding the closet of a septuagenarian and Lauren had to give her credit for style.

Paul stood up and pointed to the seat next to him. "Go ahead and sit here. I'll get you a cup of Joe too." He moved with agile grace for an older man. "Cream or sugar?" he asked.

"Yes," Lauren nodded. "Both would be lovely."

"One or two lumps?"

"One is great. Thanks so much."

Paul set a large rainbow mug in front or her that aptly said, *One in the Spirit.*

"Thanks. Nice mug."

"We have a strange assortment. The other one said *I'm with Stupid*," Paul chuckled.

Lauren laughed. "Well, I certainly don't want that one." She looked around the table. "Hello everyone. Hi Porter."

Porter bobbed his head even harder with excitement. "Halow, Beautiful." He beamed at her through bloodshot eyes.

"You don't need to talk to him," June barked. "It'll get him agitated."

"Oh, I'm sorry June. I didn't know."

"We're in between nurses right now, so I had to bring him. I might have to step out from time to time."

"That's totally understandable and not a problem," Lauren assured her. "Well, I hope you all didn't get started without me?"

"Oh no," Gloria said. "We were just shooting the breeze before you got here."

"So, this is our ministry team." Lauren smiled as she gazed at them around the table.

June snapped. "Well, we're not the welcoming committee. You're already late. Can we get the show on the road."

Lauren coughed. "Of course. I had to make arrangements for Sydney this morning. My mother's in town and she's taking care of her for me."

"Well, that's nice of her," Gloria said. "How long will she be in Vernonia?"

Lauren made a face and shrugged. "That..., I'm not sure about."

Paul chuckled. "You know what they say about fish and house guests? "He looked around the room waiting for the punchline.

"They smell after three days," Lauren finished. "Benjamin Franklin, right?"

"Right. I knew I'd like you. You know your stuff."

June tapped the table impatiently. Her long red finger nails were perfectly manicured, like little red daggers.

Lauren took the hint. "Okay, so to the point. Besides us, do we have any other church leaders? Elders?"

June pointed to Porter unceremoniously. "Here's your elder." Porter smiled and swayed forward toward her like a clown in a Jack-in-the-box.

"I see." Lauren hesitated. "So, how have you all been making decisions, getting bills paid, that kind of thing?"

"I've been taking care of that," Gloria said. She took out a manila folder full of papers and handed out copies of the budget to everyone at the table. "Giving has been down, by a lot. I think we're only bringing in about 3,500 dollars a month? This is confidential of course, but we only have about five regular tithers and three of them don't even attend this church anymore."

"Why would people who are not currently attending still be giving?" Lauren asked.

"Habit really. They're mostly older folks in nursing homes who have set up automatic withdrawals."

Lauren nodded thoughtfully. "Do we have an emergency fund?"

"We did," Paul said. "We're scraping towards the bottom of the barrel now, unfortunately."

"Yes, we are," Gloria agreed. "The account was set up to deal with emergency building issues. For example, if we were to bust a pipe or fix a broken water heater, that kind of thing. Well, unfortunately we've had to dip into it heavily just to pay monthly expenses. The General Ministry helps us out, of course, but they cap off at $2000 a month. We need about $6000 a month to pay our bills and your salary."

June frowned. "We're just months away from closing our doors. So much for the church you built, Porter." She glanced sideways at her husband. Unfazed, he continued to bob his head and smile.

Lauren covered her mouth with her hand to hide the shock from witnessing the exchange. The bite in June's words unnerved her. She looked to Gloria. "How much in the emergency fund?"

"Just a little over $1500."

Lauren pressed her fingers into her forehead in concentration. "How did we pay for the hole in the church attic?"

"What hole in the church attic?" June barked.

Gloria narrowed her eyes and gave Lauren a gentle kick underneath the table. "Oh, that. That was nothing. Luke came by and took a look at the issue and fixed it right up with supplies he already had on hand."

"What hole in the ceiling?" June repeated.

Gloria faced June directly. "When Lauren did her walk through, she noticed a hole in the ceiling. Turns out it was nothing. Luke was able to take care of a little water damage without touching any church funds."

"That son of yours. He's a handy one," Paul said. "Please extend our thanks to him. You know, I have some experience with a hammer. He could always call me to help out if he needs it."

"You?" June cackled. "You have no business with a hammer, climbing a ladder or anything else."

"That's a nice offer Paul and I agree with you," Lauren interrupted hastily. "We need to extend our thanks to Luke. That was really kind of him."

Gloria gave Lauren a playful wink and then returned to scrutinizing her financial notes.

Paul ignored June and focused his attention back to Lauren. "All I'm trying to say is we're holding church in a building that's falling apart. We're just one emergency away from going bankrupt. I don't think we can ask Luke to fix the entire building, do you? If we were going to be honest, and we should be, there's probably at least a 100,000 dollars worth or repairs that need to be done to bring this building to an operational state."

"Really?" Lauren said dismayed. "100,000 dollars?"

"At least," Paul reiterated. "We've got problems with plumbing, the roof's leaking, and we have mold and rot, maybe going all the way down to the foundation."

"The building's rotting away," June added helpfully.

Lauren could not find words as the reality of the church's dire condition became fully lucid. "Alright," she finally said. We're the ministry team. It's our job to come up with some ideas."

"Ideas?" June's voice was strident with incredulity. "Honey, we don't need ideas. We need a miracle."

Gloria frowned at June. "We're in a church, June. We're in the right place for a miracle."

June grunted a response.

Suddenly, Porter's eyes brightened and he spoke out as clear as day. "You got to bring people in. Give em a reason to come."

Lauren saw Gloria's eyes open wide in surprise.

"Porter! You're back," Paul said and patted him on the back.

June sighed. "He does that from time to time. The old Porter comes to visit now and again. Don't you honey? It's me, Porter. I'm here." June raised her hand and gently grazed his cheek. Porter rested his eyes on his wife and gave her a beautiful smile of recognition. The gesture was the first glimpse of tenderness Lauren had seen from June and for some reason it was extraordinarily painful to watch.

The moment did not last long. The old Porter returned, bobbing his head back and forth and the glazed look returned to his eyes.

June dropped her hand quickly as the brief spark extinguished. She noticed Lauren looking at her from across the table and glared.

"Well," Lauren continued. "I think Porter's right. We have to think of a reason or way to motivate people to come."

"And then give their money away," June added.

"I do have an idea," Gloria said.

"What's your idea?" Lauren asked.

"We're on pins and needles," June said with false enthusiasm.

Gloria frowned at her before looking directly at Lauren."We have a yard sale?"

"A yard sale?" Paul said with surprise.

"Yes, a yard sale." Gloria's voice was firmer with resolve.

"Who's going to come way up here for an old yard sale? We're not exactly convenient to town," June said.

Gloria sighed and looked heavenward. "You know I've been storing several of my late mother's things right here in the church. Two years ago when the interim pastor said they were going to have to reduce my salary, he said I could store things in the rooms we weren't using for awhile as a sort of concession for my sad paychecks. My mother went to this church from the time she was a little girl. She loved this place, met my dad here in the youth group. In any case, she wouldn't want me to give up on all she worked for, her legacy so to speak."

Lauren felt excitement building in her chest. "Are you saying, Gloria, you want to donate her belongings to the church?"

"I think, it's what my mama would have wanted."

"You still haven't answered my question. Who's going to come up all the way here for a yard sale?"

"Oh June," Lauren smiled. "Don't you worry about that. This is where I can help."

* * *

Lauren was still at her computer even after several hours. She smiled as she surveyed Paul Lu Roe's new Facebook page. He had begrudgingly allowed her to take several photos of him and she was proud of her work.

"Who's that?" Vivian asked over her shoulder.

"That's Paul. He's on the Ministry Team at my church."

Her mother put a large spoon of yogurt in her mouth. "He doesn't look half bad. Is he rich and single?"

Lauren groaned. "I'm not planning to date him and no, Mother, I don't think he is."

Vivian raised her eyebrows. "Then why, honey, are you stalking his Facebook page?"

"I'm not stalking his Facebook page. I just created his Facebook page so that we can promote the yard sale we're going to do at church. Look, it's only been a few hours and he already has 45 friends."

"I like his eyes," Vivian said. "He looks kind."

"He is kind. He's a sweet old man and he doesn't deserve to meet the likes of you," Lauren teased.

Vivian flicked her spoon at Lauren. "What is that supposed to mean?"

"You know what it means. Stay away from my church people. They are off limits!"

Vivian sauntered off with a humph.

In the past few hours, Lauren had created a Facebook page for both Gloria and Paul with their permission of course. She had grabbed a church directory and sent out friend invitations to everyone on the most recent registry and she had advertised on the City of Vernonia's Instagram page.

She had spent the last few days with Paul, Gloria, and Luke, removing things from storage, including the attic. She photographed the expensive rugs, lamps, sofas, and other antique furniture and had begun using her social media platforms to advertise the upcoming event and highlight some of Gloria's most impressive artifacts. She researched item after item, to estimate fair prices and sent pictures to local antique shops within a sixty mile radius. Already, several interested dealers had contacted her and were putting the yard sale date on their respective calendars.

Lauren was shocked to discover that most of Gloria's antique furniture had a estimated worth in the thousands of dollars. Throughout the week, she kept calling Gloria. "Are you really sure you want to do this?"

"I've made up my mind, Lauren. Yes. And I want you to keep the sofa and lamp for the parsonage."

"Are you sure? I just found out the antique lamp in the attic is worth around $1200."

"Really? Well, that's wonderful," Gloria said.

As she spoke to Gloria, Lauren suddenly felt a gnawing sensation in the pit of her stomach. These were Gloria's mother's most treasured items. Shouldn't they stay in the family? She thought about Luke and suddenly the yard sale didn't seem like such a good idea.

"What about Luke?"Lauren said. "I feel bad. Shouldn't these things stay in the family?"

Gloria's laughter took Lauren off guard.

"Why are you laughing?"

"Oh, it's just...Luke has no interest in these things. You should see his house, a real bachelor pad if I ever saw one. If he wants anything, we'll still have the lamp and sofa from the parsonage. It's enough. I promise. When he was married, I thought about giving him all of mother's belongings, but there was one thing that always held me back."

Lauren was curious now. "What was that?"

"His wife. That Bridget was a real piece of work."

"Oh really?" Lauren felt guilty being so nosy, but she couldn't help herself.

"That woman...," Gloria said with disgust.

"What about her?" Lauren was baiting Gloria now for more information and she was ashamed of herself.

"She was a hussy," Gloria said forcefully.

Lauren tried not to laugh. She hadn't heard that word in awhile, but then the ramifications of the statement dawned on her. "She wasn't faithful to Luke?" The surprise was evident in her voice. Luke was handsome, capable, kind... How could any woman not recognize that he was a good one and to cheat on him no less?

"He stayed with her a long time. She cast a spell on him, I think. Like a witch, that one."

Lauren suddenly felt deeply melancholy. "I'm sorry, Gloria. I'm sorry that happened to Luke and to you." She thought of Sydney and how much she hoped for her future. It was her prayer that when her daughter found that special person to love, that whoever she chose would love her fully in return and always cherish her as much as Lauren did, as much as Marcus did. When she realized that Luke's wife had cheated on him, Lauren felt physically sick.

* * *

As July came to a close, Lauren was beginning to find her stride. She certainly wasn't a smashing success, but she had managed to preach two more sermons without fainting or throwing up. In addition, she hosted an informational meeting about the church's finances to the congregants, and lay out the plans with Paul and Gloria for the yard sale which they had scheduled for late August. The attendance numbers had stayed the same, so at least her arrival had not induced the exodus Gloria had predicted.

The few members who attended the financial meeting did not seemed surprised at all regarding the precarious predicament of the church. Lauren met an elderly couple, Stan and Vicky. They were friends of Paul's. An elderly widow named Emma completed the small party. Emma was a charter member of the church, but she admitted her attendance had been spotty in recent years. She was less than 5 feet tall with a shock of white hair pulled firmly in a bun and bright red glasses. The style would have looked austere on most women, but her rounded face and features softened the severity of the bun. Lauren stood with Paul in the foyer as congregants exited into the night. Stan shook her hand as he and Vicky prepared to leave. "Don't feel too bad. It's no surprise," he shrugged. "This has been a long time in the making."

Lauren nodded. "Well, I hope maybe we can turn things around."

Vicky shook her head. "We need young people and a whole lot of money for that. This yard sale is a good start, but all just too little a bit too late."

"I think many of us around here have just sort of accepted the church is going to die with us," Stan said as he shook his head in defeat. "It's not anyone's fault. You win some and you lose some."

"Stan, I don't think I'm willing to lose this one and neither is Gloria. We have to try. The yard sale might bring some real money in and then we can start thinking about how we might get some new life into this church."

Emma smiled and elbowed Paul. "I like her energy."

Vicky sighed. "We do like your energy, but you got to remember we're old and we're not going to be able to do much to help you. It takes Stan two hours just to get up in the morning."

* * *

Despite the lack of enthusiasm, Lauren was not willing to accept defeat. The next morning, as she sipped her coffee, she engaged in some quiet prayer.

Her devotional text was on the table with the daily Bible verse. *By the grace given me I say to everyone of you: Do not think of yourself more highly than you ought, but rather think of yourself with sober judgment, in accordance with the measure of faith God has given you.* Romans 12:3. The verse felt like a slap in the face.

Do not think of yourself more highly than you ought? Lauren felt convicted by the words. She didn't believe she had been prideful exactly, but Lauren knew she was looking to herself to save the First Assembly of Disciples Church of Vernonia when she needed to look to God. She couldn't by the force of her will change the fifty years or more of history that had led the church to this place. She could only be a part of God's will in the moment.

Chapter 9

"I've learned the lesson that the worst thing
that can happen to a gambler
is to let his recent losses or wins
knock him off keel emotionally."
—Andrew Beyer

Wagering Loss

I'm an inch away from blowing a gasket, Lauren realized as she felt her mother's frenetic energy from across the room. After two weeks, Vivian's temporary visit was beginning to look anything but short-term. Her tender heart was apparently fully recovered from the loss of Bill and the money he swindled. Fortunately, she was never one to stay depressed for very long. Like spring weather, her moods could be turbulent and intense, but they passed almost as quickly as they came. At the moment, she was showing signs of going stir crazy. Pacing the house and finding fault with everyone and everything in it was now her favorite pass time. Compared to her big city life, being trapped in a tiny parsonage with her daughter and granddaughter was not generally how Vivian liked to roll.

"What does a girl do around here for fun?"

Lauren tried her best not to engage from her safe space at the kitchen table. She was working intently on her sermon notes, but as her mother continued to pace through the house opening and slamming cupboards, Lauren felt the need to intervene before she destroyed her house. "Ma, this isn't Portland. People here go to work, come home and then spend time with their families. Can I help you find something?"

Vivian frowned as she settled on a bright red coffee mug. "That's all? Work and come home? They're has to be some community life? Dances? Karee-o-kee or whatever they call it?"

Lauren sighed. "If there is, I don't know about it, but why don't you check out the town's Instagram page and find out what's going on for yourself?"

Vivian set her coffee on the table and disappeared into the bedroom. She returned with her i phone in a glittering gold case and brought it over to her daughter, "Show me."

Lauren scrolled through the apps. "It looks like you don't even have the Instagram app. Do you have Facebook?"

"Of course I have Facebook," Vivian snapped. "We're friends on Facebook."

"Oh, that's right. Well, then it will be real easy to make an Instagram page and then you can get updates on what's going on locally by following the Vernonia page."

Lauren tapped through her mother's phone till she pulled up her Facebook page. She gasped when she saw the cover photo. Vivian wore a blue sequin gown with the lowest neckline ever seen on a woman not walking the Hollywood red carpet. "Wow, Mom, do you really need to show this much… cleavage?"

Her mother stuck out her chest. "At my age I'm proud of what I got."

Lauren lifted her eyes heavenward to silently plead with God before returning her attention back to her screen. "Do you have any other pictures you might want me to use for your Instagram profile?"

Vivian was defensive as she dropped her voice to a dramatic whisper. "I like that one. Bill told me I looked like one of those old time movie actresses, like Ava Gardner."

Lauren shook her head in disbelief. "Well, it's something else." She proceeded to copy the photo onto the Instagram profile and then handed her the phone. "You're good to go. But Ma, please don't get into any trouble."

Vivian narrowed her eyes. "You know, I'm the mother, here."

Lauren gave Vivian her best sugar coated smile and spoke softly. "I'm a mother too and you're living in my house."

With a grunt, her mother marched toward Lauren's bedroom.

"Love you, Mama," Lauren called behind her.

"What a diva," Sydney sighed from the couch where she was watching T.V.

"Tell me about it," Lauren laughed. She attempted to refocus on writing Sunday's sermon, but instead found herself staring at three envelopes that were tucked discreetly into the corner of the kitchen counter. Now she recognized them as the welcome cards she had received on her first Sunday at Vernonia. *I wonder why I never opened them?*

There were three in total, a classic white, sunny yellow, and teal envelopes. Lauren opened the white envelope first and pulled out a card with a striking cover. Someone had hand painted in water colors a little snapshot of the the First Christian Church of Vernonia.

The church was drawn in all of its old historic grandeur, sparkling white with its lofty steeple surrounded by lush forest and green ferns. The artist had even included stalks of purple iris at the foot of the church. The flowers drew the viewer's eye to the purple and white stained glass windows. A blue sky and white puffy clouds framed the top of the mini painting. *If only the church really looked like this,* Lauren thought. She grabbed her glasses to make out the script at the bottom of the card. *By Emma* was captioned in rounded cursive.

Emma? Lauren realized that the diminutive, grandmotherly woman with red glasses whom she had met at the financial meeting was the artist. *She's really talented.* There was a quality in the watercolor that suggested so much more than just what she had painted.

Lauren felt her heart stir the more she gazed at the image. She opened the card and found several scrawled signatures, some illegible. The church members must have hastily signed before Sunday service. Lauren walked toward the kitchen counter and attached it to the refrigerator with a magnet. The idea occurred to her that she might frame the little painting. It was that stunning.

The teal envelope was from June and Porter. It was a run of the mill lower end Hallmark card. On the front, a cartoon dog was holding a sign that said, *We Appreciate You.* The thinner card stock and unremarkable clip art suggested the kind of greeting card one found in the discount section of a supermarket. In bold cursive letters, June had written, *Welcome,* and then signed her own name and Porter's at the bottom. *You have certainly made me feel welcome.* She suppressed a cynical laugh and set the the card aside.

Lauren opened the final envelope. The smooth texture of the front suggested it was high quality. On the cover was a vibrant picture featuring a host of hydrangeas in bright purple, blues, and pinks. The white cursive font said, *Thank you.* When she opened it a slip of paper fell out. Lauren unfolded the paper and was surprised to find a check for $50 made out to her. The card was signed, but there was also a lengthy message handwritten in blue ink with neat, angular cursive letters.

Dear Pastor Westbrook,

I cannot tell you enough how glad I am you're here. For the last few years our little congregation has been struggling so hard to stay alive. There have been problems, many problems, but we also have such lovely people. I have been attending the First Assembly of Disciples Church of Vernonia since I was about forty five years old. I'm 68 years old now, so it's been a long time. I first started coming because they needed someone to play the piano. I thought I was coming to help out, but really this church saved my life.

The sweet people here kept my heart alive during one of the worst times of my life and I will always be grateful. In any case, June told us about your circumstances and how you recently lost your husband. I was so sorry to hear about that. After June shared that news, a few of us ladies got together and we have been praying for you and your daughter daily ever since.

I want you to know that some of us know a little bit about grief and sadness, the dark places your heart can go when you've lost someone so dear to you. You are not alone. I know you're going to be busy as you're getting settled, but once you're feeling at home, I'd love you and your daughter just to come on over. You can just drop by anytime. My address is in the directory. The fifty dollars is to help you with your move in costs. Buy something special for you or that beautiful daughter of yours.

Your Sister in Christ,

Linda Martinez

Lauren held the card to her chest. Marcus' face crossed her mind and her heart fell. The sadness was always there like a gloomy visitor who refused to leave.

* * *

"Are you abandoning me here again?" Vivian called from the door.

"Ma, you're a grown woman and you have a car. Go into town."

"Well, where are you and Sydney going?" Her mother placed her hand on her hip and frowned at them as they walked toward the KIA.

"It's work, Mom. I'm visiting a lady in my congregation."

Vivian dropped her arms and shrugged. "I guess I'll keep myself busy then."

"We'll see you in a few."

"Bye Nana," Sydney said cheerfully.

Vivian frowned before shutting the door. Once they were alone in the car, Sydney smiled. "Do you really have work to do, Mom, or are we going on another outing?"

"We're doing a bit of both," Lauren admitted. "We're going to meet that lady, Linda who plays piano at church and then I'm going to take you to ice cream."

Sydney made a loud sigh. "Do we have to visit the lady?"

"Yes, we do. She's very sweet. You know she sent us a card when we first got here and gave us $50."

73

"Really?" Sydney asked. "Are you going to give me $25?"

Lauren laughed. "Nice math. I'm taking you to ice cream and I might let you get a treat at the store. Yes, you're getting your share, if that answers your question."

Since the time she was a toddler Sydney was a chatterbox, but Lauren was observing many changes in her daughter after losing Marcus. There were times she still seemed like a little girl, but at other times Lauren saw a companion, a grown up. The realization made her melancholy. She too, had grown up much too fast after her parent's divorce. Vivian was not a woman who could handle life alone, without a man that is. She started dating within weeks of the divorce, most likely even before, and Lauren was exposed to things she shouldn't have seen and shouldn't have known about at a tender age. She had vowed her own daughter would get a proper childhood. Marcus' death had foiled that plan.

Lauren loved everything about her daughter, her rich auburn hair, almond eyes, and the spray of freckles that ran along her nose and cheeks. Her hair was naturally wavy and Lauren had started braiding it when she was just a toddler in an attempt to manage her unruly locks. She had learned a dozen ways to braid hair: fish braids, Dutch braids, French braids, and rope braiding.

Sydney's hair now was parted in the middle with two traditional braids on each side. She had accomplished this feat herself. The traditional braid made her look younger and Lauren felt a twinge of longing for the past. Their daughter didn't look like her or Marcus. She was completely her own person, but Lauren saw pieces of Marcus in her sharp sense of humor and charismatic personality. She also saw some of her own perseverance and stubbornness, especially in the way she handled her Nana.

In her own way, Sydney loved Vivian, but even as a ten year old she knew when her grandmother was acting impetuous or childlike. Her daughter was wise beyond her years and loyal to a fault. Lauren was ashamed of herself for relying on her.

Linda lived in a charming yellow house on Shady Lane not too far from Hawkins Park. Her home was tucked in the corner of a dead end street surrounded by tall evergreen trees and a few scattered white pines. The front yard was a sight to behold. A low wooden fence contained a beautiful stone and flower garden. White pebbles covered the ground providing a walkway around the hundreds of plants: hydrangeas, snap dragons, lazy Susans, gladiolas, foxglove, and rhodies. The garden was beautiful, but what captured Sydney's attention were the hundreds of garden gnomes hidden throughout the yard. Some were peeking through the bushes, others were staged to look like yard workers, and yet others as young lovers.

"Look at that one," Sydney called as they walked toward the front door. Next to the gazebo was a tiny garden pond and inside of it was a gnome with a large beard screaming. "He's drowning," Sydney laughed.

"Should we rescue him?"

"Oh no," Sydney giggled. "It's funny."

Lauren wrinkled her nose, not sure what to think. "Linda, appears to have a sense of humor," Lauren said as they walked past a particularly ugly gnome on one knee asking a rather pretty, displeased lady gnome for her hand in marriage.

"Mom, maybe we should get some gnomes for our house?"

"Absolutely not," Lauren laughed. "They're a little creepy," she added with a whisper.

Lauren tapped on the front door gently. She heard movement within the house and then a voice, "I'll be right there."

Linda opened the door carefully at first, but her eyes grew bright when she recognized Lauren and Sydney. "Oh my goodness. I thought you'd never come. Please come on in."

Linda was a smaller woman, not as tiny as Emma, but petite and feminine despite the fact that she sported a very short pixie cut. As a newcomer to the congregation Lauren had given nicknames to her congregants to help her remember who they were. Lauren had dubbed Linda, *earring lady*. She was easy to remember because she always wore specialty dangled earrings. Lauren remembered smiling when she first met Linda and had observed the tiny pianos hanging from her ears.

"Nice earrings," she had said.

Linda chuckled. "Thank you. These are my baby grands. I like to wear them when I play."

With women like June and Gloria in the limelight, Lauren realized that her conversations with Linda had been both brief and limited. She knew very little about her.

Sydney spoke up. "I like your gnomes."

"Really?" Linda asked. "Some people think they're a little scary," she confessed.

"I don't think they're that scary. They're funny. I kind of like to think they're alive and they have a whole life we don't even know about," Sydney spoke in a rush of flurried words.

Linda nodded. "That's exactly right. I like to think that too. We have something in common."

Linda's home was not so different than the front yard. The walls of her living room were painted in a soft lemon pastel and the white trim and baseboards made the home feel bright and cheery. There were no garden gnomes in the house, but there were an abundant supply of Precious Memory figurines. They were everywhere throughout the house. Some were on the counters, on the furniture, and even on built in wooden shelves on the walls.

"You're a collector, I see," Lauren said.

Linda smiled. "Oh yes. It all started with Vicky and Emma. They're my best girls. I was going through a hard time when I first moved out here and I met Emma in group therapy. Well, it was my birthday and she gave me one of these Precious Memory figurines. Actually, it was that one there—Do you see the girl playing the piano?"

Lauren nodded as she examined a little girl with pigtails sitting at a small porcelain piano with an angelic smile on her face.

"Well, I was in some kind of mood that day and I opened her gift, which was beautifully wrapped by the way and I just said, *This is the silliest thing I've ever seen.* Oh my goodness…I was so rude. But it was the truth. I thought these little statuettes were downright stupid, you know…some kind of token for sentimental people, those folks who've got no sense. You know the type?

People who want to believe the world's all perfect and sweet when nothing could be further from the truth. For some reason it made me angry, furious in fact, just looking at it. Do you know what Emma did?"

Sydney and Lauren both shook their heads.

"Well, I had just started coming to the church and playing the piano and the next day just as I'm about to play, when the congregation is all serious right before worship... I notice another one of these darn things on the piano top. These tiny eyes are staring at me right before I set my fingers to the opening hymn. This time it was a little boy with a music stand. So, here I am staring at this porcelain boy with his mouth wide open just like he's ready to sing with me, no matter what I start playing. Well, I look at his silly little face and I know Emma's behind it. So, I turn away from the piano and glare at her right there from my seat on stage,"Linda laughed with glee. "Right during the middle of service with everyone staring and wondering waiting to sing. I must have glared at her for a solid minute and then suddenly I was laughing, laughing so hard my sides hurt."

Lauren smiled. "Wow."

"Honestly, never in the history of the world did a woman need a laugh more than I did at that moment. It did wonders for my soul. I found out later Emma and Vicky were in on it together. They've been giving me Precious Memory figurines ever since. About ten years ago they started in on the gnomes."

"I like them," Sydney said decisively. They cheer up the place."

"Well, that's what I think too. Wait a minute...I'll be right back." She went into the kitchen and opened a cupboard or two and the refrigerator door. She returned with a glass of milk and a plate of frosted animal cookies. As she held the plate toward Sydney, a startled expression disrupted her features. "Oh, I'm so sorry. Is it okay that I give Sydney cookies?"

"Yes, it's fine," Lauren said.

Linda set the cookies on the table and disappeared again into the hallway. She returned with a plastic crate full of knickknacks and set them next to the cookies. "These pastoral visits must get a little boring for her," she said to Lauren. "Let me see what I got here. I have a few puzzles, a magic 8 ball, a stack of Uno cards and a Rubik's cube." Linda grabbed a dishtowel and begin to wipe off dust from the plastic crate and its contents.

"Can I see that?" Sydney asked pointing to the cube.

"This old thing. Well, sure." She handed it to Sydney with surprising tenderness.

Lauren sensed hesitation in her body language. "Are you sure, it's okay?"

"Yes, yes, it's fine. It belonged to my son, Ryan."

"How old's your son, now?" Sydney asked as she began to twist the cube.

"He would have been 38 years old in October."

"What happened to him?" Sydney asked as she rammed an animal cookie into her mouth with the other hand.

"Syd, that's not..."

"No, no. That's okay," Linda said as she patted Lauren's arm. "Truth is, I'd like to talk about him more. He was an amazing boy. I was so proud of him. He was an athlete and a good student. My husband, before he died, hated to talk about him. It made him just a little too sad."

"Did he get sick?" Sydney asked with wide eyes.

"No, well...not exactly. In a way, I guess he did get sick." She pointed toward the living room where a large photo was centered above the gas fireplace. "There's a picture of him."

Lauren's gaze fell on Ryan, a plump, sable skinned young man in a blue collared shirt. He was half smiling as if making a deliberate effort to conceal his teeth.

"What beautiful brown eyes," Lauren said. They were large, almond shaped and rounded giving him the appearance of wisdom beyond his years.

"Oh yes. His eyes were pure heaven. He looks a bit like my brother Alberto in that photo. He was about 13 there."

"What a horrible loss," Lauren said. "I'm so sorry."

Linda gave her a sad smile. "Now loss is something I think we both understand."

"Yes," Lauren said softly. "I've experienced it. I'm still not sure I understand it."

Linda nodded slowly. "You're right. I don't understand it either, but losing Ryan did change me and in some ways for the better. But if I had the opportunity to bring him back… Goodness…, I would…in a second."

"Any other children?"

"No." Linda shook her head. We never really even talked about having another one. I was pushing my mid-forties when he died and working full time as a nurse. It would have been really hard and it was difficult already."

"Mom, can I go outside?" Sydney asked. Her plate of cookies was filled with crumbs and the milk glass practically empty.

"Syd, I'd rather you stay close."

"She can go into the backyard. It's fully fenced and I got a croquet set out there. You can try to hit the balls through the stakes. Have you ever played croquet?"

"No," Sydney said. "Is it fun?"

"Very fun. Follow me." Linda led them to a screen door in the back of the house that opened to the backyard. A patio with lawn furniture was followed by a large grassy space full of greenery and more gnomes. The center area was clear of gnomes, but the bushes that framed the side of the lawn were filled with the little figurines. Linda smiled as she observed Sydney's reaction. "I have a lot of them. I know."

"How many are there?"

"Between the front yard and backyard over a hundred. I've been collecting them for about ten years." Linda gestured for Lauren to sit on a padded love seat.

Sydney ran around the yard pointing and laughing. "Look at this one, Mom."

"I see," Lauren said as she turned toward Linda. "She likes your house and the gnomes. She asked me if we could get some for our house."

"Well, I probably have a few extras I could give you," Linda laughed. "That is, if you really want them."

Lauren felt sheepish. "I don't actually want them."

"They're not for everyone." Linda chuckled as she crossed the yard and handed Sydney a croquet mallet. She begin to demonstrate how to hit the ball through the metal framed targets. After playing with Sydney for several minutes she returned to Lauren's side.

They sat together for a few minutes and sipped coffee while watching Sydney hit croquet balls and run wild through the yard.

"I have to confess," Linda said amiably. "I want you to know I don't play the piano the way I used to." She extended her hands for Lauren to see. "I've got arthritis now in most of my joints. Playing is good for me; it keeps the arthritis at bay, but I've lost my timing."

As Lauren observed her swollen joints, her eyes became heavy with compassion. "I love that you keep playing. Please don't stop."

Linda chuckled and dropped her hands to her coffee cup. "You're kind. Playing used to mean an awful lot to me, but I don't feel the same passion I used to."

Lauren set her coffee down on the patio table. "I hate to change the subject, but…How did you do it?" She couldn't help herself. "How did you recover from losing him?" Linda eyed her over her coffee cup before setting it down.

"I wouldn't say I'm recovered exactly. But I'm beginning to get better at trusting God and seeing the signs." Linda hesitated and Lauren heard the sharp intake of her breath. "You know there were two casualties. Ryan of course, but also my marriage. Ryan didn't die easy. He committed suicide when he was a freshman in high school."

Images of Marcus flooded her mind. Lauren heard the smack of wood as Sydney struck the ball with the mallet. A grief washed over her heart like a cold wave. For a moment she imagined how it would feel to also lose her daughter. "I'm sorry," she managed.

"In eighth grade you couldn't keep the smile off his face, but then in high school, he became a different kid. He was moody, secretive, and he shut us out. We should have pressed harder, fought harder, but Phil and I…we didn't know about depression, mental health all of that. We didn't know about the bullying at school." She paused for a second. "Ignorance is not bliss. You know, he went into our own bathroom, in our own home, and hung himself with our towels. The same ones we'd use after a shower or to wipe up a spill. He used something so common, so ordinary to do the unthinkable."

"Oh," Lauren gasped. Almost a full minute passed before she could find words. "What happened with your husband?"

Linda's eyes looked heavy. "Phil changed. He stopped talking to me and certainly didn't want to talk about him. You see, when Ryan was alive, he was hard on him, not abusive exactly, but he wanted our son to grow into a strong man. He was critical of him more often than not, especially when he was in middle school. He pushed him in football especially. Ryan didn't have the confidence that some boys have. He just kind of collapsed when his daddy saw fault in him. It broke my heart and still does. Phil carried that guilt after Ryan died all the way to his grave."

As Linda spoke, Lauren pictured a family broken. Then her mind wandered to the elders and Reverend Martin. How could anyone thrive when the people who were suppose to help you were so eager to find fault?

"That must have been a very heavy burden to carry for both of you."

"We stayed married till Phil passed away about seven years ago, but we chose different paths. He became more reclusive and angry and when he finally retired from Bighorn Logging, he didn't hardly leave the house. We ended up with two different bedrooms, two different lives, but I nursed him and cared for him through his lung cancer, which finally killed him."

Lauren felt a deep stirring in her chest. Linda's honesty overwhelmed her.

Linda was unfazed by Lauren's silence. "Eventually, I found my way out of the tunnel. I had a career. I was a nurse for over 20 years. I made friends, I laughed, I begin to see Ryan in the beautiful aspects of my life and I could feel grateful and happy."

"I'm so glad for you. You deserve to feel joy."

"There is one area where I'm a lot more diligent and that's when I see people I love get secretive or real quiet. I get worried. I'm a lot more likely to confront them directly and let them know I care. I don't know why I was so scared to do that before."

Lauren bit her lip as her back and neck muscles tightened. "Now that part, I understand." A hard smack from Sydney's croquet mallet startled the silence. "Marcus, my late husband, had a lot of secrets."

Linda leaned forward, her round brown eyes were warm and kind, like

Ryan's in the photo. "I'm afraid to say that June made sure the whole congregation knew all about Marcus' gambling troubles and his accident as soon as the General Ministry informed us you were coming."

Lauren felt an anxious swirling in her gut. "I had a feeling that was the case. I suppose everyone believes it's my fault?"

"Why would anyone think that?"

"As a wife you're supposed to be a helpmate to your husband, a partner, keep each other out of danger, I guess. I certainly wasn't able to save him."

Linda furrowed her eyebrows in confusion. "You know, I think most people are too darn concerned about themselves to think too deeply about other people's troubles for very long. But, I can tell you what Emma and Vicky first told me about you when we had Saturday tea." Linda raised her eyebrows in a conspiratorial fashion. "They think June's a big old mean busy body and that's about the gist of it. We prayed for you. It made us feel closer to you somehow, even though we don't really know you that well."

Lauren struggled to stifle the confession that was forcing its way out of her mouth. "The police believe Marcus' death, his car wreck...that it was an accident, but I'm not always sure that I believe that. Sometimes...well, there are times I think he died because of me." *Did she really say those words out loud to a woman she hardly knew?*

Linda leaned forward, grabbed her hand and squeezed. "We could spend eternity blaming ourselves for everything we said and didn't say. For all the things we didn't understand. Honey, you can't do that. We will never do things perfectly, not ever, and that's exactly why we have to trust God, even when it's hard."

"It's so hard," Lauren said softly.

"Yes, it is," Linda agreed. When I started going to grief therapy with Emma, she gave me this verse. She rifled through a purple leather Bible and handed Lauren a note card with a handwritten verse.

For I know the plans I have for you, declares the Lord, plans for your good and not for evil, to give you a future and a hope. Jeremiah 29:11

"When you're going through grief at some point you realize you can choose to believe God cares for you and that he wants good for you or you can choose to believe he doesn't or maybe even that there's no God at all. I chose to believe and Phil chose not to. I saw both roads and I'm happy with what I chose."

Lauren ran her thumb along the index card. "It's a good verse and I do believe that God is good and that He cares for me. I guess I'm just a work in progress."

"Honey, we all are."

* * *

Lauren woke up with a start in Sydney's bedroom. Since her mother arrived, she no longer had a bed of her own. Sydney's Alice in Wonderland alarm clock read 2:32 am. A tingling sensation moved down her spine. She was on high alert and didn't know why. She looked down at her daughter who was still sleeping peacefully next to her in her full sized bed. Relief flooded her. Sydney was safe. But the instinctual fear did not completely go away. Her body ached from rough sleep. She must have been tossing and turning as she so often did these days. She rose quietly from bed careful not to disturb her daughter and walked to the window.

Sydney's window overlooked the woods, but a bright moon cast eerie shadows that shifted and moved with each strong coastal breeze. *Perhaps the wind woke me?* She peered across the yard and wondered if her mind was playing tricks on her. A dark shape was scampering into the woods away from the house. She shuddered with fear and tip toed to the living room to check the front door. It was locked. The back door was secure, but several windows had been left partially open to allow a cool breeze into the house. They were small windows, too small for anyone to use as entry into the house, at least she hoped that was the case. Most likely she had seen a deer, a cougar, or a coyote. Savage wildlife was not exactly comforting, but a person lurking outside her house in the night would be truly terrifying.

Lauren moved back to the kitchen and grabbed her favorite Briarmont mug. In the background she could hear her mother snoring from her bedroom. A cup of chamomile sounded soothing and she hoped drinking tea might calm her rattled nerves. She allowed her fingers to rest on the porcelain rim and tried to conjure Marcus' face. But her mind was troubled. The memory of a half forgotten dream clamored to break the surface of her thoughts.

"Marcus, where did you get the money?" He looked at her with mournful doe eyes, like a wounded creature. "Marcus, you have to tell me."

"I have an addiction, Lauren. I couldn't stop myself."

She choked through her anger. "Why didn't you come to me? Why?"

His body was shaking from grief or anger she could not tell. "You don't understand me, Lauren. You never could. You don't know who I really am?"

There was so much she wanted to say, so much shade she wanted to throw his way, but she was a deaf mute. The anger moved through her like a wild electrical current she could not control.

II

Part Two

New Round

Chapter 10

"Remember this.
The house doesn't beat the player.
It just gives him the opportunity to beat himself."
—*Nicholas Dandolos (professional gambler)*

House Advantage

It was one of those mornings when she felt every second of her forty plus years carved in her bones. After sleeping in late on a Saturday morning, shouldn't she feel well rested? Lauren cracked eggs into a bowl as she stared out the kitchen window into the woods. Was it more than shifting shadows she had seen in the dark? Hunching over the stove, she worked her spatula harder on the bacon and eggs in the frying pan.

Vivian came into the kitchen at just that moment. "Honey, I didn't sleep well last night. Could you get me some coffee?"

"Sure." Lauren walked the few steps across the kitchen to the cupboard and pulled out her mother's favorite red mug and the French press.

"You want creamer? I've got coconut, you're favorite?"

"Ugh! I've gained weight since living with you two. If I keep drinking that stuff I'm going to turn into a fat, old country bumpkin and then I'm going to live with you forever."

Lauren couldn't help but smile. "No creamer for you, then. Are you still looking for a man to rescue you?"

"Not all of us want to live the rest of our lives alone, darlin'. Which leads me to ask, why aren't you dating?"

Lauren took a step back from the stove and stood taller, her mouth wide open as she looked at her mother. "Mom, I lost Marcus barely three months ago. I wasn't planning to date, well...not ever. It's not even something I'm thinking about."

Her mother's mouth formed a grim straight line. "Well, maybe you should start thinking about it. You wanna be alone, supporting that daughter of yours forever? You're no spring chicken. That is for sure and two incomes are better than one."

Her mother, always the pragmatist, Lauren thought. "I'm doing just fine. I'm not the one who's homeless, remember?"

Vivian frowned and then grunted. "Why are you cooking those bacon and eggs then? It's like a full on fat festival around this place."

Lauren groaned. "I'm making breakfast for Sydney and eggs and bacon are also high in protein."

"Oh, so that's your excuse. A breakfast like that is not going to help you in the dating department." She raised her eyebrows and then sniffed her coffee suspiciously before taking a large gulp. "Well, this isn't half bad. What kind of coffee?"

"A brand called Boyds. Gloria gave it to me," she said through clenched teeth.

With coffee in hand, Lauren left her mother standing in the kitchen and settled on the couch with the plan of completing the finishing touches on her sermon. Just as she was about to consider another scripture, her cell rang. "Hello,"

"Pastor Westbrook?" The voice was clipped and professional.

"Reverend Martin?"

"Yes. I was hoping you might have a few moments to speak with me."

"Of course. Please call me Lauren." She heard him exhale through his teeth.

"Yes, Lauren. Of course. Actually, if you don't mind, I'm more comfortable with Pastor Westbrook."

"Okay I guess. What can I do you for?" She felt stupid as the words left her mouth. The Reverend was the paragon of professionalism while she sounded like she was selling fish bait at the country fair.

"Yes, well… part of my role as a facilitator for the General Ministry is to perform routine visits to our ministers in the field, especially those like you who are working in a probationary capacity. I was planning a visit to church tomorrow and just wanted you to know that I'd be there."

"Oh," Lauren said slowly. "It's only been a few weeks and I'm not sure there's much to see at this point, but of course, you're welcome to come." She felt an uneasiness settle in her chest. "What are you looking for exactly?"

"Pastor Westbrook, it is of utmost importance to the General Ministry that we are good stewards of the funds we receive. I'm sure you understand that." He paused for a moment as if realizing he was talking to a small child that may not appreciate such mature sophistication. "What I'm saying is we need to be sure that our investment in Vernonia is exercising good stewardship."

"I was of the understanding that I had a year to get the congregation off the ground. Are you saying that funds might be removed even before the year?" Lauren tried to keep the panic out of her voice.

"There, there," Reverend Martin said, his voice strangely stiff and robotic. "Let's not jump ahead of ourselves, shall we? This is just a routine visit, an opportunity for your ministry to have transparency and a chance for us to talk about your strategies and your progress with the congregation."

Lauren bit her lip. "I see. Well, I'd be happy for you to come."

"I'm hoping we can carve out some time for a conversation after the service to talk about my observations and your progress so far."

Her mind was scrambled. *Progress? What progress could she speak of?* "I will set some time aside on my calendar. Thank you for letting me know you're coming."

"Very well. Good day then. We'll speak tomorrow."

"Yes, Goodbye." She pressed the end call icon. The world seemed to speed up and slow down at the same time as dread spread over her like a storm cloud before settling in the pit of her stomach. *Lord, just help me to support my daughter.*

$$* * *$$

Lauren arrived at church early without Sydney. Vivian had informed her the day before that she planned to attend church and would be happy to take her granddaughter with her.

"I'd like to see what my daughter does for a living," she insisted.

Lauren tried to conceal her surprise. Her mother was not a church goer, never had been. She loved all things vaguely spiritual, but hated any form of religious structure.

"My church is the world," she insisted. "I worship at the temple of experience, not stuffy people singing chants about Jesus."

Vivian spoke sometimes about going to church as a child with her parents, but Lauren never got the feeling that these were particularly good memories. Her own calling to the ministry was a surprise to her mother and one she never quite understood. She remembered Vivian describing her to her various boyfriends throughout the years.

"Yes, my daughter Lauren is the religious one. Now I have to watch my language and behave like a nun in front of her. She's going to be a minister, if you can believe that?"

Lauren had to laugh. *When did her mother ever change anything she said or did to please her?* She supposed it was an interesting tale to tell for whatever company she was keeping at the moment.

Life held many ironies and one was the fact that Lauren's road to faith began with her mother. Vivian was dating a college professor at Briarmont at the time who was recently divorced. His name was Laurence Meyers and he was probably the only boyfriend in her mother's history of dating that she actually liked. He taught History classes at the college. Her mother began going out with him when Lauren was a junior in high school and she appreciated that he did not take liberties with Vivian the way other boyfriends did. He was never in her home drinking beer on the couch when she came home from school, and he did not treat her mom like a casual hook up.

Laurence was the only man she could recall that took Vivian on actual dates. When she first met him, he took them both out to a dinner and showed an interest in her studies and her future. Lauren was taking a psychology class at her high school and she remembered sharing her thoughts on Kohlberg's theory of moral development.

"I agree with his theory," Lauren remembered saying. "People make moral decisions because of what they've experienced themselves. They know what hasn't worked or what has led to problems in their own lives. They use that knowledge to prioritize what they think is morally important." Lauren was excited about her psychology class. Her learning provided the first chance to make sense of her own life. She was just beginning to understand the onion layers of dysfunction in her relationship with her mother.

Laurence nodded his head. "You're a bright young woman. I can't think of many of my college students who can even give a coherent summation of Kohlberg's theories. Have you considered college?"

"No," Lauren shook her head. "We couldn't afford that." She glanced at her mother who was engrossed in watching a neighboring table.

"I'd like another glass of wine, honey." Vivian batted her eyes at a young waiter, who seemed to find her entertaining. She had no apparent interest in their conversation.

"If you have financial struggles," Laurence continued, "there are so many scholarships available. You could rack them up quite frankly."

"Really?"

"You're the daughter of a working single mother. Yes, really." He was emphatic. "You should come to the college and tour. I'll send you some emails with applications to some scholarships. Off hand, I can think of about five that you would be eligible for."

A couple weeks later Lauren visited the college with Vivian and was introduced to a world of possibilities she had believed beyond her reach. She never imagined she would go to college. But after she met with the recruitment team and they helped her with miles of paperwork, Lauren realized going to school was more than possible. Vivian was blase, "Go to college, don't go to college. It's your decision."

The memories invaded her brain space and she forced them out of her mind. There was so much to get done before their assembly. She settled into her office chair to work on the order of service and tried not to think about Reverend Martin's impending visit. Knowing that her mother would also be in attendance did nothing to improve her mood. Suddenly there was a light tap at the door. Linda stood at the front of her office, staring past her into space.

"Are you okay, Linda?"

Linda tensed a little. "Yes, I'm sorry. I didn't want to disturb you, but I felt a bit compelled to talk to you this morning."

"Wow, you came early. Have a seat. Can I get you some coffee?"

"That would be nice, actually," Linda said as she took the seat across from Lauren.

"What can I help you with?" She stood up and poured coffee. Her only clean mug was the *I'm With Stupid* one. She handed the coffee cup to Linda apologetically. "Sorry about the mug. My last clean one."

As she took the cup, the blush returned to her cheeks. "Who are you usually with when you use this mug?"

"It's not mine," Lauren laughed. "It came with the job."

Linda smiled and then sighed. "I guess I should get down to business then. Ever since your visit, I've been feeling like God wants me to do something. Do you know what I mean?"

"I think so," Lauren said slowly. "Are you feeling a nudge from God?"

"I'm feeling drawn to a certain scripture." She placed a note card in front of Lauren with her neat angular cursive handwriting. "I've been praying over this all week."

Nevertheless, each person should live as a believer in whatever situation the Lord has assigned to them, just as God has called them. This is the rule I lay down in all the churches.

1 Corinthians 7:17

92

"Why do you think this verse is speaking to you?" Lauren asked.

"Emma, Vicky, and I have been talking for years about how we can help the church and after we visited, I just couldn't stop thinking that now was the time I was supposed to do something."

Lauren felt a warmth rise in her chest as she saw Linda's kindness. "Well... what are you thinking?"

"I believe you need someone to help with your daughter when you're preaching. That's what I think."

Lauren hesitated. "You're not wrong. I would very much appreciate help with Sydney. She's bored out of her mind during service and we don't have age appropriate options for her. What were you thinking, exactly?"

"I really enjoy your sermons," Linda said. "But I know there's other people who need to hear them even more than I do. I thought that after I play the piano, I could take Sydney to one of the classrooms and we could have a Bible lesson and games."

"You've prayed about this?" Lauren asked. "Are you sure it's not too much to take on?"

Linda nodded. "I know I'm not young. I've got arthritis. I sometimes move a little slow, but truth is I'm young at heart. I like kids more than grown up people most of the time, if I had a choice that is. You remember when I told you that I can see my son Ryan in the good things in my life? Well, when I was with your daughter, I felt him there with me, the way he used to be. After that, I was on cloud nine the rest of the day. I wondered why I had waited so long to work with kids? I know it's been a long time since I lost Ryan. He'd be a middle aged man by now if he were living, but a part of me wants to still be there with him right where I left him. I hope that doesn't seem like the sad musings of an old woman?"

Lauren smiled. "Not at all." She felt the heat of tears in her eyes, but she forced them back. "You don't have to commit right now. We could try it for a couple of weeks and see how it goes?"

Linda nodded. "You want me to start today? Because I'm ready."

She noticed now that Linda carried a large navy tote bag. The older woman unzipped the bag and gave Lauren a glimpse of her supplies which included paper, glue, games, coloring books, Bible lessons, and play dough."

"You weren't kidding," Lauren chuckled.

"There's something else too," Linda added. She pulled out a leather bound album from her tote and placed it on the desk.

"What am I looking at?"

"My late husband, Phil collected stamps. This is one of…only the Lord knows… how many volumes." She opened the album and pointed to four red stamps with the profile of a mustachioed man.

"They look old," Lauren said.

"They are old and valuable."

"*Regno D' Albania*," Lauren said aloud as she read the small print that was repeated on each of the stamps.

"They were issued during Italy's occupation of Albania during WWII. According to my research, the majority of these were destroyed when printing was shut down during the war. There are less than 200 remaining in the world and blocks of four like this one are rare."

"What an interesting piece of history," Lauren said.

"After Phil retired, he went into his hobby full time. I have a room in my house that is simply full of stamps. He spent most of his days in his study collecting, researching and organizing them. Most aren't worth a hill of beans, but a few, here and there are quite valuable. Since he died I've been trying to sort through his collection and I've sold several of them through a dealer in Portland."

Lauren wasn't sure where this conversation was going. "Sounds like a lot of work, but it sounds like possibly lucrative work?"

"I'm not just showing this to you as an interesting tidbit," Linda chuckled. "I have been in contact with the dealer about this little collection of stamps for a couple of weeks now and he has offered over $5000. I would like to donate that money toward the church to add to the yard sale proceeds."

Lauren was stunned. "Are you sure? Couldn't you use the money for yourself?"

"Well of course I could use the money for myself," Linda laughed. "But this is what I want to do. I've been wanting to do something to help the church for awhile, but it never felt like there was vision or direction to go. I never felt that a large gift would be a sound spiritual investment till now."

She pursed her lips to conceal her surprise. "You think now would be a good time to invest?"

Linda smiled. "It's now or never." She was about to leave and then she turned to look at Lauren. "I've been hearing some scuttlebutt with some of the old church members. Most of them haven't even been attending in years and I know next to nothing about it, but I can smell trouble. I just want you to know that those of us who are getting to know you, think you're doing a mighty fine job."

Chapter 11

Nobody has ever bet enough
on a winning horse.
—Anonymous

Betting

Lauren slipped out of bed just as the sun was rising and tried to prepare herself mentally for the exhausting hours ahead. Her mother usually slept in, but when she entered the kitchen Vivian was dressed to the nines in a white summer pant suit with beige sandals. Her eyes were drawn to her mother's French pedicured toenails. Vivian's chic look forced Lauren to second guess her own jean shorts and T shirt. *For a woman who was almost out on the street due to poverty, she sure seems to keep herself up with the little luxuries,* Lauren thought.

"What have you done with my mother?" she teased. "I don't think I've seen you up before 7 am, well,... never... now that I think about it. It's 5 am. You're up with the birds."

"Well isn't this the day of your little yard sale?" Vivian frowned.

Lauren tried not to gape. "Are you planning to help with the yard sale?"

Her mother shrugged. "Well, you seem like you'll have your hands full with Sydney and also all the organizing you're doing. I thought I could help keep an eye on her while you work."

"Really? Thanks Mom," Lauren said in bewilderment. "Linda will be there too, but between the two of you watching out for Sydney…I appreciate it."

"Well, don't act so surprised. There's nothing else excitin' going on around here. I can be helpful too, you know."

Lauren opted for silence, but gave her mom a smile. A yard sale was a ridiculous amount of work and she was already tired just thinking about the moving, itemizing, tagging, and bargain basement dealing she'd be doing in the hot sun. Marcus would have enjoyed the endeavor. He loved meeting new people, negotiating, and finagling over prices. Lauren took a back seat in these circumstances and was happy to do so. She didn't get any feelings of euphoria from finding a deal or talking down a buyer from his original price. She was pragmatic and task oriented. *Get the job done,* she would repeat to herself. This was exactly how she felt about today. *Get through it, Lauren. You can do this.* The pep talk was needed. After Reverend Martin's distressing news that the financial support from the General Ministry would disappear by the beginning of September, Lauren felt the pressure of what Gloria had said, 'yard sale or bust.'

Lauren was thankful for the coastal breeze. The weatherman had promised a sweltering day, but the gentle wind on her face gave her reason to hope that with a little luck, they might just ward off the heat. At this early hour, she still needed a sweatshirt. As Lauren, Sydney, and Vivian walked the short path to the church, she could not help but feel proud of her little team of workers and the hours of effort they invested in what Paul had dubbed, *Mission: Save Church.*

Together, they walked the bend from the parsonage to the church and Lauren gasped. There was no parking lot now, only a clash of bright colors. As she stepped into the clearing, her senses were assailed with the smell of sugar, candy and finished wood. There were dozens of volunteers moving at a frantic pace around the myriad of booths that formed a U around the parking lot.

"Oh, Wow,"Lauren whispered. "This is a lot of people for so early in the morning."

"Mom, It's a carnival," Sydney exclaimed. "It looks fun!" She bolted forward with frantic excitement.

"Sydney, over here," Linda called. "I need your help." Sydney made her way to her table.

Lauren waved at Linda. The older woman played a pivotal role in getting the yard sale event off the ground.

"Why don't we entertain the kids that come to the yard sale, so their parents can shop in peace?" Linda's suggestion came during the volunteer team's initial planning meeting.

At the time, the idea of setting up booths made Lauren feel exhausted. There was already so much work to do, but Linda's eyes were bright with enthusiasm and she didn't have the heart to rain on any parade.

"When I was a girl, I loved going to the fair and just playing all the games. Fishing for prizes, apple bobbing, balloon popping, the toilet paper toss, face painting…"

"Woh," Paul had said. "You got more ideas than pennies in a porcelain pig. Are you sayin' you're gonna have kids toss something in toilets?"

Linda laughed. "You just take an old toilet seat and fix it on a barrel. The children get to throw toilet paper into the barrel."

"Imagine that? They get a prize for throwing toilet paper in the privy," Paul said in disbelief.

"That sounds like a lot of work," Gloria warned.

"You gonna help me?" Linda asked.

Gloria shrugged. "Why not? Guess I don't have anything better to do. Maybe we can get Emma to do the face painting?" Gloria turned to look at Emma who had stayed silent up to this point. "Emma, our gifted friend, are you up for something like that?"

"Aah, that's sweet. I've never done any face painting before." Emma took a moment to contemplate the idea. "I'll need some supplies, but I think I could do it. As long as I can bring Lucky with me?"

"Who's Lucky?" Stan asked.

"You know, Lucky, Stan? My dog."

"What you say?"

"My dog, Lucky," Emma reiterated in a louder voice.

"Oh, that's right. That old, mutt."

"Don't listen to him, Emma," Vicky groaned.

"I can build your toilet," Luke said with a grin. "It wouldn't be the first time."

Lauren chose not to veto their enthusiasm. Instead she double downed on promotion by researching Pinterest and adding glossy pics of all of Linda's activities. She promoted yard sale items on every social media site she could think of. For the past two weeks, she fielded dozens of calls at the church from people inquiring about the event. As Lauren gazed at the volunteers running to and fro and the small line of people forming at the roped barrier waiting for the grand opening, she realized the word of mouth campaign seemed to be working.

Lauren's heart caught in her throat as she gazed at the transformed parking lot. Yard sales usually shared an uncanny resemblance to refuse sites, but the people of the First Assembly of Disciples Church of Vernonia had created something quite special. Pop up tents were in every corner. Their wares staged expertly and arranged by theme. Antiques and furniture were under two tents in the top left corner, clothing on the right, housing wares on the bottom left, and miscellaneous items on the bottom right. Between each of the corners were fun house booths and refreshments manned by Linda, Gloria, Vicky, Stan, Paul, and Emma and about a dozen volunteers.

Luke's handiwork was evident in the tall wooden frame that connected all the booths and tents together. Lauren had balked at the amount of work. "I think that's asking too much, Luke… for you to build something."

"Do we have money in the budget to construct a frame?" Emma asked.

"There's never any money," Paul assured her.

"I'm sure I've got extra wood hanging around. Everyone knows you put the new convert straight to work, don't you, Paul?" He winked at Lauren.

"There's nothing wrong with putting a young willing man to work," Paul agreed.

Lauren very much doubted Luke "had extra wood hanging around". She knew that once again he would be paying out of pocket for the privilege of serving the church just as he did when she smashed a hole through the ceiling. Something about that arrangement made her feel hopelessly indebted to him. She wasn't sure she liked it. Gloria contributed priceless antiques and Linda her husband's precious stamps, but accepting gifts from Luke felt different.

Now, as she beheld the yard sale in totality, Luke's contribution added a touch of allure that went beyond the mere ordinary. The oak beams were wrapped in bulb lights, colorful ribbon, and balloons.

Paul waved at Vivian and she made her way to his cotton candy booth. "You ever made cotton candy in your life?"

Vivian was suddenly demure. "No, I don't believe I ever have."

"You wanna help me, Ms Vivian as the honored mother of our pastor?"

"Don't mind if I do." Vivian batted her lashes.

"Here we go," Lauren groaned under her breath. Gloria signaled her to join her under the clothing tent and Lauren moved thankfully to the other side of the parking lot. "Weren't you planning to man the antique tent?" Lauren asked. "After all, we're mostly selling your items."

Gloria frowned. "I was, till she showed up." She tilted her head toward the right.

Lauren glanced in the direction of the antique tent and eyed June who was fussing over a flowered tea set. Porter was seated next to her in an archaic wooden chair. He smiled upward at the top of the tent at no one in particular.

"I didn't think she'd come," Lauren said softly.

"I can't believe she's here after that spectacle she made of our church service. That woman has some nerve."

June was certainly persona non grata since the public debacle. Lauren had not seen her in church since Reverend Martin's fiasco of a visit and Linda had stepped up to lead worship in her absence. "Do you think maybe showing up here is her idea of offering a white flag?"

"Absolutely not. She just can't stand that something exciting is happening without her. You know what she did? She went straight to my tent and took over. She just said, 'Gloria, I can take it from here' and practically shoved me out of the tent like I was a child or something."

"Do you want me to talk to her?"

"No!" Gloria was horrified. "What do you think that would accomplish?"

Lauren shrugged. "I just thought, maybe she should know how you feel. Maybe we could try to work this out?"

Gloria wrinkled her nose. "Well, truth is…" she hesitated. "The woman does know what she's doing. She arrived around five thirty this morning and did all the arranging. She wrangled Luke and a handful of volunteers and had them decorate the beams while Luke did the heavy lifting. She's got taste. I'll give her that and she's a leader of sorts. That is, if you consider barking out orders leadership—she's just the most aggravating person I've ever known."

Lauren smiled. "You don't mind her taking the tent, then?"

"I don't appreciate the way she's behaved," Gloria confessed. "But, I guess I don't mind that she runs the tent as long as she doesn't low ball my mother's things. We're raising the money for the church, after all."

"Do you think she would?"

Gloria paused for a moment and then shook her head. "If I'm being honest, I can't really imagine that woman low balling on anything, not when money's concerned anyway."

Lauren laughed. "Neither can I."

"So if you're not selling antiques, what are you going to do instead?"

Gloria gestured toward the hangers and racks that surrounded her. "Sell clothes, I guess. At least I'll be under the tent and not under the hot sun."

"That's the spirit," Lauren said with a smile.

"Where did all these volunteers come from?"

"Those are the recruits. Those two teenagers, the boy and girl in the pink, they're Stan and Vicky's grandchildren. They're running the toilet toss and apple bobbing. Not a good combination if you ask me. That's Helen by the face painting booth. She's a friend of Emma's and she's helping with arts and crafts. Over there, see the guys standing next to the wooden airplanes. That's Michael. He's actually a friend of Paul's from the Aircraft Building Association. I don't know the names of the other men. They're going to build and paint wooden planes today."

"Aircraft Building Association? Does Paul make model planes?"

"Oh goodness, not model planes, real planes. He'll tell you all about it. I've heard enough about kit airplanes for a lifetime."

"I'll make sure to ask him later," Lauren chuckled. "What's left for me to do? Should I help you with the clothes?"

"Mary Anne's going to help me with that. She's my friend from the pool and should be here any minute, but if you really want to have a job, you know who you need to talk to…?"

"June?"

"The one and only. If I were you, I'd just walk around and look busy. Maybe it's better to not be recruited, keep your hands free if you know what I mean. Good luck, you'll need it."

She left Gloria and made her way to Luke. He was sitting on a stool in the face painting booth.

"What y'all doing?" Lauren directed the question to both Luke and Emma who stood over him, paintbrush in hand.

"I'm a little nervous about face painting. I've never done it before. I asked Luke here, if he wouldn't mind being my guinea pig."

"Don't you mean victim?"

"Now, now, Luke. You remember our discussion about trust. You have to learn to trust women again."

"Oh brother," Luke groaned. "You've got to stop talking to my mom."

"Your mom is concerned about you as any mother would be."

"Okay, okay" Luke lifted his hands in mock protest. "I am your canvas and I will trust you if you just stop talking about my personal life."

"Who is this?" Lauren asked.

At Emma's feet, a small red and white dog with pointed ears reclined under the table. "That's Lucky. He's a Corgi Australian Shepherd mix. He has what they call, separation anxiety, so I take him pretty much everywhere."

Lucky sat up expectantly in response to his name. "He's beautiful," Lauren said as she bent on one knee to scratch him behind his ear.

Emma peered at Luke critically over her trademark ruby red glasses. She was so short that when she stood at her full height she was just about even with Luke's nose even though he was sitting down. She wore a tight fitted white smock and held her paint palette protectively to her chest. Her lips tightened and then she frowned. "What do you think, Pastor Westbrook?"

She looked up from where she was petting Lucky. "Maybe a rainbow or a unicorn?"

Luke glared. "No rainbows or unicorns, please."

"Shh," Emma hissed. "You agreed to trust."

Lauren stood up and smiled at Luke and then whispered in Emma's ear. "Ooh, he'll like that."

"I'm not so sure offering my face was such a good idea. What are you ladies talking about?"

"Trust, Luke. Trust," Emma repeated.

Lauren watched Emma work on Luke's stubbly cheek."

"I'm not sure you have a blank canvas with all that 5 o'clock shadow," Lauren laughed.

Emma moved the brush over his cheek in a vertical pattern."Don't you worry. I'm working my way around his stubble."

"I've been here since the crack of dawn. I didn't have time to shave," Luke protested.

"See how defensive he is?" Emma added.

"Wow, Emma. Not only do you paint well, but you also paint fast. By the way, I didn't get to thank you personally for your beautiful card. You have a way with the details."

"Dear, it was nothing."

"Emma is somewhat of a town sensation," Luke added. He winced as Emma forced his chin up. "Gentle Emma, please. I'm just a man."

"We'll see about that," she chided as she moved his chin further to the side to offer her access underneath his ear.

"Tell me more," Lauren said.

"Well, she's the town's resident artist, even has a studio downtown," Luke said through the side of his mouth.

"Really? Emma that's amazing. I had no idea."

"Don't make a big deal. It's a bit of a side hustle for me, but over the years I've done alright for an artist. The bar is low," Emma added.

"Ah, don't be modest," Luke insisted. He turned toward Lauren. "Her railway paintings have been featured in Home and Sunset Magazines. Mom, made sure I knew all about it. It's a pretty big deal in this town."

"Railway paintings?"

"Yes," Emma said. "I confess. I paint trains."

"Why trains?"

"It's something me and my hubby used to do before he passed. We traveled the country every summer by train, all over the U.S. I took lots of photos and then about twenty years ago I decided I'd try painting some of the pictures. It was something I decided to try after grief therapy after I lost my husband. They just took on a life of their own from there, I guess."

"I'd love to see your paintings," Lauren said.

Emma tried to look nonchalant, but Lauren could tell she was pleased. "The studio's open Monday through Thursday. You just pop on down anytime, dear." She put the brush down. "There, I'm done." She handed Luke a hand mirror.

Luke examined his cheek and nodded. "Not bad. Not bad. A spider web with a red and blue spider. I like it."

"I just had a feeling you were a Spiderman fan," Lauren teased.

"My favorite superhero. How did you know?"

"Every man I know loves Spiderman."

Luke narrowed his eyes. "Not very original, I suppose. But, he did have a way of saving women from falling buildings. It's a talent I've learned that comes in handy."

She blushed, but fortunately she was distracted by the sound of a car engine. Everyone watched with interest as Stan drove a massive golden Cadillac with a large red bow into the middle of the parking lot.

Stan rolled down the window as Lauren approached the boat of a car.

"What are you doing?"

"Didn't Vicky tell you?"

"Tell me what?"

"This is our raffle prize."

"We're doing a raffle?"

"What?"

Lauren remembered that Stan was hard of hearing. "I didn't know we were doing a raffle!"

Stan turned off the engine. "The wife's idea. Why you yelling?"

"Just wanted to make sure you could hear me," Lauren chuckled.

Vicky came up alongside her. "It's my mom's old car, a 1992 Cadillac Seville. It only has 32,000 miles on it. Mom didn't drive very often. She lived with us before she passed away and left us the car."

"You decided to donate it for the yard sale?"

"Well, it was just sitting in our garage. We didn't know what to do with the thing. We considered selling it, but the timing never seemed right. At one point, Stan said we should just give it to one of our grand kids in need, but none of them wanted it. I don't think Cadillacs are the cool thing for young people these days."

"It's running and it looks practically new."

"Oh, it was Mom's baby. She kept it up real nice and only drove it to go to the market."

"I have no words," Lauren said. "Thank you."

Vicky smiled. "I'm just praying that whoever wins the raffle will put it to good use and that we'll fetch a good bounty for the church."

Lauren nodded. "That's a good prayer. I'm going to join you on that one. A car could be a real miracle for someone in need."

Lauren glanced toward the entry to the parking lot. Luke and Emma were now at the far end talking to a crowd of people who were forming a queue around the rope barrier. Cars were lined up on both sides of the road.

"Wow, the line's getting a lot bigger. They're here early." Lauren was surprised.

"My hearts thumping," Vicky said. "This is exciting. Looks like you did a good job getting the word out. That's a nice little crowd for 7:45 in the morning. Don't you think?"

"Yes, it is," agreed Lauren. "I guess we better get to our stations."

"Stan and I have the raffle tickets ready. We're next to Paul, there."

Lauren shifted her gaze to Paul's booth and saw Vivian laughing. Paul was showing her how to work the cotton candy machine. They had made their first batch of fluffy blue cotton and Vivian tore off a piece of spun sugar and placed it in her mouth. Her eyes never left Paul. *That explains why she got all dressed up,* Lauren thought.

Vivian was not watching Sydney as promised, but her daughter was working the ring toss with Linda. At the moment she was trying the rings herself and demonstrating quite a knack for it. A small prize table was set up behind them with an array of stuffed animals, stickers and games.

Stan was now sitting at the raffle booth next to Paul and Vivian organizing tickets. He waved at Vicky to join him. She nodded at Lauren and left her alone next to the Cadillac. Everyone had a job to do, but Lauren was unsure of where she could make herself most useful. With reluctance she made her way to the antique tent.

"You need any help?"

June was dressed for labor. She wore tan khaki Capri pants and a white peasant tank top with a navy blue apron. Her white New Balance sneakers had an uncharacteristic gray smudge across the left toe. In her hand, she held a sketchpad and pen and eyed Lauren warily. "Isn't this your big idea? I thought you'd know where to make yourself useful."

"My job was promotion and publicity, so now I'm just looking to plug in where I can help. Gloria said you are the talent when it comes to management."

June shrugged her shoulders, but her tone softened. "Well, two antique tents is actually quite a bit to manage alone, so if you take the tent next to me that would be helpful. We might have lots of paying customers at once. Just make sure to ask me before you sell anything. See here…" June showed Lauren her notepad. "I've written all the prices of what we should be able to get for these items, so don't take anything less without asking me."

"Did you get those numbers from Gloria?"

"Yes." June raised an eyebrow.

"I gave those numbers to Gloria is all," Lauren said. "I'm the one who researched the prices."

"I've made some adjustments," she said testily.

"Wait a sec." Lauren took out her phone and took a picture of each page of the sketchpad. "I've got this for reference, now."

"Clever girl, aren't we?"

"I just don't want to mess up," Lauren said.

"Well, let's get started, then."

Lauren wasn't sure how to broach the topic. "I didn't know you'd be here today, June. You didn't go to any of our planning meetings."

"I'm still on the Ministry Team," she snapped. "Why wouldn't I be here?"

"We just hadn't heard from you. That's all,"

June glared at Lauren. "Everything I do is for this church. I might not do the popular thing, but I do what I think is best."

Lauren felt a wave of heat run through her, the desire to give June a piece of her mind. A gurgling sound interrupted the tense conversation.

"Aah eeh urg…"

Lauren peered behind June and saw Porter struggling for air. "He's choking."

June turned on a dime and was at Porter's side. She patted his back. "Porter? Porter?"

"Did he eat something he shouldn't?"

June squeezed his cheeks and forced his mouth open. Orange liquid dribbled from his mouth down his chin. She scrutinized his open mouth. "I don't see anything."

Lauren patted his back as he continued to cough through his wife's examination. "It looks like he was drinking this." She handed June the plastic blue cup lying on the table which was about a quarter full of juice.

"Were you drinking my orange juice, you silly goose? It's got the pulp in it, remember? Water, Porter, water. You can only drink water on your own." June sat the cup down and frowned. "You have to watch him like a hawk."

"You still having trouble finding a nurse?"

"I'm interviewing one at the end of the week, but so far haven't found a single one that isn't right out of training."

"With the two of us, I can help watch him during the yard sale," Lauren said.

For the first time June refrained from answering with a sharp retort, but simply nodded her head.

* * *

At 8:00 am herds of people descended upon them. The first to walk through the tent were the dealers. There were about five of them and the competition created a perfect storm.

"I'll give you $200 for the rug."

"I'll give you $250."

"I'll give you $300."

All of Gloria's inherited treasures were gobbled up at prices not far from their researched values. June bargained with the dealers like a pro. "If you want the Tiffany lamp at that price, you're going to also have to take the bookshelf for $20."

"But that's not even an antique. It's just an old bookshelf," complained the dealer who came all the way from Scappoose.

"Do you want the lamp or not?"

"Yes, but I don't want the bookshelf."

"Well, I think the woman from Cannon Beach is willing to pay more, so feel free to walk away. You're obviously not that interested."

"Okay, okay. I'll take the bookshelf." He wrung his hands in agitation.

"Good. You've made the right decision," June said. Her voice was clipped as she handed the man his change.

"Lady, if you ever want a job, give me a call. You run a hard bargain."

June narrowed her eyes as she counted change. "Sir, we're raising money for the church. God's worth bargaining for, don't you think?"

He took his change looking thoroughly perplexed, but didn't respond.

Lauren observed June's interactions through the corner of her eye. While June handled the big game, she was busy selling lesser items, answering price questions, and keeping a watchful eye on Porter. June was overwhelmed with buyers and Lauren checked on Porter several times. She even helped spoon feed him a Boost milkshake, which June admitted was most of what he ate nowadays.

Every superficial indicator led Lauren to the same conclusion. The event was a smashing success. The parking lot was bursting to the seams with people. Children were running excitedly from booth to booth and people were actually buying. Lauren took the opportunity to say hello to new people and introduce herself as the new pastor of the First Assembly of Disciples Church of Vernonia to every person she met.

She scanned the parking lot until she found him. Luke was chatting with the men from the Aircraft Building Association. Occasionally, he would stop and talk to passerbys and give each person he talked to a flier. Lauren was curious. "June, are you okay if I take a 15 minute break?" The frantic pace of early morning had eased into a steady rhythm and Delores had arrived to help June.

"Do what you need to do," June barked.

Lauren walked across the busy parking lot to the Aircraft Building Association booth. A group of four boys were sitting at the table making wooden airplanes. Luke gave her a broad smile as she approached. "Taking a break?" he asked.

"A much needed one. It's been crazy at the antique tent."

"I saw that," Luke nodded. "Saw you working with June. Everything water under the bridge now?"

"I'm not sure about that," Lauren admitted. "But, she needed help. Delores is there now and things have slowed a bit."

Luke turned toward the men beside him. "Lauren, I mean...Pastor Westbrook, meet the guys from the Aircraft Association. This is Michael, Larry, and Ed."

Lauren waved at the trio of men who looked to be in their sixties. Michael wore a bowler hat, Larry was tall and skinny, and Ed was heavyset with a long black and white beard. "Hi. It's nice to meet you. You guys work with Paul?"

"I wouldn't really call it work," Michael said. "We build airplanes and fly them."

"Wow, your wives must be very understanding," Lauren said.

The men laughed. "Larry and I are married."

"We have wives, Larry interrupted. "We're not married to each other."

Lauren laughed. "Good to know."

"But, Ed here is single," Michael said.

"And that's no shock to anyone," Larry added.

Lauren smiled as she watched the ribbing between the men. "Thanks for running this booth today. The kids are having a lot of fun."

"We just do what our leader tells us," Ed said.

"That would be?"

"Paul of course. He's the president of our club. He knows the most about flying after all the years he worked for Delta."

"Paul was a pilot?"

"Paul is a pilot," Michael corrected. "I worked with him for years. I was a diesel mechanic in my former life."

Lauren was impressed. "I'm not sure why I didn't know that."

"The guys humble," Ed said.

"Did you know Paul was a pilot?" Lauren asked Luke.

"Of course," Luke chuckled. "But I've been around here a lot longer than you."

The aviators were distracted from conversation as new children approached the booth asking for airplanes. Lauren turned to Luke. "I noticed you've been passing something out to people. What is it, if you don't mind me asking?"

"I don't mind." Luke passed her a glossy looking flier. On the front was a beautiful painted picture of the First Assembly of Disciples Church of Vernonia. She recognized the picture as Emma's work. The church was painted in glossy white strokes and the church windows gleamed with light through shades of purple and lavender. The various shades of the forest, grass and trees framed the beautiful white building. Lauren wasn't sure the church had ever looked this good. Artists were allowed their imagination and in Emma's rendering the church came out well. The flier included a welcoming message to visitors and service times. Lauren turned the flier over and gasped when she saw a flattering picture of her in the left corner.

Welcome our new minister: Pastor Lauren Westbrook

The heading was followed by a short biography and a list of her ministerial and educational qualifications which looked more impressive on paper than in reality.

"Whose idea was this?"

"My mom's. She took that picture, your first day at the office I think."

Lauren nodded her head as she remembered Gloria trying to work the camera on her phone.

Luke's voice was gentle, almost apologetic. "She didn't want this opportunity to go to waste. All these new people right here in our parking lot. Emma agreed to let her use one of her paintings and helped her produce the fliers. She's good with technology stuff, better than Mom. That's for sure. In any case, Emma's art work is kind of a big deal in this community. It can't hurt to do some promotion."

Lauren was not sure why her knees suddenly felt weak. "It's a great idea," she managed. "How come no one told me about it?"

"Mom, was afraid you wouldn't want the attention," Luke admitted. "You know what she told me?"

Lauren shook her head. "No idea."

"She said it doesn't matter how much money we make, but what matters is that the church is a place where people come to know Jesus. She seems to think you're a bit of a draw to get newcomers through the door."

"Me?" Her laugh sounded awkward. "That's flattering, but I think we'd be better off putting your picture on the flier. Look at the new convert. He's well to do and available. Get all the single women to come to our little church."

Luke smiled. "Are you trying to say, you think I'm...well how shall I put it? attractive?"

Lauren felt the heat of embarrassment rise to her cheeks. She was grasping for words. "Well, objectively speaking, you're not too bad. You know... for a fake Christian."

"hmm," Luke said. "Fake or not, I think Pastor Westbrook thinks I'm good looking."

"Oh brother," Lauren moaned. "You've got a big head. Oh look! We're right in front of the church. Why don't you just go inside for a few minutes and ask forgiveness for your unbelievable arrogance?"

Luke laughed. "You're the one who said I was attractive, not me. Maybe you need to go into the church and ask for forgiveness for your carnal desires?"

Lauren was silent with shock for just a moment. "I think that would be better advice for my mother." They both glanced in Vivian's direction. At that exact moment she was sensuously feeding Paul a handful of cotton candy. They both burst out laughing.

When she returned to the antique tent, the pace of activity was picking up. June was arguing with a middle aged brunette woman over a teapot. Delores, likewise was busy taking money from another elderly woman for a framed picture. Lauren watched Porter from the corner of her eye. He wore a broad smile and his eyes darted to and fro tracking the bustling activity in the tent. The whites of his eyes were keen and bright. She imagined he rarely had the opportunity to absorb so much stimuli in one day. It seemed to do him good.

As items sold, Lauren worked on reorganizing merchandise for display. Two women in their 50s were rifling through a pile of brass and silver candle holders. One woman with long red hair caught Lauren's eye. Conspicuous in a flowing brightly patterned cotton scarf and coppery hair, the woman was difficult to ignore. She was stage whispering to a mousy companion in a voice that all but invited eavesdroppers.

"When I saw the address for this yard sale I just about died!"

"Why's that?"

"Because this is the cult church. You know the one where..." She leaned closer to her friend and whispered an inaudible juicy tidbit into her ear.

The mousy woman's mouth dropped open as her eyes widened in faux shock. "No! They tried to pass out fliers. Who would actually go to church here...? After that?"

"Shocking, right?"

112

Lauren suppressed an urge to confront the women and demand that they share their conversation, but could think of no socially acceptable or gracious way to manage the feat. She sighed in frustration as the women wandered off to another tent. *What on earth happened at this church? What weren't people telling her?* Now she knew without a shade of doubt that those in the community they hoped to reach with the hope of God's love owned an actively negative view of the church. It would be an enormous task to change people's opinions. It was a PR nightmare and directly threatened the future of the congregation. She had no idea how to fix it.

Sidelong from the other direction, she became aware of movement. A woman was ruffling through items on a table in the back corner away from the activity in the front. She wore an over sized navy jacket, much too heavy for the weather. Her hair was frizzy and tangled framing her face like a magpie's nest. Lauren recognized her. She was the homeless woman she had seen on the first Sunday at church. The woman gave a standoffish vibe and Lauren sensed that she wanted to be incognito. Lauren pretended to fold antique doilies, but observed her covertly with occasional side glances. The woman carried a large cloth shopping bag and Lauren's mouth dropped open in surprise when she saw her place two small items in the bag.

Should she stop her? Say something? The woman was obviously a thief. Something stopped her from doing any of those things. Instead, she watched as the woman left the tent with her stolen goods safely stowed in her getaway bag. Lauren wasn't sure what possessed her exactly, but she exited the tent from the other side and followed her from a safe distance. The woman moved furtively toward the perimeter of the property toward the parsonage shielded by the tall rhododendron bushes until she met the outskirts of the forest. She looked several directions and then darted into the woods. Lauren hid behind a purple rhododendron bush about 20 feet behind her. After she saw the woman dart into the woodland, she jogged forward until she reached the place where she had stood only moments before. Lauren recognized the start of the wooded trail that led toward either the lake or the paved bike trail. The sun was high in the sky creating a sharp contrast between the church property and the shade of the forest. Lauren allowed a moment for her eyes to adjust and continued to gaze into the darkness. She registered movement and saw just a fragment of the woman's navy blue jacket as she skirted along the path toward Vernonia lake.

She was not sure why she allowed the woman to steal. In fact, she had no idea why she made the quiet decision in her head not to tell anyone about what she had seen. There was a quality in the woman that was both desperate and tragic. She felt sure she did not want to add more burdens on an already weary soul. It was a decision she would regret.

When she returned to the tent, she was not even sure what the woman had taken. The only items in that remote corner were small trinkets, mementos, photographs, pieces of church history. But something was missing. She felt a shuddering sensation in her gut.

Suddenly, Lauren remembered…the creepy spider doll. She sifted through the various artifacts on all the surrounding tables just to be certain. Sure enough, the doll was missing. *Why would anyone take that porcelain horror show?* Perhaps a collector might see value in an antique doll, but the dealers had long since left with their treasures and not one of them had shown any interest in the poppet. In the days preparing for the yard sale the dolly had almost ended up in the burn pile along with thousands of other items deemed either too damaged or worthless to sell.

Sydney had insisted they sell it as a sort of lark. "Mom, let's see if anyone will buy it?"

"No one's going to want that doll," Lauren argued with a laugh.

"Someone might," Sydney insisted. "They might see how sad and lonely it is, just like a little orphan and want to adopt it."

"Did you want to adopt it?"

"No, it's creepy," Sydney admitted. "But someone might."

They had ended the conversation with a deal. "If someone buys that doll, I'll take you to ice-cream and if no one buys it, you do the dishes for a week."

Sydney frowned. "How about you take me to ice cream and get me a pet? A dog, a cat, a parakeet. I don't care what, but I want a pet."

"I'd love to get you a pet, but were not in a stable enough position for that to happen, so ice cream will have to do for now."

I guess neither of us won that bet, Lauren thought. She had not accounted for the possibility that the terrifying poppet would be stolen.

Suddenly Lauren heard a shrill scream fill the tent.

"Porter! Porter! Where are you?"

Lauren turned to see June screaming. Her eyes darted to the wooden chair where Porter had been sitting. It was empty.

Chapter 12

"You can't change the cards
you are dealt unless
you stack the deck."
—Terry Blakeman

Stacking the Deck

Lauren stood in the foyer greeting her parishioners. The air seemed hyper charged somehow. As the congregants entered the room, some greeted her, chatted and wished her a good morning, but others stared past her or even avoided her. Paul shook her hand as he entered. "How ya doing this morning, Pastor Westbrook?"

"I'm great and you, Paul?"

"Just fine, just fine." He leaned toward her and whispered, "Something's brewin'. Pray and be on guard. I haven't got wind of it yet, but June is acting like a bride before her wedding day. That's never a good sign. She's been meeting secretly with some of the old timers."

"I thought you said you were an old timer?" Lauren teased.

"Nah. Well, I am, but these are the old timer old timers. The ones where you have to shake the dust off their church memberships. Real old timers is what I mean."

"I see." At that moment Lauren heard June's cackling laugh from the sanctuary. Lauren had never seen June in a good mood. Paul was right.

Something was amiss. *Yea, though I walk through the valley of the shadow of death, I will fear no evil, for you are with me.* She said the words from Psalm 23 in her head in rhythm to her breathing. A storm was coming. Lauren was lost in her thoughts before she felt Luke's hand on her shoulder.

"You alright?" he said gently.

"I'm good," she said quickly and then turned toward him. He was dressed in a new pair of dark jeans, black boots and a black T shirt with a navy blazer. Lauren had never seen him so dressed up. "I thought you weren't a church goer," she laughed. "What is this? Your third week in a row?"

"What can I say," he smiled. "I like your preaching. It also gives me a bit of a thrill to see how you've come and ruffled all these feathers." He glanced sidelong toward the pulpit. "They need some ruffling if you ask me."

Lauren sighed, "Well, believe me, it was not my intention to ruffle any feathers at all. I'm just trying to get through the week."

"What's up with her?" Luke nodded toward the sanctuary where June was surrounded by a group of three to four people. "She seems a little over excited."

"I'm not sure," Lauren admitted. "I'm worried to be honest. The energy is off today. There's a lot of people who can't seem to look me in the eye and new people I've never seen in my life. Today of all days," she sighed.

"Why? What's going on today?"

Lauren did not intend to spill her guts, but his deep set eyes triggered a confession. "The General Ministry is sending someone to check on my progress. I get the sense they are looking for any opportunity to withdraw the funding that keeps this church open."

Luke narrowed his eyes in visible frustration. "You've only been here about a couple months. What do they think you are, a miracle worker?"

"I'm definitely not that. It doesn't help either that my mom will be here today." Lauren tried not to sound defeated.

Luke seemed intent to speak to her more, but was interrupted suddenly by the appearance of Vivian.

"Well, this is…quaint," she said as she entered the foyer. "Ugh. No air conditioning."

Sydney followed a good four feet behind her grandmother wearing the tortured face of a martyred saint. Luke caught her world weary expression and smiled.

Lauren raised her eyebrows at her mother's attire, which revealed she had seen too many people attend church in the movies, but had very little experience actually doing it herself. She wore a tightly fitted skirt suit with bold white trim and large brass buttons. A matching sun hat made her all the more conspicuous. Her left thigh was exposed by the slightly risque slit up the side. *Looks like she watched too many episodes of Designing Women.* Well…she preferred the leg slit to the cleavage. That was for sure.

"Well, who is this?" Vivian asked as she gave Luke the once over and then the twice over. Before she could do the third, Lauren interrupted.

"This is Luke. He's Gloria's son. You know Gloria? She's the church's administrative secretary. Luke's a carpenter. He has volunteered hours to help with the building. He even did all the renovations on our little house. Luke, this is my mother, Vivian."

Her mother beamed at him with a smile that could have heated an entire northern Canadian province. Her voice was a rich, warm syrup. "I like carpenters. Well aren't you just a tall glass of water? When Laur Bear told me about her church people, I was just assuming they were all old fogies, like me. But you, well… my, my."

Lauren froze with embarrassment. "Mom, Luke did not come to church today to be ogled."

"I'm not ogling him," Vivian insisted.

"It's alright." A wry smile played at the corners of his mouth. "I like a good ogling from time to time. It's nice to meet you." He reached out his arm to Vivian. "Can I help you find a seat?" With good humor he reached out his other arm to Sydney. "Syd, should we find a seat close to the front?"

Suddenly, Sydney was shy, but she gave Luke a beaming smile.

"Hold on for a second," Lauren said. "Syd, Miss Linda would like to take you to a classroom for a Bible lesson, games, and activities after worship. Does that sound okay?"

Sydney gave her a thumbs up. "Yay, Mom! No more boring sermon."

Lauren stuck her tongue out playfully at her daughter. Sydney laughed and took Luke's other arm. They walked toward the sanctuary. Lauren watched them and couldn't help but smile. Luke had just managed to get her mother and Sydney out of her hair. *That man was an expert at getting her out of sticky situations.*

Reverend Martin had not yet arrived and service was about to start in five minutes. Lauren waved at Emma, Vicky, and Stan as she made her way to the front of the sanctuary. They nodded in return, but Lauren could see concern etched in their wide eyed expressions. There were definitely more people here than usual. Faces she did not recognize gazed at her from the pews and she heard excited chatter and hushed whispers.

The group of newcomers sat in the rows directly in front and behind June. There were two couples who were not familiar and a white haired woman. Lauren made her way to greet them and their prattling stopped abruptly. She felt the undercurrents of hostility. Porter was the same as always. He gave her a mile long smile as she clasped his hand. "Good morning, Porter. So good to see you."

"Goo...Good morning," he said in a booming voice.

"I hope you had a good week,"

He nodded and swayed back and forth. He clasped her hand so tight that Lauren had to eventually ease her fingers just slightly out of his grasp.

"Hi June. You look stunning today." Lauren spoke the truth. June was not dressed in her usual quality athleisure wear. She wore a crisp navy blazer with a matching knee length black skirt and matching tights. One inch black heels with diamonds on the toes completed the look.

June gave her a rigid smile. "It's always good to put your best foot forward even when things are hard."

Something in her tone suggested criticism. Vernonia was a casual town. Most of the congregants wore jeans, boots, cowboy shirts or flannels to church. Lauren had dressed down ever since the first Sunday usually opting for jeans, a dressy top, and boots. Being accessible and comfortable with her church people was important to her. She did not want them to feel like a seminary education made her in anyway feel spiritually or academically superior to her congregants. Her clothing and fashion would not be a distraction she told herself. After all, they were engaged in God's work together. Dressing down had been a ministry decision. She hesitated now. June seemed to be implying that she was a slouch, a person who had given up on her appearance due to the grief in her life. *Was that true? She had not given much thought to her appearance, not since Marcus...*

Lauren bit her lip. "Well, you look beautiful. I'm excited to see what you will bring to worship today."

June acknowledged her with a nod, but didn't say anything.

"Nice to meet you all," Lauren said to the surrounding company of blank faces before heading to the front. The awkward exchange unnerved her. She realized she did not have time for June's mind games and was relieved to take the seat next to Sydney. "Everything going okay, Syd?"

"Yep, Luke told me when he was a kid there was a place you could hide under the stage. It's like a whole room with a really low ceiling."

"I'd hate to crawl under there. There might be snakes," Lauren shuddered.

"I want to see it," Sydney insisted.

"No way. This old building is dangerous. You're never to explore on your own. Do you understand, Sydney Louise?" Lauren spoke in an intense whisper.

Luke sat on Sydney's other side next to Vivian. He leaned down toward Sydney and raised his eyebrows as he spoke. "If I'm working on something down there, I'll have you go with me and I'll show you while your mom's with us. That way you'll be supervised and safe and your mom won't worry."

"Can I, Mom?"

"We'll talk about it after service."

Luke leaned across Sydney so he could whisper near her ear. "It's been quite interesting getting to know your mother, Laur Bear."

Lauren glared at him before glancing at Vivian. She was oblivious to their conversation, her nose buried in her bejeweled phone. "Yeah, she's a real hoot... Her first time at church since I can remember." She turned to look at him directly. "Thank you for entertaining them. I appreciate it. Today's been completely crazy."

"Anytime," Luke said softly just as Gloria joined them in their pew. She wore lime green pants coupled with a white cotton peasant blouse.

"I woke up late today," Gloria said apologetically. Lauren did not need Gloria's commentary to see that she had rushed out of bed. Her bright red hair was not in its usual tidy up do. It was a frizzy mess that made her head look three times larger than usual. Lauren caught a glimpse of her mother looking up from her phone and caught her horrified reaction to Gloria's appearance. She did her best to ignore it.

"Should Syd and I move so you can sit next to Luke?"

"Nah," she insisted. " I see him enough already."

Luke stood and maneuvered his way past Sydney and Lauren to give his mother a quick hug and peck on the cheek. "Good morning, Ma. Everything okay?"

"Henry had a rough one last night. He couldn't sleep cause he was coughin' up a storm. I'm gonna take him in to see the doctor next week."

He placed his hand on his mother's back. "Sorry you had a rough night and sorry about Henry. Let's talk more after service." Luke returned to his seat and Gloria sat on the other side of Lauren. The older woman squeezed her hand while whispering in her ear.

"How on earth you're getting Luke in church is beyond me, but I'm grateful. Can you start on Henry next?"

Lauren's heart tightened and she felt fluttering in her chest. She moved her hand to her breast to calm its wild beating. "Believe me, Gloria. It's all God. I can't take credit for this one."

"I'm not so sure about that," Gloria insisted as she settled into her seat and perused her bulletin. Lauren felt a strange, momentary lightness. It reminded her of joy and freedom. Feelings that were a distant memory, strange in the midst of all this stress.

Her Sunday routine was to sit with the congregation while June led praise and worship. She usually sat toward the front with Sydney where she could easily move up to the pulpit to preach. On most Sundays, Gloria sat next to her in solidarity and as Luke started attending, he joined his mother. Lauren found solace in the practice and although she would be hesitant to confess her true feelings, there was comfort in having people she had grown to trust by her side.

June was taking her sweet time today. When Lauren glanced at her watch, she saw they were running about five minutes late. The one incident where she had preached past noon, her congregants had given her an earful.

My daughter's coming into town with the grand kids and we won't have time to prepare lunch.

We had to wait twenty minutes longer to get seated at our favorite restaurant.

There were a host of other complaints. The lesson? Senior citizens did not like to be late for lunch. Lauren lived in the good graces of her parishioners so she learned quickly to be mindful of their time. In light of the delayed start, she began to mentally shave off minutes from her sermon. She would preach a short one today. *What was taking so long? Maybe June was having an issue with Porter?* She glanced back at June to make sure all was well. Porter was still beaming and swaying back and forth. June was engaged in conversation with the white haired woman displaying no urgency at all. People were beginning to shift in their seats. Linda shrugged her shoulders from the piano bench as if to say, I don't know what's taking so long. When Vivian looked up from her phone and gave her a questioning look, Lauren finally took action.

She turned completely around in the pew and tried to capture June's attention with her eyes. The older woman gave her a friendly smile that chilled her to the bone.

At just that moment, Reverend Martin arrived. The entire congregation collectively turned at once to watch him enter. *How could a man give the appearance of discretion, yet still command so much attention?* Reverend Martin was skilled in the art of making public humility a form of art. He gave a polite nod and then found a seat in the back row. As if on queue, June stood up and walked to the front to begin the music.

At that moment, Lauren realized the truth. *June knew Reverend Martin was coming. She did not start the service because she was waiting for him. Why?* The other members of the ministry team, Paul and Gloria knew nothing about his visit and Lauren herself was only informed yesterday. She did not know their motives, but the writing was on the wall. June and Reverend Martin did not want her to succeed at The First Assembly of Disciples Church of Vernonia. The honored Reverend had said the words himself. They would not be sending any more ministers to replace Lauren. She was the last. For whatever reason, they wanted the church to close its doors. A spark of anger found fuel deep in her chest. *Why would they sabotage efforts to revitalize the church?* Her thoughts traveled to Gloria and Linda and the sacrifices they had made. *Why? Why?*

June now stood at the front of the church, a saccharine smile pasted on her face. "Good morning everyone. It's very nice to see all of you as well as some old, friendly faces. Thank you for being here today." She smiled directly at the small crew who had been seated around her. "I know some of you might be expecting that we start worship, but there are issues that we do need to talk about as a congregation. As most of you know I am a member of the Ministry Team. You know my husband Porter was a charter member of this church and an esteemed elder for many, many years, so I do not take this responsibility lightly. As I stand here today, I imagine that this would be what Porter himself would say to you, if he was able." She paused and tried to hold back tears before continuing. "For this reason, there will be a delay in starting our service as we discuss these issues. I hope you will all bear with me."

Lauren was confused. There was no scheduled meeting. They certainly had not discussed this in the last Ministry Team meeting. She glanced at Gloria who shook her head to indicate she too was dumbfounded.

"My friend and our sister, Delores is handing out a financial snapshot of our current budget."

Who the heck was Delores? Lauren had never seen her before. June waited as the white haired lady passed copies to each pew. "You will see that since our new minister arrived, there has been a rapid influx in spending. What's most concerning is the almost complete depletion of our emergency fund."

Lauren's hands were shaking as she scrutinized the piece of paper that included a short budget report and bar graphs. Her brain was moving like a ping pong ball and she could not focus. Every expenditure she had discussed and made with the approval of the Ministry Team was listed without explanation. The budget made it appear like Lauren was making charges for her personal benefit and without accountability.

"As you can see, our building fund is showing a rapid increase in spending the last two months. We have already surpassed our budgeted costs for the building fund back in May, but as the graph shows, under our new pastor's leadership we have excess spending not accommodated in the budget. In order to compensate for our pastor's habits, we have dipped into our emergency fund. Now, there is close to nothing left, $15.75. Perhaps enough left for Porter and me to get a cheeseburger at the old Dairy Queen." June gave a cynical laugh.

Sydney was glaring at June. She may not have understood all the ins and outs of the budget, but she was fully aware when her mother was under attack. Lauren was dazed. Her eyes felt like they were pasted open. The shock would not allow her to blink.

"We have expenditures made for office supplies, repairs, but most concerning is several payments for our pastor's use of the internet. As you can see, she charged the church $120.00 for Facebook. I don't think the church is responsible for Pastor Westbrook's pass times on social media, do you?"

A man Lauren had never seen before raised his hand.

"Yes Wesley," June said.

"We shouldn't be paying for her internet or whatchamacallit. We all know the truth. Her husband took money from the last church they were in. This is what they do."

June nodded her head sympathetically in unison with others in the pew. "Yes. Some of us see a disturbing pattern and that's why we called this meeting so we could discuss it." June glanced again at the budget. "The pastor bought a microwave, a coffee maker, a new first aid kit, and other items for her office. I just found out about $567 to repair a hole in the ceiling. A hole that had never been seen before and apparently appeared the moment our new pastor arrived and was not properly reported. That charge will need to be added as we have not received a bill yet. It appears that our secretary, Gloria tried to hide that one. And then...just look, all these separate charges for internet and social media !"

Lauren's shock turned to anger, a hard boiled rage she could hardly control. She wanted to jump to her feet and lay to waste these fruitless accusations. *No. What I really want is to wring June's neck.* Gloria too, looked as though she wanted to jump from her pew and wrestle June to the ground. She told the congregation the truth about Marcus' gambling on the very first Sunday. Now she was paying the price. Her body was shaking. She was holding Sydney's hand for dear life.

"Ow," Sydney said. She narrowed her eyes as she looked at her mother. "You, okay Mom?"

Lauren could not answer. *Didn't they know the internet charges were for the promotion of the yard sale? Gloria and Linda had already pledged thousands of dollars. The event held the promise of bringing in more funding than the church had seen in years and yet June...Why?* Her body was rigid with anger. She was hunched forward in her seat as if ready to spring at a moments notice.

Lauren heard Gloria take a deep breath as she took her other hand in hers and squeezed. "I'm angry too, but don't let them push your buttons." Her hushed whisper brought Lauren back to her senses.

Vivian's phone had long since been put away. She sat upright in her seat her eyes wide with interest.

Luke leaned forward his body tight with anger as he turned to speak to her. "Lauren, wait. You can't respond to this, not yet. I've seen this before in my world. They're baiting you."

Luke's urgency made her hesitate. Despite her powerful rage, she knew he was right.He whispered softly in her ear. "Don't say anything till you find out what they want? Just listen."

Gloria overheard Luke as well and raised her hand to speak. June tried to ignore her, but not seeing Gloria was like not seeing a parrot in the midst of a flock of crows. "Yes, Gloria," she finally conceded.

"If what you say is true and I don't believe it is, since I'm also on the Ministry Team and I'm the church secretary and anyone can see that these figures have been what you call, highly manipulated..."

June raised her eyebrow. "Is there a question, here?"

"Yes, of course," Gloria continued. "I would like to ask what it is exactly that you are suggesting?"

June hesitated as she realized she must walk this terrain carefully. "Well, the truth is and several of us have known this for a long time, we didn't really have the money in the first place to hire a new minister. We are already bleeding money and then we get a new pastor with a bunch of new ways that wants to spend every dime we got left. What are we going to have when this is all said and done, especially those of us who have been here from the beginning? I'll tell you what, a pile of debt and then we'll have nothing to show for our efforts. Our church founders deserve better than that. Porter deserves better than that."

"Bingo," Luke said quietly. "She wants the money."

Wesley raised his hand again.

"Yes Wes," June said.

"I was a charter member of this church. Over the forty years my wife Penny and I attended here we tithed regularly and now we got a new minister driving this church into the ground. So, we got no church, and we've lost our entire investment. If we sell the darn place and get out, us members will all get a share of the money."

Lauren heard what sounded like a collective gasp throughout the church and then an eruption of chatter.

"I've been here for twenty years. The money goes to charter members, not regular members, but I deserve something for what I've tithed too."

"Now, we're talking about selling the church? I though we just hired a new minister?"

"Why do charter members get the money if the church sells? I thought the property went to the General Ministry?"

The assembly descended into chaos like a fallen house of cards, but Luke was smiling. He turned to Lauren, "the claws are out."

Lauren made her way to the front. "June, please have a seat. I'll take it from here."

June frowned, but after evaluating the full on anarchy in the sanctuary made her way back to her seat with her head held high.

Lauren took the microphone. "Calm down everyone. Please calm down. We are not selling the church and we are going to make sure everyone has the information they need so we can come to decisions together."

As a high school teacher, Lauren had restored calm to chaos on multiple occasions and this was no different. She channeled a sense of serenity and waited for calm to return to the congregation. Slowly the conversations died down and the focus returned to her. "Thanks everyone. We've been given a lot to think about and I would like to have Paul Lu Roe come up for a moment and share with us a little about our church's bylaws. He is our expert in the policies of this congregation and the First Assembly of Disciples Denomination that we are a part of and he is also on the Ministry Team. I am new myself, so I would very much appreciate his summation of our finances and this situation."

For a moment, Paul looked like a deer caught in headlights, but then his features tightened and he rose from the sound booth and walked to the front of the sanctuary. He took the microphone with a firm hand. "Our church bylaws were mostly adopted in 1972," he said slowly. "Our elders at the time considered the possibility that our church here might at some point falter. As a First Assembly of Disciples Church we have an agreement that if our congregation were to fold, we would sell our property, the church building, and all church assets including the parsonage. In today's market this is likely a two million dollar property. In accordance with our agreement, half of those proceeds would go to the General Ministry, the other half would be distributed to the families of charter members who are still active attendees in the congregation today. The funds would be dissolved into a trust which would be managed by the General Ministry."

The chitter-chatter returned as people in the pews began to discuss the information with their neighbors. Lauren surveyed her parishioners and her eyes locked with Reverend Martin. His body was a tight arrow and he seemed more on edge than she could ever remember seeing him.

"Paul, how would the church come to an agreement to sell the property? Is there a process involved?" Lauren asked.

"Yes," Paul shifted from one foot to the other. Lauren gave him an encouraging smile and he continued. "All current members would take a vote. If a member does not attend for over a year, they revoke their membership and are no longer allowed to vote unless there's an underlying health concern that keeps them from attending. Also, congregants who continue to tithe are considered members even if they have not attended in a year. We would need over 80% of eligible voters voting yes in order to close the church. This would allow the Ministry Team to work with the General Ministry to move forward with the sale. The other option, if there was no longer a minister or a functioning Ministry Team, would be that the property would be forfeited to the General Ministry. They would then be allowed to sell the church and collect and disburse the funds received in any manner they see fit."

"I see," Lauren said as she walked from the front of the sanctuary to the pulpit "Thank you, Paul. I think we all see a bit more clearly now."

"My pleasure,"Paul said. "I'm also happy to talk to anyone in person if that's needed. I'll make copies of the bylaws for anyone who wishes to see them. My number's in the bulletin."

"Thank you, Paul. You might very well be getting some phone calls. Let's go ahead and make copies of those bylaws and we'll have them available for everyone next Sunday."

He made his way slowly back to his seat.

Luke gave her a brief smile. Suddenly Lauren felt brave. "I appreciate June and some of the charter members bringing these concerns to us all. Sometimes transparency can be ugly, but when we see problems at least we have the opportunity to fix them and we can rejoice in that. I will say that any spending I have done has been in the full view of the Ministry Team. We are currently preparing a fundraiser and the social media advertising has been to promote those fundraising activities. I am happy to talk with anyone who has questions about that. You can call Gloria and she will set up a time for us to meet during the week."

Lauren opened her Bible. She had a sermon planned, but she felt the quiet whisper of the spirit nudging her to speak from her heart. She abandoned her notes. "Many of us know the verse, John 3:16. *For God so loved the world he gave his only begotten son that whosoever believes in him will not perish but have eternal life.* This is the promise of the gospel. That if we give our hearts to Jesus, no matter how hopeless our current state of existence, we will be saved, restored, loved, and made right. God loves the world and he wishes to bring us into life. As much as I love that promise, the verses that follow are equally powerful."

As she preached, Lauren prayed silently in her head. *Please do not let me falter.* "Listen to verse 17," Lauren continued, *"God sent his Son into the world not to judge the world, but to save the world through him."* How easily we can forget that God's plan is to save the world, not to judge it. From the beginning when I took this post, I wanted to be honest with you about my husband Marcus. Yes, he was a gambler and I believe that addiction cost him his life. That addiction cost me a husband and it cost my daughter, a father. We pay a cost for sin. That's the truth of it. The more we try to hide that sin, the higher the cost." Lauren smiled at Sydney from the pulpit, hoping her words would not hurt her daughter.

"Verse 18: *There is no judgment against anyone who believes in him. But anyone who does not believe in him has already been judged for not believing in God's one and only Son.*"

Her eyes locked with Luke's. "I don't think Jesus came to judge us. Most of us, well... we're already paying the cost for the poor choices we've made and if we aren't paying them now, we will in the future. Don't you see? The message of God has to be one of salvation and hope, or otherwise what's the point of it? What do we have to offer anyone, if we don't have hope?"

Lauren brought her hands together in prayer or pleading, she did not know. "I'm reading Verses 19-21. *God's light came into the world, but people loved the darkness more than the light, for their actions were evil. All who do evil hate the light and refuse to go near it for fear their sins will be exposed. But those who do what is right come to the light so others can see that they are doing what God wants.* These words can feel convicting. I know none of us are perfect. We often protect our sin rather than striving to be righteous. We see that even here in our own assembly. But if we come into the light, there is hope for us. We can look at ourselves clearly and we can make changes. We can allow God to change our hearts."

Lauren shifted her gaze to Vivian, who looked at her now with wide open eyes. "My husband hid his gambling problem for years. He preached about the love and mercy of God, yet for some reason he didn't believe there was any mercy left for him. You know what? I helped keep his secret. I didn't want to experience the shame, the guilt, the consequences of coming into the light, so I hid in darkness too. I thought I wanted to protect my husband, but there was also the part of me that wanted to protect myself. When you live in darkness all you find is more darkness. I've learned that lesson the hard way."

As she closed her Bible she looked directly at Reverend Martin. "I don't judge you and I hope you don't judge me. We are here to bring hope into a broken world. Some of you may look at this church and see the thousands of dollars of repairs that are needed. Others might revel in the past when this building was a shiny relic and the future spread out in front of us all like a plain of limitless opportunity. But you know what? I like this church, just as it is. It's not so different than me, hopelessly broken and in desperate need of repair. It's got so much untapped room and potential. I don't think God has given up on this church and I don't think he's given up on me either. He hasn't given up on any of us. Pray about it this week. Selling the church is a big decision. I just think, we should allow God some space in our hearts to inform that decision. Allow for the possibility that God might be working even if we don't see it."

As she looked out on the congregation, Lauren felt indecisive. Under ordinary circumstances she would offer an invitation at the end of the service to call those seeking into fellowship with the Lord. After all the hullabaloo of today, somehow it seemed inappropriate, but Lauren felt a nudge and she followed through. "I know today has been crazy, but God is the same yesterday, today, and tomorrow. He wants to have a relationship with you. If you're feeling called or led by the spirit, you're welcome to come forward and we will welcome you into fellowship with Christ Jesus through the baptism of all believers and fellowship into this congregation.

I'm going to ask June to come up and lead us in a closing hymn.

June rose to the front looking like a bedraggled doll and Linda took her place at the piano. They began to sing, *I Have Decided to Follow Jesus.* Luke suddenly rose from his seat and walked to the front with his trademark confidence. Gloria's eyes went as wide as saucers. The shock was so pervasive that most of the congregation stopped singing mid-sentence. Lauren's heart stopped. As June struggled through the last verse, Lauren moved to Luke's side and distanced the microphone far from her face. "Are you serious?" she whispered.

Luke smiled. "As a heart attack."

"You just told me a week ago, you didn't believe."

"Things change." He gave her a teasing wink.

The song ended and June remained onstage awkwardly, not knowing if she should stay standing or return to her seat. Lauren brought the microphone back to her mouth. "Luke has just informed me he would like to give his life to the Lord."

As Paul shouted, "Amen," a ray of light shone through the stained glass window onto the faces of the people of the First Assembly of Disciples Church of Vernonia.

Chapter 13

A Gambler is nothing
but someone who makes their living
out of false hope.
—*William Bolitha*

Hope Springs Eternal

Lauren was angry. She couldn't help it. As her parishioners filtered out of the sanctuary, she relived the wide spectrum of emotions from the morning service. The fear, rage and triumph coursed through her veins in an overwhelming wave.

Vivian squeezed her hand as she left with Sydney. "Wow, Laur Bear, you never told me how excitin' church was. Count me in for next Sunday." The blush in her cheeks made her look especially radiant.

Lauren discreetly rolled her eyes. *Of course, her mother would find her trials entertaining,* but then again Vivian was showing signs of actual enthusiasm in regards to church. *I'll take what I can get,* Lauren decided. "Thanks for taking Sydney home. I have a few things I need to finish up here."

Vivian offered her a knowing smile. "I imagine you have business with the new convert." She gave her daughter a sly wink before heading out into the parking lot.

Anger was now the dominant emotion and it moved through her like an electrical current. Reverend Martin was lying in wait as soon as her mother was out the door.

"That was quite the service," he said through gritted teeth.

Lauren wondered if he was attempting to be humorous. She couldn't tell. "Yes, it was. Do you still want to talk about my progress?"

He shifted from foot to foot obviously uncomfortable. "Yes, I think we should still have our conversation. Is three O'clock okay? I have lunch plans so wouldn't be able to meet till that time."

Lauren was tempted to ask if he had meal plans with his partner in crime, June, but she pressed her lips forcefully into silence. "That would be fine. We can meet in the church office. I'll keep the door unlocked." Her voice was flat.

He nodded his head and walked out of the door. For the first time, she sensed a begrudging respect from a man who previously treated her with profound condescension. Lauren was surprised. From her point of view, the service was a certifiable disaster.

Most of the congregation had long since cleared the space. He sauntered toward her like a peacock, obviously pleased with himself. Luke leaned against the frame of the door and eyed her with close attention.

She glared at him. "That was quite the display," she said.

He opened his eyes wide in mock innocence. "I don't know what you mean. I thought churches wanted people to come to Christ, join the church, that kind of thing?"

Lauren sighed. "We are hoping for sincere conversions. I don't know what that was." She studied his face as if to jog his memory. "Remember, you just told me at the lake, you don't believe. You made me complicit by accepting your confession." She shoved her hands in the pockets of her jeans. "Luke, it feels like you're playing a game. I don't like being toyed with. The church is not here for your personal entertainment."

His eyes turned suddenly heavy and his expression softened. "Lauren, I'm not playing games. It's just…That was insane. You needed someone to step up and help."

Lauren grimaced. *He saw her as a vulnerable kitten that needed protection, a woman like her mother.* But she sensed a genuine remorse and changed her

133

tone. "I can see where you're coming from. I guess... I know you wanted to help. I appreciate that...it's just..." Her emotions suddenly overwhelmed her. "I already feel like a fraud." The tears broke the surface and Lauren brought the back of her wrist to her eyes. She felt ashamed, embarrassed by her vulnerability.

Luke's eyes narrowed in concern. His voice was gentle. "Why do you feel like a fraud?"

"Marcus was the minister, not me," Lauren said in a hushed whisper. "You know why I'm here? I'm desperate. That's why. I needed a job. I'm not sure if this is even my true calling. I feel like I've been thrown into the deep end, Luke. I'm way out of my league." She was out of breath. Her cheeks were hot with the shame of revealing too much, but she was weak and unable to control the words that poured out.

Luke grazed her arm with his fingertips. "You're the best minister this church has ever had. Lauren, I actually believe that. I wouldn't stand up in front of the church and make a public confession for someone I thought was a fraud."

The shame of crying in front of him made it difficult to look him in the eyes. She forced herself. "But you made a confession to Christ and you don't really believe?"

A tortured expression rested on his features. "Lauren, maybe I don't believe the way you want me to, but there are things I believe." He moved closer to her, his deep set eyes inches from her face. "I know that you don't treat a good woman and her child this way. It's wrong."

He spoke with a conviction that made Lauren's legs weak. She grabbed his arm without thinking to steady herself. "Sorry, it's been a long day. I don't feel too good."

"You just survived a character attack. Give yourself a break. Come on let's sit down for a sec." He led her by the elbow to a wooden bench in the foyer and took the seat beside her. They sat for a moment in silence before Luke spoke. "Lauren, I know you think I'm a handyman or whatever, but that's not exactly the whole story."

She lifted her face in surprise. "What's the whole story?" Her heart beat to an erratic rhythm as memories of Marcus flooded her—all the times he had given her a different version of the story. Lauren prepared herself mentally for more lies, more disasters.

"I had a company when I was married, a construction company. I built it from the ground up with my Uncle Brian. He was a maverick, not scared of anything. He gave me the foundation for all I know about building. My father, well I never knew him. My mom hasn't told me much about him either. All I can say is, she was a single mom and if it hadn't been for my uncle, my mom's brother, I wouldn't really have had a father figure. My last name, Reid, is my mother's maiden name. She didn't marry Henry till I was a grown man, you see?"

"Okay?" Lauren said slowly. She searched his face again. "What's the whole story you want to tell me?"

Luke sighed. "I got married in my early 20s. I was doing good. We lived out in Wilsonville. With Uncle Brian's wheelin' and dealin' and my skills and commitment to quality, we started getting a lot of contracts. We hired more and more people, got more contracts, even a few government contracts. Over twenty years,we built a successful business. Bridget and I never had kids. She was a beautiful woman and she liked socializing and spending money. I didn't mind. I was proud that I could give her that kind of life."

Lauren nodded as she listened. "Sounds like you were living the high life."

"Yeah," he said as he looked past her. "For awhile it was good. But then it also wasn't. I was working all the time. I mean all the time. Bridget didn't seem to mind. She'd pack me a nice lunch once in awhile, but she seemed okay with the long hours. I was a workaholic and kind of okay with it too. Then, a buddy of mine told me he thought Bridget was seeing a mutual friend of ours. You know...having her fun."

Lauren winced. "I'm so sorry, Luke."

"Yeah, I was too. But the strange thing was, I didn't do anything about it."

"What do you mean?"

"I didn't confront her. I just kept working and pretending I didn't know for a couple years."

"Why?" Lauren was surprised. Luke struck her as the kind of person who took action. "Did you confront him?"

Luke sighed. "No. I didn't talk to him either. Even had him and his wife over for dinner. How sick is that? I didn't want things to change, I guess. I liked who I thought Bridget was. I didn't want to know the person I actually married, not really anyway. I just didn't want to know."

Lauren groaned aloud but then sat up taller in the bench. "I get it," she said slowly. "The truth is horrible."

"Yes it is," Luke agreed. "But I couldn't run away forever. My Uncle Brian died and left me the whole company. Not long after that, Bridget filed for divorce and she wanted everything: the house, the business, half of all of our assets and alimony. She never worked, but felt that we had built the business together."

Lauren was angry just listening. "She cheats on you and still wants everything?" she shook her head in frustration.

"Yep, that's about the gist of it," Luke said with a wry smile.

"What happened?"

"I decided to get out. I sold the business. I offered Bridge half and said she could either take it and we're over and done with it forever or we could fight it out in court. I gave her the house and half the business and I moved here to be closer to Mom and live the quiet life. Haven't talked to Bridget since. Truth is, I think she was having affairs all throughout our marriage. I think I always sort of knew."

"That's horrible," Lauren said. "Do you mind if I ask why you're telling me this?"

"You're easy to talk to." Luke smiled. "Plus, I think you kind of understand."

Lauren surprised herself by laughing. "Yeah, I actually sort of do."

Luke tightened his fists in frustration. "I've got so much time on my hands now, some days I think I'm going to go crazy. That's why I started helping Ma with the church."

"You ever think about starting a company again?"

"Nah." He shook his head. "Been there and done that. I moved here cause I needed some time to process the marriage, Bridget, the company, you know...all the mistakes. Don't misunderstand me, I want to work, but working all the time is what made me go wrong the first time. I'm in my 40s. What do I have to show for my life? No kids and a failed marriage. I guess what I'm saying is, my confession today might have been premature, but I'm going to church for a reason. I'm looking for something. I'm just not sure if Jesus is what it is." His eyes searched her face.

Lauren rested her chin in her palm. "I see. Well, if you need to stay busy, I think this church has enough problems to keep you working for the rest of your life."

"Aint that the truth." He gazed at her intently. "So, what about you?"

Lauren's heart quickened. "What about me?"

"Do you have sweeping regrets?"

Her mouth opened in surprise. "Luke, that's a little nosy. Haven't I revealed enough of my dirty laundry?"

"I shared about me. I'm curious about you."

"Everyone has regrets."

"Yes. Agreed. So, what are yours?"

"You don't take a hint, do you?" Lauren said in mock exasperation.

"We've already established that," Luke grinned. "Remember two whole years before I confronted my wife with what was right in front of my nose. Ah, I coaxed a smile out of you."

"You're too hard on yourself, Luke."

He raised an eyebrow. "So…"

"I also regret not taking action in my life when I should have. Sometimes we carry things alone when we shouldn't. There were things in my marriage that I pushed beneath the surface and I thought they had gone away, but they were hiding and just getting bigger."

"The gambling you mentioned in your first sermon?"

"Yes. The gambling, but the thing is gambling, infidelity, whatever the problem…There's more to it than that, right? I keep thinking those are just symptoms of the things we're not dealing with."

"Now, that Pastor Westbrook is deep. If you don't mind me asking, what weren't you dealing with?"

"Marcus and I were graduates of Briarmont Christian college, we went to seminary and became ministers. We did the whole church life. We did the whole Christian shebang."

"And that made him a gambler?"

"Don't get me wrong. Marcus had a choice and he chose poorly, but living under the expectation to maintain a perfect image is a lot of pressure. Because of his job, Marcus didn't think he could be a real person anymore and I don't think I did either. The Christian work we were doing wasn't really about God, but stress to keep our jobs, and worry about how much people liked us. Then there was the financial burden and it just got worse and worse. After I first found out about Marcus' gambling all I could think about was how we were going to pay back the debt and all the while Marcus was just digging a bigger and deeper hole. We were headed for disaster. I regret not seeing that earlier."

"What would you have done differently?"

Lauren sat up in surprise and stared at him. "That's what I'm trying to figure out, but I think it has something to do with not hiding your struggles, especially not from ourselves and from God."

"I'm sorry you went through all of that," Luke whispered. "We have some things in common."

A small smile curled at the corner of her lips. "I caught on to that too when I was listening to you. *Realitus Escapus*."

"That sounds made up," Luke laughed.

"It means we are part of an exclusive club engaged in a quest to escape our sad realities and yes, I made it up."

Luke returned her smile. "Well, not to change the subject, but just so you know, my favorite moment of the summer was finding you with your legs hanging from the ceiling. Even in my business that was a new one."

She shook her head. "That was mortifying."

He nudged her with his elbow. "But you survived." He pointed at her and then himself. "You and me, we're survivors."

* * *

Lauren tried to remember that she was a survivor as she welcomed Reverend Martin into the church office. She had prayed for God's guidance, but she still had no inkling of how this conversation might go. "Would you like a cup of coffee?"

"Do you by chance have earl gray?"

"Yes, I do." She turned her back to him and filled the hot pot. Without embarrassment she handed him the *I'm with Stupid* mug. He frowned for a moment as he studied his coffee cup. "Would you like any milk or sugar in your tea?" She expected the Reverend to take his tea black. He seemed like the kind of man who abstained from anything that might give pleasure, but he surprised her.

"Sugar and milk would hit the spot. Thank you."

She took the milk out of the mini fridge and poured around a tablespoon in his mug. He placed his palm flat over the rim to signal her to stop. "Sorry. I almost poured milk on your hand," she said as she pulled back the carton with trembling fingers and passed him a glass bowl with sugar cubes.

He didn't respond, but his eyes were cool and indifferent as he assessed her. The sugar bowl was steady in his hands as he dropped two cubes into his tea. He stirred rhythmically as he spoke. "I don't want you to have the wrong idea about what happened today."

Lauren sat down across from him and blew on her coffee before taking a sip. She thought about Luke and how he had cautioned her during the morning assembly to listen before speaking.

"What idea do you think I have?"

The crease between his eyebrows grew more pronounced as he frowned. "I think you may be under the impression that the General Ministry is interested in this property for purely financial reasons."

Lauren nodded her head thoughtfully. "Aren't you?"

A heavy rush of air escaped his lips. He set the cup down and eyed her warily. "If this church does not have a viable ministry than it may be our best option, but that is not what I want."

"That's good," Lauren said. "When I moved here I believed there was a good faith effort on the part of the General Ministry and myself to build this congregation. I'm not sure what can be accomplished in two months to change the course of a fifty year history."

Reverend Martin nodded thoughtfully. "You're right."

Lauren read a new expression on his face, an emotion she couldn't quite figure out. His eyes were brooding and melancholy. "Reverend, is there something you want to tell me?"

He clasped his hands together and leaned forward in his chair. "Pastor Westbrook, you may think that I haven't been very supportive of you and your situation. Perhaps I haven't been. I'm sent in many circumstances to weed out corruption throughout our churches. I have seen things."

Lauren nodded. "I'm sure you have. That must be difficult."

"Yes," Reverend Martin said slowly. "Sometimes it makes me a bit of a cynic, I'm afraid. Over the years, I've come to the conclusion that often our General Ministry policies are too tolerant. We allow sin to go unchecked too long and by the time we take action to remove a minister or shut down a church too much damage has already been done. People become disillusioned, they leave the church, the kingdom of God grows just a bit smaller."

"I hadn't thought of what your job must be like," Lauren admitted. "I'm sure that feels discouraging."

The Reverend took another sip of tea and set his mug down. He wrinkled his nose as if sensing an unpleasant odor. "The First Assembly of Disciples Church of Vernonia has a rocky history. One that we didn't tell you about when you took the post. The General Ministry board discussed it and we came to the conclusion that some things are better left buried in the past, so we can all move forward."

Lauren set her mug down and raised her eyebrows. "What happened?"

"This church left the First Assembly of Disciples church for nearly 20 years. It had what we call today a *rogue minister*."

"A rogue minister? You make it sound almost exciting," Lauren said.

The Reverend frowned. "It was not. His reign, and I call it a reign because in these circumstances what we have is a king and his court. There was no spiritual accountability. The church engaged in practices that were highly questionable. The General Ministry would have shut them down, but we no longer had access to the congregation."

"I don't understand," Lauren said. "How could they leave the First Assembly of Disciples? Aren't there legal ramifications?"

"Indeed there are…" the Reverend said. "But the church members voted to leave and did so with a 90% margin. Our organization splits the ownership of churches between the FAOD and the individual congregations. In this case, if we had pressed our interest it would have gone forward in court. We did not want to air our business out in the public in such a way, so we decided not to pursue that option."

"I see," Lauren said. She peered at him over her coffee mug. "What were the questionable practices?"

The Reverend grimaced. "Pastor Westbrook, when we took possession of the church in the early 2000s we came into agreement with the church's leadership team at the time to leave the ugly past behind. We agreed we would not talk about what happened during Pastor Worth's ministry and we would move forward to a brighter future."

Lauren frowned. "I am now the pastor of this church. Don't you think knowing the history of this congregation might be helpful to me as I minister here?"

"No," Reverend Martin said with surprising force.

Lauren opened her mouth wide with shock.

He softened his tone. "There are many in the congregation today who know nothing of its past. If this old history were drudged up, it could be destructive to those in the congregation today. Pastor Westbrook, sin is like a cancer. You cannot drudge it up and play with it like a child's toy."

Lauren pressed her fingers to her lips thoughtfully. "Reverend, you know my past. You know about Marcus. Don't you think it's better to be honest with your congregation? Isn't that the way you move forward?"

He shifted uncomfortably in his seat. "Pastor Westbrook, I am certainly not promoting dishonesty. The General Ministry is simply suggesting that we not reopen old wounds."

"I see," Lauren said, even as her stomach lurched.

141

"In any case, we need to bring this conversation back to your progress. I'll admit, I thought that we would be having a discussion today about how to finally close this church for good. June has called me several times in the last few weeks to report that all is not well, but I was surprised at what I saw today."

"You were?"

"Yes. That scene today was what many in our profession call a train wreck, a genuine fiasco. I was curious how you would handle it."

Lauren frowned. Reverend Martin made her feel like a hard-shelled beetle pinned to a spreading board. "And?"

"You kept your cool, you preached a biblical message, and the church won a new believer."

The heat of shame rose to her cheeks. Luke was not exactly a new believer. Lauren bit her lip, but remained silent.

"I believe you showed me today that it is in the best interest of the FAOD to give you more time to work with this congregation."

"How much more time?"

"I believe we should have quarterly check ins, every three months or so. However, the General Ministry does feel like it's time to draw back our financial support. We've been supplementing this church for nearly five years, and we no longer feel like it's diligent stewardship."

Her heart dropped. "Reverend, you saw the budget report. I know it was manipulated, but the figures are accurate. We have no money."

"You have a fundraiser planned?"

"Yes, but our hopes were we could start making repairs to the building with the money we raise. Now, we'll need to supplement the general budget. That will set us back, a lot."

His gray eyes lacked empathy. "Pastor Westbrook, these are the challenges of leading a modern day congregation. If you can't make it work than the next time we meet we can start the process of closing the church. In the meantime, I suggest prayer and then action."

Lauren chose her words carefully. "I'm doing those things. I'm not sure that's very helpful, Reverend."

Reverend Martin frowned. "Faith is not for the weak of heart, Pastor Westbrook."

Chapter 14

Gambling is the child of avarice,
the brother of iniquity,
and the father of mischief.
—*George Washington*

Lost

June was frantic. Lauren dashed from the tent and searched through the crowd for any sign of Porter. She tried to remember what he was wearing. A blue sweatshirt and joggers, she recalled. As she scanned the crowd, she caught Luke's eye. He recognized her fear and bolted from the aviator booth toward her. June was yelling his name, "Porter! Porter!" Lauren felt the panic in her voice.

Luke was there. "Where did you last see him, June?"

"He was on his chair just two minutes ago. I was taking money from a man for some plates and I turned around and he was gone."

"Did you see where he went?" Luke asked Lauren.

"I was out of the tent and Delores was in the bathroom."

"You were supposed to help me watch him," June snapped.

"I didn't know Delores was gone…," but then Lauren stopped. There was no use in defending herself now.

Luke verbalized her thoughts. "Let's just focus on finding him."

A small crowd had gathered around June. Paul was there, Vicky, Gloria,

144

Michael and Ed. The other volunteers were watching from their stations. Their eyes wide with alarm. Lauren saw the fear she felt mirrored in all their faces. With Porter's dementia who could tell where he would go? What he might do? He was as vulnerable as a baby…defenseless. *Why had she followed the homeless woman? She should have been watching Porter.* Lauren felt the heat of guilt, her throat tight with shame.

"We need to search for him. Paul, can you walk out toward the road and check from there?"

"Will do. I'm going right now," Paul said.

"Does everyone have their cell phones? Call me if you find him and I'll text everyone. Make sure your phones are on and off silent mode."

The group nodded collectively. Lauren took out her phone and switched it off silent mode, her fingers shaking. She was grateful for Luke's command of the situation. This was not her area of expertise.

"Ed and Mike, can you go out east, past your booth and check that side of the property by the hill."

"You got it."

"On it."

Lauren wasn't sure who said what, but she watched the two men speed walk toward the other end of the property.

"Mom, Vicky," Luke continued, "I think you should walk the perimeter of the yard sale and check the church. Make sure he didn't go in there? Check every room and the space around the church. If he's not in any of those places, go ahead and call the police."

"If he's in there, we'll find him," Gloria said.

"June, I know you're shaken up, but you need to stay at the tent with Delores. Porter may just find his way back to you."

June nodded. She was fighting back tears.

"I'm sorry, June," Lauren managed. "We're going to do everything we can to find him."

June was too distraught to respond, but Lauren felt her bristle at the sound of her voice. Luke spoke to her now.

"Lauren, come with me. We'll search the area by the parsonage and the woods."

She lifted her chin to meet his eyes. "Okay, whatever you think is best."

They walked at a clipped pace. Luke was generally easy going, but Lauren realized now that in a state of emergency he was all business. He stepped into leadership with ease. She had only known him in his retired state, fishing and doing odd jobs for the church. This new Luke felt like a stranger.

Lauren walked around the parsonage several times and Luke checked the far end of the yard.

"Any sign of him?"

"No," Lauren yelled.

"Let's try the woods."

The air cooled instantly as they entered the forest. The transition from the brightness of mid-day to the shadow beneath the impenetrable ceiling of countless Douglas firs blinded her. In that moment Luke took her hand as if he sensed she could not see. An electrical current moved through her as her body involuntarily responded to his touch. *How long had it been since a man had touched her?* It seemed like forever ago. Marcus at times seemed to pulse within her, in thought, dream, and memory. Traces of his touch lingered still when she closed her eyes. The intricate pattern of crow's feet etched at the corner of his eyes and the deep set wrinkles framing his knuckles came to her mind like still life photographs. Then there were times like now where he was only a distant memory. *What did his eyes look like? His nose? His mouth? I don't remember.* Luke's hand in her hand, however, felt very real, frighteningly real.

She was steady on her feet and he released her hand. She called into the woods, "Porter!, Porter!"

Luke scanned the forest as they walked single file down the path. Lauren felt light headed and her stomach churned as she looked in every direction. "Luke, he could be anywhere."

His expression was grim as he checked his phone. "I hoped that they would have found him by now closer to the church."

"We're going to need more than two people to search the woods," Lauren said.

"Well, dementia or no, it isn't likely he went off the path. People usually follow the trail because it's simpler and our minds are trained to do it. Let's head to the candelabra tree and then we can split. I'll head toward the lake and you take the path towards the Banks trail. We'll just go down each path for a few minutes, look for him and meet right back at the tree. Does that sound okay?"

Lauren felt unsure. "I don't know the woods as well as you. I don't want to get lost on top of everything else we're dealing with today."

Luke nodded. "You won't get lost. Just go for about 10 minutes and then come back to the tree. If no one's found him then, we're going to have to do a wider search with more volunteers and the police. If I don't see you at the Candelabra tree after twenty minutes, I'll call you and find you, but we'll cover more ground if we split up."

She tilted her head to the side in tacit agreement. When she had trekked through the forest with Sydney only weeks before, these woods had seemed like a scene from a fairy tale, but in light of the search for Porter the forest had become something different altogether.

The colossal Sitka spruce loomed before them, its branches spread out like the arms of a giant octopus as it played gatekeeper to the choice of two paths. Hanging moss drooped from its limbs. Lauren shuddered under its massive presence. After the bustling activity of the carnival, the forest was a dark silent catacomb. A tingling sensation spread from her neck to her arms. She sensed danger, death and buried secrets and she did not know why.

Luke sensed her fear. He touched her arm. "It will be okay."

She gave him a brave smile. "I know. Of course. I'll see you in twenty."

Her eyes followed his confident stride in the direction of Vernonia Lake before she ambled down the path toward the Banks trail. Luke's track climbed the ridge till it collided with the lake; Lauren's trail made a winding descent into a forested valley.

"Porter! Porter!" she yelled. She was comforted when she heard Luke's distant voice also calling his name.

The air chilled as she followed the ever downward slope. The trail to the lake eventually led to a bright clearing of rock, sun, and water, but her path dipped into the heart of the forest, dark and cool. If she had been with Luke or Sydney or even her mother, the coolness would have felt like a wonderful respite from the heat of the day, but under these circumstances Lauren felt only a sense of eerie dread.

"Porter! Porter!" She continued to call. Her voice was beginning to get hoarse. Through the corner of her eye, she saw movement and the sound of dried leaves breaking under pressure. Fear gripped her heart. She turned in the direction of the motion, but saw nothing. *A deer? I hope not a cougar or bear or could it be Porter?* The thought forced her to turn from the path toward the sound. *What if Porter had wandered from the trail? What if he was this close to her and she failed to find him because she was scared of the forest?* Lauren scolded herself inside her head. She was a grown woman. Despite the folklore around forest survival stories, bear and cougar attacks against humans were exceptionally rare. Was she willing to allow her fear to rule the day when bravery might just save a life?

She looked around to gather her bearings. *If I wander off the path, I must be able to find my way back.* She noted two tall Douglas firs that leaned against one another and a large pointed rock with an uprooted tree trunk braced against its mossy side. She took out her phone and captured hasty pictures of the landmarks. *In case I get lost,* she thought. She initiated the map app on her phone, but it refused to load. "Of course," she said through her breath. "The internet never works when you need it."

Her phone revealed one bar of service. She was not ready to call Luke, not yet. Perhaps she had seen nothing. With caution, she digressed off the trail and blundered through the undergrowth. "Porter?" She no longer had the strength to yell and called his name softly. She lumbered forward and moved through a copse of spruce hemlocks. On the other side she followed a pronounced depression in the ground that led to a strange rock formation. Lauren made sure to register her bearings before descending the hill. She had reached the lowest point in the forest and entered a clearing of sorts surrounded by massive jagged rocks.

From a geological standpoint the boulders were most likely worthy subjects of study. The colossal giants bore the evidence of their survival through centuries of brutal weather, bearing the brunt of massive geological shifts through ice and fire. Lauren felt both fear and awe as she walked the path nature had forged between them. "Porter," she called again. Her voice felt like an intrusion in Mother Nature's sacred, quiet temple.

As she walked between the boulders, Lauren saw the caves hidden beneath them. Several dark openings peeked between the scattered smaller rocks that littered the floor of the clearing. Some of the caves were too small for any creature, with the exception of a bat or bird, but others were large enough for a bear or wildcat. *I'm not going in there. That's for sure,* Lauren said to herself. *I'm just going to walk to the end about twenty more feet and then I'm heading back...back to Luke.* At that moment she heard the sharp snap of a twig behind her. When she turned around to see, she saw just the last traces of movement through the corner of her eye. Terror filled her.

"Yea though I walk through the valley of the shadow of death, I will fear no evil." She whispered the Psalm softly and walked to its rhythm.

There was one thing she was sure of. Whatever she saw was not Porter. Although, she had not seen it clearly, the figure had moved quickly—too quickly for an 80 year old man with dementia. *I'm out of here,* Lauren thought. As she backtracked through the floor of the rock valley, her eye was drawn to a forlorn object straight in her path. That wasn't there a minute ago. Dread rose in her gut, making each step painful, but the object was in the middle of the path blocking her exit. *I must move forward,* she thought to herself.

A creeping dread filled her heart as she drew closer to what looked like a dirty forsaken rag. She recognized it. The porcelain doll lay on the rocky ground, a dirty discarded plaything. The dolly stared at her through one glassy eye, the crack in its porcelain face had lengthened across the cheek and spread into the hollow of a missing eye socket. The sheer horror of the sight struck her hard in the gut. She looked away from the doll and found herself staring into a woman's pale face. The woman looked at her through vacant deep set eyes in a striking shade of blue, and her face twisted in a state of agony. She opened her mouth to reveal a bottom row of rotten teeth.

Whether the woman was preparing to talk, scream or lunge at her, Lauren didn't care. She couldn't help herself. She screamed.

Her voice was strident in the dead air and she ran. Up the hill she fled into the copse of hemlock trees, running, running. A stitch in her side sent a jolt of pain through her body, but she ran anyway until she found the path.

She was panting and out of breath when she finally returned to the trail, but she was grateful. Despite the overwhelming fear and panic, Lauren had found her way back without too much difficulty. She took just a moment to catch her breath, wary of every sight and sound around her, before starting the arduous climb back up the beaten track. Luke came down to meet her before she reached the candelabra tree. Her heart leaped with relief when she saw him. Despite the frantic search, he looked confident and assured in the way he carried himself. His eyes brightened when he saw her and then darkened with concern.

"Are you okay?"

He must have noticed she was as white as a sheet. She stopped to catch her breath. "I thought I saw him," she said through labored breaths. "I followed someone off the path. It led me to this weird rocky area. There were caves and there was a woman...She came from nowhere." Lauren panted as she leaned forward to rest her hands on her thighs. "Scared me to death."

Luke's eyes widened with surprise. "You went to the caves?"

"I didn't know I was going there," Lauren said. "I followed someone."

Luke's body tensed and he pursed his lips. "That was stupid!"

Lauren looked up at him in alarm.

"Not you," he corrected. "Me. I shouldn't have had you go on your own. The caves are dangerous. I completely forgot about them. A kid was trapped in one a couple years ago. I think he was about 13 years old. He got stuck and couldn't get out. Fortunately, he was with a group of friends and they ran into town to get him help. But it took them nearly two days to get him out. Trained rescuers came in from Portland to free him."

"That's horrible," Lauren said, her breathing finally back to normal.

"You saw a woman?"

"Yes. She looked homeless."

Luke's eyes were trained on her as he spoke. "There's been a lot more homeless people in Vernonia the past few years. Sometimes they wander the Banks path and set up camp in the woods. I'm sorry I left you alone. That was really stupid. I wasn't thinking."

Lauren shrugged. "We both have our minds set on finding Porter. Plus, I'm a grown woman. I can handle walking through the woods. I just got frightened is all. I'm safe. It's not your fault."

Luke wrung his hands together in frustration. He was not willing to let himself off the hook. "No one should walk the woods alone. I shouldn't have put you in that position."

Lauren shrugged him off. "I'm okay. That's what matters. Any word on Porter?"

"Not yet," he sighed. "It means we're going to have to keep searching with police and community help. Fortunately when a person has Alzheimer's or dementia they don't have to wait 24 hours before putting out a full alert. Mom texted me and the police are there now. They have all the radio stations and local news asking people to look for him with his description."

"Poor June. I can't imagine what she's going through. This is awful. Did Gloria tell you if Sydney is okay?"

"I thought you'd be worried. Mom says she's with Linda. They're all wrapping up the yard sale. In spite of Porter's disappearance by all accounts the sale was a huge success."

"We just need to find Porter."

"I'm pretty sure he didn't go anywhere near the lake. There were lots of people down there, boaters and fishermen. I talked to over a dozen people. No one's seen him and I'm almost certain if he had gone that direction someone would have."

"Well, I guess that helps us narrow our search."

"Did you meet anyone on the path to the Banks trail?"

Lauren shook her head. "Besides the homeless woman? No one. So I guess it's a possibility, but I can't imagine an eighty year old could get that far without us finding him."

"It's unlikely," Luke agreed. "We probably should focus the search elsewhere. My hope is someone in the community finds him and calls the police."

Lauren closed her eyes and prayed silently. *Lord, I pray that Porter is okay. Please let him be okay. I pray that your love and peace is surrounding him and that he is safe from all harm. Please be with June. Give her peace in this terrible situation.*"

When she opened her eyes, Luke was staring at her. "Praying?"

"Yes. It feels a bit out of our hands doesn't it?"

Luke stared up at the sky as a late afternoon sun filtered through the trees. "Yes, it sure does."

They walked together back toward the parsonage. Lauren felt a comfort in the easy rhythm of Luke's presence, his even breathing. Everything about him was steady. Marcus had been erratic in every sense of the word. She thought of the times he would take her out on the town to dance. He was completely spontaneous. He loved to try new restaurants, dives, and new activities. Anything out of the ordinary, he was game. Those were the times she felt almost breathlessly happy. But when Marcus was depressed nothing could be done to lift his spirits. One had to wait for the dark mood to pass. She had learned to hunker down and lay low, the same way one might board up the house and sandbag the doors and windows in a level 5 hurricane. All you could do was hope and pray the damage would not be too severe.

The sky was slightly overcast as they reached the clearing. Lauren could see the parsonage now and realized she desperately needed to pee. "Are you headed back to the church, first?"

"Yea, I'm going to check in with everyone and see what the next steps are. Aren't you coming with me?"

"Yes, of course, but I have to pee."

Luke chuckled. "I see."

"Why are you laughing?"

"I've just never heard a minister talk about peeing before is all."

Lauren was exasperated. "Are you five? Minister or no, Luke, I'm a human being."

Luke laughed. "It never gets old, though. I like being on friendly terms with a minister. It sort of unravels all those layers of religious mystery and intrigue."

She stopped and placed her hand involuntarily on her hip as she glared. "I hate to break it to you, Luke. But there are no layers of mystery and intrigue surrounding ministers or clergyman or whatever. If people act like there are, they're putting on a dog and pony show. We're all just people and we all pee. If we're Christian we're just doing our best to follow Jesus. That's it."

Luke smiled. "I know, I know. It's fun to rattle you a bit. I'm just teasing. Do you want me to wait?"

"No, it's not necessary. I thought I'd just run into the parsonage and go and then meet you back at the church. Can you tell Sydney I'm on my way?"

"Will do." He looked down and a half smile traced his lips. "Take your time."

Lauren was relieved when the parsonage door was unlocked. *We must have forgotten to lock it this morning.* She bolted to the restroom and sighed with relief as she emptied her bladder. As she reached for the toilet paper, she heard scuffling within the house.

"Sydney is that you?" The scrimmaging stopped abruptly and fear gripped her. "Mom, is that you?"

She was greeted only with silence. Fear spread through her in a white heat. She buckled her jean shorts quickly and opened the door with extreme caution. She now heard voices.

"Why did you do it? Why? You have the respect of everyone. You didn't need to…"

She tiptoed across the wooden floor of the hallway and peered into the living room.

Porter was standing there. His back was to her. He faced the kitchen and he was speaking to an invisible presence that to Porter at least was just as real as Lauren herself.

"You can't expect me to let you get away with this. It's too much!"

Porter's voice sounded different. His words were clear, succinct, and laced with anger. She had never heard him speak with such clarity. Lauren kept her distance, but she spoke softly. "Porter? Are you all right?"

Porter turned at the sound of her voice. Fear struck her in the gut as she looked at his red face. There was no smile, no swaying back and forth, his body tensed, charged. His eyes were glazed, almost other worldly. He looked ready to strike.

"Porter, it's me. Pastor Westbrook. Do you know who I am?"

"I know who you are," he said as clear as day. "You're the one who ruined everything. You treated me as a fool and you took everything. You deserve to rot in hell."

Lauren was stunned for a moment. "Porter, it's me, Lauren. I'm a friend. I wish you no harm. Please, try to remember. Your wife, June. She's worried about you."

"June?" He suddenly laughed a dry cynical laugh. "You did this June? Why did you do this? I loved you."

"Porter, please snap out of it." As she said those words, he lunged toward her. Lauren ran from him toward the door and heard a thud behind her. When she turned at the door, she saw he had tripped over the rug and fallen on the floor.

Lauren dashed into the yard and touched the call icon on her phone under Luke's name. Her voice was raspy with fear. "Luke, I found him at the parsonage. I need you. Now!"

Chapter 15

I'm a great believer in Luck.
—Thomas Jefferson

Lucky Win

Reverend Martin lifted his gray eyes from the budget report and stared at Lauren from across her office desk. He tapped his fingers rhythmically on the surface of the wood. "These numbers are impressive," he finally admitted.

"We brought in around 86,000 dollars from the yard sale two months ago." Lauren tried to keep the pride out of her voice, but she couldn't help it. She was amazed at what her little church had been able to accomplish.

"So where do you go from here?"

"We set aside half to help us meet budget expenses for the next six months. We also have about $40,000 that has been restored to the building fund. There are two projects underway that the Ministry Team decided were crucial. We have plumbers coming out to fix corroded and broken pipes including a broken water heater and we're replacing the roof. There are leaks all over the place. The Ministry Team decided that was first on the list of repairs. Fortunately, we had to clear out most of the junk for the yard sale, so at least the workers have the space they need to do their jobs."

Reverend Martin pursed his lips and exhaled almost like he was whistling.

"Hmm, it seems things have gone according to plan, the best case scenario. So, what's next?"

"Next?" She widened her eyes in surprise. "I don't know," she stuttered. "I just thought I'd keep on with what I'm doing. Things are a little busy for me personally. Sydney started fifth grade at the elementary school and is adjusting to a new routine. I've been balancing my responsibilities at the church with the demands of being a mother."

The Reverend scrutinized her with his solemn eyes as he sipped his Earl Gray. He set the mug down on the table and tapped his fingers again before speaking. "Pastor Westbrook, how do you plan to grow this congregation spiritually? A pastor is responsible for helping their flock reach spiritual maturity. How do you plan to educate your parishioners? Lead them? Guide them? Help them to grow? You can't let your congregation run wild." He furrowed his bushy eyebrows as he contemplated her. "Sometimes, Pastor Westbrook, I just get the sense you are flying by the seat of your pants."

Lauren burst out laughing. "I AM flying by the seat of my pants! It's no secret."

The Reverend raised his eyebrows at her in surprise. "You don't have a plan?"

"Well, yes and no," Lauren said. "I am just beginning to get to know these people. There are secrets here and no one will tell me about the church's history. How can I help people grow spiritually if I don't understand them? I can't force people to let me in. My plan is to preach the gospel and let the chips fall where they may."

Reverend Martin did not seem to like her answer. He studied her for several moments. "You compare running a church to a game of poker. Is that what you think the Lord's work is? A game of chance?"

"Of course I don't, but I'm no longer under the illusion that I have any power over the people in this church."

He rubbed his fingers against his chin as though he was considering her seriously for the first time. "I suppose that's fair," he sighed. "What I'm really suggesting is that you consider starting an educational program, guided Bible study. I did share with you that your church had a rogue minister, one that carried your parishioners far off the path of scripture into a counter theology, one that the General Ministry and FAOD deemed as not only heretical, but destructive. The General Ministry would like assurance from you that your congregants are being guided toward a theology that is more in line with the First Assembly of Disciples with whom they have accepted funds for many years."

She was taken aback. The Reverend had actually provided her with new information about the church's history. He was tight lipped and careful with any tidbit he disbursed so Lauren did not press him for more details. "I see," Lauren said slowly. "I will talk to the Ministry Team and see if we can come up with some ideas for how to proceed with biblical education. It's not a bad idea."

Reverend Martin raised an eyebrow. "I'm relieved that I didn't provide you with a bad idea."

"No, no! That's not what I mean. I'm just saying we are growing—slowly, but surely. We have a young couple coming now with two children. They won the Cadillac Seville in the raffle and decided to give our church a try. A few weeks ago, Linda and I reached out to the mom and last week she came forward at the end of service. Her name is Mandy and her husband is Will. Neither of them grew up in the church, so providing opportunities for them to study the Bible would be a good next step and one they might be open to."

"I noticed on my last visit that you have some children attending now," Reverend Martin added.

Lauren smiled. "Yes, Sydney's so thrilled. We have the McCourt's two children and Stan and Vicky's teenage grandchildren. It's a mix of ages, but there's so much more life now."

"And what about that young man, who stepped forward on my first visit?"

"You mean, Luke?"

"Yes. What has been done to shepherd Luke in his faith? Has he been baptized yet?"

Lauren felt her heart beating through her chest. Of all the parishioners at the First Assembly of Disciples of Vernonia she had probably spent the most one on one time with Luke, yet she could not tell Reverend Martin where he was in his faith or if he even believed.

Lauren sighed. "I don't know if he's ready to be baptized. I have given him over to the Holy Spirit through prayer. I am waiting for him to tell me decisively that he wants to give his life to Christ."

The crease between his eyebrows grew darker. "Pastor Westbrook, do you know what demographic is missing from your church?" He paused as his eyes searched hers. "Young, working, and able men. Your church cannot grow without this demographic. Do you understand that?"

"Yes, but I also think we have to wait until the Lord speaks. I cannot force Luke to be baptized…"

He interrupted her. "Are you waiting for the Lord to drop a brick on your head? The man already stepped forward to give his life to the Lord!" The Reverend sounded almost angry. "Don't allow time for the devil to take a foothold. Move and get that man baptized. You're going to need him to move this church forward."

Lauren bit her lip, but said nothing. *What could she say without revealing Luke's little charade and betraying her own integrity?* "I hear what you're saying."

He rose to leave and she walked him to the front door of the church. On this blustery October day, the leaves spun wildly in the wind. The green summer forest had turned orange, yellow, and red almost overnight.

"Lauren," he said her name softly at the door.

The Reverend had never called her by her first name before. She turned around, surprised. "Reverend Martin?"

He exhaled slowly as he put on his fedora and scarf. "Over the years of my ministry I have often contemplated the wisdom of female pastors even as I've mentored them and supported them in their calling. You know, the fundamentalist churches believe it is against the scripture for women to teach men?"

"Yes, I'm well aware. There have been people even in the churches where I've ministered who have challenged me directly. They believe my calling to ministry to be sinful because of the arrangement of my chromosomes."

"You did not let their views get in your way, I take it?"

Lauren shrugged. "Marcus and I just tried to minister to them and follow our calling. I think because he was with me they were able to accept it, even if they didn't agree."

"Then, you always wanted to serve in the church?"

"I never felt militant about being a pastor. I went to seminary because I wanted to learn. The church was the first place where I felt like I could do something with my life. It was the only place I felt a sense of purpose. As a child, I felt pretty invisible. My mom was one of those people who fills all the space, so much so that there's not a lot of room for anyone else."

Reverend Martin stared at her, but said nothing.

"When I was at church serving, I felt seen by God. When I decided to serve in the church I didn't make the decision alone. I was with Marcus. We were a team. In my mind, he was always the real minister. I always saw myself as his helper, not in a subservient way, but it was where I felt most comfortable with my gifts." Memories of their early days in the ministry flooded her mind and she felt a simple joy. "When I was young, I really felt that heart for the Lord."

Reverend Martin cocked his head to the side. "And now?"

"Life got more complicated," Lauren admitted. "As far as banning women from ministry, I understand why people come to that viewpoint. If you are diligent to scripture, it's an easy conclusion to draw. Paul's letter to Ephesians comes to mind. *I permit no woman to teach or to have authority over men; she is to keep silent.*" Lauren spoke the words from 1st Timothy from memory. She paused and looked at him. "Do you believe that, Reverend Martin? That women shouldn't teach men? That they should be silent?"

Reverend Martin's lips formed a tight line as he thought. "There are many reasons to remove a minister from their calling. I've seen everything in my line of work. I've encountered sexual immorality, embezzlement, the inability to control one's anger, the inability to be truthful, abuse of power, pride…" He hesitated as he rubbed his thumb over the felt of his fedora. "Do you know what all those things have in common?"

Lauren peered at him thoughtfully. "They're all sins?"

"Precisely." He paused as he looked directly at her. "Is being a woman a sin?"

Lauren laughed. "Well, I hope not, because then I'm really in trouble."

The trace of a smile appeared on his narrow lips. "I have never been able to understand the logic of that position, because both men and women were made in the image of God. Sin and the lack of repentance is what makes us unfit to lead others, not our...make up of chromosomes, as you so aptly put it. Personally, I have always been more drawn to Paul's words in Galatians. *There is neither Jew nor Gentile, neither slave nor free, nor is there male and female, for you are all one in Christ Jesus.*"

"Amen," Lauren said.

"We live in different times than the Apostle Paul," the Reverend continued. "In those days women didn't have access to the written Word or to an education for that matter. They were not allowed the opportunity to become an authority on scripture, not in the world of Jews or Greeks in any case."

"So, you believe historical context can change how we read scripture?"

He shook his head. "No, Pastor Westbrook. The heart of scripture always remains the same in the past, present, and future. But this is a world that is ever changing and God is always working. He may choose a variety of ways to communicate that eternal message. In some cases, a woman may be the best messenger for God's unchanging Word."

"If you believe that, then why have you spent years examining whether women should be in the ministry?"

The Reverend turned away from her and gazed out to watch the leaves dance in the parking lot. "Because of the weakness of men."

Lauren did not press him to continue. She hesitated to make sure he was finished before speaking. "Why are you telling me this, Reverend Martin?"

"You may not believe this, but my heart is glad you're at this church. All those years ago when the congregation struggled in the midst of sin, rot, and decay, only one thing could have stopped the sin, kept it from growing and becoming so destructive."

"What?"

"If women weren't silent. If only they had spoken out right from the

160

beginning."

Lauren shivered in the fall breeze and closed the doors. She headed to the church office and watched Gloria for a moment from the doorway. Her red hair was piled high in what Lauren liked to call her pineapple up do with a red sash tied around her head to keep hair out of her face. Lauren was slightly mesmerized by the bright black and red paisley tunic she wore over Capri leggings. Her back was to Lauren as she tapped on the computer working on the budget. "Hey Gloria."

She spun around in her office chair like a woman half her age. She gave Lauren a warm smile. She was an attractive woman and Lauren thought she must have been drop dead gorgeous in her youth.

"How did the meeting go with the pope?"

Lauren smirked. "It went alright, actually. I think he's pretty happy about our budget. I wanted to thank you again, Gloria. For everything."

"It was no big thing." She waved her hand dismissively.

"Well, that's not true. Donating those items to the church was actually a huge thing and we would be in massive trouble if it wasn't for you, Linda, Stan and Vicky, Paul and Emma. I mean all of you guys stepped it up."

Gloria smiled. "And Luke?"

"Of course, Luke," Lauren agreed.

"You know, I think we're all having a lot of fun to be honest, the most fun we've had in years."

Lauren moved from the door and took the seat across from her at the desk. "Gloria, I know I've only been here a few months, but there is something I think you can help me with."

"Anything, dear," Gloria said lightly as she returned to the keyboard.

"I seem to keep hitting a brick wall when it comes to finding out about this church's past. Several people, including Reverend Martin have hinted that there was some serious trouble years ago and I'm beginning to feel like I need to know what happened in order to move forward with my ministry."

Gloria pivoted from the keyboard and rifled through her desk. She opened a drawer and removed a paper clip holding it so tight the tips of her fingers turned white. "We agreed all those years ago to keep that nasty business in the past," Gloria whispered.

"This would be confidential, Gloria. I wouldn't tell anyone. I just feel like knowing would help me do my job better. This may sound strange to you, but despite you and all the lovely people here, I feel a darkness in this place. Sometimes it's so powerful, I almost feel like it's going to swallow us all up. Does that sound crazy?"

Gloria released the paper clip and picked up a sharpened pencil and began to tap it on the desk. She was nervous, itching for a cigarette, despite the fact she had quit several weeks before. "I'm assuming Reverend Martin's referring to Pastor Worth. He was excommunicated years ago. I think in the early 80s. Pastor Westbrook , that was forty years ago. Do you really think that whatever he did is still relevant now?"

Lauren clasped her hands together on her lap and looked at Gloria intently. "There was an exchange with a woman at the yard sale. She said the church has a bad reputation in the community. Gloria, I didn't even know what she was talking about. Complete strangers in the community know more about this church than I do. Can't you see that this puts me at a disadvantage? You were at this church during his ministry. You can help me understand."

"I'm not sure I can, dear. It was a different time. I've put that all behind me."

Lauren searched Gloria's face.

"Okay, alright." Gloria rose from her desk and traveled the few steps to the coffee maker. "I'm going to need a cup of coffee for this." She filled the carafe with water and arranged the cream and sugar next to the coffee maker, her back to Lauren.

"Pastor Worth, from what I remember was a dynamic preacher. After each sermon he had half the congregation in tears, the men and the women. I was a very young woman at the time, a girl really, still in the youth group, about fifteen or sixteen. He had been there already for about a decade, so what I'm telling you is partially from what others told me." The coffee maker beeped and Gloria rose to pour a cup. "Can I pour you some?"

"Sure. Thanks."

Gloria returned with two mugs and two wooden coffee stirrers. "I've learned how much cream and sugar you like. Here, the blue one is yours."

"Thanks, Gloria." Lauren stirred her coffee and watched the cream spiral into the dark liquid. She waited patiently for Gloria to find her story.

"Well, not a whole lot to tell, really. He was married to a plain woman. Her name was Maggie, I think. She was one of those people you hardly notice, mousy and had a face that always looked pinched and unhappy. In contrast Pastor Worth was always smiling. Everyone loved him. He had four children with Maggie. One girl, Anne was close to my age and then there were three boys. They were half wild, always getting into trouble. Anne was more like her mother, quiet and kind of sad."

"Sounds like an interesting dynamic."

"Yea, if you were a psychologist or something, you might have seen the warning signs. Pastor Worth was a friendly type of person a little of what you call a Renaissance man. He'd help you with anything and could do about anything. He got into the fields and helped the farmers with tilling their land or harvesting. He knew how to level a horse ring, build a fence, fix a roof. That was kind of the secret of his ministry. He helped people with what they needed and then they felt appreciative, maybe kind of obligated. I can remember the way people spoke about him.

What do ya think about that new Pastor over at First Assembly?

You mean, Pastor Worth? He just helped me till my field. He's a real gem.

That's what people were saying anyway. Before long, no one could say a bad word about him. He had set up this reputation and he had connections with everyone who was anyone—Breakfast with the mayor and a seat on the school board."

"Sounds like he was a powerful man?"

"And that's when it went to his fool head. One day in church he said it was time to dissolve the elders. We didn't need them anymore. We were all believers and ought to be equal before Christ. Oh, Porter was fit to be tied. He'd only been an elder a few years and he didn't appreciate his title being taken away. He knew Pastor Worth was making a power grab, trying to get rid of anyone who might stand in his way. June and Porter were newly married at the time. They left over it…were gone for many years and then came back once Pastor Worth was long gone. My daddy was an elder too, but he thought the Holy Spirit must be speaking through Pastor Worth, so he accepted it without much question."

"And your mom?"

"She always deferred to Daddy. My family was in it for the long haul."

"Reverend Martin said there was some kind of heresy, teaching that wasn't biblical?"

Gloria crossed her arms around her chest. "Pastor Worth was permissive. He believed that grace should freely abound. I remember him saying it all the time, *Let grace abound, let grace abound.* The trouble was grace seemed to only abound for him."

"What do you mean?"

"Oh, there were different rules for him than for others. He was making all the decisions for the church, the finances, leadership structure, everything. All the people around him just did what he said, including Daddy."

"What do you mean there were different rules for him than for others?"

Gloria stood up with her back to her and returned to the counter to warm her coffee. "I guess I hardly drank a drop. Been talking too much. It's cold already." Her voice sounded apologetic. She turned from the coffee maker and pressed the mug to her lips and leaned against the counter as she looked at Lauren. "He took liberties."

"Liberties? What does that mean, Gloria?"

Gloria bit her lip. "I'm not really sure. What I do remember is a big church meeting. I was there to take care of the kids while their parents were discussing church business. There were no elders so the deacons confronted him. I heard yelling and screaming from the classroom where I had the children. I went out to see what was the matter. I just remember Maggie's face. She was sitting outside the office, her face white like she had just learned her childhood dog had died. I can't remember a time in my whole life I saw a woman look so scared and miserable."

"What happened?"

"The police arrived. They took Pastor Worth to the station."

"You didn't know why he was arrested?"

"I understand he did some time in prison, but after that everything changed. No one would say a word. I never learned the full details, just that he had done things so terrible they could not be spoken of. It didn't feel like a church at all after that, but a funeral home. People began to leave, one after the other. After that we never had a pastor for longer than a year or two and then a series of interim pastors, until you."

"Since the 1980s you've never had a pastor longer that a year or two? What kept the church going?"

"Pastor Worth's days were bountiful. The church had hundreds and thousands of dollars in its coffers and we were able to sustain ourselves for nearly two decades. We had times when the congregation grew a bit and was more self sufficient, but then something would happen and we'd be back to square one."

"Why did you stay, Gloria?"

Gloria bit her lip. "This was my home, I suppose. I left for awhile, but came back with my baby boy. My parents were so disappointed in me when I got pregnant. I guess I went back to church to please them. I needed their support, so I stayed."

"Thank you, Gloria. That helps a lot."

Gloria gave her a weak smile and then began rummaging through a small box file.

Lauren smirked as she watched her. "We need to move into the modern era. Get those stored on the cloud."

Gloria glared. "One step at a time, my dear." She pulled out an index card and handed it to Lauren.

"What is this?"

"Every once in a while we still get mail for Pastor Worth."

"After 40 years?"

"Crazy isn't it? A lot of missions organizations don't seem to update their rosters. I've been forwarding it here."

"Wait! You mean he's still alive? Wouldn't he be like 100 years old?"

"He's in his nineties. He's about 15 years older than Porter, lives in a nursing home in Newport."

"Are you suggesting I visit him?"

"I'm not suggesting anything, but you know what they say? It's best to go directly to the horse's mouth."

Lauren took the index card slowly with both hands and ran her finger over its smooth surface. Despite her fear, she felt the urgent need to see this man, to finally learn the truth.

* * *

Lauren woke from the dead of sleep to the sound of a door slamming and a car speeding away down the gravel road. Her alarm clock read 2:35 AM. There was no reason to drive up to the parsonage unless you had direct business with the pastor or had been personally invited. At this time of night, there was no good reason for anyone to be on the property. Her body tensed with alarm as she bolted to the window. She saw only the glimpse of red tail lights as a car sped away around the bend toward the church and then to the main road.

Sydney and Vivian were still asleep and the house was quiet. Lauren tip toed to the front door, struggled with the lock and opened it. Her bare arms felt the instant assault of the cool autumn breeze. She stepped onto the porch and peered into the yard. Through the moonlight, she saw nothing but rolling mist settling on the low ground. A soft thud drew her attention to the porch floor. She stared in surprise at a small white envelope which must have fallen from the crack in the screen door to the ground. In the porch light, she examined it. The envelope was blank. She opened the seal and stared at the message.

We know where you are. Why did you try to hide? You know what we want.

Lauren's heart stopped in her chest. Her stomach tightened in pain and lurched forward as if some creature inside of her was clawing to get out. She dropped the envelope. The fear triggered a memory. "Marcus," she whispered.

She saw his face, the way she remembered him when they first fell in love, his warm brown eyes and his teasing smile. His face flashed before her now. *This wasn't Marcus,* she thought. It was like her husband was possessed by Legion's multitude of demons. His face was filled with murderous rage. She was terrified. *This was not the man she married. It couldn't be. The world was crumbling around her. Everything was falling apart.*

Chapter 16

Lucky in Love, Unlucky in Cards

Gambling for Love

After making sure all the doors and windows were locked, Lauren slept fitfully. She woke without feeling rested and made coffee. *Should she call the police?* The message was clearly a threat. *Who would want to threaten her?*

Her face was buried in her coffee cup when Vivian entered the kitchen in her bathrobe. She was singing, *I can see clearly now, the rain is gone...*She grabbed a cup of coffee and held her cup protectively to her chest as she turned to smile at Lauren.

"Someone's in a good mood."

"Paul is taking me to the airport today. We're going flying," she sighed.

"Are you getting in one of those kit planes? Mom, are you sure that's a good idea?"

"He's a pilot, Laur bear. I trust him."

"Mom, I'm not sure about this. If you guys break up it's going to cause a world of trouble. I'm not sure I like this at all."

Vivian took a sudden step forward and reached her arm out to her daughter. She squeezed Lauren's chin playfully between her thumb and forefinger. "Oh my pretty girl. It's not up to you, is it?"

"He's my parishioner and I work with him. I like it when you keep your personal life separate from my job."

Vivian frowned. "Lauren, you should understand this after your marriage to Marcus. You just can't stop chemistry. It's going to happen one way or another."

"Mom, I need you to be extra careful right now."

Vivian looked at her wide eyed. "Why, honey? Who poured orange juice on your Cheerios?"

She rolled her eyes. "Someone posted a threatening message on the door last night." Lauren handed the note to Vivian.

Her mother's mouth gaped open. "Here at the cottage?" She read through the note Lauren handed her. "This is cryptic. What does it even mean? Who would write such a thing?"

"I don't know, Mom. But, it's obviously a threat. I've got you and Sydney in the house. I'm not sure what to do."

"Well, is the message true? Are you hiding from anyone?"

"No, Mom. Of course not. Should I call the police?"

Her mother frowned. "Must be some loon or teenager playing a practical joke. Was there any crime committed?"

"As far as I know leaving a message on someone's door isn't a crime, but it was the middle of the night and consider the message."

Vivian sighed. "I don't think any real harm was done. Maybe you should think about a security system?"

* * *

Several hours after her mother left, Lauren's mind still churned over the note.

"Mom, are you okay?" Sydney asked.

"I had a little fright is all. Someone left a message on the door that scared me."

"What did it say?"

"It wasn't anything to be concerned about, but someone dropped it off in

169

the middle of the night and there was no name on the note."

Sydney wrinkled her nose. "That's weird."

"I need you to be extra cautious, okay?"

"O...kay?" Sydney said.

"I'm thinking of taking Nana's advice and getting a security system."

"Mom, isn't it obvious what you need to do?" Sydney gave her the blank stare that Lauren now recognized as her daughter's gentle way of reminding her who had the real brains in the family.

Lauren frowned at her daughter. "No."

"Just call Luke."

* * *

Luke was there within an hour holding a doorbell alarm system box, his face humorless. "Any idea who sent the note?"

"No. I can't think of anyone who would do something like that? Everyone I know would have called me before coming over. Luke, I think this was some kind of threat." She took the note from the pocket of her jeans and handed it to him.

Luke frowned as he read it. "I don't like this," he said softly. "Did you see the car?"

"Only it's tail lights. It looked small, like a Toyota or something. It definitely wasn't a truck."

"Did you call the police?"

"I'm afraid they'd just laugh at me. No real harm was done, after all."

"This is your home," Luke said. "No one should be coming onto private property in the middle of the night and bothering two women and a child. Harassing someone or making them feel fearful in their own home is not okay." He turned abruptly and headed to his truck. He took his toolbox in one hand and his ladder in the other and walked back to the porch. "You call the police. I'll start in on installing the new system."

The officers arrived and Lauren filed a report. They did not seem overly concerned.

"We'll keep an eye out for other vehicles driving onto private property at odd hours of the night. If it happens again, give us a call."

"Someone has to actually get maimed or killed before they give a damn about anything anymore," Luke said under his breath as they pulled away in their cruiser.

"Hopefully it won't come to that."

"Call me, next time. I don't care how late at night it is. By car, it takes about 15 minutes to get here, but if I cut through the woods I can be here in closer to 10."

"You mean, walking?"

"Or running if need be. Yes. The trails are much more direct."

"Really? I didn't realize you lived so nearby. Where do you live exactly?"

"Near the lake. As the crow flies we're practically neighbors."

"I'll remember that and I'll call you if God forbid, it happens again."

"Lauren, let me see your phone?"

She raised her eyebrows, but handed her device over to him.

"The system is controlled by your phone," he said as he downloaded the Security App.

"Let's go inside while you do that," Lauren suggested. "Can I get you coffee, tea or anything?"

"Coffee would be good actually." His attention was still on the phone.

Lauren took the few steps to the kitchen and smiled as she ran her fingers over the smooth wooden cabinets. She returned from the kitchen with a steaming mug.

"I think I got it. Let's sit here so I can show you." Luke indicated the couch with one hand as he held her phone with the other.

She sat next to him and he inched closer to her. There was a time when Luke made her feel nervous, but Lauren realized that her fear of him had been replaced by a desire to be near him. She was surprised. He was the kind of man that made women nervous, handsome, assured and confident. Yet, she longed to lean into him, to rest her head on his shoulder, to feel safe. Her body seemed to feel like this was natural, even though her mind disagreed. She was a widow who had experienced a traumatic loss, perhaps it wasn't so unusual to long for someone to take Marcus' place, someone like Luke who seemed strong and able to protect her. But, her thoughts filled her with shame. She was still a married woman, or at least she still felt like one. She was not ready to let Marcus go, not yet. "How does it work?" she asked.

"Press here," Luke instructed. "This gives you access to the camera on the phone. Anytime, someone comes within, let's say about 30 feet, you should get a pretty good picture. The system has a trigger and the camera turns on when someone enters the zone."

"So basically, my phone's going to get activated every time anyone goes in or out the door?"

"Exactly. Most of the time, you're just going to see normal stuff. Your mom, Sydney, the UPS guy, the neighbor's cat. But you're also going to see anything out of the ordinary. So, if those clowns come back you'll have them on camera. There will be a lot more for the police to go on. You might get a license plate number or catch them in the act of vandalism."

Lauren took a few moments to mess with the app on her phone. Luke did not get up, but stayed seated next to her, watching her. He did not remove his arm from the back of the couch and Lauren felt her neck stiffen. Suddenly, she was acutely aware of how her shoulder rested on his, how their legs touched and the intimacy between them. She sat up and placed the phone on the coffee table. She turned toward him."Luke, I was thinking of taking a trip down to Newport? I'm not great with long drives, do you think you might want to come with me?"

Luke raised an eyebrow with interest. "What's in Newport?"

"Pastor Worth lives there in a retirement home."

"Pastor Worth...Pastor Worth?" Luke tried to place the name. "Do you mean the old pastor of this church? I remember him vaguely when I was a kid? He was always smiling, giving me treats."

"You remember him?"

"Yeah," Luke said. "I mean, I was really little, but I remember him."

"Oh, I thought by the time you were born, he was already gone."

"Don't get me wrong. I don't remember him well, but yeah. I vaguely remember his energy and that he was nice to me. Any particular reason you want to visit him? He's most likely a very old man."

Lauren bit her lip. *How much should she tell Luke?* "Reverend Martin told me that there's some dark history in this church. I've struggled to get people to tell me anything. Lately especially, I've been feeling like it's a stumbling block that's getting in the way of being able to reach this community. It's like trying to turn a haunted mansion into a church where people feel safe. I think Pastor Worth may be able to answer some of my questions."

Luke narrowed his eyes. "It doesn't take a rocket scientist to figure out that bad things went down at this church. Just look at the building? People don't let things fall into that kind of neglect unless there's soul ugliness."

"Soul ugliness?"

"You've seen Hoarders right?"

"You mean the show on TV?"

"Yeah. Exactly. The experts on that show go into people's houses and remove all the garbage and debris that they're just not willing to let go, but the real garbage is all the unresolved issues in these people's lives. Trauma and pain they can't let go of."

"Wow, Luke. That's pretty deep."

"I like to think so," he smiled.

"You went to the church as a boy. Did you get wind or feeling of any soul ugliness?"

Luke frowned. "June's never been nice. I remember her scolding me all the time. Sometimes I felt like her whole mission on Sunday was to find me so she could scream at me, make me feel small. One time she was teaching Sunday School and we just ran away from her. Hid for hours in one of our many hiding places. They had to search the whole church to find us."

"We?"

"It was me and Ruth?"

"Who's Ruth?"

"June and Porter's daughter. She was a little older than me. But we used to get in trouble all the time. June and Porter always thought I was the negative influence, but believe me, Ruth was a wild child."

"June and Porter have a daughter?"

"Yeah. She was an only child and a true hellion."

"I've never heard June talk about her."

"Well, she sort of went off the deep end in high school. Rebelled, did the drugs and alcohol thing and from what I understand, never really found her way out of it."

"I'm sorry to hear that," Lauren said softly. "Must have been tough on them."

"I don't know. June and Porter were always kind of prideful. They always seemed to look down on everyone else, especially my mom and me since I was the B word."

"B word?"

"A bastard."

"Luke, you're not! That's awful!"

"Well, those things follow you in a church. It's not like anyone says anything, but you feel it."

"Sounds like there was soul ugliness, if you felt that way," Lauren whispered.

Luke clasped his hands together. "I'm not going to lie, that's probably one of the many reasons, I haven't been too keen on going back to church. They weren't always good memories."

"It was brave of you to come back," Lauren said softly.

Luke smiled. "I'm not sure I had a choice."

She frowned and bit her lip.

"What is it?"

"I talked to your mom about some of this church history and the dates aren't adding up. Gloria gave me the impression that Pastor Worth and June and Porter were long gone by the time you were growing up in the church."

"Well, she might have gotten a little confused. It was a really long time ago."

Lauren blushed under his gaze. "Are you willing to go to Newport and get some answers?"

"I'm up for most adventures and I like to drive."

Lauren felt her heart quicken. For a moment she forgot about her old life. She forgot about Marcus.

* * *

Sydney was watching Saturday morning cartoons. The adults were eating at the small dining table in the kitchen. Vivian was scrolling on her phone, while Lauren was busy doing her daily Bible study.

She looked up from her Bible. "Mom, I'm planning a little day trip to Newport next Tuesday with Luke to do some church business. I was going to ask Linda if she could watch Sydney?"

"You can't take Sydney with you?" Vivian said absently, her nose still in her phone.

"She's got school."

Vivian eyes suddenly lit up behind her coffee mug. "You're going with Luke, huh? I have to hand it to you, Lauren. You have really worked this widow angle to your advantage. Well done."

"Mom? Seriously? Luke and I are friends!"

"With friends like that…who needs boyfriends?"

"Enough! He helps me a lot because he's a good person. That's it."

"If you say so," she smirked.

Lauren glared at her mother over her Bible. "I say so."

Vivian frowned. "Why are you always asking Linda to watch Sydney? I am more than capable of caring for my own granddaughter."

"Mom? You can hardly say the word grandma without gagging."

She pouted. "I don't relish growing old, but with that said, I do love my granddaughter and I don't mind watching her."

"Isn't babysitting Syd getting in the way of your dating life?"

Vivian tapped her nails on the dining table and looked heavenward as she thought about her new boyfriend. "Paul is a family man. He likes that I spend time with my granddaughter."

"So, is this some kind of ploy to impress Paul?" Lauren sighed.

She gasped. "Of course not! He's just teaching me to see things differently."

The tension rose from Lauren's shoulders to her neck. "I just don't think taking care of children is your forte, Mom."

Vivian's voice became strident. "Why don't you just say it? Say what you really mean. I wasn't a good mother! Admit it! That's what you really think."

She leaned back against her chair feeling immeasurably tired. "Mom, you know I wasn't your number one priority when I was a kid. I just want things to be different for Sydney."

"I see," Vivian huffed. Her voice suddenly softened. "I wish you could just see, Lauren that I'm trying. I may not be perfect, but I'm beginning to realize that I made a lot of mistakes and I'm attempting to make up for them."

Lauren hesitated and crossed her arms around her chest. "I'm glad you're learning…that you're trying… but Bill and Jim, they weren't so long ago. I don't want Sydney to have the kind of life I did. It's just going to take awhile to build some of that trust with you."

Vivian looked deflated and a little frail as she set her coffee mug down. "Honey, I am sorry. When you were growing up, I was always so focused on how to provide for you. I didn't think I could do it on my own. I always thought I needed a man, the richer, the better. You may not believe it, but that was my way to protect you, to keep a roof over our heads."

"A lot of those men you let into our lives weren't good people, Mom. I've tried to put it in the past, I have, but when Sydney is involved, I get protective."

Vivian's eyes were wet with tears. Her voice was shaky. "I'm not like you. You're so strong, I almost think you're a robot. When Bill took off with my money, I cried for two days and I barely knew him more than six months. Here, you've been married to a man for years, he dies in a terrible way, and I've never even seen you cry. Why is that, Lauren? What happened with you and Marcus? What really happened?"

"Mother, nothing! What are you talking about?" Lauren felt pain in her chest. "People grieve differently. You've known me since the moment I was born. I don't cry. I never did. Why do you think that is, Mom? We've already established the fact that you and I are as different as night and day."

* * *

Luke's eyes were trained on her as she walked toward his pickup truck. "You're not sure about leaving are you?"

Lauren frowned as she turned her back on Luke to look back at the cottage. "I was going to leave her with Linda, but she had an appointment and Mom really wanted to watch her."

"What's wrong with leaving Sydney with your mother?"

Lauren gave Luke a blank stare. "You've met her. So much! You don't even know."

"You turned out pretty good," Luke teased.

"That's nice of you to say."

Luke moved to the passenger side and opened the door of his forest green F150 truck. "Need a hand?"

"I got it, thanks." Lauren took hold of the grab handle and hoisted herself inside. Once she was settled Luke shut the door and then crossed over to the driver's side.

Luke's truck was a basic model, without all the bells and whistles. There were no leather seats or sunroof, but it was clean and smelled of earth and evergreen firs.

"I can tell you don't have kids."

"Why is that?" Luke frowned and his deep set eyes turned sad.

Lauren immediately regretted the comment. "Oh, just because your truck's so neat. My KIA looks like a crime scene."

He smiled. "Is Sydney the culprit or you?"

"A little of both to be honest. Since I started here, I've been so distracted. I forget to clean my car, can't remember where I put anything, the list goes on."

"Seems understandable. You got a lot going on."

They drove in silence for several minutes before Luke spoke. "Doesn't it feel good to get away?"

"Mixed feelings," Lauren admitted. "I hate leaving Sydney, but she's at school for most of the day. It does feel a little great to get away from the church, though."

Luke directed his eyes on the road. "I've been thinking a lot about what you said about that place, how it's like being in a haunted house. I think that was a pretty good description. I know that building like the back of my hand. I explored every attic, crawl space, closet in that church. Even as a kid, it was exciting, but also scary. I could sometimes feel the presence of ghosts, something eerie, something watching."

Lauren frowned. "That's terrifying. I hate the idea of a child roaming around that place alone." She gazed at his solid frame as he gripped the steering wheel. "I guess we have to try to uncover those ghosts. That is...when we're old enough and have enough strength to do it."

Luke's jaw tightened. "As long as you're willing to accept the fact that you may not like what you find."

Lauren turned to look at him. His eyes were focused on the road, his back rigid. "True," she said.

He continued, "Are you willing to poke your nose into something that might make your life more difficult? After all, you work there. You have to live in that space."

Lauren bit her lip. "It's a good question. In the past I would have agreed with you and been more likely to let sleeping demons lie, so to speak. But I've found that when you try to bury the darkness or hide in it, you make the monster bigger and more powerful. Marcus learned that too late and it cost him everything."

Luke said nothing, but tightened his grip on the steering wheel. "This conversation got kind of serious." He made a nervous laugh. "Are we making any stops along the way?"

"I don't know. I hadn't thought about the logistics, but now that you mention it, I wouldn't mind stretching my legs. You have something in mind?"

178

"I took the liberty of packing us a bite to eat and I know a rather pleasant spot off the road a bit. Do you like waterfalls?"

"Who doesn't like a waterfall?" Lauren laughed. "You made lunch? I had no idea, you were so, so...,resourceful."

Luke chuckled. "Resourceful? Is that what stopping at the supermarket is called these days?"

"My plan was to grab a bite at some fast food restaurant somewhere along the way, so in my book, yes, very resourceful." Lauren glanced at him sidelong. In a world that seemed mostly crazy half of the time, Luke seemed like one of the few sane people left. She felt comfortable and safe near him.

"Have you ever heard of Drift Creek Falls?" He asked.

"No."

"You're in for a treat. You up for a little hike?"

"I'm glad I wore my jeans. I'm wearing boots. They're not hiking boots exactly, but they should be okay as long as conditions don't get too muddy."

A few minute later, Luke pulled into a near empty gravel parking lot.

"I hope it doesn't pour on us." Lauren eyed the dark ominous clouds that hugged the coastline.

"I'd say we have about forty-five minutes before this weather system unleashes its fury."

They ate their sandwiches and gulped sodas at a picnic table under an umbrella of fir trees.

"You wanna risk it?" Luke asked.

"How long of a hike is it?"

"Not far, about one or two miles. Or...we could stay safe and warm in the truck and just continue toward Newport?"

"There's a waterfall at the end of the hike?"

"Yes, there is and a suspension bridge."

"And it's beautiful isn't it?"

"It's not bad." The corners of his mouth turned slightly upward hinting at a smile.

"Worth getting wet for?"

"I'd say so," Luke smirked.

"Okay then. Let me grab my hat." Luke unlocked the truck for Lauren and she rifled through her backpack before she found her green beanie. She tied her hair back and then adjusted the hat firmly over her ears."

"Cute," Luke said with mock approval.

"Shut up," Lauren said. The force of her own words shocked her and she laughed.

"Oh Wow. The pastor's getting mouthy with me again."

Lauren touched him on his forearm. "I hope you know this is part of our teasing banter. I'm not this rude to most people."

"I get it. This is just how you treat the fake Christians," Luke teased.

"No. It's not that. You're more than a parishioner to me. You've become a friend."

"A friend? Ouch." Luke pretended to take one to the heart and laughed.

As they walked the trail single file, Luke in the lead, Lauren suddenly realized the implications of what he had said. *Did Luke desire more than friendship?* Of course it made perfect sense. She was single. He was single. But somehow, her role as minister had made her feel protected from having to entertain any real advances from a man. She was a woman of God and a widow. That made her off limits. It offered her protection from having to deal with complicated matters of the heart. Didn't it?

I'm an idiot. Lauren was struck with the reality of all she had missed. *Did Luke believe this was a date? Did he believe her invitation to accompany her on this trip was an overture toward romance?* The thoughts began to whirl in her head in an overwhelming wave. Even more frightening was the realization that Lauren needed to be honest with herself. Was it possible Luke was only responding to the flirtatious signals she had unintentionally conveyed? How unintentional were they, really?

She was attracted to him. But how much of her attraction to Luke was genuine affection for Luke and how much of it was grief over the man she had lost? Was she no different from her mother? Was she too, just looking for someone, anyone to fill that empty space where she once had a husband, companion, and a lover?

They walked in silence. Lauren's head was churning in a stew of troubling thoughts, but she could not ignore the beauty around her. The stream bubbled on either side of them as they climbed a path that wound gently upward through large deer ferns. The recent rains restored them to their full glory and Lauren was mesmerized by the myriad of arching fronds that framed the trail. Soon, they met the stream again, but this time the only way across was a wooden suspension bridge. For some reason, Lauren was overcome with fear. She stood paralyzed at the foot of the rickety structure as Luke crossed it with ease. He was already half way across when he turned to look at her. For some reason her body was shaking.

"The waterfall's right there. You can see it from the bridge. Lauren, are you okay?" His eyebrows were creased in worry as he moved back toward her.

"I don't know what's wrong," Lauren whispered. "I can't seem to move."

"Are you scared of the bridge?"

"Yeah. I don't know why. I've never reacted this way in my life." She managed a laugh even through her terror.

Luke was there, holding her as though it was the most natural thing in the world. "It's okay. I'm sorry," he whispered in her ear as he held her to his chest. "I never should have brought you here. I had no idea you were so scared of heights."

A voice in her head told her she should tell Luke to stop, to keep his distance. But she couldn't. It felt good. As he held her, she closed her eyes. "Luke," she finally managed to whisper. "It's okay. It's not your fault. I had no idea I was this scared. This has never happened to me before?"

"Should we go back?"

The heat of anger moved through her body as Lauren revolted in frustration against herself. "No way," Lauren whispered firmly into his chest. "I'm so mad right now. It's just a stupid bridge. I came here to see a waterfall. I'm going to cross it."

Luke lifted her face gently upward with his thumb. "Okay. You can do this." He released her from his embrace. "Can you walk, now? It's just one foot in front of the other."

Lauren tried to move toward the bridge. She made a couple of steps forward before her body refused to cooperate with her. She shook her head in disbelief. "I don't get it. I'm practically paralyzed with fear," she whispered. Her hands were visibly shaking.

"I have an idea," Luke said. "Put your arms on my shoulders." He turned away from her and offered his back.

Lauren did as she was told and draped her arms unsteadily around his neck. He hoisted her up on his back and began to walk toward the bridge.

"Is this okay?"

Lauren's heart was beating hard through her chest. "No, but keep going anyway," she said through gritted teeth.

Luke laughed. "Yes, ma'am." He began to walk slowly across the bridge carrying Lauren's full weight. She heard the rain in the trees before she felt the heavy cold drops on her back.

"Luke, I need you to go faster. I feel like I'm going to throw up."

Luke quickened his pace and Lauren closed her eyes. When she opened them again they were on solid ground."

"Thank you, Lord," Lauren whispered as he gently released her. He rested his hands on her waist for a moment.

"Are you steady."

"I think so," she nodded. At that moment the clouds unleashed their full power. In a matter of seconds the bridge was slick with rain and the heavy drops pooled into rivulets that channeled their way back to the stream. The sound of the rain made her feel suddenly alive.

"You realize we're going to have to cross it again on the way back?"

"That's great, Luke. Thanks for reminding me. Very helpful." Lauren yelled through the rain.

Luke's eyes danced. "Lauren, you are quite a woman!"

"And I find you quite annoying!"

Luke laughed. "We make a good pair, don't we?"

As they hiked down the trail toward the falls, the rain subsided to a drizzle. Lauren was half soaked when they reached the end of the path. They stared in silence at the waterfall that towered above them. The force of millions of tons of water hitting jagged rock created a deafening sound that eased the throbbing in her head. She stood mesmerized, her eyes drawn to a deep pool of blue water enclosed by jagged rocks. The rocks suffered damage from the forces of water and gravity, but the pool was calm and undisturbed. Lauren leaned forward against the guard rail and allowed the mist to cool her already wet face. She felt Luke more than she saw him. He stood next to her staring into the same blue pool.

"What do you think?"

"It's amazing."

Luke's arms were around her again. Half in surprise, she turned and faced his chest.

"You were brave," he whispered in her ear. "The way you faced your fear." He traced his fingers to the side of her face. Slowly, he removed her beanie and ran his hands through her wet hair.

"Thank you for helping me across," Lauren whispered.

He was kissing her now. His lips were firm, but gentle, his hand lightly lifting her face toward his.

Lauren was struck by a strange euphoria that forced her body to react while her mind slumbered. She kissed him back without hesitation. Luke made her feel seen, alive, resurrected from the hands of a monstrous guilt that refused to let go.

Lauren was lost. She was not sure how long they stood under the waterfall kissing passionately like teenagers, but suddenly Luke pulled away from her. He straightened his back and his eyes tapered in concern as he studied her face. "Lauren, are you okay?"

"What do you mean?"

"You're crying."

"I am?" Lauren brought her hands to her face and felt warm tears. "I am."

"You didn't know?"

"No," she confessed.

"Lauren,..." Luke's voice was a raspy whisper.

III

Part Three

Gambling in the Dark

Chapter 17

For what does it profit a man to gain the whole world
and forfeit his soul?
—Mark 8:36

Not Sorry

L uke was quiet. She could not read him. They were standing apart. Just seconds before all she could hear was the sound of her heart beating against his chest in a wild rhythm, but now the roar of the waterfall overwhelmed her. He guided her away from the falls where she could hear his voice. "There's a lot we need to talk about, but now doesn't feel like the right time." His face was twisted, half hidden in the shadow of the trees. He was fighting with himself, she realized, wrestling with what to say and not to say.

Lauren tried to find the words to reassure him, but none came. They hiked back to the bridge where Luke wordlessly picked her up in his arms and carried her to the other side of the bridge. Lauren was struck with the same terror, but this time she closed her eyes and buried her face in his chest. Her fear was muddled by other thoughts. The kiss and Luke's silence since seeing her tears were all she could think about.

Once they were in the truck the quiet continued. Luke turned on the radio almost as if to discourage conversation. She hated the silent treatment and cursed herself for allowing their relationship to move past the point of no return. She should have put proper boundaries in place, told him clearly she was only interested in friendship. The problem was it wasn't true. She didn't know what she wanted, but a part of her wanted Luke. She couldn't deny it. Now everything was ruined. Their friendship was apparently over.

* * *

Morningside Assisted Living Community was a gloomy place about five miles outside of Newport. The two story wooden structure was sprawled at the foot of a hill about three miles inland from the ocean. Lauren thought it would be nice if the residents could catch a glimpse of the coastline, but the property was surrounded by hills. Seagulls, however were everywhere and a few had even made their nests in the awning. A sunny day on the Oregon coast was rare. In Lauren's mind painting a building gray seemed a poor choice for a place that was gray almost all the time already.

Luke opened the door for her. "You have a plan?"

She was relieved to hear him speak. "I'm going to make a friendly visit and just see what information spills out organically."

Luke bit his lower lip. "You don't think he'll think it's odd that two complete strangers have come to visit him?"

"No. In these homes people are in and out all the time. It's pretty lonely for most residents, so they don't seem to mind. Most people are just happy for the company."

As they entered the reception area, an older woman sat at the front desk sipping a two liter soda. She raised her penciled in eyebrows as they entered. "Who you here to visit?"

"Byron Worth," Lauren said with confidence.

"You family?"

"No, we're from his church?"

"His church?" The woman's eyebrows shot practically to her hairline. "Theresa!" She yelled to a woman in the back office.

Another middle aged woman appeared with blonde wavy hair. "What?"

188

"These people here, say they're from Byron's church. Can you believe that?"

Theresa's eyes also widened in surprise. "Byron goes to church? Now, that is a new one?"

"I should correct myself a bit," Lauren interjected. "He used to be the pastor of our church many, many years ago. I'm here to give him some mail and visit with him a bit."

"Wait," the brunette woman said, her mouth wide open. "Are you telling me that Byron Worth was a pastor?"

"Yes." Lauren absorbed their amazement. "Why? Is that a surprise to you?"

"Honey," the blonde woman said. "Byron Worth has the mouth of a sailor. He's angry and from time to time a bit, well…how do I put it? Handsy with the ladies."

"Oh," Lauren faltered. "Is it okay if we visit him?"

The brunette woman laughed. "Well we're not going to stop you, but we might say a prayer for you."

"I think you're the first visitors he's ever received since he arrived here a few years ago. He has no family that I know of," Theresa added.

Luke frowned. "Wow, it's sure not the way I remember him. He used to be Mr. Congeniality."

"Sign here." The brunette woman pointed to a line on the page. "He's in room 105. Make sure you wash your hands thoroughly before entering his room. Have either of you been sick in the last two weeks with any cold or flu symptoms?"

"No."

"It's about 30 minutes till dinner service starts, so you might want to keep the visit short."

"Okay. We got it," Lauren said.

The halls of the retirement home were poorly lit and she felt fear building in her gut as she searched for room 105. "Luke?"

"Yeah? I'm right behind you."

"Are you feeling as nervous as I am."

"This place is creepy," Luke said under his breath.

"Are you mad at me?'

"No, Lauren. I'm not mad. Things are just complicated."

"I know," she whispered.

Room 105 was at the end of the hall and Lauren knocked gently on the door before entering. "Mr. Worth?"

He was seated next to the window in a drab room hunched over in a wheelchair. He looked like he might have been dozing off.

"I'm sorry to disturb you, Pastor Worth."

"Who the hell are you?" He croaked.

The man in the wheelchair was broken. He was skinny, almost emaciated and his body looked like it was slowly caving in on itself. Old age had made him unrecognizable. She would not have been able to identify him today from the old picture in the attic. Despite the condition of his body, his eyes were alert, deep set, a bright blue and clever, almost birdlike.

"I'm Lauren and this is Luke. We're from your old church, the First Assembly of Disciples of Vernonia. We have some mail for you from the Christian Missions Association. I guess they're not very good at updating their mailing list." She handed the envelope to him.

He glared at Lauren. "Just put it over there." He waved his frail, age spotted hand toward a table in the corner that was already piled with envelopes.

She set the envelope down and then turned to him. "We thought we'd visit, if that's okay with you?"

He assessed her coldly. "You from First Vernonia, you say?" he coughed.

"Yes. I'm the pastor. This here is Luke, he's a friend."

"It's good to meet you," Luke mumbled

"You're the pastor?" His eyes widened in disbelief. "A lady pastor? Things are really going in the crapper aren't they?"

Lauren ignored the insult. "Are you okay with us pulling up a couple chairs from the hallway?"

The old man shrugged as if nothing really mattered.

"I got it," Luke said. He stepped outside and came back with only one chair. "I think I prefer to stand." He placed the chair in front of Pastor Worth for Lauren and she took a seat. Luke shifted from foot to foot and Lauren could sense his uneasiness.

Pastor Worth's eyes darted between the two of them with cold intensity.

"Can I get you anything?" Lauren asked. "Maybe water or coffee?"

"No," he barked. "You're in the waiting room for death, there's nothing you can give me that will make it more comfortable."

Lauren's mouth gaped open. "I'm sorry," she finally managed. "It must be difficult here."

He shrugged. "You get used to it, believe it or not."

"The women at the front desk told me you don't get a lot of visitors."

He grunted."Lady, when you're 96 years old, you're the only one left. Everyone else is under the ground."

"Makes sense," Lauren nodded. "Your children?"

"Haven't seen them in years. Went off with their mother. I didn't see them after that."

"I'm sorry to hear that."

"I don't know you. What are you apologizing for?"

"Nothing. I just didn't mean to upset you. I did want to ask you some questions about the church if that's okay?"

Byron gave her an unpleasant smile that made the hair on her neck stand on end. "What would you like to ask me, pretty lady?"

Luke's face was now openly hostile as he witnessed the turn in the conversation. He stood closer to Lauren and placed his hand protectively on her chair.

She continued. "I think you know my mentor, Reverend Martin. He told me there was some trouble back in your day and I was hoping you might be able to shed light on what happened."

"Oh, so that old coot told you there was trouble did he? Reverend Martin." Byron spat out his name in contempt. "That man wouldn't know trouble from a day at the circus, the old fool. Always going around correcting everyone else like he's not as dirty as the rest of us." Pastor Worth chortled and Lauren found the sound of his voice deeply unsettling.

"I've heard other stories too. I just would like to know the truth."

"The truth! That's a good one. Mrs…."

"Westbrook."

"Mrs. Westbrook, what do you think the truth is, anyway?"

Lauren's answer was a rush of words. "What really happened all those years ago? The reason people are so quiet. The reason they're walking on eggshells."

He did not seem to hear her. "What's that?" Byron was pointing a shaking finger at her.

"What's what?"

"That thing on your neck?"

Lauren brought her fingers to her neck. She felt the gold cross of her necklace in her fingertips and then the soft curve of the ruby ring. "I found it at the parsonage. I've been trying to find its owner."

"I gave it to her," he barked.

"You gave it to who?" Luke asked.

"To June. That vixen. I gave it to her. She caused all the trouble. You just ask her. That woman was a Delilah, a Jezebel."

"What do you mean, Pastor Worth?"

Just seconds before, he was animated, engaged, alert, but now the old man turned taciturn, his eyes dead. "I'm tired," he said. "I don't want to talk anymore."

"But Pastor Worth..."

"Lauren, it's time to go." Luke rested his hand on her shoulder.

* * *

They sat in the parking lot. Lauren was still breathing hard. "That was... weird," she finally managed.

"Yeah. That guy was creepy, not a man of God, that's for sure. Sick in both mind and body as far as I could tell."

"June?" Lauren let her name hang in the air for a moment. "Luke, what do you think happened between them?"

"I think it's sort of clear what happened between them."

"They had an affair?"

"He gave her that ring."

Lauren unclasped her necklace with shaking fingers and removed the ring from the chain. She handed it to Luke.

"Expensive." Luke examined the ruby and diamonds and then handed it back to her. "Hard to imagine the two of them. Don't think I want to imagine it, frankly. Life hasn't been kind to him. That's for sure."

"You know, when I first met June I was wearing it. She noticed the ruby around my neck."

"Oh yeah, what kind of reaction did it get from her?"

"She wanted to know where I got it. She definitely had her feathers ruffled when she saw it and June doesn't ruffle easily."

"No, she doesn't. That woman's a force of nature," Luke agreed.

Lauren examined the ring. "It really is a lovely ruby, a real showpiece. You know, June's a lot younger than him, by at least 15 years. He was married with kids."

Luke's eyebrows furrowed. "Why would he give her something she couldn't wear in public? Porter would have asked questions about where it came from."

"I don't know. Maybe he just wanted her to have it. I think maybe Porter knew about the affair."

"Why would you say that?"

Lauren bit her lip, not sure if she should reveal a secret. "Remember, I found him that day in the parsonage after he got lost. I thought he was just babbling in a state of dementia, but he was talking to someone. He came to the parsonage, Luke. He came there for a reason. In his muddled mind, he came there to confront someone."

"Pastor Worth?"

"Exactly. He was talking to him and he was so angry. That's why I was so scared after I found him. The Porter I saw that day was not the Porter I knew. He was a version of his younger self, a scary version."

"What did he say?"

"Something like you ruined everything. You deserve to rot in hell."

Luke shook his head. "We're getting into people's personal lives, their secrets. Are you sure, this is something we need to explore?"

"I'm just confused."

"They had an affair. He left the church, lost his job, family. She returns to her husband. It's scandalous for sure, but not unheard of."

"No. There's more. Your mom said the police came and arrested him. People don't get arrested for having affairs. They have to do something illegal."

"Are you planning to go back in there and ask him what he did that was illegal?"

"No."

Luke started the truck. They drove for a few miles without speaking.

Lauren glanced at him sidelong as he drove. "Thanks for talking to me again. You scared me when you went silent. I don't want to lose you, Luke. I don't want to lose your friendship."

A rush of air escaped his lips in a prolonged sigh. "I need to say something to you and I don't want you to be offended."

"Okay?"

"I think maybe you have PTSD. Have you seen a counselor or talked with anyone since what happened with Marcus?"

Lauren's shoulders tensed. "No. I haven't had time for that. I've been too busy getting a job, taking care of Sydney, and now my mom..."

"It's a lot. I get that. I think you're having some trouble processing. I enjoy spending time with you. I like you, more than I should probably. But, I think I'm just adding more confusion to your healing process."

Lauren turned away from Luke and stared out the window. She watched the rolling hills and trees. "You're right," she finally admitted. "I've felt really disconnected for a long time. I like you too, but we can't..."

"I know," he said softly. "Starting a relationship when you're still healing... It's like making a really important decision when you're drunk. Not a good idea. I'm just really attracted to you. I wanted it to happen. There's a part of me that still wants it to happen. But the timing. If I go there again with someone, it has to be right."

"What's the point of getting older, if you don't learn anything? It's okay, Luke. You're right. I don't even know what I want. If I'm honest every time I try to feel something, especially if I think about Marcus, I go numb. It's like I feel so much, I can't feel anything. Does that make any sense?"

"Yeah, actually. It makes a lot of sense."

"Luke, I'm a mother and I have to work. I don't really have time to deal with my mind not being okay. I don't know what to do about it."

Luke pulled the truck to the side of the road. He placed the gear in park and turned toward her. "Lauren, you can't run away from this kind of thing. It will catch up with you."

She did not recognize her own voice. She heard a small laugh like a hand bell escape her lips. It sounded like her mother's laugh, the one she made when trying to make light of whatever she shouldn't be making light of. "How come you know about PTSD?"

The hint of a smile was gone. He clasped his hands to the steering wheel and stared out the window as he spoke. "Most of us don't get through life without trauma. After my divorce, I got hit hard. My issue was mostly insomnia. I couldn't sleep to save my life. When I did sleep, it wasn't restful. Even did a little sleepwalking and woke up in some weird places. One time even out in the woods, creepy stuff. I woke up not knowing where I was. I've tried a lot of prescription drugs with varying results. Anyway, I've read up on it and Post Traumatic Stress Disorder hits people in different ways. The fear at the bridge, the crying without knowing it. All that stuff signifies a delayed response. It's like you're out of sync, reacting now to what you should have reacted to weeks ago."

Lauren rested her head on the car window. "Sounds about right," she finally said. "I don't like it."

"Like what?"

"Having so little control of my own feelings. I feel like I'm a loose cannon and I could go off at anytime." Lauren clasped her hands across her lap. "The sleepwalking sounds terrifying. Were you able to get better?"

He turned from the window and looked at her directly. "That's the thing.

I've improved, but I'm not sure I'm recovered. I still struggle to sleep especially if my mind gets caught in a loop where I relive my marriage or mistakes I made. Apparently all my problems come out in my sleep."

"Sounds like I'm not the only one with PTSD."

Luke grinned, but then became solemn. "Actually, what's helped me is praying, if you can believe that?"

Lauren raised her eyebrows in surprise. "Really?"

"That's what I've been trying to tell you, Pastor Westbrook. God's been working on me."

She was curious now. "Not to be nosy, but what do you pray exactly?"

"Exactly?" Luke repeated. He thought for a moment and then opened the storage bin in the center console. He pulled out a small brown leather Bible. "I started with Psalm 23. Here. He showed her several passages highlighted in yellow. You know this verse? *Yea tho I walk through the valley of the shadow of death, I will fear no evil.*"

Lauren smiled. "I know the one."

"I thought you would," he laughed. "I know it's a famous passage, but I always liked those verses. I started by just reading the words over and over, but then it kind of branched out to therapy where I was able to just talk to God, be honest about everything. Do you know what I mean?"

"I do," Lauren said. "I feel a little guilty. You're reminding me that I need to get back to talking to God myself."

"You're a pastor. I thought you talked to God every day?"

Lauren shrugged. "I open my Bible every day. But recently, it's been to put a sermon together. You just reminded me that my relationship with God might just be a little on the rocks."

Luke furrowed his eyebrows. "I doubt that. Lauren, you've been through a lot. Sometimes it takes quite awhile just to get your brain back in working order. But you know I don't think I'd have been able to talk to God right away. At least not right after the divorce."

"Why do you say that?"

"I'm no expert, but when you talk to God you have to lay yourself pretty bare. At least it seems that way to me. It takes us a little while to fully process grief before we can do that. Don't beat yourself up. Sometimes we can focus so much on the needs of others we forget to take care of ourselves. We don't realize that we might not be where we need to be with God."

* * *

As they pulled into the driveway she was surprised to find her mother already standing on the front porch. She rushed toward Lauren as she opened the truck door.

"She's gone, Lauren. She's gone. I don't know where she went."

"What? Mom, what are you talking about?"

"I picked Sydney up from school. We came home. I was on the phone with Paul in the bedroom and when I came back to the living room, she was gone."

"No," Lauren's voice was a whisper. "She wouldn't…She wouldn't go running off. Sydney knows better than that? She didn't tell you where she was going?"

"No. I've looked all around the parsonage. I've been screaming her name."

"Did you call her? She almost always has her phone on her?"

Vivian nodded. "Yes, but her phone is in her bedroom."

"She didn't take her phone with her? How long has she been gone?"

"About an hour?"

"An hour? Why didn't you call me?"

"I thought we'd find her," Vivian's voice was soft.

"You haven't changed. Not one bit," Lauren snapped. Luke's hand was on her shoulder.

"We'll start looking."

"I already called Paul to help us look," Vivian added.

A chill traveled through her body, so cold it made her tremble.

"Luke," she whispered. "We have to find her."

Chapter 18

The lot is cast into the lap,
but its every decision
is from the Lord.
Proverbs 13:8

Short Stick

The parsonage was now the center of a major operation. In the tiny sitting room, people paced, frowned, and prayed. Linda held Lauren's hand while Emma patted her back.

"It will be okay. We'll find her," Linda whispered in her ear.

Vivian was talking to a police officer in the kitchen while Paul and Luke made plans to comb the immediate area with a small search party.

Lauren was numb. Her mind was scattered, her heart triggered. She could feel her pulse beating wildly through the thin skin of her wrists, but she felt disassociated from the scene. "Please God. Help her to be alright. Sydney, just please be okay?"

Luke returned to her side. "We're going to search the church and the woods. Paul has called every member of the church to also be on the lookout."

"Luke?" Lauren whispered. "The car, the note...What if they took her?"

Luke's voice was firm. "You can't think like that, Lauren. She's okay. You have to have faith that she's okay. She's a kid. They run off sometimes."

Despite his words of encouragement, Lauren noticed the tightness in his jaw. Energy coursed through his body and he paced the tiny sitting room like a boxer on steroids.

Linda took her hand. "Lord Jesus, we pray for Sydney's safety. We pray and trust that she is in your hands. We know you love her. Protect her and keep her from all harm. In Your name we pray, Amen."

"Amen," Emma repeated. "Both of my kids took off more than once when they were around her age. They just wandered off. Sometimes they just get so caught up in what they're doing; they just plain forget they have a mother and a father worried sick about 'em. It's going to be okay, Lauren."

"I hope so, Emma." Her voice was hollow.

Officer Torrence made her way through the small crowd. "Ms. Westbrook, ma'am? We've put out an APB for your daughter. That's a broadcasting alert. Your mother has been kind enough to provide a picture and description of your daughter. She also filled me in on the recent incident with the car and the note you received. I want you to know, it is unlikely that those two events are related, but we will be keeping a lookout for the car and all suspicious activity. I just want you to know in over 90% of cases, we are able to find the child within a few hours."

"That's good," she whispered. "It will be dark soon."

"Yes, ma'am."

"Sydney wouldn't stay out after dark. She knows I would worry. She's not like that."

"I understand that, Ms. Westbrook. That's why I think we will most likely find her soon, especially with everyone looking."

"Thank you, Officer. I hope with all my heart you're right."

Linda squeezed her hand. "You want me to sit with you?"

"No," Lauren said. "I need to look for her too. I want everyone looking."

"Someone needs to stay here in case she comes home," Officer Torrence said.

"I'll be here," Vivian choked.

Lauren watched her mother in shock. She was weeping, her face red as she sat hunched over the kitchen counter. Her conversation with the police officer had obviously left her drained and exhausted. Normally, if

Vivian cried she managed to shed tears while still looking beautiful and put together, but her mother was ugly crying, sobbing. Paul was patting her back in an effort to comfort her. She clasped her hands together and began to pray. In all her life, Lauren had never seen her mother pray.

Luke's arm was around her now. "I'm going to go look, now. Keep your phone on you, okay? I'm going to call the second I find her," he whispered. He held her close for a moment and she felt his lips just barely touch her forehead. "We're going to find her." His hand grazed across her cheek as he wiped the tears from her eyes. She was not aware she was weeping till that moment. "You should stay too, with your mom," Luke said gently. "You're not in a good state of mind to be on the search." Lauren nodded her head, but she wasn't listening.

* * *

The house was empty now except for Lauren and Vivian. Everyone was searching for Sydney. Lauren's grip was so tight on her phone her fingers hurt. At that moment, a terrible thought entered her mind. *The caves. Sydney loved to explore. What if she had gone there for an adventure and was now trapped? Sydney may have thought she would only be gone for a half our or so, but if she got trapped without a phone...?* The thought filled Lauren with dread. She could not bear the idea of her daughter spending a night alone in a dark, cold cave. Memories of the crazy woman and the doll flooded her. There was no way, she would leave her daughter in such a situation, no way in hell.

Lauren grabbed her jacket in a state of maternal panic and fled through the door. Her mother called out to her in a broken voice, "Lauren, where are you going?"

"I'm just going to step out for some fresh air, Mom. I'm going crazy with worry in here." Lauren shut the door behind her without looking back. She crossed the porch and took the first step only to jump over the rest of the stairs. Her feet sunk into the soft foliage as she ran toward the woods and down the path, neglecting her own safety. She was gliding across the surface of the rough terrain. The usual discomforts and muscle pains had vanished as adrenaline pulsed into every muscle. All she wanted was to find her daughter, to keep Sydney safe.

The sun was setting and the forest lay in the semi-darkness of twilight. The ground glistened from the recent rains. Lauren ran, but slowly enough to maneuver the roots and debris on the forest path. She would not allow anything to get in the way between her and Sydney. *I should call, Luke,* she realized. *I should let him know where I'm going?* But the fear that gripped her heart would not allow her to stop for the instant it would take to call or text him. She could not even spare one moment, not if it meant a delay in rescuing Sydney from the terror of darkness. The hands of fate unfolded before her in a haze of ethereal twilight. She could see nothing but Sydney.

Lauren heard only the sound of her feet on wet leaves and her own uneven breathing. Her thoughts were an unfinished prayer, *Sydney, Sydney, Sydney.* In her head, she heard only her daughter's name.

The candelabra tree loomed over her like a hydra from a classic Greek tale. In the eerie light, its branches snaked and twisted like a dozen arms reaching to grab whatever creature they could find to drag into the moist earth below. Lauren shuddered under its gaze and made a sharp right away from the lake and into the bowels of the forest, leaving the tree to watch her retreating figure. She slipped and fell. The ground was slick from the rains and the legs of her jeans were now wet and caked with mud. She didn't care. Again, she was on her feet and she ran. Her legs carried her off the path toward the caves. She begin to cry, "Sydney! Sydney! Are you out here?"

The rocks were now just barely visible in the waning light, their distinct lumpy shapes darker than the the dark indigo blue of the sky. She realized her surroundings were now simply a menagerie of dark and darker shapes. There was not even a visible star or ray of light to provide contrast to the night sky, only the last faded glow of a disappearing sun. Deeper into the valley, she descended. She was getting smaller and the rocks were growing bigger. They encircled her now. *I have been transported in time and place to Stonehenge to participate in some pagan festivity,* she thought. Her back tensed and a shiver traveled down her spine as her eyes deciphered through fading light the place on the ground where once the doll had rested. It was the day of the yard sale, she recalled as she remembered the lump of tattered rags that stared at her from the ground, forlorn and foreboding watching her through one eye and a lopsided smile. The homeless woman's face was now seared into her brain and her features flashed through her head, the pale skin and bottom row of rotten teeth. She felt the darkness of that place in every pore of her skin.

"Sydney!" she continued to call. By memory, she remembered the opening of the cave, the place where Luke had told her a child was lost. *It had taken two days to pull him out,* Luke had said. Her fingers pressed against the surface of the wet rock. With trembling fingers she grabbed her phone and tapped the flashlight. She shone the light into the darkness of the opening.

"Sydney? Sydney? Are you down there?" Cautiously, she poked her head further in the cave and shone the light of her phone as deep into the cavity as her arm would allow. There was no sign of her daughter. She saw only a sharp declivity that led to what looked like an open space below and a large pile of loose rock that reached its summit near where Lauren stood at the mouth of the cavern. She was just about to turn around and head home when she felt a presence behind her. A sense of danger filled her body and she whirled around to meet her fate, but it was too late.

She felt the brunt force of two powerful arms pushing her brutally forward. She fought for balance, but was not able to right herself. Lauren was falling head first into the mouth of the cavern.

The phone was ripped from her hand as she tumbled forward down the declivity into the belly of the beast, but there was no pain. Her body was fully juiced on adrenaline. Only vaguely did she experience the various assaults on her head, arms, and legs as she tumbled down. It was as if she was seeing her life through the eyes of an omniscient watcher. *She must be having a nightmare after seeing a scary movie before bedtime. This couldn't actually be happening? Sydney could not possibly be gone and she was not actually falling into the heart of a bottomless cavern?* She finally stopped rolling. As she closed her eyes, the world stopped.

"Lauren, Lauren," Marcus spoke to her softly. He stroked her head and she felt his lips lightly graze her forehead.

"Marcus?"she whispered. Or was it Luke who was speaking to her? It was hard to tell.

Marcus wasn't really there. The truth overwhelmed her as she managed to roll onto her back. She stared into nothingness, the heavy blackness of what she imagined was the entrance to hell. She was not conscious, not really. Her arms, legs, fingers, toes…They refused to move even as her brain signaled to them. Her eyes were closed, but she knew even if she were able to open them, there would still only be darkness. She had followed her fear and it had led her to this place. *I will die here*, she realized.

Moments before, while she was running through the woods, she knew she should call Luke, call her mother. She had chosen not to. Lauren had made a conscious choice, as if in the deep recesses of her mind she knew the cave was part of her destiny. Lying unconscious, she was completely alone; she could finally see the truth.

When did she know that her life was a lie? They were in bed together, but neither of them could sleep. She bolted from the bed in frustration and headed to the kitchen. Marcus was on her heels. "Lauren," he said again. "I'm sorry. You know I'm sorry."

"You always say your sorry." Anger coursed through her veins. "But then you do it again, and again, and again…" Her voice trailed off.

"I'm an addict," Marcus pleaded.

"An addict?" Lauren laughed. The cynicism turned her blood to a black oil that hardened every part of her. Claiming he was an addict, made him a victim. He abdicated all responsibility for all the pain and suffering he caused. She felt no compassion for this man. His face was contorted in an expression of agony. He was her husband, but he was a stranger. Her voice was clipped. "You are an addict, but you still have choices, Marcus. You're still a husband who has allowed his wife to pay back his debt, an addict who refuses to be honest and tell the truth, an addict who is supposed to be a minister of God, who steals money from his own congregation to feed his ego!" She whispered the words in a rush of hateful intensity. "I don't think there's anywhere to go from here, Marcus. You refuse to get help. I can't help you..., not anymore. I can't be in this anymore."

Marcus glared. "I didn't want you to take the extra job at the school. I wanted to be a good provider, but I...Lauren, this was never what I wanted."

"Do you think this is what I wanted?" she cried. "It's not just the money, Marcus."

Marcus stared through her. His face a blank slate, but his eyes still wet with tears. "You're going to leave me. You hate me." He sounded like a child.

"I don't hate you," she said slowly. "No. I... I just don't respect you." The words came in a discarded breath.

His breathing was cut short. He winced in pain. Lauren felt a momentum welling inside her "I thought you were different. I thought I was marrying a Christian, but you're no different than any of them."

"Any of them? Who are you talking about, Lauren? Any of who?"

She stared through him. "Her boyfriends."

"You're talking about your mother? Your mother's boyfriends?" He stared at her with a look of incredulity.

"I'm not like them. I love you."

"This isn't love," she said, her words barely audible. She continued. "Sometimes I look at you, while you sleep at night and...I hate you."

He gasped and his eyes widened into deeper pools of anguish. "What do you want me to do? Drive off a cliff? End your miseries by killing myself?" His voice was rising with passion, anger, and something else she couldn't trace.

He wanted her to take the words back. She could see it in his eyes. He wanted her to say that she loved him, that she wanted him alive, well, and happy. They would work on this together and help each other through it. They would remember their wedding vows and love each other no matter what. Lauren's heart was cold. "What do you do?" she asked. "When you're there? What are you doing?" She tried to incarnate the monstrous thoughts

204

into flesh. With her words, she formed the monster's head, arms, torso, legs and feet. "You're drinking? drugs? Are there other women? Everything you say to me is a lie."

"No!" Marcus exclaimed. "It's not like that. The world just has too many closed doors, limitations everywhere you look. You make one choice and fifteen others are dead to you forever. I just want to be free, sometimes."

"Free of me?" Lauren could not hide the hurt.

"Lauren, I love you. But our marriage makes me feel trapped sometimes, the church, the expectations. It's a heavy burden. But, I love you, just…" He scrambled for words. "Very imperfectly."

"I don't believe you." Lauren said. She was deflated. He was all passion, but she was dead. "You go there and do God knows what; then you come back to our bed? I get an extra job, I cover for you at the church. I pick up the pieces. I clean the mess."

"Lauren," he gasped. "When I'm gambling, I lose control, but it's not who I really am. You have to believe me."

The words made her cringe. "You are what you do, Marcus. It is exactly who you are!" She spat the words with force. She remembered Sydney sleeping in the bedroom across the hall and whispered. "You need to leave. It's over."

Marcus' eyes flickered for a moment and then went dead. They stared at each other, frozen in the moment reading the pain and sorrow in each other's expressions. Lauren forced her legs to move. She retreated to the bathroom, locked the door and sat on the toilet. Her face was buried in her hands and she did everything in her will to hold back the tears. The vibration of his footsteps and the squeak of wood betrayed his presence. She heard the scuffle of his movements through the walls and then the hollow thud of the door. Lauren was grateful he had not slammed it. Perhaps, in the last moments before that fateful drive, he remembered his daughter sleeping or maybe he just didn't have the fight in him to protest. As for Lauren, she had been containing the force of an ocean inside of her heart for too many years. In the back of her mind she wondered if she should have chosen this time to call him out on his actions when he was so low, when his job and everything else in his life was in the balance. No, she had been holding on to the anger, the frustration, the disappointment, and the dark knowledge that he loved himself far more than he could ever love her for too long. Lauren realized she simply could not suppress the burden she carried for one more second. She retreated to the bedroom where she collapsed on the bed in exhaustion and grief. She cried in her sleep and awoke to Officer Hernandez's silky voice over the cell phone telling her Marcus was dead.

Lauren tried to turn her head toward his voice. He was in the cave with her now. She felt his presence through the heavy haze of darkness. "Marcus," she whispered.

"I'm here." His voice was relaxed and filled with the bright humor she remembered from their early years together.

"I'm sorry. I'm so sorry, Marcus. I love you. I really do. I didn't know how much till you left me," she wailed the words. Her cries echoed from the walls of the cavern.

"I know," Marcus said again. "It's okay." She felt his fingers tracing her forehead, moving the strands of hair from her eyes, and then the gentle pressure of his lips on her forehead. "I love you too," he whispered in her ear.

"Have you come to take me?" she mumbled.

Marcus laughed his magical laugh, "No, Laur bear. No. You've got more work to do. God's not done with you yet." He laughed and his voice was music.

"I'm too tired," Lauren groaned.

Marcus laughed again. "You're going to be okay." His voice was softer. "It's time for you to let me go."

"Don't leave me, Marcus. I can't do this alone. Don't leave me here." Her words were hardly intelligible.

"We can be at peace now, Lauren. We can. I know you've forgiven me and I've forgiven you. You were right to protect Sydney and yourself."

Her heart tightened. "I don't feel peace," she whispered. "I'm...I'm stuck."

Lauren felt the warmth of his presence embrace her and his breath in her ear. "You have to forgive yourself." Marcus lingered for a moment and then he was gone. Lauren was alone.

Chapter 19

Yet you do not know what tomorrow will bring.
What is your life?
For you are a mist that appears for a little time
and then vanishes.
—James 4:14

Vanishing

After a period of not knowing whether she was asleep or awake, Lauren began to adjust to the thickening darkness of the cavern. The flashing images of vicious creatures lying in readiness to devour her no longer plagued her thoughts. Her bones ached, but as she lay perfectly still, she was able to suppress the pain. Marcus was with her, in spirit. She felt him. The awareness of his presence gave her some comfort as she closed her eyes and prayed in rhythm with the beating of her heart. She prayed for Sydney, Luke, Linda, Reverend Martin, Vivian, and all the others in the church. And she prayed for Marcus, thanking God that she knew he was finally at peace. She saw each face clearly in her mind and focused on blessing the people she cared about and praying for their good.

From far away, she heard her name, "Lauren! Lauren!" The voice filtered through the haze almost like a call from another world. She accepted the voice, just as she did the blackness and the cold. *No one knows where I am.* Suddenly, she felt a stabbing pain in her head as fireworks seemed to explode within her skull. *Wake up! Wake up! It's Luke!* Lauren's eyes opened in awareness.

"I'm here," she whispered. She intended to yell, but her voice was ragged and weak. A scene from a movie came to mind. *What was it? Just thinking hurts.* A vision of Kate Winslet in the frigid water of the Atlantic ocean flashed through her mind. Kate was waking herself from the stupor of a death sleep to cry out for help toward a small fleet of rescue boats. *I'm Kate,* she realized. *Oh, wait...It was Rose in the Titanic movie. I'm Rose,* she realized. *I have to let him know I'm here.* A vision of her daughter flitted through her thoughts. *Oh, how she wanted to reach out and hold her close! Sydney... Sydney needs me.* There was a light shining above her in the cave. She could hear the distant sounds of people. They were here for her.

"Luke!" She finally managed to cry weakly. "I'm down here."

"Quiet!" a voice said.

She recognized the muffled sound, *Luke,* she thought.

"I heard something," he said from above.

From somewhere deep inside her, Lauren felt a sudden strength. "Luke!," she cried again.

She squinted as the light found her face.

"Lauren? Lauren! Are you okay? I'm coming down."

She didn't have the strength to say more. He knew she was there. It was enough.

Paul's voice was just barely audible, "You need to wait till the paramedics come. They'll be here in a few minutes."

"No, I'm going down. Help me anchor the rope."

Light illuminated the cave as Luke descended into the depths. In a matter of seconds, he was beside her. She felt his hand gently stroking her face and then his fingers on her throat as he measured the strength of her pulse. "You sure know how to drive a guy into a panic, Lauren." His voice was dry, but she sensed his relief.

"Sydney?" Lauren managed in a hoarse whisper.

He placed his hand firmly on her shoulder. "Don't move. We have rescue workers coming." His voice did not waver. "She's okay. We found her. She was in the church the whole time. When you're feeling better, I have a story you're not going to believe."

"She's okay?"

"Yes, she's okay, not a hair out of place, but I'm not sure about you. What crazy notion made you come here, Lauren? Wait, don't answer that. You don't need to overdo it."

"Thank you, God," she whispered.

He shuffled through a first aid kit and brought a compress to her head. He held her firmly. "Don't move. You're bleeding. We're just going to sit real still till they get here. I'm with you, okay?"

"Luke?" Lauren croaked.

"Don't strain yourself. Everything's okay. Why do I always seem to find you when you're bleeding?" Luke stroked her hair as he held the compress firmly to her head.

"I was pushed," she whispered.

Luke's voice rose in alarm, "Someone pushed you in here?"

Lauren wanted to nod but couldn't. "Yes," she managed.

His lips traced her forehead, before he spoke gently in her ear. "Okay," he murmured. "Lauren, I'm going to find out what in God's name is going on. That's a promise."

* * *

After the paramedics came, Lauren remembered little. She could recall answering a few questions about her name and family. A oxygen mask was promptly placed over her head and then a shot in the arm before she was lifted onto a stretcher. Suddenly, she felt so exhausted she could no longer fight to stay conscious.

Her eyes opened to an explosion of colors. Flowers were arranged throughout the hospital room on every available surface. Lauren's eyes focused on the sight of violet hydrangeas. The blooms leaned so far from the bedside table, they almost touched the skin of her bare, bruised arms, which were almost as purple as the flowers. *Gloria,* she thought as she recognized who must have brought them for her. The corners of her mouth lifted into a smile. Events from the day before flooded her thoughts in an intense mirage of images. *Sydney!* Lauren thought desperately. At just that moment, she heard her daughter's voice.

"Mom!" Sydney ran through the open door and almost knocked over a harried nurse in the process. The woman glared at her before clutching her supplies to her chest.

"Syd," Lauren croaked. "Are you okay?"

"Mom, I'm fine. What about you?"

Sydney leaned into her mother's arms almost knocking over the hydrangeas. Lauren stroked her hair with her one free arm. She took a moment to assess her own condition. "You know, Syd. I'm not really sure. My head hurts like I used a hornet's nest as a pillow."

Sydney laughed. "Well, you almost did. You fell head first into a cave. Mom, that's not very smart, you know."

Lauren rubbed her forehead as she shook her head. "Only because I was worried sick about you, you little booger."

Sydney was sheepish as she retreated from her mother. "Yeah, I'm sorry about that."

"Where were you?"

"She was at the church the entire time," Luke said from the door.

"Luke," Lauren was surprised by the joy she heard in her voice at the sight of him. He looked better. His face was more relaxed and at the moment he was pretending to glare at Sydney. "The two of you cause more trouble than any two women I've known in my entire life, just like two magicians in a disappearing act. We are never to repeat a day like yesterday, is that understood?"

Sydney, not without humor, glared back at Luke. "It was all your idea anyway, telling me about that secret room underneath the stage."

"Is that where you were?" Lauren asked.

"Yes, she was. And what did you find, Sydney?" Luke prompted.

"Mom, someone's been living there right underneath the pulpit?"

"What?" Lauren asked, dazed.

"There was food, magazines, books, blankets, all this stuff and you know what else?"

Lauren shook her head, baffled. "No, what?"

"A secret passageway!" Sydney's voice was breathless.

"There's a passageway underneath the church pulpit?"

Luke was solemn as he nodded his head. He narrowed his eyebrows. "Someone's been living there a long time by the looks of it and using the passageway to get in and out without being seen."

"Who?" Lauren said in disbelief.

"We don't know. Police are over there, investigatin'," Sydney blurted.

"Where does the passageway lead to?"

"Behind the church there's what looks like a vent, but it's a separate entrance that takes you under the church and into the room below the stage. These old buildings used to build escape hatches like that one," Luke said.

"So behind the church, kind of near the woods?"

"Exactly. A person can just sneak in and within seconds their hidden in forest. They can get on the trail and go to the lake, to town, anywhere… No one's the wiser."

"You never noticed the room when you were doing the renovating?"

"I never went under the pulpit. I was working on the attic and some other rooms. It was on my list to check out, but I just never got around to it. I knew about the place from when I was a kid. You know we used to play hide n seek and sardines and all those exploring games, so I know that church like the back of my hand, but I haven't actually gone down there in ages. I kind of assumed, someone would have sealed it off by now, but considering the neglect of that church, I guess I shouldn't have been surprised."

Lauren frowned as the full risk of the situation became clearer to her. "Sydney, that was incredibly dangerous. That person could have attacked you. What if they were there when you were down there?" She remembered the day when she first explored the attic, the feeling of a dark presence in the room with her.

Sydney's eyes went wide like a deer's. "I didn't see anyone."

"Mom and Linda finally found her," Luke continued. "She was crawling out of there like nothing ever happened about the same time you were falling into a cave, without your phone, I might add."

Lauren bit her lip and looked at the foot of her bed suddenly ashamed. "I'm sorry, Luke. It was stupid. I got so panicked and worried about Sydney, I couldn't think straight. I remembered you telling me there was a child who had been stuck in that cave. All I could see was my daughter trapped in a scary, dark place and my mama instincts just took over. I did have my phone...It just broke when I fell into the cavern."

Luke's jaw tightened for a moment before relaxing again. "All that matters is you're both okay." His deep set eyes rested on her. She could see his relief.

"How did you know where to find me?"

"Your detective daughter."

"Mom, when we couldn't find you, I used my phone to track your phone. It said your phone wasn't on, but it showed us the last place you were which was in the woods. Grandma was a total mess. She kept saying she was going to have a heart attack."

"Hey Sydney, why don't you grab your mom some candy from the vending machine and maybe a soda. It would probably be a nice treat after all she's been through." He rifled through his wallet and handed her a ten dollar bill.

"I don't think the machine takes anything but ones," Sydney moaned.

"Check with the nurse's station and see if they can help you get change. I need to talk to your mom for a sec."

"Okey dokey." Sydney rolled her eyes, but complied.

"Where did she get that expression?"

"I think from Paul," Luke smirked. "He's the only person I know who says, *okey dokey.*" Luke's eyes suddenly turned serious and his voice became soft. "By the way, your mom was with you all night, sleeping by your bedside. The doctor said you were fine and she could go home, but she insisted."

"I don't remember a thing after the paramedics," Lauren admitted.

"They gave you some serious sedative and pain meds. I think they expected you to a be a lot more banged up than you were."

"So, everyone's okay?"

"Linda stayed the night at your place with Syd. She came by this morning because Sydney wanted to see you, but also so Vivian could go home and take a shower. I called her when I saw you were up, so she'll probably be here any minute."

Lauren nodded slowly. "Thanks for telling me that. She's changing I think. I never used to be able to count on her." Lauren clasped her hands together feeling the strength of her knuckles underneath her fingertips."It wasn't really my mom's fault Sydney went AWOL, was it?"

Luke's eyes were gentle. "I think it could have happened to anyone. Sydney's a bit of a free spirit. It's kind of hard to keep track of her every second. But, then again, I don't have the same history with your mom that you have, do I? I'm sure that the way you feel is perfectly reasonable considering your history together."

"I've been trying to forgive her. Some days I'm better at it than others."

"Oh man, you're preaching to the choir," Luke chuckled. Suddenly he reached his hand out toward her and took her hand in his own. "Lauren, yesterday, when I found you, you told me you were pushed into that cave. I didn't want to say anything in front of Sydney. I don't want to worry her, but I need to know what happened?"

Lauren's face fell. "Luke, it was terrifying." She paused as she searched his features. "I didn't actually see who pushed me. I was at the opening of the cave and I was leaning forward with my phone's flash light. Suddenly, I just felt this really creepy feeling like someone was behind me, ...someone big and bulky...There was a plasticky sound like someone was crinkling garbage bags. Anyway, I turned around just as they pushed me really hard. I lost my balance and just fell in."

"Did you see what they looked like?"

"It was so dark and I had just been staring at the light on my phone. When I turned around, I just saw a big black shape, but Luke, whoever it was shoved me like there was no tomorrow."

Luke's eyes were trained on her. He grew more solemn as she spoke.

"Lauren, I have a theory, but it's a little outlandish, so I'm not sure I want to say anything out loud."

Lauren squeezed his hand. "You think you might know who did this?"

He shook his head. "I can't wrap my head around it exactly, but I have a hunch as they used to say in the old detective movies."

"Luke, don't leave me in the dark. It was my daughter who went missing and I was the one who fell headfirst down a pile of rocks. If you've got a theory, I want to know what it is."

"I get that, but I want to make sure I'm on the right track. Look, according to the doctors, you're in here for a few days. They think you're going to make a complete recovery, but until your concussion recesses a bit, you're not completely out of the woods. That's what your mom told me last night anyway after she talked to the doctors. How you didn't break every bone in your body, Lauren, is a miracle."

At that moment, a doctor entered her room.

"Ms. Westbrook? I'm Dr. Yamamoto. I'm so glad you're up. I hope, I'm not interrupting anything."

"Oh, no. Of course not," Luke said quickly. "I was just leaving."

Lauren nodded toward the middle aged professional woman with gold, wire rimmed glasses. "Nice to meet you, Dr. Yamamoto, just one second." She strained her head back toward Luke. "Whatever you find out, let me know right away."

"I'll tell you as I go. I'll be completely straight with you."

Lauren frowned as Luke backed toward the door. At that moment Sydney returned with a Dr. Pepper and a package of M&Ms. She placed the drink on the bedside table next to the hydrangeas and put the candy on her mother's lap.

"The nurse out there said it was the breakfast of champions," Sydney said with pride.

Lauren laughed. "I believe that's called, sarcasm."

"Mom, I know what sarcasm is," Sydney insisted. "Are you going to eat it?"

"I will. I will. My stomach feels just a bit queasy, if I'm being honest,"

Lauren admitted. "I might have to save it, till my stomach settles."

Dr. Yamamoto smiled at the exchange from behind her clipboard.

"Vivian should be here pretty soon," Luke said from the door. "Should I leave Sydney with you so you have a little more time together and then she can go home with your mom?"

Sydney caught the warning look in Lauren's eyes. "It's not grandma's fault. She was in the bathroom when I left the house. I didn't even tell her where I was going."

Lauren nodded. "It's okay." Luke gave her a quick thumbs up before leaving the room.

Dr. Yamamoto turned toward Lauren. "So, you had one heck of a night?"

Lauren managed a smile. "So, I hear. That's the last time I hang out in a cave."

"I would say that's a good idea. Have you spoken to your mother, yet? I debriefed her last night, but just thought I'd stop by to check in with you when you woke. I was here last night, so I'm not officially on duty now."

"I haven't seen her yet, not since I woke up, but…"

"I'm here. I'm here." Vivian rushed into the room and ran to the other side of her bed next to Sydney. Her energy was frantic. "Oh, Laur Bear! You have no idea how worried I've been. Look at you. You're awake. Oh honey!"

Sydney backed away to make room for Vivian.

Lauren was overwhelmed by the force of her mother's hug and then several kisses on her cheeks and forehead.

"Ow, Mom," Lauren protested.

Sydney watched the exchange with interest, a broad smile on her face.

"I was just filling Lauren in on what I told you yesterday," Dr. Yamamoto said to Vivian. She turned her attention back to Lauren. "You are an incredibly lucky woman. You had quite the fall. Besides being black and blue nearly all over, X rays revealed some cracked ribs and some internal bleeding in your abdomen, but nothing like what could have happened under the circumstances. Right now, our biggest concern is that lump on your head. You do have a sizable concussion and your medical team would feel better if you stayed at the hospital for about 48 hours for observation."

"Thank you," Lauren nodded. "I appreciate all you've done to fix me and to help my family."

"Of course, Ms. Westbrook." Dr Yamamoto paused for a moment and ran her hand through her chin length bob before placing both hands in the pockets of her lab coat. "There is an officer out in the hall that would like to speak with you? Is that alright? She says it will only take a few minutes."

Lauren bit her lip."Yes, you can send them in. Thank you Doctor"

"I'll be back this evening to check in with you again."

Vivian's eyes were wide. "Lauren, why do the police want to see you?"

"Well, Ma, if you stick around you'll get to find out." Lauren recognized Officer Torrence as the same officer who had helped with Sydney's disappearance.

Sydney's eyes also widened. "Did you do something against the law?"

Lauren considered sending her daughter out of the room for a moment and then decided against it. Someone had purposefully pushed her into a cave. Her life had been treated at best carelessly and at worst, malevolently by another human being. If there was a person in the world who had homicidal intentions toward her, perhaps it was not wise to keep secrets. *Something wicked this way comes,* she thought. She would not allow evil to sneak up in the cover of darkness without warning any longer. When Marcus was alive, there had been so many secrets. There were the secrets Marcus kept from her, the secrets she kept from Marcus, and the secrets they both kept from Sydney. Lauren did not have the energy for one more lie or half truth.

"Ms. Westbrook," Officer Torrence said smoothly. "I'm really sorry to bother you at the hospital. I'd like to talk to you about what happened last night." She glanced briefly at Sydney and Vivian before returning her gaze to Lauren. "We can talk alone?"

Lauren shook her head. "No, it's okay. They can stay."

"Your friend, Mr. Luke Reid, reported that you told him that you may have been pushed into that cavern? Is that correct, Ms. Westbrook?"

"Yes."

"Someone pushed you! Oh my God!" Vivian gasped.

"Can you tell me what you remember?" Officer Torrence continued.

"I was looking for Sydney." Lauren felt her daughter grasp her hand. "I decided to check the woods because Sydney, my daughter I mean, loves to explore. Suddenly I remembered the caves. You see, Luke had told me that a child had been stuck in them and not able to get out and I just had this terrible thought that Sydney was there."

"Did you see anyone or anything?"

Lauren shook her head. "Not this time."

"What do you mean, not this time?" Officer Torrence questioned. "Was there another time?"

"Yes. Back in August, I encountered a homeless woman in the forest, near the caves."

Officer Torrence narrowed her eyes. "Can you give me a description of this woman?"

"Honestly, it would be kind of hard to tell you what she looks like. She's larger, almost the size of a man and wears a dark windbreaker... Ma?"

Vivian's back was shaking. She was crying.

"Grandma, are you okay?"

"Officer," Vivian choked. "I believe I have information that might explain who pushed Lauren."

"Mom? What are you talking about?"

Officer Torrence raised her eyebrows. "Do you know something about this homeless woman?"

"Homeless woman? No... I...I haven't been fully honest."

"Fully honest? Mom? About what?"

"About Bill?" She burst out sobbing again.

Lauren was bewildered.

Officer Torrence seemed to take Vivian's outburst in stride. "Ma'am, is there something you need to tell me?"

Chapter 20

Do not lay up for yourselves treasures on earth,
where moth and rust destroy
and where thieves break in and steal,
but lay up for yourselves treasures in heaven,
where neither moth nor rust destroys
and where thieves do not break in and steal.
For where your treasure is,
there your heart will be also.
Matthew 6:19-21

Thieves

Vivian's face was ashen and her hands trembled.

"Ma, what's going on?" Lauren's head was pounding as she felt a tidal wave of dread building in her chest. "What happened with Bill?"

"Well, I think I already told you...Bill was a bit of a con man, but I left out some pertinent details." Vivian's voice sounded profoundly exhausted as she sunk into a chair next to Lauren's bed.

"Ma'am, I'm going to need you to start from the beginning. Who is Bill?" Officer Torrence stood poised at the foot of Lauren's bed with a pen in hand and a small notebook.

"He was my boyfriend up in Portland. Murphy was his last name, Bill

Murphy. I …I learned the hard way that he was about as shady as a three dollar bill. We met at a rodeo and started dating. We moved in together a few weeks after that. He was a real romantic at first…at least, until I gave him everything." Vivian wilted under Lauren's gaze. "Don't say it! I already know. It was stupid!" She slumped deeper in the chair as she hid her face in her hands.

"You gave him money?" Officer Torrence clarified with a raised eyebrow.

"I gave him 15,000 dollars from my own pension and he gambled it away in days. We were supposed to be going into business together, bull breeding and such, but he gambled it on horses at the track or God knows what else. To be honest, I'm not even sure the whole bull story was even true. He just out and lied to me, I guess. He was just another one of those men who sees a stupid, desperate woman and thinks, 'Oh there's someone I can use.'"

"You didn't tell me that, Mom?" Lauren said softly.

"You're right, I didn't." Vivian clutched her hands together in her lap and sighed as she sat up a bit straighter in her chair. "You already think I'm such a fool. Why would I give you more evidence?"

"Ma'am, how do you believe this Bill person relates to your daughter being pushed into a cave? I'm not sure I'm seeing the connection."

Vivian bit her lip and continued to rub her hands together. "He was looking for me?"

"Why was this Bill looking for you?" Officer Torrence pressed.

Sydney now sat on her mother's bed and leaned forward towards her grandmother with eyes wide with interest.

"He had some money. I knew where he kept it."

"Ma, you didn't?"

"He had just taken my entire retirement and he didn't even say sorry. He just said I knew the risks what I was getting into. So, I thought maybe he should learn what he was getting into when he met me."

"Grandma, what did you do?"

"Hush, Sydney," Lauren warned.

"He kept a wad of cash in a mason jar under the sink. I saw him squirreling away money in there, you know….when he didn't know I was looking. I had no place to go without a lick of cash and I needed to leave, so I waited till he went off to the rodeo and I took that jar and left town."

"You left Portland on the run with his money?" Lauren could not hide her dismay.

"How much did you take from him, ma'am?"

"Ended up being close to $8000, all cash mostly hundred dollar bills which wasn't even near as much as he took from me?"

Officer Torrence whistled softly between her teeth. "You still have that money?"

"Most of it," Vivian confessed. "I honestly haven't had too many expenses since my daughter took me in. But a few weeks ago..."

"What happened, Mom?"

"I got a message from him on my Facebook account. You know, that direct message thing with the purple circle and the lightning. It was real threatening. Let me show it to you." Vivian reached for her phone with trembling hands and tapped on the screen through teary eyes. "Here. There's the whole thread." She handed the phone to Officer Torrence.

She raised her eyebrows as she scanned the screen. After a brief moment, she took out her own phone and captured some photographs of the messages and then scribbled annotations in her notebook.

"Please Officer, can I see the messages?"

"She can see them," Vivian nodded.

Officer Torrence handed Lauren the phone. "He sounds like a real nice guy," she said under her breath.

Lauren scanned through the messages with Sydney breathing excitedly behind her shoulder.

"I wanna see!" Sydney insisted as Lauren tried to move the phone out of her eye range.

"I don't care who knows," Vivian sighed. "Sydney should know the truth about her nana."

Lauren's stomach knotted as she read the threats. *You know what you took and I know where you are,* read the first.

Me and my buddies are up near Vernonia Lake having a picnic. Ever heard of the place?

The last message began with a snapshot of the parsonage from a distance and then a brief message, *A quaint little house, don't you think? But I wouldn't want to live there without a man protecting the place, would you?*

Lauren felt a chill move through her body. "Mom, this guys a total psycho, creep! The note on the door. It was him, wasn't it?"

Vivian's eyes were frozen and Lauren could see them fill with moisture. She rose from the chair and paced nervously back and forth.

"Why didn't you tell the police then? You acted like you had no idea..."

"I'm sorry, Laur bear. I really am. I was wrong. It's just...things were getting so much better between the two of us. I finally felt like...well, for the first time in my life like you didn't hate me. I had a relationship, a real relationship with you and my granddaughter. I know I don't always make it obvious, but I love it here. I didn't want to ruin it!"

"You love it here?" Lauren shook her head in disbelief. "What exactly did you think would happen by not telling anyone? Did you think he would just go away? You didn't think that maybe after the text messages, a visit to our house in the middle of the night, the same house where your granddaughter sleeps mind you, that maybe you were in over your head?"

Vivian's words were rushed through her tears. "I hoped he would go away! I never saw him do anything violent. I didn't really think he'd hurt anyone? I just thought he wanted to scare me a little."

"So"...interjected Officer Torrence with a raised eyebrow. "You believe this Bill followed your daughter into the woods and pushed her into the cave as revenge for you taking his money?"

Lauren glared at her mother as she spoke. "Well, someone did put a threatening message on our door in the middle of the night. Whoever it was wanted to make their presence known and scare the living heck out of us! He knew where we lived. I can't think of anyone else who would want to harm me," Lauren admitted.

"I'm sorry," Vivian mouthed as her eyes pleaded.

"You put my life at risk and Sydney's in addition to your own. What were you thinking? Is 8,000 dollars worth the life of your family?"

"No! Of course it isn't!" Vivian cried. "That's why I'm telling you now. I was stupid and doing what I always do…running away, not dealing, but things are different this time."

"What's different, Ma?"

Vivian moved a few feet away from Lauren and clung to the iron railing at the foot of the bed next to Officer Torrence. She looked directly at Lauren. "Things are changing. I'm changing. I know not as quickly as you'd like, but I met Paul, started going to church, and mending things with you and Sydney. I know it's not perfect, but for the first time in my life, I feel like…like, there's hope."

Lauren's head was pounding. She suddenly felt exhausted.

"You okay?" Officer Torrence asked.

"Today has just been a lot," Lauren whispered. "I'm sorry, Officer. You certainly don't need to be a part of our family drama."

She shrugged in a nonchalant manner. "Ma'am, this is nothing, but if my professional opinion means anything, you're alive and you have a chance to be a family. A lot of folks don't get that chance, so count yourself lucky."

Lauren said nothing as the heat came to her cheeks.

"I think I have enough to get started here," Officer Torrence continued "I'll do a check on Bill Murphy and will go from there. I will call back later for a little more description on the "homeless" woman and we'll see what we can piece together. Thank you for your time. Good luck and get your rest."

The door closed softly behind Officer Torrence. Lauren stared at the door, but felt Vivian's eyes on her.

"Lauren," Vivian said softly.

She turned her head to look at her mother's weepy, raccoon eyes, but she didn't really register her.

"Paul asked me to marry him."

"What?" It was as if she was awakening from a drug induced stupor. Her mother's words jolted her into reality.

"He proposed a few days ago. I was going to tell you, but then you went on the trip, Sydney got lost, and this…" She gestured toward the hospital bed.

"Does Paul know about Bill?" Lauren said bitterly. "All this drama around you?"

Her mother surprised her. "Yes. I told him and he still wants to marry me. He wants me to give him back the money, put this chapter behind us and move forward. Lauren, Paul's a different kind of man, a good man."

Lauren felt tears in her eyes. Something inside her that was tightly bound shifted.

"Mom," Sydney's voice was tentative as she snuggled closer to Lauren. "Grandma's getting married. I'm going to have a grandpa. Paul's the best. This is a good thing, right?"

Lauren closed her eyes and for a moment. Her mind traveled back to the cavern and she remembered Marcus' soothing tenor in her ear. "Sometimes you have to forgive yourself," he had whispered. *And forgive your mother too,* she thought. She remembered her desperate fear in that place and God's provision for her in her darkest moment. She managed a smile. "Mom, Paul is a good man, the best in fact. I'm really happy for you."

Despite her headache she stared fully at her mother's face. She saw a lot less make-up these days, but there was something glowing and a texture almost dewy in her cheeks despite her melted mascara. Her frown lines were still there, but something in her face had softened. She was no longer a woman on a mission. Her mother seemed at peace, almost relaxed in spite of the heated tenor of their conversation. Lauren stared hard at Vivian, before allowing a small smile to warm the corners of her mouth. "Don't screw it up."

Vivian's shoulders relaxed. "You know, I won't this time and once we get married you'll get your place to yourself."

"You're waiting till marriage to move out?" Lauren said in surprise.

"Paul's idea," Vivian shrugged. "He lives by the book. He's always calling me the Pastor's mother like I have some halo or something."

"It's a miracle," Lauren laughed despite the throbbing in her head.

"Do I get to be in the wedding?" Sydney asked.

"Of course," Vivian said. "Next to the bride, you are the most important person."

Sydney wrinkled her nose. "More important than the groom?"

"Just as important. How's that?" Vivian laughed. "Flower girl, bridesmaid, you name it."

* * *

Lauren hated being held captive to her mother's driving. After a California stop and a turn down a neighbor's driveway, they finally pulled up next to the parsonage. Sydney was speaking a mile a minute from the backseat intent on bringing Lauren up to speed on everything that had happened while she was in the hospital.

"Juan brought a frog to class and hid it the whole day in his pencil box. It jumped out when Mrs. Lesky was writing on her Smart Board. It was crazy!"

"Poor thing," Vivian cooed mindlessly. Lauren recognized the dazed look in her mother's eyes. She was in a chimerical state thinking about Paul, the wedding, and her happily ever after which might explain the unfocused driving.

"Mrs. Lesky didn't' freak out. She just picked it up and put it outside, but everyone was laughing hysterically and we got out of at least 10 minutes of the math lesson because that's how long it took to get the whole class to focus again."

Lauren nodded without truly listening, her eyes were too busy absorbing the colored balloons and streamers that cascaded across the porch. Gloria, Emma, Linda, and Vicky were standing under a *Welcome Home* sign on the front porch. Lauren eased herself out of her mother's compact.

"Let me help you," Gloria said, slightly frantic as she bolted from the porch to the car. "You need to take it easy."

Lauren felt sore all over and moving hurt despite the pain meds Dr. Yamamoto prescribed. "What are you all doing here?" Lauren laughed.

"We wanted to welcome you home, of course," Linda said. "Sydney and I decided to do a little decorating."

"You like it, mom?" Sydney asked as she brought in Lauren's carry on.

"I do, Syd. Thank you. It looks lovely."

"But we're not going to stay long," Emma added. "Several folks in the church made you food. We organized your kitchen, so you should just be able to pop a dish in the oven when you're ready to eat without any bother or fuss."

Lauren leaned on Gloria just slightly for support as they walked toward the porch steps. "Thank you. You really didn't need to..."

"We most certainly did," Gloria whispered. "No way were we going to let you fend for yourself after all you've been through."

"We've got fresh sheets on the bed and you've got a fully stocked refrigerator, hon," Vicky added.

"Thank you," Lauren managed.

"This sure is a nice community," Vivian said as she slung Lauren's purse around her shoulder.

These women were fixtures now, so familiar that she could almost take them for granted.

Conscious of her ordeal and exhaustion, the women only stayed about 15 minutes. Sydney was in her bedroom working on a class project and Vivian who was as worn out as Lauren was making a cup of tea in the kitchen. For the moment, she had the room to herself. Her only plan was to ease her sore body onto the couch to watch T.V. and catnap. Just as she was about to relax and put her feet up, there was a knock on the door.

"Coming," Vivian said from the kitchen. "Oh, Reverend Martin," her mother exclaimed from the door. "I'm not sure this is a good time."

"It's alright," Lauren said from the couch. "Come in, Reverend."

He was dressed casually in a blue sweater with brown leather elbow pads. His balding head was covered with his fedora and he was bundled in a scarf. He looked a bit sheepish as he entered. "I'm sorry to bother you," he said as he approached her.

"It's okay. I'm feeling a little sleepy, so if you had come any later, I'd probably have passed out. So, now is as good a time as any. "What can I do for you?"

"Can I get you coffee or tea, Reverend?" Vivian called from behind her as she returned to the kitchen.

"No ma'am. I won't stay long," Reverend Martin sighed. "I'm very sorry about what happened to you." He took a seat in the armchair across from the couch. He stared hard at her for a moment. "Do you have any idea who could have done this?"

"The police have a couple suspects in mind and they're looking into it. You probably heard about the person who has been living in the church."

The Reverend raised a bushy eyebrow in surprise. "Uh, no. I hadn't heard."

"Sydney was exploring and found a room beneath the sanctuary. The space shows evidence of someone living there at least till quite recently.

He shook his head in disbelief and frowned. "Extraordinary...Sometimes I think this place is cursed. Do you know how many interim pastors we've sent to this church?"

Lauren shook her head.

"Dozens! And they've been chewed and spit out of the mouth of this congregation like chicken bones." He sighed and his shoulders stooped as if he carried a heavy burden.

"So, Reverend...What brings you all this way?"

The crease between his eyebrows deepened. "Pastor Westbrook, I owe you an apology. In my own life, I want you to know I pray. I talk to God and I listen. Not as much as I should, but there are times I know the Lord wants me to hear Him.

Lauren nodded. She no longer felt sleepy as curiosity coursed through her veins. "What do you think God is saying to you?"

"I've come to offer you a new position. I have been praying and reflecting and I believe I was wrong to send you here."

Lauren noticed a change in his eyes, a melting of the steel as he spoke.

"You see, I didn't think you would succeed. Perhaps there was even a part of me that wanted you to fail. I didn't believe you were the real thing, a real servant of God. I doubted you because I doubted your husband." He clasped the sides of the arm chair with new intensity. "But who am I to judge such things? God doesn't use who I think is appropriate. God does what's best in His own eyes. I've allowed cynicism and bitterness to blind me." His voice became barely audible. "I haven't served the Lord as I should."

Lauren surprised even herself by laughing. "Reverend, I haven't always served the Lord well either. I've been distracted and focused on myself and carrying around terrible burdens from my marriage while trying to minister to this congregation and be a mother to a 10 year old daughter who I half suspect is smarter than I am. I think I'm quite a mess." They faced each other in silence for a few moments before Lauren continued. "Your apology means a lot to me,"she managed. "It takes a wise person to say sorry and please know, I appreciate it. I don't like to admit it, even to myself, but your good opinion of me matters more than you know, probably more than it should."

"You have it," he said as he rose shakily and walked a couple steps closer toward her and the door behind her. "There's a congregation in Warrenton. It's a larger assembly and a healthy church with a functioning leadership body. I've recommended you. They very much would like a female pastor. We're looking to make the transition in the next couple of months."

"Oh,"Lauren choked. "Thank you, Reverend Martin. I am touched that you would think of me, but I don't know if I have the heart to leave Vernonia."

"I was afraid you might say that," he frowned.

"I will pray about it," Lauren offered.

"Yes, please do that. With a slight nod of his head, he exited and Lauren slumped into the couch suddenly exhausted. How could she leave Vernonia? Lauren was not exactly sure what God had in mind for her, but she did not feel like her job was complete. There was more to do, even if she didn't know exactly what.

* * *

Her mind slowly returned to consciousness as if through a thick fog. The room was dark and she wasn't sure what time it was. The pain medication she was taking made her feel groggy and not at all in tune with her surroundings. Vivian entered the room frowning. She sat a cup of tea on the coffee table in front of Lauren all the while standing over her looking stricken.

"Ma, what's wrong?"

"I just got a call from Officer Torrence."

"And...?"

"Bill Murphy did not push you into that cave?"

"How do we know that?"

"Because he was sitting in prison in Lincoln County for a DUI?"

"What about the guys with him?"

"All of em were in county lock up for drug possession waiting to get booked. They had to stay in lock up the whole night."

"And the homeless woman...?"

"They're looking into that lead now. Taking fingerprints and waiting on lab results. It might take awhile."

Lauren nodded grimly. "Square one. I guess we'll know when we know."

Vivian moved around the coffee table and gently adjusted Lauren's legs so she could sit next to her on the couch. "I want you to know, sweetheart. I returned the money. Paul added to the deficit I had and we left it with the police officers to give to Bill when he gets out of lock up. He shouldn't be bothering us anymore."

Lauren grabbed her mother's hand. "That's good, Mom. It's real good. I'm proud of you."

***

Lauren was feeling stronger every day and after a week had passed she was getting around almost like before the accident. Luke was over most days to visit for an hour or two and Lauren found she looked forward to his visits. He brought coffee and they sat on the front porch talking about anything and everything. The air was different between them, now. Lauren felt more relaxed. After her experience in the cave, she felt a peace about her marriage to Marcus and what God had in store for her future. Lauren realized fully now that the fear, the loss, and guilt she carried were an inescapable burden. She was lost carrying the load of it. But now… Lauren was learning to release those burdens to God. In order to feel like a whole person, she needed to heal. In Luke, she had found a friend.

Reverend Martin had volunteered to take the pulpit while Lauren recovered and she found the break almost delicious. Luke sat across from her on the porch swing, his foot resting on his other knee as he sipped coffee and assessed Lauren with a concerned glance.

"You feeling better?"

Lauren sat on the bench bundled in a fuzzy blanket. She held her coffee cup to her lips and suppressed a shiver. In Oregon, a person did not let cold, rainy weather keep them from enjoying the outdoors. "I am," she said slowly. "My shoulder still feels super sore and I still look like a punching bag underneath all these layers, but I'm definitely healing." She sat her mug on the porch railing. "You know it wasn't Bill after all?"

"Yep. Your mom told me. That has me even more concerned. I was hoping you'd let me see your phone and take a look at the security app."

"Yeah, sure." Lauren reached underneath the blanket for the phone in her pocket. "You have that look like you know something I don't."

"I'm not ready to reveal my theory quite yet," Luke nodded. "It's kind of far fetched so I wanna make sure I'm not losing my mind first."

She tilted her head in curiosity. "With a disclaimer like that one, I feel like I have to know now."

Luke cut her short. "Not without a little more evidence."

Lauren watched his expression as he scanned through her phone. Suddenly his eyes raised in surprise.

"What? What?" Lauren asked.

"I think I know who our intruder is?"

Chapter 21

Ask, and it shall be given you;
seek, and ye shall find;
knock, and it shall be opened unto you
—Matthew 7:7.

Stakeout

A cold chill traveled down her spine. "What do you see on my phone?"

"Here, see for yourself," Luke shifted in the porch swing to make room for her.

Lauren wrapped her blanket tightly around her shoulders and labored her way to his side.

"Do you ever check this thing?" He sounded almost agitated.

"I don't really understand how it works and my old phone got destroyed in the cave, remember? This is the new one. I finally got my apps all updated from the cloud after Syd helped me."

Luke was scrolling through a series of thumbnails on her screen. "Some of the videos are still loading." He continued to scroll. "Do you see here? Each of these are live motion recordings from when the cameras detected movement around the parsonage. Look. You can see Sydney here and this is your mom getting into her car."

Lauren registered each image and then stared at two shiny eyes peering from the next video in the cue. "What's that?"

"I think it's a raccoon. Appears to be sneaking off after doing a raid on your porch. You can see it's striped tail. Uh, wait… Take a look at this one."

Lauren squinted as she tried to make out what exactly she was witnessing. "What did I just see?"

"Watch again." His voice was firm and humorless.

Lauren tracked the movement on the black and white screen as Luke replayed the video. "You see that?" He ran his finger across the glass. "That's the front yard going toward the woods."

She squinted again. " I see something! Is that a face? Oh no!" Her stomach jolted uncomfortably and her shoulders clinched. "That's her!" The gray screen paused at her touch, and she was now able to make sense of the white circular shape in the background of the frame. The muscles at the base of her neck tightened as her body recognized even before her mind, the pale wide face and dark feral eyes that flashed across the background of the screen. From the video alone one could not determine the gender, but Lauren would never forget that face.

"Do you recognize her?" Luke's voice was soft.
"It's the woman from the woods who had the doll. Luke, do you think she's the one living in the church?"

He narrowed his eyes at the screen. "It would appear so. She's headed from the church into the woods."

"You know her?"

Luke sighed. "I think I recognize her, but I'm not sure."

"Who is she?"

His eyes darkened. "Someone I used to know, I think. But I can't be certain. It was a long time ago."

"Luke, you're being cagey. You don't want to tell me who she is?"

"It's not that. It's just…It's sensitive is all. I just want to be sure."

Lauren shuddered as she watched for the second time, the woman's lumpy shape move with surprising speed through the back of the frame. "It's like she's staring at the parsonage. What time was this?"

Luke's voice was flat. "Two in the morning, the night before you were pushed."

The fear once again traveled her back. She was shaking. "I'm almost positive that's the woman who pushed me, Luke."

His arm was around her and he drew her toward his shoulder. She rested her head there for a moment remembering what it was like just for a second to rely on another person. He tilted his head closer to her and whispered in her ear. "I believe you."

"What was she doing in front of my house in the middle of the night? Is she stalking me? Why would she want to hurt me?" Lauren's words were an intense whisper, a voice for fear.

Luke's tone was gentle. "I don't think she meant to hurt you. You can tell she's not right. Even in the pictures and when you got a glimpse of her at church and at the yard sale, you got the impression that she was out of it. She's not okay."

"No, she's not," Lauren agreed. I need to tell Officer Torrence. This is our primary lead now that we know Bill couldn't have done it. Luke, she might hurt someone else? I don't want Sydney or Mom going outside if she's violent."

"In most cases I would say call Officer Torrence immediately. But..." his eyes were heavy, almost tired. "Could we consider gathering just a little information before we set a fire under this thing."

She stared blankly at his face.

"What if she hurt someone else?" She repeated.

"I hate that this woman hurt you and I want to put an end to it. I want to do it the right way, the most effective way. I'm asking for one more night. Can you give me that?"

Lauren sighed. "I don't understand why?"

"I think we're dealing with someone with a mental illness," Luke said gently. "The police coming after her, would maybe make her more volatile, not less."

"What did you have in mind?"

"You have plans tonight?"

She turned her head back toward him. "No. Why?"

"I think we should do an old fashioned stake out. Get all the information we can."

* * *

By the time Lauren heard the sound of Luke's truck pulling into the driveway, the sun was in its golden hour casting warm light even through the chill of the coastal air onto the porch.

As Lauren moved toward the door, Vivian said with exaggerated cheerfulness, "You two have a good time."

"Yeah, Mom," Sydney chimed in. "Have fun with Luke." Her eyes sparkled with mischievous delight.

Lauren was just about to tell her mother and daughter that this was certainly not a date, but when she opened the door, Luke held out a bottle of wine.

"You ready for this?"

"What's the wine for? I thought we were doing a stake out?" The suspicion in her voice seemed to catch him off guard.

He nodded solemnly. "We are and it's going to be cold. This is just to warm us up."

Lauren remembered the trip to Newport , the food and preparations he had made and realized that Vivian was not wrong. This did appear to be a date, at least in Luke's mind. He was already through the door. "Hello Syd, Vivian…"

"Hi Luke," Sydney chirped.

Lauren turned toward her mother and Sydney, annoyed by their eager expressions. "Just a sec." She grabbed Luke by the hand and drug him out the door onto the porch.

"Stop pushing and shoving," Luke said with a slight laugh.

"There's someone out there trying to kill me and push me into caves. I'm not sure I'm in the mood for a bottle of wine! I thought we were doing something serious and now it's like we're going on a date?"

234

"Would that be so horrible?"Luke said with a smile. He dropped the grin as he observed her humorless expression. "Look, I'm okay with us taking it slow. I mean…molasses slow is okay. But I want to spend time with you and I think you want to spend time with me too."

Lauren's face went hot as she stammered. "I'm just not sure I can move from a stakeout mindset to date mindset so easily is all."

"Well, that's why I brought the wine. It's a Napa Valley Cabernet Sauvignon and it's amazing. You can taste the black cherry with just a hint of wood and vanilla in the background. It's also not cheap."

Lauren glared at him. "So, now you're a wine connoisseur?"

"Okay. I'm just trying to lighten the mood. We are going on a stakeout, but it is going to be cold and a bottle of wine will be nice. Lauren, you deserve something nice. That's the truth of it. Plus, I have something to show you."

Despite her better judgment, she felt her resolve softening. "This better be good." She left him on the porch while she went back inside to grab her coat.

"Have fun," Vivian called after her.

The mist was settling into the crevices of the foothills as they walked toward the woods. They moved past the Candelabra tree and then down toward the Banks trail, but instead of turning west toward the caves, they veered right toward town, which was a two mile hike down the steep hill. "Where are we going?"

"I realized today," Luke said lightly, "I've been to your house a million times and you've never been to mine. It just didn't seem fair. I want you to know where I live."

The words were simple, straightforward and Lauren did not know how to respond. Her chest felt warm and suddenly it was hard to breathe.

"Why aren't we driving?"

"It's more direct to walk and this way we get some fresh air."

They swerved off the trail toward town and moved north in the direction of Vernonia Lake on what was more of a deer trail than a true path. Through the gaps in fir branches the golden light filtered through darkness, casting a mix of amber glow and shadow over the forest floor. They hiked up a mossy hill and then Lauren saw the gate. It was a rustic structure with a handcrafted wooden latch. Luke opened it expertly and they progressed forward on a small path that wound its way through a mossy carpet. About 50 feet from where they stood, Lauren saw the cabin.

Luke's house was built on an incline that allowed for a tree filled view before settling into the sapphire of Vernonia Lake below. The cabin was bathed in yellow light from the setting sun. Although a modest dwelling, Lauren was still awestruck by the beauty of the craftsmanship and the loveliness of the forested surroundings. The siding of the house was configured from uncut logs that fit together perfectly, like an intricate puzzle.

"You built this, didn't you?" Lauren almost whispered.

"I did." Luke said, his tone matter of fact. "After Bridget left...you know, the divorce and everything, it was the project that kept me going. Even when I was sleeping, I would dream about it, picture how I would lay each log, each beam. Honestly, it was kind of an obsession for a whole year. I was living out here in a trailer like a crazy hermit, cutting logs and screaming at the stars."

"You screamed at the stars?" Lauren teased.

"Sometimes," Luke admitted.

"Well at least you were honest about what was happening to you, facing the loss of your marriage head on. You were probably light years ahead of me," she confessed. "I hold everything in."

As they approached the porch, Lauren couldn't help herself, she reached out to touch the wooden beam of the arched entryway. "It's beautiful," she whispered.

The corners of his mouth turned just slightly. "Glad you like it." He opened the door for her and they entered a great room with a vaulted ceiling. "Wow!" Lauren stared up at the rafters taking in the massive wooden beams that carried the weight of the entire structure. "Gorgeous," she said. "I can't believe you did this all in a year."

"Me either," Luke answered, "but like I said, I was obsessed."

The great room was clearly the heart of the house. At the far end of the space was a kitchen, one that Lauren had to admit, almost appeared as if it should grace the cover of an architectural magazine. Luke's sense of design seemed familiar and comforting, but he also had an eye for beauty and simplicity. The kitchen was not sterile, but full of warmth which emanated from the honey and cinnamon tones of the maple cupboards that lined the wall. The appliances were enclosed by a large island with ample counter space made of the same concrete as Lauren's kitchen. She ran her fingers over the smoothest most polished concrete she had ever seen.

Toward the south end of the great space, the living room centered around an over sized window that opened the room to the forest. A brown leather couch with an antelope pelt draped over the back faced the window and there was a built in window seat that Lauren imagined would make a person feel like they were sitting directly in the forest. Through a small break in the trees, one could just make out the blue surface of Vernonia Lake.

"Can you see the stars?"

"When it's not foggy, you can see the stars almost as clear as day."

"Luke, this is really something else…like living in a fairy tale."

"I lived here as a kid." The nuance of his admission interrupted her thoughts.

"How could you live in a place you just built?" She stood now at the window looking toward the setting sun over the lake.

"Not this cabin, but the land. The property belonged to my grandparents. They had an old fishing cabin here and when Mom got pregnant with me, they let her move here, where she was out of the way, I guess. Old rickety thing,…falling apart half the time."

Lauren frowned, as she grasped a sense of what it must have been like to be an unwed mother in the 1970s, especially in a small church community. "I'm sorry for both you and Gloria. It must have been alienating."

Luke chuckled. "Are you kidding? It was great! I got to grow up in the woods, fishing and hunting. My uncle would come out every once in awhile and show me something new. One time he gave me a slingshot and taught me how to make traps for squirrels and rabbits. Mom let me explore and figure stuff out on my own. I couldn't have asked for a better childhood. It's why I wanted to come back here. It always felt like home."

"And for Gloria?"

"I think she was pretty lonely. She stayed single for a long time. She wasn't bad looking either so it surprised people. I don't think she really started dating till I was in high school and then met Harrold. Now, she's not alone anymore. I have to say, I'm happy for her. She was a good mom to me even when it wasn't easy."

"Yes, she was." Lauren said softly. "Sounds like she always put you first."

Luke set the bottle of wine on the table and opened a cupboard. He emerged with two wine glasses and a bottle opener. "For the most part, she did." Luke gestured toward the wine. "I'm taking some supplies with us." He wrapped the bottle and glasses in a dish towel and placed them gingerly in a leather knapsack.

"We're not staying here? Are we going to do the stake out in the font yard?"

Luke's eyes were bright. "Even better. Zip up that jacket."

The sun was almost fully set as Lauren followed Luke behind the cabin further up the hill on the deer path. She watched her feet carefully over the moss, rocks and tree roots under the waning light. As they walked through patches of fog, she shivered under her coat. At the crest of the hill, the forest seemed to illuminate before her eyes. Luke walked ahead of her, but he turned and grabbed her hand to help her up a sharp incline marred by exposed tree roots. On the other side of the swelling was a large tree filled with light. On second glance, Lauren recognized a tree house strung with white Christmas lights.

"Oh wow," Lauren whispered under the soft glow of warm white light.

"When I was a kid, it was just a few boards nailed into the trunk and tree branches, but after the cabin was finished I gave it a bit of a remodel."

"Yes, you sure did." Lauren was completely awestruck as she gazed upward. "It has window shutters and a little door. It's the sweetest thing I've ever seen."

Luke smiled, pleased. "Glad you like it. You want to do the honors and climb first?"

Lauren frowned and then teased. "I'm not so sure. I haven't had good luck with ladders when you're around."

Luke chuckled. "I think you got it wrong. If you're on a ladder it's best if I am around, don't you think?"

"I can't argue with that," she laughed.

The ascent up the trunk of the tree was long. The great oak tree was nearly a 100 feet tall and the house itself was nestled in its branches. Lauren was careful with her footing and glad for the hand railings on both sides of the ladder that made her climb up the trunk easier with only the Christmas lights to illuminate her way.

Once inside, the excitement overwhelmed her. All four sides of the cabin contained a great window that provided views of the lake, the forest, and the city of Vernonia in the valley below. The roof boasted a skylight that opened to the starry sky, filling the room with moonlight. The furniture was sparse, but included a shag rug and several plush bean bags. In one small corner was a book shelf filled with books and other knickknacks.

Luke entered the room a moment later with a cautious smile. "What do ya think?"

"Wow, just...Wow! This is incredible! I wish I could go back in time to when I was a kid. This would have been absolute heaven."

"I built it with my Uncle when I was 14, but there have been some renovations since then."

"I don't think I ever want to leave," Lauren said as she ran her fingers across the wooden bookshelf and then turned toward the open window.

"You think that, until nature calls," Luke chuckled. "Inside plumbing is a bit of a challenge for a structure like this one."

"I can imagine." Lauren found a spot on the rug and collapsed against the bean bag. She gazed upward into the skylight at the stars that now sparkled through the clearing between puffy white clouds. The moon was incandescent and brightened both the sky and forest.

"I think you can see everything from here."

Luke eased his way next to her on the carpet, propping himself up on the bean bag and pulled the wine and glasses from his leather knapsack. "That's the idea. It's the perfect place for a stakeout. We can see people coming and going through the woods and I brought these." He pulled out a pair of binoculars from his knapsack.

"You didn't? I'm beginning to feel like we're in an old movie, just like Rear Window?"

"Jimmy Stewart and Grace Kelly?"

"The very one."

"That's a classic Hitchcock film. I think it's exactly the vibe we're going for." He handed her the glass and poured. Lauren took a cautious sip. He was right. The wine was good and warmed her throat and chest.

They sat in silence for a few moments, watching the stars, the binoculars flat against her chest and Luke stretched beside her, their heads sharing the same bean bag. She felt the urge to lean into him, but wasn't sure she was ready for what might happen if she did.

"I'm sorry," he whispered.

She turned on her side toward him. "Sorry for what?"

"It wasn't fair of me to expect you to be over him. I was upset at you for grieving for your own husband. I wanted you to myself."

"Marcus?"

"Yeah. He turned toward her now. They were eye to eye. "It's totally natural to be stuck on him. I just didn't know what to do with it. When you've been with a person who cheats, you feel like a second class citizen. You never feel like you're the first choice. I didn't ever want to feel that way with a woman again, the way I felt with Bridget. I was a little too hard on you for just being human. I should have thought about what it's like for you, losing a spouse. All I'm saying is, it's natural, it's okay that you're not ready...that you still love him."

Lauren's face was hot. "Luke, you should never have been made to feel like a second class citizen. You're honestly...awesome. Bridget didn't know what she had." She reached her hand toward him without thinking and touched his cheek lightly with her fingertips.

His eyes searched her face and he covered her hand with his own and moved it to his mouth. He kissed the soft skin of her wrist as his eyes searched hers.

Her lips parted in a surprised breath and then his mouth covered hers. They kissed for a minute before Lauren broke away. She pulled her face away from his and settled her head on his chest.

He stroked her hair gently and they were silent.

"Did you really mean it?"

"Mean what?"

"That we could go as slow as molasses."

"I meant it," he said softly. "I'm pretty sure you're worth the wait." He rested his thumb across her chin and lifted her face to his.

The intimacy overwhelmed her as the heat flooded her cheeks, but she couldn't suppress the pleased smile. She tried to conceal it by burying her head into his chest. He allowed her to hide there for awhile. They did not stay there long. Lauren rose to her feet. "I think it's time to get this stake out going." She handed Luke the binoculars. "How are we going to do this?"

His forehead creased in thought. "I'll take the south window facing town. Do you want to take the west window facing the parsonage? That way we'll see anyone walking from your house and we'll see where they go."

They stared out the tree house windows into the night. Lauren still felt the warmth of his kiss and her thoughts were racing. *Am I ready for a relationship with Luke?* Parts of her felt beyond ready to leave the chapters of sadness and grief behind her. Marcus had released her in the cave from the guilt of that night, but she knew that he was still with her, would always be with her. She was not sure if losing him would cast a forever shadow on her life, if his loss would rob her of any joy with another partner. She forced her thoughts back to the moment. "What do you see?"

"Nothing right now." He narrowed his eyes as he brought the binoculars back to his forehead.

What was Luke thinking right now? From the corner of her eye she watched him as he stared through the trees. He was different from Marcus in almost every way. Where Marcus was spontaneous, Luke was steady. Where Marcus craved the limelight, Luke retreated into nature. At this season in her life, Lauren needed stability, someone steady. She needed Luke. Before, she had blamed him for their attraction. Who was she kidding? She was as much responsible as he was. Lauren was in love with him. The realization coursed through her like lightning.

"Lauren," Luke whispered. "Get over here."

She hurried to his side. He placed the binoculars in her hand. "Over there!"

Chapter 22

The Lord is near to all who call on him,
to all who call on him in truth.
—Psalm 145:18

Truth Seekers

Lauren gazed blindly into the forest. At first she saw only the outline of firs against the night sky. Through the moonlight she could barely decipher a figure shuffling forward on the path. The chill traveled up her spine. "Is it her?"

"You tell me?" He handed her the binoculars. She pressed the frames to her forehead and adjusted the dial to focus the lens. Her eyes were drawn to the gaps of moonlight between dark trees, but she spotted the movement of a dark stooping form with wild hair. The black caped figure darted doggedly along the path.

"It's her," Lauren said, struggling to make her voice audible through the tightening of her throat. "What do we do next?"

"Come on." Luke gestured toward the ladder.

"Where are we going?"

"We follow her?"

"Luke, are you mad?" She shook her head in protest.

"We'll keep a safe distance," he assured her. Luke's first action when they arrived was to turn off the Christmas lights so the sky was revealed in all its celestial glory. The cover of darkness was also needed for a stakeout. Lauren had no desire whatsoever to climb down a dark ladder in the pitch black of night. She followed Luke, muttering slightly to herself in frustration. The moon's glow provided enough light to see each rung and she was grateful at least for that. *What was he thinking? Traipsing after a crazy woman in the middle of the night?* Yet, she also was itching to know who this woman was. She wasn't sure she could spend any more time in the dark. Her deepest need was to know the truth about this woman and why she had pushed her. She needed to know why.

Luke was waiting for her on the ground. As she turned from the ladder to face him, he offered his hand. He held a finger to his lips cautioning her to stay quiet. She took the hand he offered and soon they were moving swiftly through the woods parallel to the path. Lauren could not see their quarry, but Luke led with confidence. *He knew this forest like his own blood,* she realized. No doubt he had combed every square foot as a boy. He seemed to know instinctively the location of every overgrown root and branch even off path.

"Do you see her?" she whispered.

"I can just make her out. She's headed for town."

Lauren glanced at her smartwatch. *Where was this woman going at 1:27 in the middle of the night?* Curiosity overrode her fear. Every person has a story. *What is wild woman's story? How did she get to this time, this place, this condition?* Despite her fear and anger toward the woman, Lauren felt a sudden compassion. She prayed silently in her head. *Please, Lord, I don't know her situation, but help her. Lead her to a place of clear thinking and peace. Help her, wherever she is at. I pray that she would no longer be the cause of violence and chaos.*

They were descending from the woods now, into town. Lauren could see street lights through the branches as they followed the main path into Vernonia. Luke stopped every once in a while to make sure they were a safe distance away and out of sight. They were walking quietly now. Luke laced his fingers through hers to reassure her and Lauren admitted to herself she was no longer afraid, but still highly alert. She was conscious of every breath, determined to bring no attention whatsoever to herself that might alert their target. A mist curled into the low spaces of the valley and Lauren could see the woman walking down Main street under the shadows made almost cinematic by glowing street lamps. They followed behind staying to the side of the road under cover of store fronts. The dark figure veered suddenly to the left.

Luke held her hand tightly and moved her toward a dark corner in the direction where wild woman had disappeared. They stayed there for a minute. His eyes were focused and intense and Lauren noted the tightness around the corners of his mouth as he followed her path with his eyes. "Come on," he whispered.

They scampered across the street like thieves. Lauren was hunched forward with her eyes to the pavement. They moved in this fashion for about a hundred feet before they met the property line of some business. Luke cut through the manicured lawn and they found sanctuary in an overgrown rhododendron garden. Lauren could just make out the woman, scampering toward the building. They watched from their refuge as she made her way toward the back of the structure. She climbed a makeshift ladder and then crawled into a window.

"What is this place?" Lauren whispered.

They moved out into the open toward the front of the building. Lauren noticed a plaque on the side on the left of the front entrance identifying the facility: *Vernonia Mental Health Treatment Center.*

"She's a patient here," Luke said in a hushed whisper.

"She's sneaking out. How is she getting away with it? Places like this do routine checks."

"Ruth is smart," Luke said absently.

"Ruth?"

He sighed. "Let's get some coffee at the 24 hour Diner. It's time to tell you what I know."

* * *

Lauren was grateful for the coffee, and took off her gloves to feel the warmth on her freezing fingers. She eyed Luke with eager anticipation. There were so many questions and she hoped to God he had answers. "Ruth...?" she pressed as she stared intently at his deep set eyes from across the booth. She brought the steaming mug to her lips and blew on liquid that was too hot to drink.

"Ruth..," Luke sighed the name. "Where do I begin? To be honest, I think I told you a little about her already. I grew up with her in the church. She was June and Porter's daughter."

"That woman is June and Porter's daughter?"

He raised his eyebrows. "Yep, I know. That's why I wanted to be sure."

"When did you first suspect...?"

"I thought I saw her from the corner of my eye that first Sunday in church. That was your first Sunday. I didn't recognize her exactly, but I noticed a large woman in the back and I just thought there was something familiar about her. But...I didn't really put two and two together till we found Sydney and all the stuff in the church. I just realized whoever was living in the church was reading books and so quiet, the way she used to be. When we were kids, Ruth was like a spy. She could conceal herself for hours and no one could find her. That girl knew every hiding place in that church. It was her refuge from June and Porter I think. One day they couldn't find her and there was a bit of a panic after service. Everyone searched for hours, yelling her name all over the place. She came out a few hours later. She wouldn't tell anyone where she was hiding, wasn't a lick sorry for freaking out the entire congregation. June and Porter were fit to be tied."

Lauren's mouth tightened into a frown. "Are you saying that on that Sunday when she was in church, June was sitting in the service with her own daughter and didn't even acknowledge her?"

Luke nodded slowly as he considered it. "I didn't acknowledge her either. I didn't recognize her. The question would be does June still visit her and keep contact or are they estranged? If they have frequent contact then I'd say she would have recognized her for sure and was deliberately ignoring her, but if she hasn't seen her in years, then maybe not."

246

"Do you think it's possible her daughter would be in a treatment center in the same town, possibly for years, and she wouldn't visit her? That she doesn't know she's here?"

"We are talking about June? She doesn't have a high score on the empathy scale."

A heaviness settled in her chest. "That's just so sad."

He raised his eyebrows. "You don't understand. If that woman is Ruth, she has made a complete transformation. She doesn't look at all like the Ruth I remember. For one, she's a lot heavier. Ruth, when she was a girl, was neat as a pin—always wore her hair in braids. June kept her that way. She always wore dresses and those little black shoes with the straps."

"Mary Janes?"

"Like a doll." Luke continued. "She wasn't a happy camper. Always had her nose in a book or hiding from her mom and dad. But, she was nice to me. We grew up together—Basically the only kids in the church for quite awhile, but then eventually June and Porter left. It was the last I heard of Ruth, but we got news of her every once in awhile through the grapevine. She was a lot smaller than the woman we saw today, not exactly thin, but tall and wiry."

"Did you hear about her struggles with mental health?"

"Not exactly. Just during high school, a friend of mom's said she was into drugs and alcohol. We didn't know much, but just that there was some trouble. When Porter and June came back to church, Ruth was an adult, had moved on. They were just another nice retired couple with grown children living their lives. I only saw them on the occasional Sunday I visited mom, on holidays and special occasions when I was with Bridget. June and Porter never talked about her."

"Never?"

"NEVER!"

"Did you ever ask them directly about Ruth?"

"Yeah. I would always ask how she was doing and to say hello for me. That kind of thing."

"What would June say?"

"Oh, just the typical throw away responses like, "She's got a job in Portland and I'll let her know you asked about her. I could tell she didn't want any more questions."

"What about your mom? Do you think she knows more?"

"Well, it's possible. Mom does know a lot about other people's business. She's also real good about keeping secrets. That's why she knows what she knows. She doesn't betray a confidence."

"She doesn't care much for June, though? It's hard to imagine June confiding in her...But if she knew something, do you think she would tell us more about Ruth? It's going to come out anyway. We have to tell Officer Torrence and the hospital needs to know she's sneaking out and getting into trouble."

He frowned as he stared into his coffee. "If it was a matter of safety, Mom would tell you whatever you needed to know." Luke stared out the window. "It's kind of depressing," he muttered. "I would have hoped for a much better life for Ruth."

"Yes, it's horrible," Lauren agreed. "Luke, what's the right thing to do in this situation? Do we talk to June? She probably should know her daughter's wreaking havoc on the town of Vernonia."

He managed a half smile and his eyes brightened. "Well, I don't think we need to tell her quite like that."

Lauren sighed. "Unfortunately, it's not just a matter for the police. June is a member of our congregation. I have a personal duty as her minister to talk to her, pray for her, help if I can."

Luke raised his eyebrows in surprise. "Up to this point how receptive has June been to your efforts to help her?"

"Not very," Lauren admitted.

"So what's going to change now?"

"I really don't know. I guess my hope is that she'll see she's not alone that she doesn't have to keep Ruth a secret anymore. Maybe it will give her some relief? Maybe this explains why she is the way she it,...so hostile and angry."

Luke stared at her, his eyes wide with meaning. "You think your involvement in her life will help?"

"Okay, Okay. I get your point. Maybe my involvement isn't going to stir a revelation in her soul, but I do think reaching out and trying to have a conversation, a private, caring one, is the right thing to do. That's all I'm thinking."

"The right thing for her or for you?"

They sat in silence for a few minutes. Lauren was suddenly overwhelmed by fatigue. The night's events had been almost too much. "Luke, I don't think I can walk all the way home. Your truck is at my place. That's nearly a three mile hike mostly uphill."

"I think it's closer to four miles, but I was thinking about that. Don't worry I have a plan."

About 20 minutes later, Paul walked into the diner a broad smile on his face. "You two are up a little early aren't you? Did your car break down?"

Luke rose from the booth and shook his hand. "Thanks for coming to get us. We've been up all night. We were hiking."

"Ah, to be young again," Paul said.

"Go ahead and have a seat for a few. We're still finishing the last few drops of our coffee." Luke sat back down and slid to the far end of the booth to make room for Paul.

The older man eased his way into the booth, wincing slightly as he seated himself next to Luke. "Up all night, huh? Well, I hope you had fun?" Paul offered Lauren a wide smile highlighting the whites of his teeth.

"We had an eventful evening," Luke said dryly, but I think we're both about ready to crash. Thanks for offering us the ride."

"No problem. I love getting calls from you early in the morning. I'm up every day at 5 at the latest and these days sometimes even earlier. I'm glad to help."

"Am I detecting a little sarcasm?" Luke laughed.

"No not at all. I just have to give you a little bit of a hard time, for fun." Paul looked directly at Lauren. "I suppose you've heard the news about me and Vivian?"

"Yes," Lauren nodded through her fatigue. "I'm happy for you, Paul. Really I am. Sydney's over the moon."

He brought his hand to his forehead in relief. "Phew! I was worried. I had a feeling we had Sydney's okay, but I didn't know if you'd approve."

"Mom is a lucky woman," Lauren said softly. "You know she's a handful. You're going to have to be kind, but also tough." She bit her lip afraid she had said too much.

"Don't I know it," Paul chuckled. "I'm not naive, I know she's had her struggles and so have I if I'm being honest. You don't get to be our age without a pound of baggage, but Pastor Westbrook, when you find another person who makes you laugh and experience real joy, I think you've found something special."

Lauren couldn't suppress the smile. "Yes, I think you're right. You make her happy and I'm glad for both of you. Now that we're going to be family, you need to drop the Pastor Westbrook thing. Just call me Lauren."

Paul nodded. "That's going to be tough. Will do, Lauren."

A waitress stopped at their table and Paul ordered coffee in a "to go" cup. "For the road," he said to Luke. "Since you have me up at the crack of dawn."

"We want you fully alert for the drive, so go right ahead," Luke said.

Lauren frowned into her own coffee which was now lukewarm. "Paul, do you know much about the mental health clinic down the road from here?"

"The Mental Health Center?" Paul shrugged. "Not much...hmm...It's a newer facility, been here for about ten years or so. I've heard that they are pretty full, not a lot of empty beds. Why?"

"Luke and I noticed the facility as we were walking tonight and realized that we didn't know much about it? Do you know what kind of patients live there, whether they're violent?"

Paul shook his head. "There's both an in treatment and out treatment center. Never heard of a violent incident, although during COVID they did have an outbreak that was in the local news for awhile, but that was people getting sick. There is a a drug and alcohol treatment center and a wing dedicated to mental health conditions. That's about all I know, but do you know who knows everything about it?"

"Who?"

"Linda. She used to work there. I think she was there a couple years before she retired. Everything I know about the place is from things she's told me from working there."

"Are you thinking about doing a pastoral visit?"

Despite her exhaustion, Lauren's mind awakened. "Something like that." She gave Paul a beaming smile.

* * *

"Mom!" Sydney whined. "Can you make breakfast? Nana already left."

Lauren groaned. "Oh Sydney, I'm so tired. Can't you give your mom maybe another half hour to sleep?"

"It's almost noon!" Sydney wailed.

"Seriously?" She had hoped to sleep a few hours and then still make the most of the afternoon, but the day had already gotten ahead of her. She went through her mental checklist: She wanted to see Linda and was planning to call June.

"Ok. I'll make you breakfast. Would you go to Linda's with me? I need to see her for a few minutes."

"I will, if you agree to take me to Dairy Queen."

Lauren threw her pillow playfully at Sydney. "You are such a pill. Everything's a negotiation with you and I'm too tired to argue. When did you get so mouthy?"

"I learned from the best!" Sydney said with a smile.

"I never taught you to wheel n deal. I taught you to be a respectful, obedient child!"

"I was talking about Nana."

"Never mind. Now it all makes sense," Lauren teased.

She made a quick meal of bacon and eggs and they were out the door to Linda's. As they passed the church, she was suddenly overwhelmed by the feeling that she had forgotten something, something very important. She stepped on the brake and allowed the car to idle in front of the sanctuary entrance.

"Mom, what are you doing? Aren't we going to Linda's?"

"I have a weird feeling like I'm missing something."

"What did you forget?"

"I don't know. That's why I'm giving myself a moment to think. So hush, and let me think." Lauren stared at the church through the hum of her car engine. So much had changed in the months since her arrival. She was looking at a church that no longer looked like a forgotten relic. Metal scaffolding was set up on the north east side to accommodate the painters who were giving the exterior a bit of a face lift. The windows looked clean and the church now had a lived in appearance. Lauren felt a sense of amazement. "Syd?"

"Yes, Mom!"

"What did you see under the pulpit in that room?"

Sydney suddenly became animated. "There were tons of cans of tuna fish."

"Tuna fish?"

"Yeah, some empty and some that hadn't been opened. It smelled bad, like that lady with all the cats."

"You mean that lady from our old church?"

"Yeah, the one that Dad would visit and sometimes buy groceries for."

"Mrs. Wilson?"

"Yeah, that's the lady."

"What else?"

"There were tons of books? Actually a book shelf with a bunch of books."

"What kind of books?"

"Mostly like the ones you try to read me. The ones that have gold on them and kind of look like Bibles."

Lauren frowned. "Do you mean like classic literature books?"

"I think so. Like those books you used to read to me in the summer. They looked a little like that Robinson Cooso book you tried to read to me."

"Robinson Crusoe. Sydney, that's a classic."

"Classically boring."

Lauren glared at her playfully. "Anything else you remember?"

"Just that it was kind of dirty. There was a mat with a blanket and a gray looking pillow. It smelled gross because of the tuna and there were some pictures?"

"Pictures?"

"Yeah, like old photos or something."

"Do you know who was in the pictures?"

Sydney shrugged. "Not really. The pictures were either black and white or they kind of had that yellow, old look."

Lauren felt her heart racing, but she wasn't sure why. "Let's stop in and take a look? What do you say?"

"Do we have to? I want ice cream."

"I never got to look at the hiding place. So I'm kind of curious. We can have our own little adventure."

"Okay," Sydney agreed reluctantly.

Lauren followed her daughter into the sanctuary toward the stairs that led to the pulpit. She had never noticed what looked like a cupboard at the side of the stairs. "It looks like a cubby. I don't see a handle."

"There isn't one. You have to pull it out," Sydney said. Her daughter, with her small fingers was easily able to grasp a hold of the handle-less door and open it. The wood cut out opened to Sydney's pulling and revealed a dark hole.

"Weren't you scared to go in there? I can't believe you would have the nerve to go into such a dark, creepy space. Syd, promise me you'll never do something like that again!"

"I won't. It was kind of scary, but I just had to know what was in there. Mom, don't you ever get curious, so curious that you just can't help yourself?"

Lauren groaned in response. "Your mom here almost died in a cave, so I get it. I'm curious too. That's why we both have to learn to control some of our impulses. You know what people say about curiosity?"

"No."

"Curiosity killed the cat."

"What does that mean?"

"It means that sometimes our curiosity can lead us into danger."

Sydney frowned as she thought. "I guess that makes sense. We're here alone in the church. Maybe you should let someone know we're here, Mom?"

"Point taken. Good call," Lauren agreed.

She grabbed her phone from her jean's pocket and called Luke. He did not pick up. "Sorry to bug you, Luke. Syd and I are in the church and we're taking a look at the crawl space under the sanctuary. I've got my phone, but I wanted someone to know where we are. Both Syd and I are trying to be safer. Okay. That's it. Call me when you get a chance."

Sydney got on her knees and was about to crawl under the stairs. Lauren stopped her. "Syd, I'm going first. We're not sure what's in there."

"Do you think she's in there?" Sydney whispered.

"I doubt it. I think she knows her hiding place was found out since the police were here." Lauren did not want to mention that she had seen Ruth return home in the middle of the night a few short hours ago, so it was highly unlikely she could return in such a time frame on foot. She traced her finger over her phone's screen to activate the flashlight and crawled forward. The space opened into a room under the pulpit. From floor to ceiling it was only about four feet in height, but was spacious in terms of width, nearly 1000 square feet by the looks of it. Through her flashlight she could see wadded bedding, a bookshelf with books dispersed across the floor, and open cans scattered all over the space. The police had taken a few samples for evidence, but since the room had not been technically linked to a crime, it had been left mostly in tact. Lauren brought her arm over her nose. The fishy smell of tuna was almost overwhelming in the small space.

"Syd, stay toward the corner. I don't want you to touch any of the bedding, okay?"

"Don't worry. I won't. Gross!"

"Where's the door to the outside?"

"Just keep going straight."

Lauren crawled forward to a place where the room narrowed into a hallway and she saw shafts of light. *I must be past the pulpit now beneath the side room, the changing room for the baptismal,* she thought. It was a small add on partition built at the side of the church.

Lauren found the light and pushed on the vent. It opened without too much urging and she was momentarily blinded by the sun. She was standing outside the church in the far corner of the building. If she continued to walk, she would be covered in trees and forest within seconds and then one could travel to the Lake, town, or Bank's trail undiscovered under the veil of forest.

Sydney crawled out behind her. "Isn't it cool, Mom?"

"It's wild," Lauren said. "I can't wrap my head around the fact that someone was basically living underneath the very spot I was preaching every Sunday."

"And eating lots of tuna fish," Sydney added helpfully.

"I can't believe I didn't smell it."

Lauren stared out into the green of forest, her mind scattered with incoherent fragments of thought. *Why did Ruth come here? After so many years, why did she decide to hide in the church? Was she just so far gone mentally that she had become a creature of old habits? Perhaps memories of her childhood called her here, a place she felt safe? Or was it something else?*

Lauren remembered her face and was haunted by the image. The day she was lost in the woods, Ruth had opened her mouth showing her rotten teeth. Lauren thought she was about to scream. *Was she actually screaming or had Lauren misread the situation? Was she trying to tell her something?* The image was terrifying, but there was also something unresolved, a mystery she now felt desperate to uncover.

Lauren turned back toward the dark room and with the light from the vent now shining through the blackened tunnel into the dark room, a bulky shape caught her eye. Gradually her vision adjusted and she saw what looked like a shrine in the corner of the room. A space with a small makeshift table made from concrete cinders and on top of it an array of framed photos. Luke had not mentioned the pictures.

"Syd stay here for a sec." She ducked and crawled back into the tunnel her phone flashlight in hand if needed.

Lauren made her way to the shrine and shone her phone flashlight over its contents. She picked up the first framed photo and held it under the light. An involuntary gasp escaped her lips. She recognized the picture of an older man holding a little girl in his lap. The girl held the doll with it's petticoat and little Mary Jane shoes. Lauren felt a sudden fear, similar to the one she felt when she first saw the picture in the church attic. "Sydney? Where are you?"

"Mom, I'm outside, do you want me to come back in?"

"No!" Lauren called. "Why don't you stay out there and just keep an eye out for anyone."

"Can I go to the swings?"

"Yes. I'll be out in a minute."

She directed her attention back to the picture and scrutinized it carefully. The man was Pastor Worth and the handwritten inscription still identified him. There was a familiar quality to the girl. Her eyes were striking, unusually deep set and a light color, blue or green. The faded photo and poor light made it difficult to be sure, but Lauren knew they were blue because she had seen the eyes herself in the woods near the cave. *This was Ruth as a child.* Luke told her that she had looked "as neat as a pin" and Lauren could see that in the photo. The child was beautiful, but there was a vacant quality in her expression. Lauren had not noticed at first, but the child looked strangely detached. Physically she was posing for a picture with her pastor, but her mind was far away.

Lauren examined the other photos under the light. Another one was of a couple standing outside the church. They were younger for sure, but Lauren recognized June and Porter staring into the lens. June stood upright with perfect posture. She wore a chic sports jacket with flared jeans and stared at the camera with the trademark haughtiness Lauren recognized. Porter stood next to her in suit and tie, his smile more reserved, a coldness in his eyes that seemed out of character to the smiling man she saw every week in church. She concluded from the photo that back then they were the epitome of the cool church couple, if there was such a thing. The kind of people in a congregation who had status, power and influence.

She placed the framed photo carefully back down on the cinder block and picked up the third picture, another 5 by 7 in a silver frame. The photo was once again of Pastor Worth this time standing in the church sanctuary and holding the hands of two children. Lauren recognized the same beautiful girl with dark curls and deep set eyes. On the other side of Pastor Worth was a little boy. Lauren ran her forefinger across the boy's face. She recognized him as well, the mischievous grin, intelligent and thoughtful eyes, and the lighter sandy hair. *Luke! He's adorable. There was nothing from the photo that did not match exactly what Luke had told her. He and Ruth had grown up together in the church. They were the only kids for a while. She smiled again as she looked at they boy's face, but something was off about the photo.* Lauren wasn't exactly sure what she was picking up on. She set the photo down.

Luke must have meant a lot to Ruth if she kept his photo. The pictures looked worn like she spent time looking at them. Lauren sensed there was more here, but she couldn't figure it out. The smell of tuna combined with the cramped space was becoming unbearable and Lauren made her way outside back to the door anxious to leave Ruth's hidden room behind her.

Chapter 23

These things God has revealed to us through the Spirit.
For the Spirit searches everything,
even the depths of God.
—1 Corinthians 2:10

Shot in the Dark

Lauren sat on Linda's floral patterned couch sipping hibiscus tea.

"Oh Pastor Westbrook, I can't even tell you how much you've been on my mind. I'm so glad you decided to visit. How are you?"

"I'm good," Lauren insisted. "I'm healing pretty well and honestly taking a couple weeks off from preaching has been a nice break."

"Good for you. And much deserved." Linda walked from her kitchen and sat across from her on the matching floral love seat, placing her own cup of tea on the coffee table in front of her. "Just when everything seemed to be going well, the enemy throws a wrench into the good work. I can't help but think it's a spiritual attack and that's why I've been praying for you especially hard."

"Thank you, Linda. I really appreciate that."

"You want any cream in that tea? I have a little milk frother that will blend it up really nice almost like a latte."

"Oh, that sounds lovely, but no thanks. Actually, I came over with a question. I hope you don't mind?"

"Of course not. Ask away."

"I don't know if you've noticed her before, but there's a woman who has visited our church a few times. She looks kind of rough."

"Are you referring to the person who has been living underneath the church?"

"I guess the rumor has spread then?"

"I would say so. Most of us were out looking for Sydney that night she went missing. Then you got lost too. It's not an evening any of us will forget anytime soon. When Luke found Sydney she was talking a mile a minute about what she found in that room down there. Anyone who was there looking for her, which was half the church, heard all of it. People were just getting riled up about the intruder, and then we got the news that we lost you and everyone's attention got redirected toward another search and rescue. Now that you're both okay, I can safely say it was the most exciting night this town has had in recent memory."

"Well I guess I'm good for something,"

"No, I'm sorry," Linda said. "I know it must have been a living nightmare for you, missing your daughter and then being attacked. We were all worried sick. Anyway, I didn't want to get into all that. Go back to your story. What were you trying to tell me about the woman?"

Lauren chose her words carefully. "She's a patient at the Vernonia Mental Health Center. Paul told me you used to work there?"

Linda's eyes widened in surprise. "I did. I retired a few years ago from nursing all together, but I ended my career there. I worked at the hospital in the emergency room for years and someone convinced me at the time that the Mental Health Center would be a nice change of pace."

"That wasn't the case?"

Linda chuckled. "Well, not quite. I worked in the emergency room at the hospital, but that's a whole different bag of potatoes than a Mental Health wing. I had never worked exclusively with patients with non verbal autism, schizophrenia, or bipolar disorder before. All I can say is, it wasn't boring."

"Do you know the woman I'm referring to? She's been to church at least one time that I know of and was also at the yard sale. She has wild hair and wears a big rain jacket."

"You mean Ruth, don't you?"

Lauren's mouth opened wide. "You know Ruth?"

"Course I do. I'm not supposed to speak about former patients because of confidentiality rules, but she was one of my patients at the Center. For the record, I only saw her one time at church around the time you first got here if I recall correctly."

"Linda, I have reason to believe that she's the one who's been living underneath the church?"

Linda frowned and shook her head. "No, that's not possible."

"Why do you say that?"

"She was under constant supervision. At least when I was there. Pastor Westbrook, this is all off the record, okay? I know I'm retired, but I'm not totally comfortable discussing patients. Without going into specifics, I will say she had a condition that made it unsafe for her to be on her own."

"Was it a condition that could make a person violent?"

Linda's eyes narrowed in thought as she chose her words carefully. "There were many clients at that facility who needed to stay on medication in order to counteract paranoid and violent thoughts and behaviors. Unfortunately, the patients with such conditions were often the most resistant to taking their meds." Linda raised her eyebrows for emphasis.

"I see. Thank you, Linda. This is more helpful than you know. Did you think it was strange when you saw her at church?"

"I noticed her when I was playing the piano just the one time. She didn't stay very long, but left before I had time to say boo to her. In that moment, I figured she must be doing very well. Patients are allowed to go on field trips and outings when they are regulated and taking their meds. I assumed that she must have made significant strides since my days at the Center, maybe even moved to a group home environment since she didn't have any immediate family. It has been a few years since I last saw her. I assumed she came to church with a licensed caretaker, but there was something off about her."

"Off?"

"She didn't look good. Her hair was wild and uncombed and she just didn't look like she was taking care of herself." Linda sat her tea cup down and then dropped her hands on her lap suddenly. "Oh Lauren, you think she's the one who pushed you, don't you? I should have told someone or called the Center when I saw her, but it never even entered my mind that she could be a runaway, but it seems so obvious now. Oh goodness."

"Linda, I know she's the one who pushed me. Luke and I followed her from the church and we saw her entering the window of the Mental Health Center in the middle of the night. For her own safety, I called The Center anonymously and let them know I saw her climbing in through the window. I didn't tell them she pushed me. I'm not sure I want to turn her into the police either, especially now that I know about her mental health. I don't believe she meant to hurt me, but the care at the facility has been negligent. It's hard to believe that she could be gone for hours without anyone noticing."

"Goodness. They're going to put her on really heavy meds now. The truth is, Ruth is smart enough to know her caretaker's rounds like the back of her head. It's outlandish, but not impossible that she was sneaking in and out for a long time."

Lauren clasped her hands together. "Do you know much about her background?"

Linda shook her head. "Not that much. What I did know was such a sad story. No one ever visited that girl. According to the other staff, her family abandoned her as a young woman. They couldn't handle the erratic and violent outbursts. I guess there was an incident where Ruth ran away from home. She was gone for weeks and weeks. The family was frantic. They finally found her on the street, completely out of her mind. At that point, they realized they were in over their heads and turned her over to the State and that was the last Ruth ever saw of them. By the time she arrived at the Center she had already lived in numerous facilities."

"Is that an unusual story for patients in the home?"

"There's some that never do get visitors, but most do. Families realize that once their loved ones are getting quality care and medication, they can return to some semblance of normality again, at least have a relationship. When Ruth was medicated and in her routines, she was lovely and incredibly bright. She loved books and music. I was rather fond of her. I used to share my book club books with her. She loved them and would even discuss the plot and characters with me."

"Linda, can you think of any reason why Ruth would hide in our church? Why she would come here?"

Her eyes widened in surprise. "No. Maybe she was drawn to the music or just wanted a place where she could be by herself?"

"You don't know of any connection she has to anyone in the church?"

"Like I said, she had no family."

"But you think she was mentally aware of herself and her surroundings?"

Linda leaned back into the love seat and exhaled sharply. "Ruth suffers from paranoid schizophrenia and has had some catatonic episodes as well. When she was off her meds, she could be paranoid, violent, irrational, hysterical even. There were even hallucinations, but it wasn't like she didn't know who people were or didn't understand what you were saying to her. She had what I liked to call an intelligent kind of mental illness, if that makes sense? Almost like you become so hyper aware of everything that you're aware to an extreme. As an example, most of us are aware of hostility and kindness, but Ruth was overly aware. So, if someone glared at her, in her mind, she might believe she was actually physically assaulted. You act in extremes, if that makes sense. That might explain why she pushed you. She may have thought you were a threat to her in a state of paranoia."

"I see. But you don't know of any personal connection that she had to this church? Any reason she'd come here?"

Her mouth opened and then closed. "Nothing that I'm aware of."

"Linda, what was the Center's policy on visitation from clergy?"

* * *

262

Luke squeezed her hand gently as they entered The Vernonia Mental Health Center. "Here we go," he whispered.

A receptionist glanced up from her paperwork. "Can I help you?"

Lauren flashed him her ID and visitation card. "I have written permission from the Oregon Chaplain's Association for a clergy visit with one of your patients."

The man nodded as he looked over Lauren's paperwork. "Ruth is in room 102. You just go down the hall to the right. Did Michael, our chaplain, tell you about this patient and what to expect?"

"Yes. He said no sudden movements, calm voice and to leave and let the nurse know immediately if she gets upset."

"Oh good. It's nice that she has a visitor, but she can get agitated. She's also on pretty heavy medication right now. She had an episode recently. so we're taking extra precautions. Normally she's highly verbal, but today she might be pretty out of it."

They walked the hall in silence. Lauren paused at the door and turned to face Luke. "Do you want to go in with me?"

He shook his head. "Based on everything you told me Linda said, I get the feeling if she recognizes me, it might be upsetting for her, but I'll be right outside the door if you need me. You just holler."

"Do you think she'll recognize me? She saw me in the forest and the night of the accident."

"I don't know. That's why I'll be right here if you need me, just to be safe." He squeezed her hand again.

The door was already ajar and Lauren peeked through the crack. Ruth was visible from the side. She was not in bed, but sitting in an armchair facing a dead TV. Her fingers moved in circles as she twirled the strands of hair that framed her face as she mumbled incoherently. Her hair was wild, but a care provider had made the effort to comb it into some semblance of order in the form of a messy bun at the back of her head.

"Hello? Ruth?" Lauren eased her way into the room, but left several feet between herself and the patient.

Ruth swiveled the arm chair slowly in her direction. Lauren stared at her

striking blue, vacant eyes. Her mouth was closed, but Lauren remembered
how Ruth looked that night in the woods when she had searched for Porter
and discovered the doll. Her eyes were wild and the mouth a deep, dark pit.

Lauren fought her fear. "I'm here to visit you. My name is Lauren and I
am a minister at the First Assembly of Disciples Church."

Ruth's eyes lingered on her face for a moment before she swiveled her
chair back toward the dead TV. Lauren could not tell if she was registering
her existence or not. Cautious not to stand between Ruth and the screen,
Lauren walked a few steps toward the center of the room.

"I know you've visited our church a few times. It's a good place to go
when you need help. I'm glad you found your way there and that it's been a
safe place for you. Anyway, I thought we could pray together, if you're okay
with that?"

Ruth mumbled something unintelligible at the TV, but remained calm. She
was under the influence of anti-psychotic medication, so it was impossible
to gauge her clarity of mind. The hospital chaplain warned her that Ruth
might be non verbal, even childlike when he approved her visit.

Lauren dragged a folding chair from the corner a few feet from her arm
chair. "Ruth, what should we pray for today? Is there anything you need?"

Once again her questions were met with silence. Lauren sat quietly for
a few minutes next to Ruth and said nothing while she meditated. She
then said a quick prayer aloud. "Lord, I pray for Ruth. I pray that you will
surround her with your love. Give her sound body and mind. Please give
her peace even in the storm. I pray that she would not feel alone, but feel
your loving presence. Bring good people into her life and restore her. In
your name we pray, Amen."

Lauren lifted her head from the prayer and noticed Ruth staring at her
intently. Lauren met her gaze and offered a smile. Ruth pointed at her
now and spoke. "Mama," she said. "Mama, Mama, Mama...She turned back
toward the TV, but continued to mumble.

"No Ruth. I'm not your mama. I'm Lauren, remember?"

"Mama..."

"I'm a minister, Ruth. I'm here to visit you."

"Mama." Ruth turned toward her again and pointed. This time she made a sudden movement forward and her hand almost touched her chest. "Mama," she whispered.

Lauren forced herself not to back away in fear. Reflexively, she brought her hand to her chest and her fingers traced the ruby ring around her neck, the one June refused to claim. Lauren could not explain why she continued to wear it, but there was a force inside her that spurned to take it off until she unraveled its full mysteries.

"Oh, you see this? Is this your mama's?"

Ruth's eyes were no longer vacant. There was a spark of recognition. Lauren brought her fingers to the back of her neck around the clasp. She struggled with the fastener and finally managed to remove the gold chain. Separating the ring from the chain, she placed it in her palm and handed it slowly toward Ruth.

Ruth's eyes were wide and glassy as she stared at the ring. She spoke more clearly, "Mama."

"I found this near the parsonage. I thought it might be your mama's. Would you like to hold it?"

Ruth didn't answer, but her eyes refused to leave the ring. Lauren gently and slowly reached out for Ruth's hand. "I'm just going to place it in your palm, if you want."

Ruth held the ring now and Lauren saw for the first time a genuine smile. "Mama," she whispered.

Encouraged that Ruth was both calm and more aware, Lauren pressed the conversation. "I..uh... think I found some of your things in the church. I wanted to ask you about them. She rummaged for a moment through her tote bag and revealed the framed photos.

"This is your mama, right?" Lauren held the photo of young June and Porter in her hands and pointed to June.

"Mama," Ruth repeated.

"Such a beautiful mother," Lauren said softly.

"She..., she leave me."

Lauren turned in surprise toward Ruth. Her eyes were different, even

265

more alert as she looked at the photo, like she was emerging from a drug induced sleep.

"I'm so sorry, Ruth," Lauren whispered.

"This is your daddy?" Lauren pointed to Porter.

"No."

"That's not your daddy?"

"No, no Daddy, no Daddy, no, no…." Ruth eyed the other photos on Lauren's lap and reached toward another photo.

Lauren handed it to her.

"Daddy, Daddy" she said.

Ruth held the photo of Pastor Worth with Ruth on his lap and ran her index finger over the man's face. "Daddy," she repeated.

"Oh," Lauren blurted. "This man is your daddy?"

"Daddy," she said again.

Was Pastor Worth really Ruth's father or was this the invention of a confused mind?

Lauren examined the photo with new eyes. "That's your doll?"

"My Daddy give me. Sa, Sarah."

"The doll's name is Sarah?"

"Sarah."

"She's a beautiful little dolly."

"Daddy's mama."

She was confused for a moment. "Oh, that doll belonged to your grandma?"

"Sarah."

"Sarah," Lauren repeated. Pastor Worth stared at them intently from the photo. His eyes were striking, deep set, yet so blue. Lauren could not unsee what she saw now. Ruth had her father's eyes. They were distinctive, unusual, and in Lauren's mind conclusive. *How did Ruth know the truth?* She couldn't imagine June telling her that Porter wasn't her real father. The woman lived on appearances. Ruth was smart. That's what Luke had told her. Ruth had rebelled all those years ago and now Lauren understood why.

Ruth reached toward Lauren for the last photo. "See it."

Lauren handed her the photo. A strange guttural sound filled the room. She looked up in alarm at Ruth before realizing she was laughing. "Luke," she said.

"You remember Luke?"

"Luke," she repeated. "My Luke."

Lauren wondered if she should call for Luke. Ruth obviously recognized him and thought of him fondly.

"Luke-family."

"Yes. You grew up together, didn't you?"

"Luke, Luke, Luke…"

They sat in silence for several more minutes before Lauren decided it was time to go. As she rose, Ruth spoke clearly. "I'm sorry."

Lauren spun to look at her. The icy blue eyes were now trained on her, the fog temporarily lifted. "What are you sorry for, Ruth?"

"I push you. I didn't…I didn't mean to push so…so hard."

Lauren touched Ruth's arm gently, afraid she might pull away. But Ruth's eyes were calm and steady. "It's okay, Ruth. I know you didn't mean to hurt me. Do you know why you pushed me?"

"I just wanted to tell you, tell you… I'm here. I'm here. Ruth is here," she repeated the words over and over and suddenly she was agitated.

"It's okay, Ruth. I see that you're here. I see you." Lauren stroked her arm gently in an effort to calm her.

"I'm here, I'm here, I'm here….." she repeated more rapidly.

A caretaker was a the door. "She's getting agitated, ma'am. You probably better go. Looks like the window for visiting has closed."

Chapter 24

The better the gambler, the worse the man
—Publius Syrus (85-43BC)

From the fullness of his grace
we have all received one blessing after another
—John 1:16

Grace

"We are all so broken," Lauren whispered as she pulled up in front of the church.

The old photo had triggered her thoughts. She wanted to be alone. Luke understood. He didn't stop her when she fled the parking lot. He didn't push her even though his face betrayed his eagerness to hear details about Ruth. He gave her the space she needed.

Lies, lies, and more lies. It was the common theme in her marriage with Marcus. Now, as she stood outside the church, she was overcome by the weight of it all. How would Ruth's life, her own life have been different, if they had heard the truth from the people they trusted the most from the beginning?

Gloria's flaming hair was bent forward over her desk in concentration when Lauren entered the church office. She looked up from her notebook and beamed at Lauren. "What are you doing here? Luke told me you had some plans together."

"I need you to tell me about this." Lauren pulled the framed photo of Pastor Worth with the child versions of Ruth and Luke out of her tote bag and placed it on her desk.

Gloria's eyes widened in surprise, her mouth slightly agape. She glanced at the picture in silence and then managed a stilted laugh. "You diggin' up old photos again?"

"The woman who has been living under the church is Ruth Lee, June's daughter. She had this photo in her cubby below the pulpit. She's a patient at the Mental Health Center downtown. I just got back from visiting with her."

Gloria's complexion turned the shade of peeled almonds. "It's Ruth?" Her voice was barely audible.

"Yes. I don't think you were honest with me before when you told me about Pastor Worth."

Gloria shifted her gaze to the floor. "What? What do you mean?"

"Please don't do that. I don't have time for it. Ruth told me."

Gloria looked up again and her eyes hardened. "Well, Ruth isn't exactly right in the head is she, if she's living at The Center?" The flash of anger was gone and tears suddenly welled in her eyes.

Lauren changed tactics and pulled a chair up to Gloria's desk. "Look, I know what it's like to live a lie. Don't you think it might be time to come out of the shadows?"

"No." She shook her head. "You don't understand. It will hurt people."

"Gloria, Ruth is for all practical purposes in an asylum. Porter is in full fledged dementia. So much time has passed. What do you think the truth will do that hasn't already been done?"

"Luke," Gloria whispered.

"Luke deserves the truth."

"He'll hate me."

Lauren's voice softened. "No, Gloria. He won't. Give him some credit."

She looked away from Lauren's face and stared at the surface of her desk.

"What do you want to know?"

"Tell me again about Pastor Worth? This time the truth."

* * *

They made their way to the almost never used church parlor where Lauren ushered Gloria to the couch. Lauren parked herself on a powder blue armchair and waited for Gloria's story to unfold.

"It started with June." Her lips trembled. "They were having an affair. No one knew at the time. No one could have imagined. It would all come out later. June walked around this place like a peacock, not too different to how she does now. The church was a big deal back then, several hundred people, a little empire in a small town. She had the minister and the lead elder wrapped around her little finger. She was the queen of the church and she liked it that way, walked around here like Jackie O."

"What happened?"

"She got pregnant."

"It wasn't Porter's?"

Gloria shook her head. "Nope. That baby was Pastor Byron Worth's. Maybe June didn't know for sure who the father was. But everyone congratulated Porter and June, the happy couple. Pastor was married with kids and June was married too with a child on the way. I figure she just thought they'd have each other in private and keep their families in the dark, forever if necessary. She had a nice little arrangement going."

"There was quite the age gap?"

"Yes. Pastor Worth was in his mid to late 40s and June in her 20s." Gloria hesitated.

"But...?"

"She didn't know about Pastor Worth's other indiscretions."

"Indiscretions?"

"I was 14 at the time. Pastor Worth started visiting our Sunday school class and takin' an interest. He took me and some of the other gals on some outings. We went fishing and one time to a youth retreat in Idaho. And, well… two of us girls in the youth group ended up pregnant. One of 'em was me."

Lauren felt sick to her stomach. "Oh Gloria. That's awful. It's disgusting you went through that."

"I thought I loved him. I didn't want to tell on him and hurt his family. He did make me feel special, spent a lot of time and money on me, and told me I was beautiful. I was determined to protect him." Gloria was staring at her suede boots, but she looked up now at Lauren. "You're not surprised? You knew? Pastor Westbrook, how did you know?"

"Ruth told me Luke was her family. I looked at the photo. Luke's eyes. They aren't the same color as Ruth's and Pastor Worth's, but they are deep set and striking. He has his father's eyes too. Once I recognized his eyes everything fit into place."

"You haven't told Luke?"

"No. That's something you have to tell him."

Tears streamed down her cheeks leaving a trail of mascara. "I don't think I can."

"I know it must seem that way. But Gloria, let's start with what happened?"

"I didn't tell on him. My parents were distraught. Called me a harlot, a whore, demanded to know who the father was, but I wouldn't tell. My dad came razor thin close to beatin' me and he wasn't that kind of man. They eventually sent me away to a home to have the baby. They wanted me to give it up for adoption, but I wanted him. I had given up everything else, so I wasn't going to give up Luke. My parents went to Pastor for advice and he convinced them to let me keep the baby. They thought everything he said was the Gospel truth. They didn't know that he promised me."

"Promised you what?"

"He said if I didn't tell my parents he was the father he'd convince them to let me keep the baby."

"He was a deeply sick man!"

Gloria nodded her agreement. "Yep he was a monster. He enjoyed the power he had over so many people."

"And the other young woman?"

"That was Leah. She had some complications. After she got pregnant, her family left the church. Everyone just assumed they were ashamed and no one heard a thing from them for a long time. But Leah ended up having a very difficult pregnancy. She was the same age as me, 14 a little younger and a lot smaller of a girl. When it came time to give birth, she wasn't able to have a natural delivery. The baby was breached and the doctor had to do an emergency C section. Leah didn't make it."

"She died?"

Gloria's hands were shaking. "Yeah, she bled to death." Her voice faltered. "But the baby survived, a little boy. Leah's parents ended up raising him."

"Did they know Pastor Worth was the father?"

"I don't know if Leah told them or not, but I know they suspected it."

"So Pastor Worth was still preaching?"

"Yep. Life went on as normal for almost 10 years. I had Luke and then I came back to church and I became the tragic unwed mother. My parents were the saints for putting up with me and every Sunday I stared into the face of my baby's father, keeping that secret and believing someday he'd leave his wife and choose me, choose Luke."

"Oh Gloria."

"I was a teenager and not a particularly bright one. That church was the center of our family life and my parents did so much for me, especially with supporting me with Luke. I never even considered leaving."

"And June?"

"She was busy with baby Ruth, who was only a few months older than Luke. No one knew it wasn't Porter's baby. I had no idea, but I think June suspected who Luke's father was. After I got pregnant, she was always hostile with me. And when Luke was a toddler, always scoldin' him. At the time, I just thought she disapproved of me being an unwed mother, but now I think it was more than that. In her heart she knew the kind of man he was."

"He was an addict," Lauren said. "How did the truth finally come out?"

"Well we went on for years like that. My parents let me move to their cabin and I got a job at the quarry in the office. It's kind of crazy what you can live with, but I guess I just begin to pretend that it was all in the past, a youthful transgression and I let myself believe that Pastor Worth just made a mistake and that he wasn't doing it to other women, other children."

"But he was?"

"All hell broke loose. I told you about the deacon's meeting when there was yelling and screaming and the police came."

"I remember. You told me Pastor Worth was taken off in handcuffs. Why was he arrested?"

"Leah's parents were able to get a paternity test for her baby, which was not a baby any more. They were suspicious, and the boy looked like his daddy. With those results they went both to the police and to the deacons. It was irrefutable evidence that Pastor was the father. A clear case of child abuse and one that ended up in a pregnancy that took Leah's life. That baby also never had a mother. It was tragic all around. And...other allegations had come from other members."

"Other allegations?"

"A couple other girls from the past came forward. There was another teenager who was now a woman living in Astoria who birthed his baby."

"Wow! He was a serial abuser. Did he do any prison time?"

"He did about two years before being released on parole. Fortunately it ended his career in the ministry."

"Poor Leah. It's awful."

"I've had nightmares about it over the years," Gloria admitted. "She didn't deserve that. Her fate could have been mine. I will never comprehend it."

"How did the congregation find out that Ruth was also his daughter?"

Gloria sighed. "That was vengeance on Pastor Worth's part."

"Vengeance?"

"That or revenge. Porter was the only elder left, you see. He was the one who confronted Pastor Worth about Leah and the baby and then several of the other allegations that had surfaced. He had gone to the trouble of investigating and talking to Leah's parents. He interviewed me too, but I lied to his face. I was eavesdropping that night from the next door room where I was watching the deacon's children. The walls were paper thin. I remember Porter saying, *You have that dead child on your hands. You have sinned and you haven't repented. You are headed for hell!*

"Strong words."

"Porter was the only man in that church who wasn't milk toast. Byron Worth wasn't going down without a fight."

"What happened then?"

Pastor Worth said back to him as cool as a cucumber. *You think you're so high and mighty, standing in judgment over me when you're not half the man I am. Even your wife knows it. She doesn't want to be with you. She's sleeping with me. And you're such a blowhard fool you think Ruth is yours? You weren't man enough to get June pregnant. You weren't man enough then and you aren't man enough now!*

Lauren could not stop the involuntary shiver that ran down her neck. "Ouch. That's awful! Poor Porter".

"And poor Maggie, Pastor Worth's wife. She was there listening to the whole confession and then watched her husband go off in handcuffs."

"Do you think she was really surprised?"

Gloria bit her lip and then blurted. "Who knows what a wife really knows? I'm sure she had her suspicions in the dark shadows of her brain, but whether or not she allowed herself to know is a different matter. When I saw Maggie like that that's when I knew for sure that whatever I experienced in a bedroom with Pastor Worth wasn't love. I felt so guilty. He had caused everyone so much pain and suffering and I was a part of it."

"I've been in Maggie's shoes. Who wants to think the worst of your husband? But eventually lies become too big to hide any longer."

Gloria nodded. "Rumor has it that Porter confronted Pastor at the parsonage a few weeks later when he was out on bail. Apparently their meeting got physical. Porter found love letters and jewelry from Pastor to his wife. He had it out with him and then Porter and June were gone in the night with Ruth."

"I can't believe they came back?"

"Unfinished business for both of them, I suppose."

"Oh Gloria. It's a terrible story. I visited Pastor Worth up in Newport after you gave me that address. He's practically 100 years old, but still vicious and cruel. I got chills just having a conversation with him. I don't think he would take responsibility for any of it, even now."

Gloria wrinkled her nose in distaste. "It doesn't surprise me. In his mind he was never wrong about anything." Gloria's gaze wandered the room as if seeing it for the first time. "Pastor Westbrook, If you see arrogance in a man or woman who claims to be of God, you know they're not serving God alone, but two masters."

Lauren recited the scripture almost without thinking. "Love is patient, love is kind. It does not envy, it does not boast, it is not proud. It does not dishonor others, it is not self-seeking, it is not easily angered, it keeps no record of wrongs. Love does not delight in evil but rejoices with the truth. It always protects, always trusts, always hopes, always perseveres."

Gloria nodded. "Exactly. If our eyes were open we would have seen the truth about Pastor Worth, but the whole church was so excited about building the empire, being a success. We forgot to think about why any of it mattered."

"Gloria, how on earth did you come out of this still a woman of faith? Christians have left the faith for so much less? You were abused by a man of God?"

"But I wasn't." Gloria straightened her posture. "I was abused by a man who claimed to know God, but didn't at all. He didn't struggle with sin, but embraced it like a long lost friend. He was a wolf in sheep's clothing. But when I was going through the pregnancy, the loneliness, all of it, God was the one who was there for me. He was the only one who knew the truth, the only one I could confide in honestly. My faith was my comfort and it made me strong. My faith led me to Harold who is the kindest most loving man I've ever known. That was God fixin' what was broken in my life. I was fortunate to recognize the difference between what is false and what is real, but I know not everyone does."

"Your parents stayed. Did they ever know who Luke's father really was?"

"I always thought deep down they knew. How could they not? Leah and I were friends in the same youth group and both pregnant around the same time? I didn't think they could face it, the fact that they put me in the path of an evil man, one they had trusted with so little discernment. It was too much for them. I kept the secret for them as much as I did for Luke. I'm not sure they would have been able to live with that truth. They're marriage didn't last, you know. About two years later Mom left Dad. They did their best to rebuild the wreckage Pastor Worth left behind, but the church was never the same; they were never the same. They hid everything so deep the light could never get to it. They were terrified of their own shadows."

"I can't help, but think they both carried a lot of shame and guilt."

Gloria sighed. "They were good people, really, and I learned a lot from them. I will never put all my faith in a pastor, man or woman, no offense."

Lauren smiled. "None taken. I prefer it when people don't put their faith in me, thank you very much."

Gloria sat forward now. He did not have God in him, Pastor Westbrook. He was an evil man. I know that now. I never wanted Luke to know that his birth father was such a horrible human being. He used God to abuse women and children and he abused God's church."

Lauren moved from the chair and sat next to Gloria. She placed her hand on the older woman's shoulder. "Luke is nothing like him. He's kind and good. Gloria, he's strong enough to know the truth."

Gloria clasped her hands together as if she wasn't quite sure what to do with them. "I've carried it for so long. I didn't want him to be burdened with this. I found it easier to just make up a different story. One where he wouldn't have to question who he was or wonder if he was like his father. One where he didn't see how stupid and foolish his mother was. I didn't think it would be a sin to carry the secret for his sake."

"I know your intentions were good, Gloria. But hiding the truth is never the answer. You have to give Luke the credit that he can be trusted with this. He loves you. We deserve the truth from the ones we love."

* * *

She wasn't sure what to expect when she stepped into Black Bear Coffee to meet Reverend Martin. He was already seated in a booth by the window waiting for her. Lauren ordered a house coffee and squeezed into the seat across from him.

He greeted her with a genuine smile as he trained his grim eyes on her. "So you've decided to stay."

"I know. It sounds crazy after all that's happened, but I feel called here."

Reverend Martin stroked his chin thoughtfully. "You know the truth now. Do you really want to stay?"

"I think I do. We're finally getting to the good part."

He raised his eyebrows in surprise. "The good part?"

"Yes. We're finally walking in truth. Maybe the church can finally heal."

"How is Luke?"

"He was pretty upset when Gloria told him. He left town for awhile. Went off into the woods for a couple of weeks to hunt, fish, be alone with God. His mother's been lying to him his whole life. I know she had her reasons, but the world looks different to Luke now. He met his father briefly. He knows the kind of man he is and he's got a sister with a lot of struggles. He has other brothers and sisters too and he has to decide whether or not to find them. He's still figuring out how to come to terms with it all."

Reverend Martin stirred his tea rhythmically. "Is he better now?"

"Yes. I think so. He's been visiting Ruth almost every day. He's working to have her moved to a different care facility, one that would allow her more choices and activities. Ruth seems so much happier and they've been able to reduce some of the anti-psychotics."

"That's good, that's good. So, she's doing better?"

"I went with Luke a couple times to visit her. She's a lot more alert and can resume some of the activities she loves, like reading and exercising, but this time safely."

"You know now, why she pushed you?"

"I think so. She was trying in her way to connect with June and Luke, but she didn't know how. June gave her up to the state almost 20 years ago after she ran away from home. They were living in Portland at the time. She and

Porter didn't know how to handle her schizophrenia and Ruth was refusing medication and refusing to follow their rules. Considering the dangers on the street, I really think they thought it was the best situation. They were in over their heads, gave up all rights to her. In a strange twist of fate, she ends up in a facility in Vernonia of all places."

"Sounds to me, like an act of God."

"It's unbelievable. Ruth began to fall back into her childhood routines when the caretakers weren't looking and she found her way back to the church. The ring, the pictures, the doll. They were all Ruth's way of trying to tell me who she was. She was trying tell me she was here and to find her family."

"Poor child," Reverend Martin sighed. "The things we do to try to find our place in the world, to feel like we belong. How is June doing with all of this?"

"I don't know for sure, not great. I met with her a few weeks ago and told her about Ruth. She turned so white I thought she was going to pass out. I gave her the ring too. The secret is out and I think it's pretty humiliating for her."

"Has she seen Ruth yet, reconnected with her daughter?"

"Not yet, Reverend Martin. I'm praying for a good outcome. I think it's all I can do, now."

Reverend Martin sat his cup down on the table and fixed his stare on her again. "Do you think a church can really ever survive a Pastor Byron Worth? I'll be honest, Pastor Westbrook. I've seen it before and almost a hundred percent of the time, the church doesn't make it after such a scandal. It either dies or becomes something unrecognizable, something not godly."

Lauren sipped her coffee in thought. "When I first came here, Reverend, I'll be honest, I thought the church was dead. Our God is one of resurrection, but I didn't really believe this church could be saved. I don't know what the future holds, but I do know that our God is the God of miracles. Gloria and June were both so wounded and God is bringing about healing in their lives. He's bringing healing to Luke and Ruth, to my mother and Paul and so many others."

Reverend Martin smirked as though he had a private joke. "And to you, Pastor Westbrook. Don't think I haven't seen a change in you? God is working in your life, healing and restoring you. You were almost like a shell when I met you. It wasn't surprising after what you'd been through, but there is joy in you now. Do you think that's just by chance?"

Lauren smiled. "No. I know it's true. My marriage to Marcus was complicated. I carried so much guilt when he died. I think I'm finally at a point where I'm able to let some of that go." She pressed her lips together. *Should she tell him?* "When I was in the cave, I saw Marcus."

Reverend Martin's eyes widened in interest. "You had a vision?"

"I did. When things were there darkest, most hopeless, when I thought I was never coming out, Marcus comforted me, kept the pain at bay. He told me he forgave me and that I could let him go."

"Can you let him go?"

"Probably not ever completely. But I feel a peace now, I didn't before. I accept Marcus for who he was,the good and bad. I still love him. The truth is we made a lot of poor choices. I always wanted to please him. I was scared to do the hard things in our marriage."

He said nothing as he stroked his chin listening. Lauren hesitated for a moment. "I know now, Reverend Martin that we need to face those hard things, even when we're scared. I...I have an apology to make to you."

His woolly eyebrows lifted in surprise. "You have an apology to make to me?"

"Yes. The first day we talked about Marcus and the money he took from the church. I knew about it. I told you, I didn't know, but it wasn't the truth. Marcus told me the night before he died. I should have gone to you immediately, but I didn't. I wanted to protect Marcus and I wanted to protect myself."

Reverend Martin set a black leather notebook on the table.

"What is that?"

"This my mentorship notebook. It's where I record notes from my meetings with my mentees."

"This thick section here is all about you."

Lauren frowned. "Wow. Was I really that problematic?"

Reverend Martin opened it to a bookmarked page and used his pen to make an annotation. He sat it down and placed it in front of Lauren. "What does that say?"

"Mentorship complete." Lauren looked up surprised. "So we're done?"

"Well, yes. In the official sense. I no longer have any concerns about you moving forward at Vernonia."

Lauren stared at the golden clasp of the open leather notebook.

"Even after what I told you about the money?"

"It wasn't a shining moment for you, Pastor Westbrook. What can I say? We are ministers, not angels. Your husband had just died. It's natural that you would want to cling to his good memory. But you're willing to tell the truth now. That's all we can ask for."

"Reverend Martin, this might surprise you, but I'm a little sad about this news."

He closed the notebook. "Are you saying you'd like to continue our meetings?"

"Well from time to time you've actually given me good advice."

A spark flared in his gray eyes. "I'm so happy to hear I'm useful on occasion. Well, perhaps I could squeeze you in for a meeting from time to time." He stared at her intensely from across the table. "But they would be different."

Lauren raised an eyebrow. "Different how?"

"We would meet as friends."

Lauren smiled. "I would like that Reverend Martin. I would like that a lot."

He reached inside his briefcase to return the notebook and pulled out his fedora. He rose to leave. "Thank you, Pastor Westbrook."

"Thank you for what?"

"For reminding me that God is the judge. Even an old timer like me can learn humility. You brought this place back to life even after Pastor Worth, if that isn't a testimony to the power of God, I don't know what is."

"Thanks for not giving up on me, Reverend."

"The challenge isn't over here at Vernonia. I'm here for you if you need me, Pastor Westbrook. All you have to do is call."

"I know that."

* * *

"You ready, June?" Gloria asked from behind the wheel of her car.

June's face was pale. She was frozen in the passenger seat. "No. I can't see her."

"You can," Gloria urged. "She's your daughter and she loves you."

June looked heavenward. "I left her. I abandoned her. She'll never forgive me."

"You don't know that." Gloria sat with June in silence for a moment. "Come on. Let's pray together." Gloria reached for June's hand.

"No. I can't," June snapped.

"Stop being stubborn, you old bat. You and I, we're survivors. All that daughter of yours wants and needs is someone to love and care for her. It's just gonna take time is all."

Gloria's lips were set in determination as she grabbed June's hand in her own. "Lord, I pray that you would take this woman, your daughter June into your grace. Take this stubborn, fussy old woman and give her the right words to say to a lost daughter. Ruth was lost and now she's found. I pray that you would be with that girl and heal her mind and body. Take all of June's anxiety and wailing and give her the words she needs to say so there can be healing in this family. Soften this woman's hard crusty heart and work in her life. In the name of Jesus we pray, Amen."

June was fighting tears, but she finally allowed herself to cry. "I did everything wrong, Gloria."

"No, not everything. You're here now. You have the chance to see your daughter. It's a gift, June. Take it."

* * *

"Do you take this woman to be your lawfully wedded wife?" Lauren asked. "I do."

Paul was dashing in his black tux, but Vivian was a vision in white. "Mom, Grandma looks amazing," Sydney stage whispered from her spot next to the bride.

"Ssh," Lauren warned. "I'm trying to officiate a wedding." She directed her attention back to her mother.

"Vivian, do you take this man to be your lawfully wedded husband?"

"You bet I do," Vivian blurted. The congregation laughed.

Vivian wore a lace lavender dress, tapered in the middle around her narrow waist. Her wedding dress was the most modest garment Lauren had seen her wear in recent memory and she was stunning. Lauren struggled at first to fight the tears. For so many months she had refused to cry, especially for herself, but now as she saw her mother, so beautiful, so happy she was fighting to keep herself from blubbering.

"You people are making it hard for me to complete this wedding," she confessed.

The wedding guests laughed again.

Luke moved from his position as Best Man to her side and squeezed her hand as he whispered in her ear. "So, at the end of the day, you're just a big softy, aren't you?" He handed her a tissue and then in an exaggerated stately fashion returned to his place beside Paul. Lauren smiled through her tears and found her voice again. "I now pronounce you husband and wife. You may kiss the bride!"

Paul took Vivian in his arms and gave her a gentle, but passionate kiss.

"May I proudly introduce Mr. and Mrs. Lu Roe."

The guests went wild, clapping and hollering, with even a whoop from Emma. Lauren felt a warm glow as she looked at the faces of the people who were now her family: Gloria, Linda, Emma, Stan, Vicky, Paul and Vivian. Porter was in the front row bobbing his head and June smiling because she really meant it. Her daughter, Ruth stood next to her like a new creation in no visible way the same woman who had once pushed Lauren into a dark cave. Her hair was pulled back from her face exposing rosy, healthy cheeks and she was laughing. Lauren could recognize her for the first time as the girl holding her doll in a childhood photo. God was certainly a God of miracles.

Luke moved back to her side and took her hand as the happy couple made their first walk as husband and wife through the crowd of guests. Lauren laughed through her tears until her eyes met Luke's.

"If Mom can have a happy ending Luke, anyone can," she whispered.

He raised his eyebrows in mock surprise. "You mean, even us?"

"Yes, Luke, even us."

"Well that's good to hear, because I think we have a pretty good thing going." He traced his fingers across her wrist and Lauren rested her head against his shoulder.

Sydney groaned. "Oh no, does this mean another wedding?"

Luke knelt to her level. "Would that be okay with you?"

Sydney wrinkled her nose. "I guess. Can I can get a puppy?"

Lauren laughed and took Sydney's hand in her own. "Nothing is impossible."

The End

About the Author

If this story resonated with you, a short review helps other readers who've lived through similar loss find this novel. Even a sentence matters

Debby Handman writes women's fiction that explores the psychological aftermath of loss, betrayal, and starting over, stories of grief and the work of rebuilding a life. Debby is a missionary kid, pastor, musician and teacher who lives in Oregon. She finds joy in raising her two sons, teaching and writing. Photo by Alesha Culp photography.

You can connect with me on:

 https://debbyhandmanauthor.com

 https://www.facebook.com/profile.php?id=100068952940858

www.ingramcontent.com/pod-product-compliance
Lightning Source LLC
Chambersburg PA
CBHW051940220626
47052CB00004B/727